NOX DORMIENDA

AN ARCTURUS MYSTERY

Nox Dormienda

(A LONG NIGHT FOR SLEEPING)

Kelli Stanley

FIVE STAR
A part of Gale, Cengage Learning

GALE
CENGAGE Learning™

Detroit • New York • San Francisco • New Haven, Conn • Waterville, Maine • London

GALE
CENGAGE Learning

Set in 11 pt. Plantin.
Printed on permanent paper.

LIBRARY OF CONGRESS CATALOGING-IN-PUBLICATION DATA

Stanley, Kelli.
  Nox dormienda (a long night for sleeping) : an Arcturus mystery / Kelli Stanley. — 1st ed.
    p. cm.
  ISBN-13: 978-1-59414-666-4 (hardcover : alk. paper)
  ISBN-10: 1-59414-666-7 (hardcover : alk. paper)
  1. Physicians—Fiction. 2. Murder—Investigation—Fiction. 3. Agricola, Gnaeus Julius, 40–93—Fiction. 4. Great Britian—History—Roman period, 55 B.C.–449 A.D.—Fiction. 5. Romans—Great Britain—Fiction. I. Title.
PS3619.T3657N69 2008
813'.6—dc22   2008010695

First Edition. First Printing: July 2008.

Published in 2008 in conjunction with Tekno Books and Ed Gorman.

Printed in the United States of America
1 2 3 4 5 6 7 12 11 10 09 08

For my small but fierce family, who never let me give up:
Patricia Geniusz Stanley, Van Stanley and Tana Hall.
And for Mac, and my much-missed Paris, who were there
for the journey, but not the destination.
Sit terra vobis levis, deliciae meae.

ACKNOWLEDGMENTS

Writers dream about this page. It's like an Oscar speech, except we don't win a new television for brevity. We make our editors happy, but that's a different story.

Getting a novel published—particularly your first novel—requires a lot of work from a lot of people. Everyone you meet along the way has the power to inspire you, to keep you from sinking into the proverbial Slough of Rejection Dejection—or push you in a little deeper. By the time you get to write your fantasized acknowledgments, you're brimming with gratitude. At least I am.

So if you're with me this far, please keep reading. A writer's favorite reader is the one who sticks around for the thank-yous.

Nox Dormienda and the Arcturus Mystery series would never have been conceived without San Francisco State University. The SFSU Classics department was my home away from home for a few long years. Under the tutelage of Professor and former Department Chair Pamela Vaughn, dearest friend, mentor and all-around angel, I found my vocation, as well as a love of Latin. It was in a class taught by Emerita Professor Barbara McLauchlin that Arcturus made his first appearance: her infectious humor and wonderful soul made a classroom an environment for creativity. Dr. Phil Stanley, a long-lost cousin, inspired my archaeological leanings, and Dr. David Leitao taught me Greek—something for which I'll always be (painfully) grateful. Many thanks as well to my fellow students for their friendship and insights. SFSU saw me through undergraduate and graduate degrees, and it will always be a place close to my heart.

The academic community is a generous one. For the chance to develop as a scholar, writer and speaker, thanks go to the California Classical Association, the American Philological Association, the Women's Classical Caucus, the University of Melbourne, the University of London and the Institute of Classical Studies, the American Classical League, the Pacific Modern and Ancient Languages Association and SFSU's own Classics Students Association. *Multas gratias* to my good friend Mary-Kay Gamel at University of California, Santa Cruz, the wonderful Charlayne Allen of University of California, Davis, Ruby Blondell of the University of Washington, and Dr. Steve Oberhelman. Great thanks to Susan Fox at the Roman Bath Museums in Bath, for coming in on a Sunday and helping with research for the next book! You'll be thanked again when it comes out. An extra special thanks to the most brilliant Roman historian in the world, who also happens to be a wonderful human being: U.C. Berkeley's Dr. Erich Gruen.

The Arcturus Mysteries are set in an ancient culture, but their style is indebted to a more recent era. Huge thanks are owed to a man who has done more than anyone else to preserve that era for us: Eddie Muller, president of the Film Noir Foundation. I renew my noirish inspiration on a yearly basis during his Noir City festival in San Francisco, and on a personal level, thank Eddie for his generosity, vision and support. Thanks, too, to some of Eddie's recent guests—the gracious and delightful Coleen Gray, the sweet and funny Farley Granger, the courageous and beautiful Marsha Hunt. And of course, much awestruck gratitude to the images on the screen: Rita, Barbara, Orson, Marlene, Garfield, Power, Mitchum, Bogie and Bacall. May they, and the other immortals of the twentieth century, live as long as Jove and Venus.

To the man who taught me how to write, I owe a debt that can't be repaid. Raymond Chandler was a classicist, a scholar, and a gentleman, and wrote some of the toughest, most lyrical lines in prose. To him, and to Dashiell Hammett, who started it all, I take off my fedora: they are the holy men of noir.

Thanks to Steven Saylor, for showing us all it could be done, and making such an excellent job of it—and for personal inspiration and generosity. Thanks to J.K. Rowling for insisting that Harry Potter be translated into Greek and Latin, and for helping resuscitate the act of reading. Thanks to HBO, for keeping the Vestal flame burning on television. Thanks to England, for always feeling like home. Thanks to San Francisco, for being home.

Thanks to Sal Dichiera, Lee Woidt and Chris Phillips at Amazing Adventures in San Francisco for their camaraderie, and for finding bits of collectible history to help inspire the next mystery series. Thanks to Bob Moyce of Phoenix Studios Productions, for web design help. A big, sweet-smelling thank you to Christopher Lynch, perfume god extraordinaire, and supplier of glamorous goodie bags at the launch party. And a toothy grin and a toast of bourbon for Jim Ferreira, who shoots the dishy dames and tough guys of the mean streets better than anybody this side of Fritz Lang. "The bird is mine!"

On a personal note, I have supportive friends to thank: the Toscaninis, Jeremy, Kris, Paige, Joan, Nancy, Michael and George, and Jackie Whittaker, for always making us feel like members of an incredible, wonderful family; Joan Sutton, for your faith, love and support through anything, including language tests; and Stuart Vaughn, for everything, but especially a particular walk in the rain in mismatched shoes.

To John Helfers, of Tekno Books, and the folks at Five Star Publishing: thanks for believing in a Roman doctor with a hard-boiled attitude. To Gordon Aalborg, my esteemed editor and a terrific writer, who convinced everybody else to believe in Arcturus—I can't thank you enough. Maybe "G" does stand for "God." To my wonderful agent, Irene Kraas, a superb representative and a truly good person: thanks for all your help and for believing in me.

Finally, many thanks to my parents, who have never lost faith, never given up hope, and can now say "I told you so." They are my strength, my resolve and my perseverance. And to T.S.H., my partner in all things, who has given me criticism when I needed it, guidance when I sought it, and love every day of the week. I love you all.

To paraphrase George M. Cohan, "Arcturus thanks you, Bilicho thanks you, Venutius thanks you, and I thank you." Now, on with *Nox Dormienda*!

Kelli Stanley
San Francisco, March 2, 2007

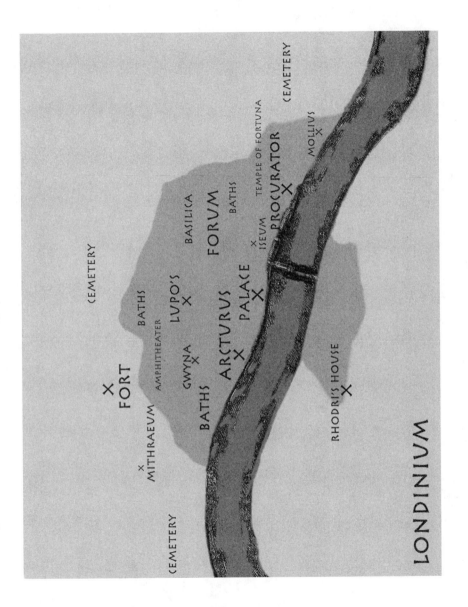

LONDINIUM

ONE

Yesterday began like most yesterdays in Londinium in December. Venutius roasted some partridge eggs for breakfast and served the stuffed figs with cheese curds. I was hungry for plain oat porridge. We ate, anyway.

There were people waiting to see me. There were always people waiting to see me, especially in December. Rheumy eyes, runny noses, aches and creaks of all descriptions—the list was long and the day was short. Bilicho made it easier by figuring out who really needed me and who just wanted a peek at the governor's *medicus*. I always disappointed people who expected to meet a prodigy.

"Aulus Scaptia."

"Pipe-maker. Loss of appetite, losing weight, hair falling out. Looked a little pale. Legitimate."

"Decimus Clodius Super."

Bilicho chuckled. I looked up.

"Sorry. Just that he's more of a Minor. Clerk at Headquarters, keeps the bank records. Wrist hurts, but make it quick. He'll talk your ear off about how important his time is."

"Valerius Milo."

This time a snort escaped from Bilicho. "Hangover. And hanger-on—he's a friend of a friend of the governor, and in Britannia to see the 'Savage North.' Constipation problem, too. Give him some flax-seed oil; that'll keep him busy."

"Who else?"

13

"Sulpicia Lepidina, and her three children, all with coughs. She's the wife of a helmsman stationed on the coast. Recommended by somebody in Legion XX. Nice woman, on the dimwitted side."

The morning staggered by, still looking for a party. Saturnalia was officially over two days ago—unofficially, there were still cockfights and dice throws, more wine-soaked quickies and the odor of vomit filling every alleyway. Valerius Milo wasn't alone. Mint and barley-water tonic flowed like last night's *vappa,* and I was starting to run low when a couple of knife-wounds walked in. The men left, with no payment and a promise of chickens. I had too many already. Brutius finally shut the door.

I asked Bilicho: "How many?"

"Fourteen. Three emergencies, two political hand-holdings, five digestion problems and four chronic cases. Not bad."

Another day, another *salutatio.* Agricola always let me see whomever I liked—as long as I'd see whomever he liked, too. He was the governor, and I was the governor's doctor. I was about as exclusive a dish as peacock tongue, but I didn't let it go to my head. Drunks and senators all look the same without a toga. Sometimes the drunks look better.

The partridge eggs made a reappearance at lunch, accompanied by a pheasant. The pheasant looked a little surprised at the pairing. Bilicho and I were discussing just how savage Milo would find Britannia after his laxative took effect, when Brutius ran into the room.

"What is it?"

"A . . . a woman, sir. At the door."

He said it as if he expected her to hurl herself over the garden wall. "The *salutatio* is over. Is she from the palace? Is it an emergency?"

"I don't think so. She's a rich lady, very beautiful. She's not bleeding or anything."

I grinned. He wouldn't want to bother me even if the woman had a *pilum* stuck in her back.

"Well, what does she want?"

Brutius wrestled with the question until it almost had him pinned. I turned to Bilicho. "Send her to Serenus if she wants a prescription. We're through for the day."

I drained my cup and Venutius poured more wine. Rich women meant trouble. Some wanted attention, some were bored, but most were just looking for what their husbands were giving the wineboy. I'd been groped, fondled, pinched and grabbed, and treated to the sight of more nude women— unasked—than a towel-holder in a *caldarium*. It usually started with a funny feeling in the stomach, which inevitably led to a fast stripdown and offers that would embarrass Messalina. Not even Messalina could get to Bilicho.

I nearly choked on the Falernian when he reappeared, his face red. He said: "It's not a medical visit."

We looked at each other. Another case. Another sort of case, the kind Dioscorides never told me about. I gulped the wine before Venutius could mix it.

It had been awhile. But we never waited long, and we never looked too far. Mercury brought them to the doorstep like a cat with a rat. It was a present from the Blessed Ones, a big smelly rodent that I usually had a hell of a time burying. Virgil was right: never trust Greeks, gods or cats bearing gifts.

Bilicho looked at me like a dog hoping for a bone to drop. I shook my head. "You're hopeless. Bring her in."

Venutius and Brutius left for the kitchen, and I rearranged myself on the couch. I was picking some dried egg off my tunic when I heard footsteps. A woman entered, a pace ahead of Bilicho. She paused in the doorway when she saw the food on the table. I paused when I saw her. Brutius hadn't exaggerated the beautiful part. Money enhanced the impact. I felt my doctor face slipping.

I grinned at her, and hoped I didn't look stupid.

I said: "Please—join me."

She hesitated, and looked back at the door, as if she'd changed her mind. Then her shoulders relaxed, and she nodded. The white fur mantle slipped off. Her body was wrapped in silk. The tunic was aqua, the *palla* was midnight blue with a light purple border, and I was running out of adjectives. The gasp was out of my mouth before I could swallow.

She sat down on the couch like she was afraid she'd break it. I didn't care if she did. Bilicho cleared his throat. She looked at me. I nodded and he left, throwing a curious look over his shoulder as if he expected me to catch it. I let it land on the pheasant. He finally crawled his way to the kitchen.

The woman was a native. Her face reminded me of Camulodunum—the good part of the memory. Blonde hair was tied back in an old-fashioned knot at the nape of her neck, and the carnelians on her sleeve glittered red against white skin. I enjoyed watching her reach for an olive.

I wasn't supposed to ask her name until after she'd eaten; that is if I wanted to be a good host. For some reason, I did. She picked at the food like she couldn't taste it, and her eyes fell on my mother's medallion. I'd worn it for a long time— since the day she was killed—and I usually forgot about it. I reached a hand up to feel the healer's symbols carved in the blue-grey rock.

She'd been crying. The red couldn't hide a blue deep enough to drown in. She leaned forward, her breath short, quick and ragged. Whatever was coming out was coming out now.

She said: "I'm here to warn the governor."

I've been more shocked, but I couldn't remember when. I pulled myself upright. My heart was thumping louder than a cymbal player in a three-sister dance act.

I was responsible for the general's health. His legs, his hands, his mood, his manner, whether he shouted himself hoarse or tried to get his wife pregnant or got off a horse to take a piss. I took a deep breath as far as it would go. She spoke fast.

"A man named Vibius Maecenas arrives from Dubris any day. He's a freedman of the Emperor, a fat, greedy fool of a Syrian." She glanced around the room, as if she expected Domitian to pop out of a chair.

Her voice sank to a whisper. "He's also the Emperor's spy. And he's here to harm Agricola."

I stared at her again. It was a story that deserved some Falernian, and I was glad it was still on the table. I poured myself a drink, but she waved one away, her mouth stretched thin with impatience. I took my time with the wine. I didn't know what she'd expected, but apparently I wasn't it.

"You must do something right away. I came to you as soon as I could."

"Who else have you told?"

The question surprised her. "No one. I told your servant—"

"Assistant."

"I told your assistant it was a family problem. No one else."

"What about your husband? Father? Other family members?"

She reddened, and studied a painted pot on the corner shelf. "My father . . . I came against my father's wishes. No one can know I was here." She paused, and a spasm of pain caught her face and held it. The words helped break its grip. "My . . . my husband is dead."

I chewed my cheek and kept staring. The face was a proud one. It didn't like asking for help. "How did you get this information?"

I could smell lavender, and the moist, still odor of fear on her body. Her hands were grasping the edge of the couch. She looked into the hearth fire as if she knew what it felt like to burn.

"The Syrian is my *sponsus*. My father arranged it. He's old and ill. My husband was killed before he could give me children."

She pulled her eyes from the flames and met my own. "I'll slit my veins before I carry that monster's seed."

The ferocity was familiar. A cornered cat. A tigress in the arena. The medallion drew her back again. I wasn't surprised she recognized it.

"That still doesn't explain how you found this out. Or why you came to me instead of the governor."

One of the logs in the fire popped a small explosion of sparks. Neither one of us noticed.

"You're his doctor—his friend. You have a reputation for solving problems. You were pointed out to me and I—I liked the way you looked."

Our eyes met again and were formally introduced.

"Is that all?"

"What do you mean?"

"I thought maybe Agricola's men ask too many questions."

Her face got cold, and a wave of red washed over it without thawing it out. The words got harder.

"Think what you want, but you're a fool if you don't warn the governor. Agricola's brought peace, good fortune—he's given us the hand of Rome, not her fist. My—my husband believed in him. What do you believe in, I wonder?"

"I'll tell you what I don't believe in. I don't believe in beautiful widows interrupting my lunch and feeding me lines about Syrian spies. I think you want my help because you don't want to marry him."

The color drained from her lips. Blue ice raked my face.

"I don't need you. I can look after my own affairs. I want

him to die. I'd kill him myself, before he touched me."

Maybe it was the way she was standing, with her shoulders back and her fists clenched into white balls at her sides, or maybe the frozen voice trying hard not to shatter. Or maybe because as a child I'd seen women standing like that in the face of death.

"All right, I believe you. You don't need me and Agricola does. So explain how you know this."

She waited until she could breathe again. "I can't tell you. You'll have to trust me."

"Trust you? I don't know who you are, lady. I don't even know your name."

"Claudia Catussa—to the Romans. Gwyna to my own people. Which man are you today? Julius Alpinus Classicianus Favonianus or Arcturus?" The sarcasm seemed to help her. She was good at the Roman versus native game, but I'd played it all my life.

"You can call me Arcturus. And if I trusted you like my own—sister—I'd still need to know how the hell you found it out. And I will . . . eventually. Is there anything else you know—anything at all—about the Syrian's plans?"

Her tongue ran over her lips, while she thought about how much to say. "Something about . . . about a new governor."

That made too much of the wrong kind of sense. Agricola played the game, and he knew how to win. But he also knew how to pretend to lose. His success was Domitian's success, and the day it became his own would be his last. But the army loved him—maybe too much—and he was about to conquer the North. So the Emperor would want an eye on him. Or a knife at his throat.

Londinium was already stinking with rumors. Some swore he'd be here forever, Domitian's favorite general, but more were laying even odds that he'd be replaced before next season—

before he could achieve his dream of holding the whole country in his hands. For the glory of the Emperor, of course.

I looked around. We were both still standing in front of the fire.

She said: "I have to go."

The fine lines around her mouth hadn't been there before. Her *palla* was on the floor. We both bent down to pick it up, and her hand brushed my arm. The hair was standing up where she'd touched it.

I could smell lavender again. I draped the *palla* around her, and maybe my fingertips lingered on her shoulders. She turned to face me. Her eyes searched mine, looking for something. She moved closer, and I felt the heat of her body through the silk. She stood on tip-toe, and a softness I could barely remember caressed my cheek.

She whispered: "I do need you. Be careful, Ardur."

I closed my eyes, inhaling a fragrance from the past. When I opened them, she was gone.

Two

I couldn't work. I could barely think. Focus. Focus on Agricola. I called Bilicho.

"It's about the governor. I'm not sure what exactly."

He grunted. "Women who look like that—"

"What do you want them to look like? My Aunt Pervinca, the Gorgon? Follow her. Find out as much as you can about her."

He looked startled. "Why? I thought you said this has to do with Agricola? What's the mystery?"

"Something about a spy. For Domitian. A Vibius Maecenas, a Syrian. Supposed to marry that girl." I blamed the tightness in my chest on too many partridge eggs.

He studied me as if I were some sort of new hemorrhoid salve. I could feel my face flush and get irritable.

"What is it?"

"You're afraid to do it yourself."

I rubbed my cheek, and gave him a sour look. He grinned in return.

"I haven't seen you like this in years. I don't know if I've ever seen you like this."

"Well, don't stand there gawking at me. Tell Coir to go down to the market and ask around. Her native name is Gywna—Claudia Catussa to the Romans." I caught his arched eyebrow. "And don't look so damned pleased with yourself."

He sucked his teeth for a moment, suppressing a smile, and then headed for the kitchen. I could hear him call for Coir.

He'd better hurry if he was going to catch Gywna.

Gwyna. I didn't want to think about her. What I needed was a fresh, cold slap in the face. My favorite old cloak was wadded up underneath a chair cushion, and I put it on and stepped into the atrium.

The air bit my face, and the thin sunlight did nothing to help. I looked around, and wondered what the hell I was doing. A loud purr interrupted me. Fera was watching the wood doves with dinner on her mind. I scooped her into my arms, her black body heavy with a thick fur coat.

I petted her for a while, before she got impatient and went looking for a rat, leaving me to deal with my own—the latest gift from the god of mischief. I stood up and frowned at a broken statue. The house was unfinished, like most things in my life. All right, Arcturus, where did that come from? I reminded myself not to talk to myself. Focus. Focus on the house.

I wandered up to the wall separating the courtyard from the street. It was covered in graffiti, but no one had scrawled over Postumus and his claim to have screwed ten girls on the very spot. His legend was still secure, and my atrium still wasn't.

One of these years I'd finish the wing, and the house and gardens would be completely private, and I wouldn't have to worry about waking up one night to the sound of Postumus grunting in the herb garden. One of these years. Right after Domitian made me Pontifex Maximus.

A loud clang from the kitchen startled me. Just Venutius, whistling and clanging and preparing more food, and I hoped to God it wasn't more roasted eggs. I massaged the knot in my forehead.

My eyes landed on the *Lararium* huddled in the corner, shivering from neglect. If the protectors of the household decided to move out to plusher accommodations, I couldn't blame them. I muttered a small, feeble prayer for forgiveness, and wiped the marble with my arm until the first level of grime was gone. The incense cup was full of ashes. When had I last made an offering? Why the hell did I avoid it? I forced the questions back down the hole they crawled out of. Focus. Focus on the *Lares*.

I brought some myrrh from the workroom and shoveled some charcoal from the hearth and carefully laid the incense on a red-orange ember. The sickly sweet smell started to waft upwards, and I stepped away, nearly gagging. Myrrh always had that effect on me, but that wasn't the reason I didn't come out here. I shoved that thought down the hole, too, and this time latched the cover. Time to turn the corner.

The chickens were scratching desultorily, but they weren't sacred chickens and I didn't believe in signs, anyway.

I played with Pyxis and her puppies and let them chew on me, which gave us all a little comfort. I closed the kennel gate, and walked back through the atrium.

The myrrh was still burning, a thin grey wisp spiraling into the heavy air. The hell with focusing. The hell with Agricola, the house, the *Lares*. I was shaken up inside like a small pair of dice in a too large cup—tossed by a drunk on a losing streak. Thirty-three years old, and still stupid. Trying to figure out just how stupid I was occupied the rest of my afternoon.

I was still trying to figure it out when I got hungry and came in to eat. Bilicho hadn't returned, but Coir was back from the market. Venutius laid out a large bowl of surprisingly good leek soup, along with some coriander bread and hard cheese.

I motioned for Coir to sit with me. I'd seen statues less stiff, and she was avoiding my eyes. For a slave, she was giving a good imitation of a jealous woman.

"What did you find out?"

She kept her voice even.

"She's a well-born lady. Her husband was on the council.

Her father was, too, before he became crippled. No one expects him to live much longer."

"Go on."

"She's to be married to some foreigner—some Easterner," she said with distaste. "Some say there's a man who won't let it happen."

"What man?"

We were both surprised by the tone of my voice.

"That they wouldn't tell. A native. Someone in trouble, from the way they were talking. The lady spurned him, but he still loves her. She's a fine one, all right. Giving herself Roman airs and such."

"Did they say anything else useful?"

"Just that her family has money problems, like everybody else." Her mouth was pinched. "She's too proud for her own good."

I chewed my lip until I noticed she was still there.

"Fetch Draco for me."

She turned to go, then hesitated.

"Yes, Coir? What is it?"

"I was wondering—I was wondering—"

"Yes?"

"If you . . . if you'd need me later."

We both knew what she meant. It would help her get over the jealousy tonight, but if she was getting too attached—and obviously she was—tomorrow would be worse. I always freed the girls eventually, but I'd just bought her. And she was too good in the examination room to get ruined by the bedroom.

I shook my head, and she left, her eyes lowered. I felt pretty noble about the sacrifice.

Draco interrupted me in the middle of self-congratulations. He was still eating a drumstick from the pheasant of this afternoon. Wiping his lips, he stuck it back in the fold of his tunic. "You wanted me, *Dominus?*"

As bodyguards go, he was bigger than most. I was lucky Agricola worried about my hands, because I could never have afforded him. I could barely afford his feed bill.

"Bilicho isn't back yet. Stay awake, and guard the door tonight. Call me immediately when he returns." It was already after the first hour of night. I was starting to worry about him. And not only about him.

Draco drew himself up to his full height, and threw out his formidable chest. Incredibly, it looked like he'd outgrown his tunic again. Soon I'd start believing in two-headed calves.

"Yes, Master. Should I arm myself? Is there any danger?"

"No, don't arm yourself. Just keep your eyes open." The literalness was lost on him. "Remember—the instant he comes home."

Draco bowed, and left me alone with thoughts that were too loud and too shrill for company. I decided to go to sleep early. The sun had already left for a cold dip in the Styx, but his work day was getting longer again. Maybe the worst of winter was over. Maybe this was nothing serious. Maybe Domitian really would make me Pontifex Maximus. Coir walked in as soon as I stood up.

"Brutius already lit the furnace, sir. Your bedroom should be warm. Would you like him to prepare the *caldarium?*"

"No, not tonight. Take the lamp, will you, Coir?"

She followed me into the bedroom. The mattress was spread with a warm, green blanket. She stood by, her eyes focused on nothing, holding the lamp. The flame was casting a glow on her already ruddy skin. The hell with nobility. I could feel bad in the morning.

We were both drenched in sweat before I could sleep, and she must've left for her room as soon as I dozed off. All night long she'd been another woman. My dreams turned dark, and were running into familiar nightmare territory when the sight of Draco's large, pockmarked nose inches above my face shocked me awake.

"Bilicho?"

"No, Master. But there is an official waiting for you in the examination room."

I threw on a leather tunic, and some trousers. Draco helped me into my outdoor boots. Bilicho should've been home by now. He was following Gwyna, and if she'd been telling the truth—what if she'd been attacked? What if he was hurt? What if they were both hurt?

I cinched my belt too hard and the pain helped me focus again. Bilicho was a professional. And the girl—I'd think about the girl later.

Draco was still trying to drape a cloak over me when I stepped into the hallway. From there, I could see a man in a muddied cloak, poised in front of the brazier, warming his hands. He looked up. I recognized Caecilius Avitus, one of Agricola's best intelligence officers.

"There you are. Sorry to get you up, Favonianus."

"What is it? Is Agricola all right?"

His black eyes roamed my face and Draco's. "Yes, of course the governor's all right. Something—something has happened, that's all. I need your help."

I studied Avitus for a few moments. His hair was grayer than I remembered, and I'd never noticed the scar on his right hand.

"Well, what is it? Is someone ill?"

Avitus stared at Draco and said nothing. I motioned for him to go, and he clomped out of sight with a worried look. The *beneficarius* turned toward me.

"This is a very delicate matter. Your absolute discretion and secrecy are required."

"Of course."

"Do not discuss this with anyone. Not even the governor."

"I don't think—"

"You will. It's for his own protection."

I'd heard one too many mysteries already. And his pompous manner gave me an itch.

"Stop speaking like a goddamn oracle and explain yourself. You know my record. I've handled touchy situations more than once."

Avitus frowned and scraped his muddy boot on the floor. He didn't want to be here, either. "That's why I came to you. I need you as a doctor, and an—expert."

"I'll get my tools."

He shook his head. "I don't think they'll do any good."

We took a roundabout way to the city. Not much was awake. We passed a combination inn and brothel, and got caught in the light from the ground floor. A scream—whether of joy, pain, anger, or just wine—made me jump. Avitus pulled me into the shadows, while a drunk wavered through the door. He looked like a tradesman. He stumbled, and fell against the wall, singing an obscene ditty.

"Galla's hole is nice and fat,

'Cause on a Legionnaire she sat.

For an *as* on me she'll sit—

But I get the hole that's full of shit!"

He was starting to scratch some graffiti on the wall, when a woman's voice screamed again, and a chamber pot flew out the upper story window, barely missing him. Amid a subsequent stream of curses, Avitus tugged at my arm, and we crept up the muddy alley behind the brothel, heading northwest.

We threaded our way through the knot-like cluster of the marketplace. Apartments gave way to Roman houses, houses to British round huts, and soon any roofs at all were few and spread wide apart.

We finally arrived at the top of a low hill, and Avitus stopped. As far as I could guess, we were somewhere near the fort. Glancing to his left and right, the *beneficarius* walked three paces ahead and stomped on the earth three times. He stepped back, expectantly. A sliver of light from what had been solid ground suddenly pierced the night. I watched in awe as a hand pushed open a sod-covered door, and the earth yawned open, illuminated with the yellow-orange light of torches.

The sudden glare blinded me. Avitus whispered something, and when my vision cleared was beckoning me towards the door in the earth, holding a torch in his hand. I peered in, and saw rough steps carved out of rock and earth, leading downward.

"We must break a sacred rule tonight, and allow an uninitiated man into the temple. The reasons will be clear shortly. But pledge me, Favonianus, that you won't speak of our god. To anyone."

He was tense enough. "I swear by Dius Fidius. Now where the hell am I?"

He didn't answer, and started to climb. The steps were formed from compacted dirt mixed with rock, and were uneven and treacherous. The moist, black soil absorbed the dim light of Avitus' torch. I barely made out the flicker of more lights at the bottom, some seven or eight steps lower.

When I managed to scramble down the dirt ladder—it was more ladder than staircase—I was in a man-made cave. Stone panels cut with strange carvings of animals and birds dug into the walls, and columns of rock braced a timber ceiling, helping to support the massive weight of earth above. A small group of men clustered around a marble statue in an apse. It was a finely carved portrait of a man in a Phrygian cap. He was slitting the throat of a bull. I was in a mithraeum.

Rumor was that Pompey brought it over from the East. Everyone knew it was popular with the Legions, but that was all they knew. Mithras liked his secrets, and Domitian didn't like Mithras. The Emperor didn't get along with other gods.

The figure on the right came into focus. Lit by the torches of two legionaries stood Bilicho, his hands tied with rope, his eyes blindfolded.

First relief, then surprise, then anger set in. Avitus knew Bilicho by sight. And he'd kept his mouth shut, hoping to cage a crumb or two of information while we stumbled over each other in the dark. The *beneficarius* would have to look elsewhere for a meal.

"Why are you holding my freedman here?"

He didn't even have the grace to be embarrassed. "We found him outside, nosing around. And he won't tell us why. Not yet."

We stared at one another for about ten seconds, and then I smiled and turned to go.

"Good night, Avitus. Send him home when you're done."

He looked a little panicked. "We didn't bring you here just to see him."

I paused, a foot on their dirt ladder. I turned to look at him.

"Then quit scratching your balls and get to the goddamn point."

One of the sentries looked shocked. It wasn't the hour for military etiquette.

Avitus pinched his lips together and made a brusque movement with his head to follow him. After a few steps I stopped.

"Let him go, Avitus."

He was striding ahead, but glared back at Bilicho and then me, and didn't argue. "Undo his hands. But he'd better talk."

One of the soldiers bent down and cut Bilicho's binding with a dagger. He rubbed his chaffed wrists, and grimaced.

Avitus, impatient, motioned me forward. "Mind the pit," he growled.

I glanced to the left. A deep hole, just the size for burial, was dug out of the raw dirt and filled with rocks. Only the quivering light of Avitus' torch lit the small anteroom in front of us. I could barely make out a bigger-than-usual altar shape with something large and shapeless on top.

The lines scoring Avitus' face deepened. "Tomorrow, the eighth day before the Kalends of Ianuarius, is the birthday of our god. I'm an initiate of the Sixth Level, and it's my duty to prepare the temple. A few hours ago, I came in here to begin. This is what I found."

He stood back, but shone the torch directly over the altar. There, trussed like a calf for sacrifice, was a fat, middle-aged man, his eyes rolled upward, a cloth tied around his mouth. His throat was slit in imitation of Mithras' slaying of the bull.

THREE

The man was dead—that much was obvious. His throat was slashed almost to the spinal chord. Avitus blanched, and turned away when I bent the nearly severed head backward to study the depth of the wound. Any sharp, solid blade could have done it, but to saw through the rolls of fat in the man's neck required strength.

A substantial amount of blood had poured over the altar, adding a grisly touch of color to the stone. Some of it had coagulated into pools, while more had just dripped down the side. The blood worried me. There was too much of it, and in the wrong places.

"Has anyone moved the corpse? And do you usually hold some sort of blood rite on this altar?"

Avitus was debating how much I needed to know.

"No one moved or touched anything. I posted some sentries, and they discovered your man prowling around outside when I was on my way to you. He wouldn't talk, so we brought him in here." He looked up. "I know your methods. I told the men not to remove this . . . this pollution." Avitus looked like he might be sick in a moment.

"And . . . my other question?"

"No." He croaked it harshly. "Sometimes . . . blood . . . but not here. Not ever."

I nodded. Relief made him unbend a little. "You understand why I came to you? We can't risk this getting out. The men are already restless, and they'll blame the natives. There'll be trouble for the governor."

"You're not usually so worried over what happens with the Brits, Avitus."

His eyes dug to the back of my skull. "I'm not. They're your concern. Agricola's mine."

"He's mine, too. I'm his doctor, remember?"

"Look, Favonianus. We've had our differences. But we both want what's best for the general, and I need your help. Serenus can't keep his mouth shut, and you know it."

The *vigiles'* surgeon sported the bedside manner of an embalmer and the discretion of a circus tout. If he examined the body, the bookmakers could lay odds on the dead man's last meal. From the looks of him, I'd put a *sestertius* on the honeyed dormice.

I looked at Avitus. Triumph glinted from the corners of his mouth.

"And then there's the problem of your assistant."

The *beneficarius* could make my life difficult if he wanted, at least until I could get to Agricola and beg him to have Bilicho released. But he needed my knowledge, and he couldn't afford to be too nasty.

I stared at him. Somewhere underneath it all, we liked one another.

"Give me the goddamn light."

A surprisingly boyish grin lightened his face, before it remembered how tired and frightened it was. He stuck the torch in a socket carved into one of the braces, and leaned against a dirt wall. Then he left me to my work.

The blood was all wrong. Severed arteries spew with violence—one battle can teach you that much. This looked poured on. I sniffed. I dipped a finger into one of the pools, and sniffed again, rubbing it between my fingertips. Avitus grimaced, and turned away. I knew human blood—spurting or oozing, thin or thick, dried or caked. I knew its taste, its smell, its colors. This wasn't human. I glanced at the *beneficarius,* who was studying a spiderweb in the corner. A small lick confirmed it. An animal's, probably sheep or pig. An even smaller voice told me to keep the information to myself. And anything else important.

Walking around the altar, I squeezed the man's feet. The knots of hemp around his knees and ankles were tight, and he was lying on his back. The stiffness hadn't set in that far, yet, but the feet were suspiciously still pink. I checked his hands. The cord was cutting into his wrist, too, and tied—like the others—in a British knot. The fingers were clenched, and when I tried to unbend them they fought back. He was cool, almost cold to the touch. I moved up to look at his eyes. The flat, deep brown was shiny, but a milky film was starting to form. The pupils were dilated. I knew Avitus was getting impatient for some answers, so I bent back up and spoke. "I think he's been dead for about four or five hours."

He nodded. "That would mean somewhere between the first and third hours of night. Anything else?"

"I need a bit more time. I'll be as quick as I can."

The *beneficarius* grunted, and slouched down, crouching, on the earth floor. It had been a longer night than usual for him.

I turned toward the corpse, and tried to picture the once-living man. He was fat, probably about forty to fifty, and swarthy. The brown of his skin was due to sunshine. The color covered his fleshy arm, stiff and extended from under his saffron tunic, in an uneven, mottled pattern.

A long mink mantle lay open and exposed beneath him. A few large, gold rings were nearly swallowed by the fat of his fingers, and an ivory and gold earring, in the shape of a woman, dangled from his right ear. I leaned over his tunic and sniffed. I knew better than to think any smell would linger in what was left of his throat. But a faint odor of something sweet—not beer, not wine, something else—wafted by me and disappeared. I glanced over at Avitus. He was nodding off, probably catching his only sleep for the day.

I moved around, back toward the man's feet. They were shoeless and swollen, and the color still troubled me. And they were fairly clean. That bothered me, too. I shoved my hands under his thick, hammy calves, and touched something damp and earthy. I grasped and pulled, and came out with a muddy slipper—the kind fat, rich, lazy men like to lounge in. Laying it beside him, I searched for another. No luck. I turned to his feet, and pushed hard on a spot below his big toe. The pink color remained.

Turning him over would make me certain, but I was worried about waking Avitus. If I found something—and I thought I might—I didn't want him to see it. The altar was wide, and I was able to shove the corpse on its side without too much effort. The body squeaked a little, as they sometimes do, and I wasn't breathing lightly. I looked up, worried, but the *beneficarius* was still sleeping.

I pushed up the man's tunic, and as I did a leather pouch peeped out from his right hip. He'd been lying on it, and whoever had done this to him hadn't bothered to take it. I braced his body with my left hand, and with my right, carefully disentangled the pouch from a belt which had been all but obscured by a roll of fat. It was heavy. Keeping my eyes focused on Avitus, I slipped it into the fold of my cloak, and hoped the *beneficarius* wouldn't notice the bulge on my left side.

Now I turned my attention to his back. The shoulders were rounded, looking as though they'd stooped in a perpetual cringe. If he'd been killed in this position, the blood should have settled here, in his back and buttocks. From the gore where his neck had been, all the way down to the crack of his ass, the color was the same as the rest of the body—a waxy, ashy grey.

I grunted as I lowered the corpse back down on the altar, and Avitus woke up. He snapped his head back and forth, like a ferret in a chicken house, eyes wide and large and alert. After a couple of seconds, he realized where he was. He pulled himself to his feet slowly, stretching his long arms and legs. He yawned. "What else?"

"He's just arrived in Britannia, and he's probably from the East—Egypt, maybe, or Cyrenaica. And he's got money—lots of it."

The *beneficarius* grunted. "I could have told you that. Any papers? What he did, who he was?"

I was smooth. "No idea. But I can tell you that he wasn't murdered here, if that makes you feel better. Someone dispatched him somewhere else, and then that same some-one—or maybe a whole new set of someones—brought him here, tied him up, and poured animal blood over the altar of your god. There would have to be at least two, to carry him."

Poor Avitus stared at the body like he hadn't seen it before. He'd wanted me to spoon feed him a tidy little robbery and murder, with the discovery of his temple an unfortunate and somehow accidental side-effect. But the fat corpse on the slab was no accident.

"Are you sure?"

I shrugged. "As sure as I can be."

"Goddamn it. We're all senior men. Who'd betray the temple? Who'd betray the *pater*, the governor himself?"

He choked on the sacred information and leaned against the wall and brooded. I was tired. With a look at that pouch and a talk with Bilicho still ahead. I decided to throw him a bone.

"Who said it was personal? Maybe some local saw the earth glowing. Maybe he thinks sticking a corpse in here will shut you down and hurt the legions. Maybe it was a joke. Who knows?"

The *beneficarius* stopped pacing. The bone was there for the chewing. He sniffed it, gnawed it a little, but decided not to wag his tail over it. Then he looked at me, and remembered I was fresh meat.

"Let's go see what your freedman has to say."

If I was worried, I didn't act like it.

"Let me straighten out the victim first."

I had noticed what looked like a fragment of papyrus clutched in the fat man's fist. I unscrewed the stiffening fingers of his right hand, the side hidden from Avitus' view, little by little. As I bent down to tuck the robe around the sagging flesh, I made one last effort to dislodge the paper. It was clammy to the touch, and I palmed it easily. I placed my other hand over the man's eyes.

"May the earth rest lightly upon you," I said piously.

Avitus had already turned toward the larger, better-lit room where Bilicho was waiting. I glanced down at the scrap in my hand, and caught a few words in the flickering light. The ones that stuck in my throat, the ones I was almost expecting, hit me hard enough to knock the air out of my lungs. Whatever document the piece had been torn from had been about a certain "C. Vibius Maecenas."

I shoved the paper in my tunic fold, next to the leather pouch. Bilicho was up ahead, still standing, his eyes covered, next to two soldiers. But I was the blind man—all I could see was a tense and lovely blonde, murmuring words in a low, cold voice, words I wished I'd never heard: "I want him to die. I'd kill him myself, before he touched me."

FOUR

Even in the dark cold, sweat trickled down my neck. I shivered. One thing I knew: whatever Gwyna's role, it wasn't the theatrical butchery of Maecenas' throat-slitting. She wasn't strong enough. And the rest I didn't have time to think about.

Avitus was watching me. Bilicho couldn't see me at all. The soldiers were angry and frightened and stiffer than Maecenas. This was supposed to be a nice mithraeum.

The *beneficarius* had his courtroom face on. It was time for opening arguments, and we'd better come up with a good defense—one that kept Avitus in the dark, where he was so obviously comfortable.

"These two men discovered—what is his name?"

I wanted to tell him his pretense was about as convincing as the Emperor's hairpiece. Instead I said: "You know him, Avitus. His name is Bilicho. My medical assistant. Recently manumitted."

It was too early for answers, and too late for too many questions, but Avitus was asking them anyway.

"He was seventy-five feet from the temple. There's nothing else around. The fort is two miles away, and the nearest farm is even further. It was as black as Hades, and he had no torch, no lamp, no flint. Is he going to tell us what he was doing here—or are you?"

The lip of one of the soldiers was curling like a woman's wig. There was one way out that I could see, and I hoped Bilicho would stumble through it.

I ignored Avitus, and walked close enough to feel Bilicho's breath. One of the guards made a move, but Avitus frowned and the soldier took his hand off the pommel. The *beneficarius* needed me. And I needed Bilicho.

I stuck a glower on my face, and made my voice a growl. "What did you spend it on? Wine? Cockfights? Whores?"

His face asked for directions, so I showed him the door.

"You were supposed to buy supplies. And be in bed, not tramping around the countryside. So go ahead. Explain what you did with my money. Explain how stupid I was to free you. It'll be all over town tomorrow."

He hung his head. I thought he might be hiding a grin.

"I'm sorry, Master. Arcturus, I mean."

I glanced at Avitus to see if he was buying yet. It wasn't fresh, and we'd have to try harder.

"What did you do? Why are you here?"

He stooped lower. "Tavern," he mumbled.

"Torture isn't just for slaves, freedman. Speak up!"

"I was at the tavern," he said loudly. One of the soldiers sneered.

"Which one?"

"The one with the big whorehouse. In the middle of town, by the market. 'Lupo's Place,' I think it's called."

"And? What were you doing? How long were you there?"

Bilicho tried to make himself smaller.

"All . . . all day. I spent the money."

I looked at him, too disgusted to speak. The soldiers moved a few inches away, as if they were afraid he'd rub off.

"On what? Drink? Dice?"

He visibly brightened. "I won some money back!"

"How nice. Fortuna smiled on you. Or was that the name of the whore you screwed?"

He almost groveled. "I'm sorry. It won't happen again."

"You're goddamn right it won't. I freed you, you son-of-a-bitch." We waited. Nobody said anything. I was improvising a forgiving master routine when Avitus interrupted me.

"How did he get here? He hasn't answered the most important question."

Bilicho answered as if he'd written the script. "Someone stole my purse. I'd won some, and was going to keep throwing until I had everything I started with." He eyed me like a kicked dog. "I couldn't go home and face"—he paused—"until I was sober and had the money."

"Who stole your purse? And how did you come here? We're three miles from town."

"I'm—I'm not sure. I thought it was two men. Two native men," he added. The soldiers looked at Avitus.

"They were watching me close when I was winning, and after they left I noticed my purse was gone. I asked someone what direction they went, and I thought I could catch them. But after I left the city, I got lost, and I—I kept hearing things. All of a sudden I saw the earth on fire. I thought it was Pluto coming for me!"

Bilicho's superstitious terror was a nice touch. One of the legionaries chuckled.

"He can afford you better than I can. Why didn't you explain yourself to Avitus? You know who he is."

The floor barely held him up. "I was ashamed," he whispered.

I stared at him for a few seconds, with what felt like a good mixture of embarrassment, contempt and pity spread across my face. I turned to the *beneficarius*.

"There's your answer. I was in bed—as you know—and thought he was at home. Looks like an unhappy coincidence."

Avitus grunted. "It looks that way." He nodded to the soldiers. "Does he have his purse with him?"

I tried not to watch Bilicho. I hoped Avitus couldn't see the knot in my stomach. The taller one spoke. "I searched him, sir. There was nothing."

The *beneficarius* grunted again. "I guess you can go, Favonianus. We'll both be busy tomorrow. Crenus, Arian, you escort these two home." He threw a hard glance at me. "For their own safety. Yorko and Didicus—take the body outside and bury it. Smyrnaeus—you and I will clean."

The escort disappointed me. We'd have to take the satire on the road, and I wasn't up for a tour. At least we wouldn't have to play in that particular hole again.

We climbed the steep earthen ladder. One of the men cut Bilicho's blindfold a little too roughly. I stepped hard on his foot, and made profuse apologies.

As we walked out of the clearing, the soldiers close behind us, Bilicho started weaving toward a large oak tree. I wondered why, until he brushed against it, and gave a sudden cry.

"My purse!"

The men came running behind us. They watched as he opened it, and showed the brass coins. I clucked my tongue at him in mock disgust.

It was a long trip back. I couldn't talk to Bilicho, so I thought I'd talk to the soldiers. The short one, a centurion named Crenus, was out. He grumbled too much, his men probably hated him, and I hoped his foot still hurt from when I'd stepped on it. That left Arian. He was tall, and wore the gear of an insignia bearer.

I said: "I haven't seen you before."

He met my gaze—we were about the same height.

"I was wounded last year in the night battle, when the Northerners attacked the Ninth. Nothing serious. You operated on a friend, though."

"How is he?"

"Dead. Under your hands."

I decided to ignore his tone. "What was his name?"

"Would you remember it?"

My hand made contact with his shoulder before I could stop it. He waited, surprised but ready, while I stood in front of him. Close in front of him.

"I may not remember the name of every man I treat, *Signifer*. But I damn well remember the names of the ones I couldn't save."

Bilicho flicked his eyes from the soldiers to me. We were on the outskirts of the city by now. Crenus had stopped grumbling for a moment.

"Lucius Cerealis. He was—"

"About to be promoted to *optio*. At the end of the summer campaign. He'd been looking forward to the extra pay—he was saving up for a farm in Gaul. That's where he wanted to retire."

"You remember—"

"Yes, I remember. Cerealis was one of the lucky ones. He was conscious for long enough to let me know where his family was."

Exhaustion honed my anger, and I watched it slice into Arian.

"You're not the only one in a goddamn battle. I fight like hell to save men already dead. Your friend had been cut in two with a double-bladed axe. His guts were ground sausage, and I couldn't keep him from bleeding to death. But yes—I remember his name."

I looked down to find my hands clenched. I was getting too old for this. I started walking again. Bilicho fell in beside me, and the two soldiers, saying nothing, kept a distance all the way home. I had had enough of conversation for the night.

FIVE

The two men saluted me when we finally arrived. I watched Arian, who kept his eyes down as he and the centurion faded into the gloom. I unlocked the door to find my bodyguard facing me in a battle position.

"Draco! I used a key!"

He shook his massive head. "When you went away with that man, I thought it best to prepare for anything. Especially with *Dominus* Bilicho not at home."

He took his job seriously. Maybe too seriously. When we could breathe again, we walked into the *triclinium* and found a few lamps still lit.

"Build up the fire. Wake Brutius and tell him to watch for the rest of the night. And tell him to light the kitchen hearth, too."

Draco tenderly sheathed his cast-off *gladius* and brought in enough logs for a blizzard. We shrugged off our muddy mantles, and I took out the dead man's pouch and piece of parchment. By the time Bilicho brought some more lamps from the examination room, Draco was finished.

"Anything else, Master? Food? Drink?"

"Nothing. Go on to bed."

The mention of sleep made his eyelids heavy. He lumbered through the door, and entered his own room down the hall, shutting it with a light clack.

I turned to Bilicho. "What the hell happened?"

He grinned. "Don't you want to congratulate ourselves first?"

"You, you mean. Sorry about the story. You know soldiers—they don't like freedmen."

"No one does. Yet somehow we breed like rabbits."

I leaned forward. "Listen—there's a dead man on top of their altar. And he's Vibius Maecenas."

I described how the body was laid out, and told Bilicho what I had found, and what I knew—what there was of it.

"Jupiter's balls. So that's where he went."

"Who?"

"The Syrian. He must have slipped out when I was inside."

"Inside what? What happened?"

Bilicho took a few seconds to get it in order. I knew it would be a long story—it always was, with Bilicho. But it was also always worth the wait.

"I caught up with the girl and followed her home. It's a nice house, small, older style. Looks run-down, though. Old door hinges, for one thing, and some of the wall beams are rotten. The roof probably leaks. So my guess is they need money."

I nodded. That tallied with the market gossip.

"I decided to hole up in an empty market stall across the street. I waited about an hour, thinking nothing interesting was going to happen, and then a man in his early twenties sauntered up to the door. Black hair, well-built, definitely a native. And he was wearing good clothes—too good for that neighborhood. A slave answered when he knocked—a bearded man, red-haired, kind of wild-eyed. About fifty. Bad teeth, too. He probably stank—the younger one kept a distance."

"Then what?"

"The slave wouldn't let him in—kept shaking his head. I could tell the man was getting angry, and even from across the street I could hear raised voices. Then he reached for something inside his cloak, and the slave vanished and shut the door like a conjuring trick. The other one just folded his arms and waited.

"About a minute later, the door opened a crack, and he slipped inside. So then I figured I'd better find out more about him, and the corner bakery seemed like a good place to start."

Bilicho paused for a moment, and picked at a tooth.

"I think that bastard baker adds rocks to the dough. Anyway, he was a typical nosy neighbor and told me Claudia's family— just she, her father, an underage brother and a couple of servants—are down on their luck, and have been for a year or so. 'I wouldn't mind a piece a' her,' he croaked at me. A real gent. Apparently the only piece he gets is her tongue, and not where it would feel good."

Bilicho saw my face get red, and hurried a little.

"Ur . . . the young man. The baker said he's been after Claudia since her husband died, about a year ago. That's when their finances went to hell, too. His name is Rhodri. And he's got a lot of money, for a Roman-hater."

I looked up. Bilicho nodded.

"He's made no secret about it. The baker hemmed and hawed a bit, but hinted around that this Rhodri is involved with the old religion. Well, of course he hates Agricola, because of Mona. He fought there, apparently, and he's living proof the governor didn't exactly succeed in killing off all the Druids. So naturally Rhodri hates him and everything the Romans do."

I could understand why. I'd almost left Agricola over it. "Go on."

"Well, I'd gotten this much out of the old man for the price of an *as* or two and a chipped tooth, and was on the point of trying to find something else to buy that wouldn't kill me when out of the corner of my eye I saw the girl leaving the house."

"How long afterward?"

"I'd been talking maybe half an hour. So I see her, wrapped up in something considerably less fine than she was when she came to you, and I thanked the baker with promises of drinks to come. Then I followed her up the street. Her head was covered, and she was in a plain brown mantle, worn at the edges, but I could tell it was her and not a slave woman from the walk and the shape. She knew where she was going—didn't pause, didn't look for markers, didn't ask for directions. So I figured she'd been there before."

"Go on." I was getting nervous.

"I stayed behind her pretty close. Went through some nasty alleys—I don't know if I'll ever get the pig shit out of my boots. She was making for the center of town, right off the main market, and bold as a peacock marched straight into Lupo's Place."

"So you *were* there this evening!"

Bilicho nodded, and allowed himself a pleased smile. "On business, not pleasure."

"Why was she there? What possible reason could she have for going to a—" I stopped. I felt my face turn red again.

"She wasn't . . . selling herself, was she?"

Bilicho looked at me with a modicum of pity. "No, Arcturus, she wasn't. At least I don't think so."

"What do you mean, you don't think so? Was she or wasn't she?"

"I—don't—know. Let me finish telling you what I do know, and you can figure it out."

I glared at him until I felt better.

"I followed her in, and bought a drink and a semi-decent chicken leg and cheese. The cheese tasted more like beer than the beer did, but it was better than the bakery. She talked to the innkeeper for a few minutes, then walked upstairs—that's the inn. The whores are kept on the ground floor, in back of the tavern. The barman saw me looking at her.

" 'Good-looking little squeeze, that one,' he said. 'Too bad she's marrying a fat, hairy foreigner. Persian or something. Rich

45

as Croesus, but not as pretty—even now!' He laughed at his own bad joke, and the stench that came out of his mouth was enough to make me wish I hadn't bought the food.

" 'Why doesn't she marry her own kind?' I figured the native approach would keep him talking, and I made sure not to speak Latin.

"He scratched a wart on the side of his nose, then blew it. 'Ah, there's them that wants her but can't afford her. Least-ways, not yet. Young man, nice-looking, British, of course.'

" 'Of course.' I leaned over the bar and placed my elbow next to his. 'Is that where she's going now? To meet her lover?'

"He leaned in close, and I held my breath so I wouldn't get sick. Thinking about it still makes me want to light some incense."

I made an impatient noise. "You'll live, Bilicho. And the drama is over, so hurry it up."

He eyed me with annoyance, and continued. "Well, to make a long story short he told me she was going upstairs to meet her fat, hairy betrothed."

"You mean Maecenas? He was staying at Lupo's?" I scratched my cheek until it hurt. "He had the money for something bet-ter."

"A cattle barn would've been better than that place. So I start asking the barman about him. He didn't know where Maecenas called home, but had a vague notion he was important to high-ups.

" 'I've even heard it said'—he leaned in close again—'that he's come here from Rome, and knows the Emperor personally.' He was nodding like an owl at the importance of his own information, and I clucked my tongue to show how impressed I was. After this he started repeating himself, so I looked around the room, trying to see who else might know something. Then I saw Claudia again, walking down the stairs.

"She wasn't in a hurry, and I thought she saw me, so I turned my head as quickly as I could and drank. It had been about half an hour from when she walked upstairs—probably less. It's hard to tell inside, they don't have clocks in taverns—keeps people from going home.

"Anyway, I left in a hurry and followed her outside. I still wasn't sure if she'd seen me. She was going back the same way she came—heading straight for her house. After I trailed her for a block, it just seemed more important to stay with the Syrian. So I turned back."

"What happened next?"

"I walked back in the tavern, and tried to spot the innkeeper. He's different from the whoremaster, it's a separate business. He was watching a dice game near the stairway, so I joined in and made a few throws."

"You gambled, too?"

Bilicho grinned in return. "Part of the act. I won a *sestertius*. I played for two rounds, and then stood up to talk to him. I was pretending to be a messenger for some big-shot merchant.

" 'Excuse me, sir, but I could tell from your air of authority that you're the proprietor here.' I could've been running for office, I was so greasy. He stuck out his little pigeon chest, and puffed himself up.

" 'Yes, I am. What can I do for you?'

"I made a show of looking around the room. Well, part of it was for show, and part of it was real. I didn't want to be overheard, and I wanted him to know it.

" 'I'm here on a mission of some secrecy for a . . . business-man. I have a message for the gentleman from the East. The one upstairs.' I was sure there wouldn't be two traveling Eastern-ers at Lupo's Place, even if there were more in Londinium.

" 'Ah, you mean the Syrian gentleman? Vibius Maecenas?'

"I landed on the name like I'd already known it. 'Of course,

47

who else?' I elbowed him a bit to be chummy.

"He leaned against me. 'You know that he's here on the Emperor's business.'

"I dug my elbow in deeper and nodded. 'And you know, I'm sure, he's to marry Claudia Catussa.' He nodded back, as smug as a bookmaker on collection day.

" 'So may I see the gentleman? It's rather urgent.'

"The innkeeper turned red. 'I'm afraid you'll have to wait. He's with—er—one of the girls right now. I think they call her 'Stricta.' It means 'tight,' you know.' "

Bilicho frowned, and his chin stuck out like it was looking for something to fight.

"Well, I told him I knew Latin better than he did, and that I'd wait for a while until the 'gentleman' was disposed to see me. The Syrian certainly hadn't wasted any time—barely fifteen minutes since Claudia left, and he'd already picked out the most expensive whore."

"How do you know she's the most expensive?"

He turned bright red. "I asked."

I ignored the implications. "Then what happened?"

"Nothing. For an hour or so. Claudia left as the sun was setting, and here it was the second hour of night and I was hungry and bored, waiting to see this Maecenas. The innkeeper didn't know anything else, beyond that Maecenas was rich, thick with Domitian, and here on some errand of mystery.

"I decided to leave and come back home. But when I walked through the tavern door—and after spending time in that dump, the night air was a real blessing—I heard some strange noises from the rear of the building."

I raised my eyebrow again.

"It wasn't that," he added, with a slight blush. "Unless Lupo's trying something new. This sounded like—I don't know—something scraping the walls or the floors. And something heavy, walking very slowly. It was odd—odd enough to make me want to find out more."

"And?"

"I started walking toward the back. There's a small alley behind the building—they probably have a rear exit. The noises got louder as I walked closer, and then stopped. Then I hear what sounds like a horse stomping, and a kind of muffled squeak, and this time toward the road to the west, on the other side of the building. Then all of a sudden there's a scream and a shout from the tavern, and I ran back inside. Who do you think I saw?"

"The Syrian?"

"No—Rhodri. He was standing in a face-off with some drunken soldiers. The natives in the place were moving to his side of the room—it was a real little war. One of the Romans pushed Rhodri, and he punched back, and all hell broke loose. I ducked, fortunately, because someone threw a stool at me. Then I made my way to a quiet corner where the innkeeper was hiding.

" 'What happened?' I asked.

" 'That Rhodri. Always after trouble with the Romans. And he's still in heat for the little blonde bitch. She's pretty, all right, but why the fuss? And who's going to pay for the damages?' I left him wailing and counting up the broken dishes and furniture.

"The real fighting lasted maybe five minutes—typical tavern brawl. Rhodri got in his licks and then sprinted upstairs. Two of his friends stayed at the bottom of the stairs, so I didn't follow.

"Finally, Lupo himself—the whoremaster—came out of the shadows and roared—that was enough to scare shitless anyone left standing. He's a great, big, ugly monster with one eye and a mass of scars—looks like the Cyclops, but not as handsome.

"That calmed it down, and just in time. The tension between

the Romans and the natives in that place was like Greek fire—anything could have set it off. I waited for a few minutes to see if Rhodri was coming down or not. I figured he wasn't up there to inspect the rooms. His men were getting nervous, but he never showed, and I was wondering what happened with the Syrian. So I decided to go back outside.

"I crept over to the rear of the building, listening for more noises. Nothing. It was too dark to see clearly in the alley, but I could make out what looked like some tracks going around the back and toward the western road.

"Well, call it a hunch. But I wanted to follow those tracks and see where they led. It was mostly all guesswork—I couldn't see, couldn't hear, and couldn't smell a damn thing other than the pig shit on my boots. I didn't even know what I was following.

"Soon enough, I wound up in the middle of nowhere, in a dark country meadow, tracking what I thought was a horseman way up in the distance. But I couldn't be sure. By the time I got to that tree where I stashed my purse, I'd lost the trail."

"When did the soldiers find you?"

"They didn't find me, I found them." He chuckled. "I saw the earth open up and figured it was a mithraeum. Supposed to be some evil-worshipping underground cult, where all the young men get deflowered. Anyway, I knew I was in way over my head, and heard several voices, including Avitus'.

"I figured I'd better be quiet until we talked, and I was pretty sure Avitus would bring you up there if he recognized me. Then I saw those two lumbering giants. They couldn't find piss in the *Cloaca Maxima*. I thought up a story about being robbed, stuck my purse in the crook of that tree, and let myself be caught."

I rubbed my eyes and grinned at Bilicho. "You always manage to surprise me."

His mouth twisted into a misshapen smile. "The day I stop,

kick me out of the house. I'll be no good to you. Are you going to Agricola?"

I frowned. "Maybe. I'd like to make sure he's all right—we haven't spoken since before Saturnalia."

Bilicho yawned like a shaggy hippopotamus. "Sleep first, then decide."

I sank on the couch and yawned in return, then saw what was on the table and flung myself back up. Bilicho checked to see if I'd sat on Draco's *gladius*.

We pulled the basket chairs around the table and moved in closer. I opened the fragment of papyrus and anchored each of the ends down with a lamp. The paper had been torn diagonally. From its size, and the quality of the papyrus, it looked like a formal letter, the kind that usually arrives with military orders or other command messages. A dollop of red wax remained at the top edge.

"His name is the only full word we have—here at the top," I muttered. "This looks like *'leg'* afterward—probably *legatus*. Hmm. That would declare him an official emissary. Here's the next line—"

"—*erio Domitiani*. By the order of Domitian!"

"Good. That fits. The rest of the missing lines would describe his office and list Domitian's titles. I can just make out a few more letters here, right in the tear. Hmm. *'—Olae'?*" I looked up. "It could be *'Agricolae.'* That means the message was to Agricola."

"Or about Agricola."

"Maybe." I carefully rolled the papyrus back up and turned toward the calf-skin pouch. It was sleek and expensive, beautifully tanned, and sewn with expensive gold thread. I weighed it in my hands.

"Heavy. We'll find more than brass or bronze in here."

I pulled open the leather strings, and emptied the contents

on the table. Bilicho gasped. At least thirty freshly minted gold *aurei* poured out, mixed in with about twenty silver *denarii*. The coins looked like the new type we'd heard about. Domitian had increased the amount of gold without increasing the face value, and the more valuable money almost never made its way up to Britannia. I stared at it. It didn't get here by swimming.

The murder motive couldn't have been robbery—at least of the monetary kind. But what was the Syrian doing with so much? Even a woman of Gwyna's beauty wouldn't fetch a price like this, even if she came from one of the scion families of Rome. Even if any were left.

The metal was a little too bright for my eyes. Next to it was a ring and a small pair of ivory dice. I picked up the ring. It was a signet, gold, thick, ostentatious. Malachite is hard to carve, and the initials were not elegant. I could make out the "V M" intertwined with a grape vine. I shook the pouch again, but it was empty.

"Nobody could spend this stuff. At least not on the street. And not without changing it."

I put everything back in the pouch. Bilicho added a slow-burning log to the fire, while I walked into the chilly corridor and took what seemed like a long walk to my bedroom. I opened a locked chest. Only I had the key to it, and I kept it around my neck, next to my mother's medallion. I nestled the pouch underneath some souvenirs of Delphi. Avitus would have to pull more strings than Orpheus if he wanted to search my house.

I stumbled and almost dropped the lamp on the way back to the dining room. Bilicho was sitting in the chair, nodding off. We were useless. I nudged him gently.

"Go on to bed. I'm staying here."

"Why?"

"I need to think before I fall asleep. It's bigger and warmer in here than my bedroom."

Bilicho shrugged. "It's your stiff back." He stood up, stretched, popped a joint in his shoulder, and made his way out the door.

"You sure you'll be all right?"

"There's the mantle if I get cold later, and I'll probably crawl into my own bed soon enough. Get some sleep."

I heard him mumble in agreement as he walked down the hallway. I yawned again, and after wadding up one of my cloaks as a pillow, burrowed into the couch with a still-damp mantle as a cover. Tucking my hands beneath my head, I stared at the ceiling. Vibius Maecenas was dead. Murdered and mutilated. Agricola's temple—a symbol of the Roman Army—desecrated. I closed my eyes, but it didn't help. All I could think about was the smell of blonde hair on a summer's day.

Six

Rosy-fingered Dawn never visited Britannia in the winter time. It made her neither rosy nor excited to get up in the morning. All I could see was grey. I'd been thinking about yesterday for nearly an hour and a half.

In front of me was the governor's palace. Four of the governor's bodyguard waited in front of the heavily fortified door. One glanced at me as I stood on the river bank, belching out clouds of smoke in the frigid air.

The palace sold Rome like a fishwife sold mackerel: there was nothing subtle about it. It was big, obnoxious, and covered in reasons why you should get down on your hands and knees and kiss the ground because Julius Caesar had decided to take a piss across the *Oceanus Britannicus*. Green and white marble in front, black columns, painted statues—you coughed up the money before you remembered you didn't like the taste of fish.

It was unfinished, but it didn't matter. Even the guards were decoration—the palace was the real threat. Agricola had softened it with the generosity of other buildings: the baths, temples, the arena, law courts—everywhere you looked, you saw the benevolent smile of your governor, Britannia's *paterfamilias*. And now, all of a sudden, everyone wanted to be Roman—at least the upper classes. The lower classes preferred to stay invisible.

I shifted my weight. The governor was a brilliant man. For the last five years, the sunshine of Rome had shone down on little grey Britannia, and peace was just around the corner. The South was officially subdued except for a stubborn few, who clung to the past like men on a life raft. They'd kill a soldier here, burn down a building there. But the distrust and resentment they fed on was lurking right beneath the surface. Even in Londinium.

Agricola didn't worry about it. Tribal memory was as stubborn as a rock, and he'd worn it down to a pebble or two. Time would do the rest. He wanted the North; he'd get it this summer. He'd build a line of forts, and keep the South safely Roman.

He was a man with much to lose.

I turned back. The palace looked the same as it always did. The guards were alert but bored, the threat and the promise of Rome still intact. I would see the governor—but not now. Better to wait for Avitus.

I was a man with much to lose, too.

Roosters were crowing all over the city by the time I got home. Venutius made some warm oat porridge for a change, and dug up a few dried plums and bread rolls to go with it. Unfortunately, the porridge wasn't the simple mixture it pretended to be. I smelled it, and my stomach shriveled in horror. Goat milk and *garum*. There is such a thing as too much creativity in a cook.

I was gnawing on a stale wheat bun when Bilicho came in, still looking sleepy.

"Did you see Agricola?" he asked, and sat down, reaching for a plum.

"Beware of the porridge this morning. No—I decided against it. I expect Avitus will arrange a meeting with the governor, and I don't want to crowd him."

"So where do we start?"

"The inn—"

Venutius came in to clear away the untasted oats, gave the still-full bowls a stricken look, and dragged himself back to the kitchen. We tried not to watch.

"—the innkeeper, the whore—even Lupo. Anyone who came into contact with Maecenas. And I want a look at his room right away."

Bilicho leaned back in his chair, munching a date, his forehead creased. "It looks like two crimes. One, the Syrian. And two, the temple."

"Could be. We can't rule anything out." I rubbed my eyes. "Here's what we've got. A fat, hairy, and very dead Syrian, freedman to Domitian, part-time spy and full-time sycophant. Carrying a message—probably imperial—to Agricola. It's gone, taken by somebody. He was also carrying enough cash to buy a small army of his own, and build a homey villa on the side. But nobody took the money. He wasn't killed in the mithraeum. Maybe he was killed at Lupo's, and then delivered to the temple. Maybe he's his own message. He must've really had something, if two sets of people are fighting for the credit of murdering him."

"You sure he wasn't killed in the temple?"

The bridge of my nose hurt from frowning. "They used sheep or pig blood on the altar. The bastard was already dead—the throat slice was for show. I wish I'd had more time with the body—I should've found another wound."

"Could it've been suicide?"

"You mean he kills himself, someone finds the body, steals the document but not the money, and mounts him on the altar like a choice heifer?"

Bilicho grinned. "All right. What about poison?"

I looked at him. I remembered the sickly sweet odor from the Syrian's mangled neck. For some reason, I didn't mention it.

"Possibly," I admitted. Then I changed the subject.

"And then there's the damn message. Why didn't he deliver it? Imperial messengers—if he was one—are supposed to go straight to the palace. Why was he at Lupo's?" My elbow knocked over a cup of *mulsum,* which started to ooze across the table. Bilicho wiped it up with his sleeve before Venutius came in with a towel.

Bilicho was watching me. "You're as jumpy as a *flamen* with a scrotum itch."

"I've been jumpier. Let's figure out the timing. He was killed about four or five hours before I saw him—sometime between the first and third hours of the night. You said he was with a whore."

"Stricta." The color rose in Bilicho's cheeks. I pretended not to notice.

"So he was with Stricta after Gwyna left—"

"—Until Rhodri started the brawl and ran upstairs."

We looked at each other. Rhodri led us back to the one subject I wanted to avoid. Bilicho leaned back even further in his chair. My eyes met his, a little defiantly. With a barely perceptible shrug, he turned his attention to the food.

He asked: "What do you want me to do?"

"Find out all you can about Rhodri. Where he lives, how he gets his money. He's got a motive for the murder, and a motive for the mithraeum. He hates the Romans."

Bilicho smacked his lips loudly on a plum pit, and looked at me with a pitying expression. "Probably not as much as he hated Maecenas—for personal reasons."

It was my turn to change color.

"Spit it out, Bilicho. She wanted Maecenas dead, now he is, and her boyfriend was right there. That's as obvious as a middle-aged redhead. Remember—she came to me. To warn Agricola. And she was telling the truth, I'd stake my life on it."

His face told me I might have to. I ignored it.

"If Rhodri killed the Syrian, why take the document and not the money? And what about the mithraeum? Couldn't he find an easier way to humiliate the Romans?"

A memory snuck over and hit me from behind.

I said: "Yesterday was the ninth day before the Kalends. That's the New Year in the Old Faith."

Bilicho whistled. "I should've remembered that. Sure makes it seem like the whole thing was planned. And by a native."

"But no one knew the Syrian would arrive when he did. You know how ships are in this weather." I rubbed my neck.

"None of this makes sense. And maybe you're right, maybe we're dealing with two crimes. But goddamn it, don't treat me like a child." I met his gaze. "I know a suspect when I see one."

"I'm sorry. I've just never seen you like this. Over a woman, I mean."

I smiled sardonically. "It happens, Bilicho. Even to you, it will happen."

He snorted and ate another date.

I told Venutius I'd eat lunch in town, and asked for a simple dinner that night. He looked depressed, but better a depressed cook than a half-dead master. I was beginning to think he'd make a good poisoner.

It was a feast day due to the solstice, so no *salutatio*. I asked Bilicho to post a sign directing all cases to Serenus. I had a feeling we'd be busy for the next few days, and Avitus hadn't notified the *vigiles* yet. Serenus wouldn't kill anyone. He wasn't that talented.

I didn't own a litter, but a bodyguard was status symbol enough. Draco could come with me, and we'd both dress for the occasion. My mantle was thick and purple with a trim of green grape leaves, and I wore it over something even louder—my toga. The purple stripe flaunted my rank with all the subtlety of a campaign speech. I looked like a pompous ass.

Draco was as giddy as a virgin on her wedding night. His short tunic in grey wool was hemmed with a simple pattern of blue stripes. I let him wear his sword, and an inlaid bronze arm bracelet that showed off his biceps. He looked like the bodyguard of a pompous ass. We were finally ready for the whorehouse.

Some heads turned along the way. Purple stripes didn't travel those streets—at least not in daylight. Most people were at home, and the city was quiet, except for soldiers, slaves, worshipers of various gods, and the common variety of bath-loiterer.

Draco tried to steer me away from the largest piles of mud and shit, but my ankle boots would never be the same. A few stable flies that had survived the cold were starting to form a queue behind my feet when we finally reached Lupo's Place, conveniently located at a main crossroads just northeast of the baths and near the center of town. I recognized the building. It was the same inn-cum-tavern-cum-brothel Avitus and I had passed on the way to the mithraeum.

I expected an audience when we walked through the crude door, and was surprised to find it empty. Taverns were always full. Unless they knew something that I didn't.

A thin-chested man was watching me, his mouth open as he apathetically wiped the bar with a flannel cloth. A drunk hunkered down over a bowl of steaming wine in the corner. He was the only person visible, but I thought I could feel more than two pairs of eyes.

Draco scanned the room, and took a stance. I told him to wait by the door until I was finished, and to pretend to be mute. No one could leave without going through him, and most walls were softer than Draco.

I strode up to Pigeon-Chest. He glanced nervously at the

drunk in the corner, and spoke in a thin, cringing voice.

"C-Can I help you to something, sir? Anything in my humble tavern that would satisfy your stomach?" He made a pitiful attempt to appear worldly. "Or perhaps it's not your stomach that needs satisfying?"

I frowned and he bit off the laugh in his throat. The glint of gold on my finger blinded him for a second, and with my left hand I clinked the coins in my purse.

"You are the innkeeper?" I was as sour as Cato's mother-in-law.

"Y-yes, sir. I manage the tavern and the inn, the whorehouse is Lupo's."

I gingerly sat down on a stool. I was going to hammer the Rome of Domitian down their throats. Bilicho had extracted all the information a native could. But somebody, somewhere, knew more, and it would take a rich, obnoxious Roman to find it.

"Who is he?" I pointed to the drunk.

"Him? That's just old Madoc. He's a tanner by trade, when he practices it. He's drunk most of the time since—since—well, he's drunk most of the time," he concluded in a hurry.

"Since when?"

Pigeon-Chest gnawed his lip. "Since a few years ago. He was in a battle, against—against—"

"Against the Romans?"

"Uh . . . yes. But pay no attention to him, sir, he's not important, and he can do you no harm."

I bristled at the suggestion, and the innkeeper nearly squealed. "I didn't mean nothing, sir, I—I—how about some wine? I serve an excellent mead . . ." Time to relent a little. "Nothing, thank you. I'm here because you spoke to a servant of mine last night." I emphasized the last two words, and looked at him like we both knew what I meant.

His weasel eyes darted around the room, and his tongue came out to lick his lips. "L-last night? Is it about the fight? Was he hurt? I'm sorry, I tried to stop them, but—"

"No, it had nothing to do with the fight. He spoke to you earlier. About one of your guests."

I lowered my voice. At the mention of "guest," Pigeon-Chest got canny. His eyes wore a flat, lizard-like black. He knew something.

"What guest?"

The stammer disappeared. I glanced over at Draco, who took a step closer into the room and looked over in our direction. Pigeon-Chest paled. I leaned in closer.

"I think you know the guest I mean. I'd hardly believe you had more than one at a time in this dungheap. Now, I have business with the gentleman. I suggest you show me to his room."

"I—I could call him down—"

I grabbed his arm. It takes a strong grip to clamp open wounds. He winced. As we walked upstairs, I gestured to Draco to remain where he was.

The hallway was dirty and empty, with pornographic graffiti scratched everywhere. Some of it was anatomically impossible. Lupo's offered women, boys, and apparently dwarves, when they could get them.

"Are you sure this is an inn?"

He noticed my disgust, and cackled with nerves. "Our customers like to take advantage of Lupo's business, too."

We arrived at the last door on the left. It faced the rear of the building, and was adjacent to a back stairway.

"Where does the stairway lead?"

"Outside, to the mews." He avoided my eyes as he knocked on the door. He knew it would be empty.

"Did the—gentleman—request this particular room? All the

others are empty."

"Yes. Sir? Sir?" He was making a pretense of calling Maecenas. And lying.

I put my hand on the door. "Open it."

He looked up at me, his eyes round and shiny and full of fear. He was terrified, and not just of me. He fished in his filthy tunic—it looked as though he'd slept in it for several days—and pulled out a ring of keys. Fumbling a bit, he fit one in the lock and opened the door.

I walked in, while he cringed on the threshold.

The room was bare. I checked the chest and found no sack, no bundle of belongings. The cot was rumpled, but neat. No sign of struggle, no mess. I looked at the floor. Pigeon-Chest memorized my movements as if he wanted to get the details right. No blood on any of the floorboards. Someone had done a thorough job of erasing Maecenas' presence like so many words on a wax tablet.

I walked to the small, dirty window that overlooked the alley below. The glass was cheap, and I'd seen clearer panes made from cow horn. What light struggled through caught a tiny gold thing in one of the cracks of the floor. It was a triangle or point of some kind, maybe part of a *fibula*. I hadn't recalled seeing one on Maecenas last night. I looked at it closely. The gold was high-quality, the original pin a trinket of a well-to-do man or woman. Or maybe a prize of someone not so lucky. I put the piece in my pouch.

"Where is he?"

"I—I don't—"

I advanced on Pigeon-Chest with a scowl. "The bastard owes me money. I sent my servant here to collect it last night. Where the hell is he?"

The innkeeper shrank against the wall. He was trying to figure out what he could tell me and still stay safe.

"He—he's disappeared. No one's seen him since yesterday."

"No one?"

He shook his head in confirmation.

"Did anyone see him leave?"

"No. He must've gone in the middle of the night."

I unbent a little. "Did he owe you money, too?"

His flat, shiny eyes got brighter, and he found he could talk again—businessman to businessman.

"No, he paid for several days in advance. Is-is it true that he was a freedman of—of—the Emperor's? That he was marrying a native girl? That he's here on some sort of s-secret business?"

I poked my head out the door and looked down the hall. No one in sight. The action made the impression I wanted.

"That's what *he* said. Whether or not it was true . . ."

I left the thought dangling in mid-air. He took the bait.

"Oh! I see. So you loaned him money, thinking—"

"I loaned him money. That's all you need to know."

He retreated, hastily. "Of course, of course." Puzzlement creased his bulbous brow. "But the girl, she came here last night."

"Who?"

"The one he was supposed to marry."

I forced myself to shrug. "So? It's not like it takes much to impress a local. He probably paid a few *sestertii* and got himself a good breeder."

The innkeeper nodded. I swallowed my disgust, and it was hard to keep it down. Then I pounced.

"How did you get taken in?"

He stuttered some more, and the lizard-lids came back over his eyes. "I—I forget who told me. He may've told me himself. Yes, he said so, when he paid for the room. Said 'This money came all the way from the Palace,' and I said, 'The Governor's Palace,' and he laughed kind of nasty and said, 'No, idiot, the

Emperor's Palace on the Palatine Hill in Rome,' or something like that. And he talked about the woman he was marrying."

I didn't want to hear what he'd said about Gwyna. Pigeon-Chest was hiding something, maybe something small, but it wasn't coming up this morning. I turned abruptly and strode to the doorway.

"I need to talk to anyone who saw him last night. He may have mentioned something. I'm not about to let fifteen *aurei* slip out of my grasp."

His eyes bulged. "Fifteen *aurei?* That's more money than I've ever heard anybody here having—probably more than even Agricola owns!"

I pursed my lips and started walking back through the hall. "He saw a whore last night, didn't he? I want to talk to her."

He shrank, suddenly, frightened beyond what I could do. He was in front as we started down the stairs, and I could see the reason. At the foot of the stairs was Draco, with his arms folded, and towering over even him was what looked like a Cyclops.

Huge, craggy features jutted out like spines on a hedgehog. A thicket of black, wiry hair sprouted from the top of a gargantuan but pointy head, and a mass of scar tissue was all that remained of a left eye. An entire ox-hide clothed his huge, misshapen body. He carried no weapon. He *was* a weapon. A monster, created by the gods to make the strongest man piss on himself at the sight.

Fortunately, I'd seen worse. And, to the shock of Pigeon-Chest, the sound coming from the hole in Lupo's face was laughter. He seemed to be joking with Draco. I shoved the innkeeper out of the way.

"Lupo, I presume? How do you do." I grasped his hand, a courtesy I hadn't extended to Pigeon-Chest.

His voice was surprisingly gentle. "You want something?"

"Yes. The bastard who was staying here last night left owing me a great deal of money. I'd like to talk to whichever girl serviced him."

Draco stepped backward. He'd evidently forgotten what I told him about pretending to be mute. Now he placed himself between Pigeon-Chest and me.

Lupo thought for a minute. He wasn't as slow as he pretended, but then neither were we. "Galla. He saw Galla last night."

I laughed bitterly, took out three *denarii,* and placed them on the bar. "I should have known better. My slave told me the Syrian had 'Stricta.' This should be enough to buy your whole operation. Now, let me see her."

Lupo wasn't used to tough talk. Draco stepped out from behind me now, his hand on his belt, his muscles tensed. He was smaller than Lupo—what wasn't?—and much more agile. Lupo was grotesque, but no fool.

"Stricta. All right. You see Stricta."

He lurched off in the direction behind the bar, and I wondered what sort of joke he could've told to make Draco laugh.

We left Pigeon-Chest behind. He scooped up the coins, but I didn't think he'd try to dupe Lupo. Another figure came out from the kitchen, a gap-toothed man of middle-age—probably the wine-server. He huddled behind the bar with Pigeon-Chest. I glanced in the corner. Madoc was gone.

The rear cubicles were too small, dark and cramped for anything other than a three minute poke, but it looked as if the women were actually living in them. The graffiti was worse down here, and so was the stink. Bodies, bodily fluids and sour wine mixed in a heady aroma that made me almost dizzy with nausea. I guess the women got used to it. I guess they had to.

The front cubicles looked the smallest—more like pantries than rooms. I could hear some noises from one or two—mostly male gasps and groans, and an occasional dramatic pounding on the wall. A cheap and tawdry whorehouse, one of several in Londinium, and one of countless thousands across the Empire. Some better, some worse. Though I couldn't imagine any much worse than Lupo's. Even the life of a whore should be worth more than a flea-bitten straw mattress on a stone ledge, with only watered-down vinegar to dull the pain and two-inch roaches for a sympathetic ear.

Stricta was a little better off. She'd been given an actual room at the end of the hall. The murmur of women's voices, even women's laughter, was coming from her cubicle. Lupo's thundering footsteps could be felt in the floorboards before he entered, and the laughing stopped. He pushed the cheap flannel curtain aside and walked in. I was close behind him. Draco stayed a discreet distance in the rear.

Lupo pointed at one of two women, a garishly made-up, henna-haired whore of an age impossible to determine. She was still plump around the cheeks, so she could've been younger than she looked. A stale perfume of spices, pennyroyal and dried violets swam around the tired room, unable to escape.

"You—Stricta. This man wants to talk to you about the Syrian."

The woman looked surprised, and then stared at me. I stared back. The other woman, a small, intense brunette, a little less garish, fled.

What passed for a grin creased Lupo's face. "Stay here. Talk. You paid for her." With that, he lumbered off.

I poked my head from behind the red flannel drape and told Draco to stay, and then turned back to the woman in front of me. She was attractive, in a desperate, mean way. Her hair looked like it once was really red. The eyes were blue, dull, but with a spark of cunning. She seemed oddly familiar.

"How much did you pay for me?" she asked, stretching out

on a cot with a provocative leer.

"Three *denarii*."

Her eyes widened. "You really are a rich boy, then, aren't you?" For some reason, she found this funny, and tilted her head back to laugh.

It was more like a laugh-scream, a strange, almost angry voice. I remembered, then, where I'd seen, where I'd heard, this woman. She wasn't Stricta. She was Galla, the girl of the drunken ditty.

SEVEN

I was lucky to recognize her. Her voice was distinctive, and even though Avitus had dragged me away from last night's comedy, I remembered the stream of curses and piss the whore tried to pour on the drunk. I'd underestimated Lupo. It wouldn't happen again.

Galla was staring at me with curiosity. No doubt she hoped for a bonus. She grinned knowingly, laid back on her cot, and spread her legs. Unlike Gwyna, she couldn't afford silk underwear. Apparently, she couldn't afford any at all. The sight was far from arousing.

I walked the few paces to the cheap straw mattress—glad the stuffing had been changed recently—and sat down, next to her, facing the wall.

"Here—what is this? I thought you paid for me. Stricta," she emphasized. "Don't you wanna see why tha's my name?"

I shook off the exploratory hand she'd snaked around my lap. Her hands were older than her face.

"No offense—Stricta," I added, with equal emphasis. "I paid for information. That's all."

She studied me, surprised, from a kneeling position. I stood up and faced her. She met my eyes, shrugged, rearranged her thin, spotted tunic, and sat down. A cautious, animal-like wariness came over her.

"So whaddya wanna talk about?" She slurred her Latin, and

68

now spoke with a pronounced native accent. She smelled of fusty wine.

I held up a finger, and stepped to the door. I craned my head around the corner and saw Draco, still alert, but revealing an unhealthy fascination with the odd noises coming from a cubicle up the hall.

"Draco!" I whispered.

He jumped, blushed, and strode toward me.

"Yes, Master?" he breathed in a booming undertone.

"Shhh. Quieter. Where did that other woman who came out of here earlier go? The dark-haired one?"

"I remember. She was small. Looked a little like Coir. She and Lupo walked into that end room." He pointed to the first curtained stall off the tavern, the farthest from where I was. "Then Lupo left, and she's been there ever since."

"Good. Now listen to me, and this time don't forget what I tell you."

He hung his head and blushed. I couldn't be too hard on him. Maybe Lupo told a hell of a joke.

"Stand in front of her cubicle and don't let her leave. If Lupo—or anyone else—comes through here, yell."

He nodded. I turned back into the room, where Galla had lit some shabby incense and poured herself something fermented.

"Wan' some?" She offered the drink with an expansive gesture, as if she were a hostess on the Palatine.

I smiled, and shook my head. What she was drinking smelled like the cheapest *posca*. She swigged it from a chipped, cracked *kylix*—a bit of eastern drinking ware that probably belonged to Stricta. The *posca* probably belonged to Stricta, too.

"Tell me about the Syrian who was here last night."

She drank again, smacking her lips. Then she shrugged. "Not much t'tell. He had a lotta money. Saw some little blonde thing he's gonna marry. 'Course, she didn' give 'im what he needed," she added knowingly. "Tha's why he called me."

Galla must've already been half drunk when I walked in, and the boozy vinegar she was gulping finished the job. That should make mine a little easier.

"Did he say why he was here?"

A wary look again crossed her face and body. She sat up straighter. She'd been rehearsed.

"Business deal for Domitian. Friend of the Emperor. A freedman. Here to marry tha' girl. Came—oh, day b'fore—night before—last. Don' know why—he didn' pay to *talk* to me." She aimed a leer at me.

"What did he do when he was done with you?"

"Whaddya think? What they always do. He wenta sleep. Then tha' Rhodri started trouble," she added with an afterthought. That didn't sound like part of the script.

"What about Rhodri?"

She stared at me and frowned. The wine was starting to make her a little volatile. "He's one 'a us. Not one 'a you. I ain't sayin' nothing against 'im. He wants that li'l bitch . . . her father sold her. Sold her for money to tha' Syrian." She hiccuped. "Tha' makes her a whore, jus' like me."

"Were you with the Syrian when Rhodri came in?"

"No. He finish'd early." She giggled. She was improvising.

"How long between when you were done with the Syrian and when Rhodri came upstairs?"

"Who knows? I go from one t'other. I work all night. After th' Syrian, I had one a' my regl'ars."

"A tradesman?" I asked.

She sobered up a little. "Yes. I have many re-gu-lars." She stretched out the word in an effort to speak more clearly. Fear crept behind her eyes.

"Do you know where the Syrian is now?"

She paused before replying. Insinuation perfumed the rancid

atmosphere. I reached into my purse, and took out a *denarius.*
Walking over to the *kylix,* I dropped it in with a plink.

She grinned. "You're a good man. I'm s'pposed t' say he left
for Durovernum on business. Changed his mind, maybe, 'bout
the girl. But—I heard—" her voice dropped to a low whistle—
"He's dead. Murdered."

She fished the *denarius* out of the cup and drained it. "Maybe
you killed him!" She laughed her angry laugh again at her own
bad joke.

"Maybe." I walked to the cot, and it agitated her.

"Whaddya want? I was jus' jokin' around—I tol' you what I
know, even extra."

"I appreciate it. If you remember anything else, there'll be
more." I gestured to the *kylix,* and sat beside her, and spoke in
the native tongue.

"Listen. Forget you talked, to me or anybody else. If you're
asked, say you haven't. And if someone makes trouble for you,
find me." I handed her two more *denarii* and her eyes bulged.

"Lupo's put you in a bad spot. Don't let him make you play
Stricta for anyone else."

She rose from the cot.

"H-How did—"

"It doesn't matter. Find me. Ask at the marketplace for where
Agricola's doctor lives."

Her mouth hung open, and I could see she didn't have many
teeth. I wondered how long she'd been living like this—and
how much longer she could expect to live. I got up to leave. She
just watched me. The shock had nearly sobered her.

"I'm going to find Stricta. Stay here, keep quiet, and tell
Lupo you did what he told you to do. Remember—come if
there's trouble."

I left her to hide the *denarii* wherever she could and entered
the hallway. A retired veteran was walking toward me with a

dyed blonde whore in a skimpy crimson tunic. He glanced at Draco and me, but the woman succeeded in pulling him behind the drapes of her stall.

Draco was still standing near the cubicle with the real Stricta, keeping an eye on the entrance to the corridor. I pushed aside the cheap green linen that hung from the doorway.

Inside, the small brunette I'd glimpsed earlier was perched on the far corner of an even cheaper mattress than in her own room, holding her arms tightly around herself, and rocking in a quick, repetitive motion. The smell of fear overwhelmed the other odors.

She looked up like a wild thing when I entered, and shrank against the wall as if she expected me to hit her. She was actually pretty. With her nickname, she must not have been in the business long. Her skin was olive and her face was Greek.

"I'm not going to hurt you. Don't be afraid of me, Stricta." It was the voice I saved for the fatal cases. She understood the tone. Never letting her eyes leave my face, she edged toward the bed. I tried Greek.

"Are you Egyptian? I can speak to you in Greek, if that is easier."

At the sound of the other language, her tired brown eyes found a spark of something, and she stared at me.

"That's good. You can understand me. Listen. I am your friend. I am Galla's friend, too."

She frowned, and a little more spirit crept into her face.

"No, she did not betray you. But I knew she was not Stricta. I have seen her before."

There was a long pause. She finally spoke in Greek, with a heavy Egyptian accent.

"Who are you? And what do you want with us?"

I wanted to get her out of there. She'd been beaten recently—bruises still showed on her thin arms, even behind the dark complexion. Her lip was swollen, and the garish white makeup that covered her face couldn't hide the marks of violence. But she moved like a priestess. Despite her pain and the omnipresent stench, she made the squalid room feel like a temple.

"My name is Arcturus. I'm the governor's physician. Something happened here last night to the Syrian. I'm trying to find out what."

She nodded. She appreciated the truth.

"I know. He was murdered."

"Do you know when?"

She shook her head and lowered her eyes.

"Do you know why he was here?"

Again, she shook her head. Kindness wasn't enough. I tried money. I reached into my purse and pulled out six *denarii*. I'd spent that much on Galla.

Her face darkened at the sight of the coins, and she brushed me aside. They insulted her. I should've known better.

"Go now. I have nothing to tell you."

I placed the money on the bed, and took her hand. "Who did this to you?"

Her eyes hurt too much to read them. "If I talk, I lose my ears. Or my eyes. Or anything else a whore doesn't need. Please go. I have nothing to say."

"Stricta, listen. You don't have to stay here. You can come with me. I will protect you. I have many slaves—one of them is very strong, he's outside. Please—promise me if they beat you again you'll find me. I live by the river, not far from the governor's palace. I can buy you."

She shook her head before I was finished. "No. They will not sell me now. If I am quiet, they will be merciful."

I took her by the shoulders, and she flinched. "Don't believe that. Lupo asked Galla to pretend to be you. Both of you are in danger. I can protect you both."

She looked at me with a kind of desperate hope, but then I heard Draco. Someone was coming. She reacted more quickly than I did.

"Take the coins!" she hissed, grabbing them from the bed. I pocketed all but one, which I kept in my palm. I raised my voice.

"So—Galla—you look like you could handle—"

Lupo lumbered in the room with another man, a young Roman immaculately dressed and coiffed. He moved with the lightness of a backstabber and stank of perfume. He seemed to hold Lupo with an invisible chain. I had a feeling he was the real owner of the entire business, inn, tavern, and whorehouse. The fact that I was seeing him at all meant I was doing something right.

I stared at his smooth, soft face—marred only by the closeness of his eyes. I turned to the Cyclops.

"What is this, Lupo? I'm not accustomed to being interrupted when I pay for a woman—"

"You pay to talk to Stricta. This not Stricta."

I studied the giant like a *haruspex* examining a particularly foul liver. "I paid three *denarii*. That should be enough money to buy your entire shithouse of a business—"

"Not quite," the young man interrupted. His voice was easy and pleasant, the voice of someone who spends his time selling dried-up mines and two-thirds shares in leaky ships.

"My name is Caelius. And you are—?" He meant it as a demand, not a question.

I smiled. My first look should've been enough to warn him. "I was under the impression that we don't use names in an . . . establishment like this one. So you're actually proud of your business. A citizen, are you? Why don't they call it 'Caelius' Place'? Such a nice ring to it."

He turned a gratifying shade of purple. Small, mean eyes

darted back and forth, looking for a target, and I expected the pink tongue that licked his lips to have a fork in it. He wasn't showing fangs. Not yet.

"And who I am is not really the point, is it? I paid money— *good* money—"

I poked him in the chest with the *denarius* still in my hand. Hard. Lupo took a step forward, but Draco was right behind him.

"—to find out some information about a lying, cheating, smelly bastard that, unsurprisingly, chose to stay here last night. He always had a taste for shit."

I moved close enough to smell the unguent on his cheeks.

"I play with real money, not the bark you people wipe your asses with. I talked to Stricta, who tells me he left. The Syrian was only interested in oiling his prick—she doesn't know anything else."

Sweat was starting to ooze from Caelius' face. I watched a drop form on his forehead and slowly drip down his cheek. I moved in a little closer.

"The money was spent, so I decided to have a go at this little thing here. She's not completely worn out, unlike most of the hags I've seen crawl out of these rooms. And then you come in and interrupt me before I can get her clothes off." I took one more step. This time, he backed up.

I said: "You're lucky I don't haul you into court."

Lupo was watching us, confused and alarmed. He kept looking toward Stricta, and concern etched a pattern in his caved-in face. But then, he wasn't the monster.

Caelius had no dignity to recover, so he was scrambling to pick up the pieces of his shattered aplomb. He would've sold his mother's eyes to find out who I was and what I really wanted. I almost wanted to tell him. But I was sure he'd long since blinded his mother for a chance at something else.

"Very well, I understand. Lupo thought—well, never mind what Lupo thought."

Lupo looked at him with bewilderment. This wasn't Lupo's idea. Caelius' small, girlish mouth was smiling the toothy grimace of a man afraid of something. It was something dirty, something he was equally afraid of losing and getting. Money was a part of it. I could smell it on him, despite the sandalwood. He probably slept with it at night.

He said: "If you like her, take her. I apologize for the intrusion."

I shook my head. "Forget it."

I moved forward to enter the hallway. He thought about blocking my way, but reconsidered and stepped back, a pleasant smile on his pleasant face. The cruel lips and eyes and twitchy hands were desperate. He'd do anything to save himself. I wondered if he'd be able to save himself from me.

I made it deliberate. I said: "I don't like whores that look like boxers."

He raised a plucked eyebrow. "Oh? Is she bruised?"

"Oh? Are you blind?" I mocked him. "I get my money's worth. If I want bruises, I'll make my own."

That got his attention. I was, after all, a man he could understand.

"We have more—"

"No thanks. There are other whorehouses in Londinium. Maybe your competition will appreciate a paying customer."

"You must be new in town."

He thought he'd scored a point.

"Must I?"

This time my smile didn't bother to hide anything. Caelius got a little pale. "It's not been a pleasure, gentlemen. If I find the Syrian, he'll owe me even more money. For forcing me to talk to you."

I let my eyes memorize the pores in his nose. Then I gestured to Draco with my head. He fell in behind me and we made our exit.

The innkeeper was craning his neck, trying to catch a glimpse of what was going on. The tavern was nearly full. Natives and Romans, merchants and auxiliary soldiers, all formed small pockets. There was a murmur when Draco and I walked into the room.

If anyone had any information, I'd make it worth their time. I marched up to Pigeon-Chest, slapped my palmed *denarius* on the table, and in a loud voice proclaimed that I'd give ten *denarii* to anyone who could help me find the fat Syrian bastard. Then I ordered a drink, which gave the crowd enough time to get a good look at us. Caelius was watching my every move.

I swigged a cup of watered-down mead and readjusted my toga. With a dramatic gesture of farewell, I finally got the hell out of Lupo's Place.

EIGHT

The fresh air felt good. Lupo's had been an ordeal, and not just for my nose. I leaned against the brick wall of a small grain *horrea,* and tried to put it all together. I was worried about Stricta and Galla. Caelius wouldn't have gone through such an elaborate ritual of hiding something if there wasn't something to hide. But if Maecenas was killed there, why not let Rhodri take the blame? Why pretend the Syrian left? Why hide the connection when the mithraeum did it for them?

I rubbed my forehead, and only succeeded in getting dirt in my eye. It was time to move on. I was already tired.

The streets were crowded now. A group of young natives—more boys than men—were lounging against the wall of a fuller's shop, making rude gestures to the soldiers passing through or heading for the whorehouse.

Some cavalrymen rode by hard, and one of the horses kicked up some of the muddy shit I'd tried to avoid. It was muddier and shittier than before, and it landed on the cloak of one of the young Brits.

The girl with him held her hand to her face and giggled, and he turned as red as his hair. He shouted a particularly vivid curse at the soldier. The *eques* checked his horse and turned in his saddle. His hand was already on his sword when I told Draco to grab the reins.

"What the—Who are you?" he demanded. "Get the hell out of my way."

"I wouldn't address a superior officer that way, *Eques.*" I was not in the mood for bullies. He stared at me.

"You? An officer?"

"Maybe you didn't notice the senator's stripe. That ought to be enough." I took a few steps closer to his horse. "My name is Julius Alpinus Classicianus Favonianus. I hold the rank of centurion."

Some dim recognition dawned on his swarthy face. "The *medicus.* Agricola's *medicus,* that's who you are."

"Don't advertise it." Draco's hand was still on the reins. I looked back at the boy. He'd done a good job of coating himself with filth in an inept attempt to wipe it off. His friends were still laughing at him, in between sneaking a few glances in our direction.

I faced the black beetle eyes of the cavalryman. "Throw him a coin. His cloak is ruined."

The *eques* shot a wad of spit on the ground that narrowly missed my foot. "You overstep your authority—*Medice.* Those bastards lie in wait for us, hoping to start trouble." He leaned forward in the saddle and bared his yellow teeth. "We don't run away from it."

I ignored the smell of week-old garlic. Then I smiled. "Such a brave man. I'm impressed." His eyes flicked back and forth from me to Draco. Draco said nothing, but his fist was turning purple. He'd evidently remembered he was supposed to be mute.

I made it conversational. "Courage is a Roman virtue. But you know—so is generosity." My finger traced an old lash welt on the neck of his stallion.

"Myself, I'm a generous man. For example, I'll forget you said I'm overstepping my authority. And I'll forget you're disobeying orders from the governor about fighting with the natives. I'll even forget you're ignoring a direct command from me."

I felt his knuckles crack when I grasped his hand and threw it off the sword pommel.

"Throw him some money, *Eques*. And give me your name. Because next time, I won't be so generous."

The beetles crawled over my face. He pulled a pouch from a saddlebag, and plucked out a few *ases*. The natives were watching us, now, waiting. He was watching me, and abruptly flung the coins into the crowd. They scrambled in the mud to pick them up, jeering and whistling at the soldier.

He leaned over in the saddle and blew more garlic in my face. "My name—*sir*—is Gnaeus Quatio. I won't forget, either. *Pathice!*"

He dug the spurs into his horse, and sped off, kicking plenty of mud on my mantle and Draco's cloak. I held out an arm to stop Draco from sprinting after him and pulling him off. I'd been called worse, and by better people. I didn't mind making enemies. It always helped me think, and here it was, still morning, and I'd already made two.

But Caelius and Quatio would have to wait. I'd been dreading the next visit since yesterday. If dread and desire can exist at the same time.

I looked at Draco. His solidity was comforting. The sun was at its zenith, and Londinium was as bright as it was going to get. I knew where to find her from Bilicho's directions. But what I'd do when I did find her was anybody's guess.

By the time Draco drew alongside me and nudged me in the ribs, we were nearly there. I was grateful for the interruption.

"Master—there's someone following us. I think from Lupo's. Do you want me to seize him?"

He looked a little wistful at the prospect of a fight. I'd been hoping someone would track us out of Lupo's—whether with something to sell or something to hit us with.

I shook my head. "Let's wait here."

We slowed to a crawl, and I looked around like I was lost. A heavily swathed figure—dressed in layers of old, nearly decayed tunics, bound with leather straps—emerged from the shadow of a nearby wall and drew close. It was a moving, shapeless bundle of once multicolored cloth, now a uniform spotty grey, but torn and repaired until the patches were stronger than the linen. A head wrap hid the face and hair. I recognized Madoc.

A hand brushed my shoulder. He gestured with his head to follow. We turned the corner of a garden wall, and leaned into a recess.

He unwrapped the shaggy brown-red beard and mane I'd seen this morning. But his eyes weren't drunk, or stupid, or even old. His back unbent, and he stood with a soldier's bearing, his body looking much stronger than it had at Lupo's, when he was pretending to be a sloppy drunk, and I was pretending to be a pretentious bastard. His voice, when he spoke, was deep and melodious.

"I saw what you did. With that *eques*. Why?"

I stared back. "If you know who I am, you know why."

His eyes drifted down and lingered on my mother's medallion. I'd forgotten to take it off that morning.

"I know who you are. But some say you turned against your own people long ago."

He knew who I was, all right.

"Which people? I'm a Roman—and a Briton." I wasn't in the mood for this. I couldn't afford to lose my temper again.

"I'm a man, Madoc. My mother married a Roman. I was adopted by another Roman, who was born in Gaul. That makes me—what exactly?"

He looked surprised when I addressed him by name.

"It makes me a man. One among thousands, in Britannia

and Gaul, in Phoenicia and Nubia and Bithynia. I'm a native and a Roman. A Brit and a Roman. And I've never turned against any of my so-called, goddamned people."

He waited for my color to die down. I hoped I hadn't lost all chance of getting some information.

"Romans and Britons." He shook his head. "I do not think you can be both. But I know you tried to help. At Mona."

Mona. My nightmares came back at Mona, the ones where they were swinging the ax at my mother and all I could do was scream. It's funny how memories turn into dreams.

I looked at him. Madoc had fought there. I'd been caught in between. I turned my back on the carnage, and on Agricola. I'd tried to reason with the governor—make him see that the wound would never heal, that destroying Mona would never destroy the Druids.

Rome's greatest strength was in embracing other faiths and making them her own. The only thing left for Rome at Mona were the puddles of blood and the desecrated, chopped down oak groves. I'd never forget the smell of burning wood and corpses, the smoke filling the sky while the waves lapped against the shore. Mona was a bad dream. It was a worse memory.

I said: "It wasn't enough."

"So now what do you do? Now whom do you help?"

Something in his voice . . . I stared at him. Was he referring to the Syrian's murder?

"I help—peace. I don't want war between my people."

He gazed at me thoughtfully. "But who are your people, *Meddygon?*"

This time I stayed in control. He was testing me. Now I remembered why I hadn't gone to a rite in so many years.

My eyes met his with a stubborn frown and I answered in the native tongue. "All who desire justice. All who value life. And all who seek the truth."

The reply seemed to satisfy him. After a minute, he began again.

"The Syrian you seek. He is dead."

"He was murdered. I have to find out why."

He shook his head. "Accept what is. You do not always need answers."

I felt my lips pinching. I'd forgotten how irritating the priests of the Old Faith could be. Or was he just trying to warn me?

"The dead man was important, Madoc. To the Emperor. If I don't discover who murdered him, it could be blamed on the natives. And it will hurt Agricola. I know he's made mistakes, none worse than Mona. But he's done much good for Britannia. He's my friend. And another governor might be worse."

Madoc's face stayed stony, but I caught a look of alarm in his eyes. Maybe some self-preservation had penetrated his thick British skull. Or maybe he was frightened, too.

"You have been a friend to us. I respect you. I tell you this: there are other believers, different believers, who hate both Roman and native. They hide in the darkness. They hold only one god holy. They wish to destroy all others. Look for them when you seek the truth." With one last piercing look, he wrapped his head, and vanished down the narrow lane.

NINE

Draco and I watched him go. He blended into the wattle-and-daub houses like a politician at a resort town. Interesting. And irritating.

He'd been trying to protect someone. I could feel it. Who? And how the hell did he know about the murder? Was Rhodri guilty? Was he protecting Rhodri? I shook my head. Always more goddamn questions.

So the Druid blames another cult. One—he says—that hates Romans and the Old Believers. The only group I knew of who worshipped one god, in secret, were Christians. An offshoot from the Jews. A one-god belief, and if there was one god above all others in Rome, he was squatting in a palace on the Palatine Hill. So they kept quiet, if they wanted to keep alive.

Mithras was more reasonable. His temples could be a little damp, but he didn't care how many other gods you went out with as long as he got his share of the sacrifice. He was a normal kind of deity. Not like the jealous gods of Judea.

I scratched my chin with my thumbnail, and thought it over. There'd been no trouble from that part of the world since Titus stamped out the rebellion of another faction. The Jews were supposedly embarrassed by the whole affair.

Of course, the Christians embarrassed them, too. The Jews had spent generations adjusting the careful balance between Rome and their god, between what they owed the Empire and what they owed their priests. Then a clique decides to commit suicide by not paying taxes and not giving allegiance to the Emperor. It was insane.

When I was a boy in Rome, I saw some, once, queue up in the amphitheater to be killed by Nero. Then I threw up on a shriveled old senator and Classicianus took me back home. I couldn't understand it then, and I couldn't understand it now. Because if reports were true, they were doing the same thing for Domitian, and happy about it because they got to meet their god sooner. I could wait a lifetime to see mine, and I had a few to choose from. And none of them was worth dying for.

Debating the behavior of a strange cult brought me no closer to a solution or to Gwyna's house. I was hungry, and it was time to find some food. Draco's stomach already sounded like a dog fight. We continued down the road to find Bilicho's bakery closed. We'd have to depend on our hosts for lunch, but at least we wouldn't need a dentist.

Across from the baker and a little further down stood a Roman-style house. It was old and hunched over, and probably built when Londinium was founded. It had managed to escape Boudicca's fury, but not the more patient malice of time. I turned to Draco.

"Stay outside the door. Whistle if someone wants in."

He nodded, while his belly groaned in privation.

"I'll ask them to bring you some food." I tried to brush off as much mud as I could, and told him to do the same. After readjusting my toga, I was ready.

"Knock on the door."

He was about to try again when I heard a shuffling noise. The door opened with a squeak, swinging precariously on two hinges. A blue eye, topped by bristling red eyebrows, peered belligerently through the crack at Draco. I stepped closer, so that it could see me.

I said: "I'm here to pay a call on Claudia Catussa."

The eye scrutinized me carefully. The door opened a bit wider. "That your slave?" a voice growled.

"Yes."

It examined me again, afraid it had missed something the first time. The door opened a little wider, and I could see a face. A full red beard hid most of the craggy, cantankerous features of a man in his fifties or sixties. His beard was stained with wine and food, and he was clearly missing most of his teeth. I remembered Bilicho's warning.

With a final groan, the tortured door opened wide enough to let me in. He had to prop it open at an angle, due to the missing hinge. Both eyes crawled over Draco from head to toe, hoping to find something objectionable. Finally, he nodded once.

"Enter."

"My slave will wait on the doorstep. We don't wish to be any trouble."

He snorted, as if that were unlikely. With another abrupt head movement, he motioned me inside. I caught the odor of chickpeas and pork, and so did Draco. He sniffed the air like a Molossian hound, and longingly peered through the opening. Red-Beard seemed to take delight in closing the door in his face, but was hampered by the fact that it was a slow process.

The interior surprised me. From the outside, it looked like a modest Roman house with an atrium. Everything was squared that wasn't warped or broken. The inside, however, was that of a native round house.

A circular room, supported by wooden pillars, seemed to be the main eating and living area. Constructed around a large hearth, it was too warm and too dark. A small opening in the roof let in a little sun, while a hallway surrounded the center room and led to several other doors. Branches of mistletoe hung in the traditional places. The chickpea smell was drifting from behind the hearth.

Red-Beard stumped ahead of me toward the fireplace. He walked with a limp—one leg looked shorter than the other. I followed him.

Sitting near the fire, on a hefty couch covered in furs, was an old man. His long, stringy hair had once been blond; it was now a faded straw, tinged with silver and white. His beard was neatly trimmed, and he was sitting up and staring at me.

The clothes he wore had been young once, too: a Roman tunic, trimmed with molted rabbit fur, and old-style leg wraps. A torque and a set of gold *phalerae* hung on his withered body like old cronies swapping war stories.

His sharp, beaked nose jutted between two milky eyes that had once been the same blue as his daughter's. He reminded me of an eagle who could no longer hunt for itself. There was pain in his face, and rage, made all the worse because of its helplessness.

He looked me over with pride, since that was all he had left. I kept a respectful distance, and nodded my head. Red-Beard grunted.

The old man's voice said he was dying, and it said it wouldn't be long. But it was still a voice that commanded, not questioned.

"Who are you? Why do you wish to see my daughter?"

"Julius Alpinus Classicianus Favonianus. I'm usually known as Arcturus. I'm the governor's physician." I let him take that in before adding more.

"I'm here because your daughter's *sponsus* was murdered last night."

His impassive face flickered a moment. "Sit down."

He gestured to an old, well-made chair that wore some battle scars of its own. He tried to sit up straighter, and the effort tired him. It also infuriated him. He turned to Red-Beard, who waited with the devotion of a favorite dog.

"Leave us, Meuric. And tell Sioned that we will have

one"—he looked at me questioningly. "Did you come alone?"

"I have a slave outside."

"—two guests for the midday meal." Meuric—Red-Beard—lowered his head and backed out through a door by the hearth. The old man studied me for a few moments.

"I am Urien. I am Gwyna's father."

I nodded again. I knew what the name meant. But I'd already figured he'd been an important man among his people—probably a local chief.

He leaned forward. "I have always—*always*—been a friend to Rome. You see these?" He gestured with a long, graceful hand to the bronze torque and the *phalerae*.

"The Emperor Claudius himself gave these to me. I was an ally of Verica, the Atrebate King. I led many of my people, the Trinovantians, into battle for the Romans against the Catuvellauni. But that was many years before your birth," he muttered. "No one remembers."

"Your length of service and devotion to Rome must be honored by all who see you."

His face twisted into a bitter smile. "No one sees me. I cannot stir from this bed; my legs are useless. All, all have forgotten me. Even Agricola, who could use my wisdom to help heal deep wounds. No, I am forgotten, even before I am fully dead."

I pitied him. That was my first mistake.

"I will ask the governor to visit you."

A flash of anger passed through the milk of his eyes and curdled any remaining softness.

"I do not need or invite your patronage. If he wished my advice, he would have come already. But I am not valued. I am not remembered."

His shoulders twisted with pain. "But you didn't come here to hear the laments of an old, dying man. You are here because Vibius Maecenas is dead."

"Murdered."

He looked at me, his face more interested than before. "How do you know it was murder?"

"I'm a *medicus*. It's my job to know. I saw the corpse, and he'd been killed."

"How?" Urien sounded more like he wanted confirmation than answers. I gave him the obvious.

"His throat was slit."

"Ah." For an old, dying man who couldn't get out of bed, not much surprised him.

"Did he have money with him?" He shot the question suddenly, and surprised me. My second mistake.

"Yes. No. I—I don't know."

He didn't say anything. He folded his fingers together and stared at me hard, as if he were waiting for something. I was beginning to wonder how much those milky eyes could see. And I tried to remember I was supposed to ask the questions.

"Did he owe you money?"

He raised his eyebrows. "Of course. Surely you knew that he was to marry Gwyna. That is why you're here, isn't it?"

A parry and a jab. I was bleeding on the floor. I tried again. "Maecenas was a foreigner—how did you meet him? Why betroth your daughter at all?"

He smiled and spun it around like a praetorian on parade. He was enjoying himself. "You've seen my daughter, no doubt. Do you find it hard to believe that the stories of her beauty traveled to Rome?"

I shook my head.

"I thought not. Vibius Maecenas is—was—a friend of a friend's. Marcus Caelius Prato. I'm sure you know of him—he is the owner of the brothel and tavern in which Maecenas, unfortunately, spent his last evening. Maecenas had written him to find out if there were any beautiful women of good birth in

Britannia. It is an unfortunate but indisputable fact that our family's fortunes have been in decline since Gwyna's first husband was killed. I had several subsequent offers for my daughter's hand, and Maecenas' was the most lucrative. That was all." He waved off any objection with a dismissive gesture.

But that wasn't all. He'd told me too much. A man of his birth, his pride, should not so easily admit to needing money. And what was that bastard Caelius doing with this dying old man?

Urien was watching me again. Amusement animated his face, and made him look more alive.

"What happens to you now that Maecenas is dead?"

He shrugged. "Someone else—with money—will wish to marry Gwyna. Maybe you." His laugh was as dry and mirthless as a leaf from last autumn. It chilled me. The old man was still dangerous.

"Is that why you won't give her to Rhodri?"

I hit a nerve. "What do you know about Rhodri?"

Now I took my time. I was worn out, sore and hungry, and couldn't afford to make the wrong move. Urien, even crippled and nearly blind, was too skilled an opponent.

"I know that he wants to marry your daughter. And I know that he was at Lupo's last night. Rhodri may've been the last man to see Maecenas alive."

He smiled at me sardonically. "Then he'd better be careful. I told you, no one marries my daughter without paying a very large bride price. Rhodri is not penniless, but he is far below Gwyna's worth."

"Was the marriage the only reason Maecenas was here?"

He shrugged again. The gesture was painful and unnecessarily elaborate. "Who knows? One hears rumors. There was a rumor circulating that he was a bearer of bad news for Agricola."

I leaned forward. "What kind of news?"

A fit of coughing—real or not—racked Urien's thin body. At the sound of his gasps, a middle-aged woman—I assumed Sioned—entered from the kitchen, bearing two large bowls and a plate of bread.

She was short, doughy, and grey-haired, and hovered over him, glaring at me each time his chest gurgled. When he could breathe again, he motioned for her to leave.

"Sioned and Meuric are the only servants we have left. They are my people. Meuric served under me in the war. Unfortunately, Sioned and he are childless, and so are dependent on me."

Too much information again. Why was he telling me this? To emphasize no one in the house had any reason to kill Maecenas? No one, that is, except the woman who was sold to him.

He gestured toward a bowl. It smelled good. Small pieces of roasted pork swam in the chickpea mixture. Out of the corner of my eye, I noticed Sioned creeping toward the front door with another helping. Draco would be fed.

We ate for a few minutes without talking. It gave me time to think. He obviously didn't know about Gwyna's trip to see Maecenas last night. He'd have already offered an explanation.

I cleared my throat. "I wish only health and fortune to you and your daughter. The unexpected death of her *sponsus* must grieve you both. If you have any information that would help me find his killer, I'd be grateful."

He sat down his bowl, and wiped his lips punctiliously with a napkin.

"Yes. I thank you for your good wishes. They do not buy food for the table, however. We will sorely miss Maecenas' money. Be that as it may, I can only think of one person who would wish him dead."

"Who?" My arms tightened.

He gazed at me steadily with a faint—very faint—twitch of his lips.

"Our governor. Agricola."

I jumped up, knocking my bowl to the ground.

"What?"

"I wouldn't have fed you if I'd known you were going to waste it," he growled. "What I have heard—and this is just the gossip that comes to a shut-in old man—is that Vibius was carrying papers to Agricola from Domitian. The papers were orders, telling Agricola to relinquish the governorship. Everyone knew they were coming, there've been rumors going about for months. Unfortunately, they seem to have arrived in the person of Maecenas and he appears to have borne the brunt of the bad news."

His face twitched again into a bitter imitation of a smile. "So you see, young pup, however unlikely it is, our governor has the best motive for killing him."

Urien basked in my confusion, rolled around in it like a cat in a sunbeam. While he called Sioned to clean up the mess and refill my bowl, I fell into the chair. I felt as clumsy as a *retiarius* caught in his own net. The old man was right.

Rumors had been flying for months that it might be the governor's last year. Agricola and his supporters had the best motive for murdering the messenger and destroying the documents. Provided they knew Maecenas was carrying them. And from what Urien said, that wasn't exactly a secret.

Killing Maecenas was risky, but the only way to keep Agricola in power. Once those orders were delivered, read and accepted, any delay in following them would guarantee a civil war.

Sioned handed me a full bowl with a look that suggested she'd put in some poisonous mushrooms. I barely noticed. Too many goddamned questions again. Why didn't Maecenas go to the palace right away? Why stay at Caelius', and not be lodged like a normal imperial messenger? And the money—the question of the money gnawed at my mind like a ship rat with a rope.

Urien's opaque eyes glinted with malice, and for once I knew what he was thinking. Maybe I had a motive. Maybe even two motives. If I didn't know better, I'd suspect myself.

I finished the meal in one long gulp, and stood up.

"Thank you. I'll keep you informed of our progress."

His sunken chest wheezed with satisfaction. "I assume you wish to speak to my daughter?"

"Yes. Is she here?"

"I believe she is in her room. You may go to her." I could see him calculating how much my clothes were worth. The lines on his face carved out the imitation smile again. "I trust your intentions."

I bowed. He clapped his hands, and Sioned emerged from the kitchen. He told her to take me to Gwyna. She wasn't happy, but gestured for me to follow. I left Urien in front of his cold fire. I wondered what I'd find behind his daughter's door.

TEN

Sioned led me through the hallway on the right side of the round room, to the upper corner of the corridor. She turned her head, to make sure I was behind her, and gave me a look normally reserved for bill collectors. I don't think she cared for my toga. She tapped lightly on the door three times.

"My lady? You have a guest. A Roman."

She made it sound like a disease. I heard the rustle of frantic movement behind the doorway, and Gwyna thrust open the door. Her face still came as a shock.

The finery of yesterday was gone. She was dressed in a brown linen tunic, old and spotted with stains. No jewelry on her fingers, no furs caressing her body. But she took my breath away.

She looked at me like she'd never seen me before. She nodded at Sioned. "You may leave us."

Sioned reluctantly bowed, and Gwyna motioned for me to come in. The room was simply decorated, with a small mattress, a writing desk, some shelves with scrolls and tablets, and a few scattered souvenirs of better times. There was also a blond boy, about ten, sitting at the desk and staring at me.

She blushed a little. "Hefin, go to your room. We'll read more later."

The boy jumped off his stool.

"Who are you?" he asked, reaching out a hand to feel my muddied cloak. "I saw your slave outside. He's big."

"Yes, he is. Bigger than me, even. My name is Arcturus. I'm a *medicus.*"

He nodded sagely. "I know what a *medicus* is. Are you here to marry my sister?"

It was my turn to blush. "I'm a friend of your sister's."

"Lots of men want to marry her. Rhodri wants to—"

"Hefin! Go to your room!"

He gave Gwyna a look of injured dignity. His head held high in an uncanny imitation of his father, he marched from the room and shut the door behind him. She paused for a moment, still looking toward the door. Her shoulders were tense. She turned to me, and met my eyes head on.

"I'm sorry. Hefin is—"

"A child. And your brother. You're teaching him?"

"Yes. We can no longer afford a real tutor."

"You don't need one."

She looked down, and reddened again, and plucked at a spot on her tunic. The room was hot and it was hard to breathe. The memory of how we said good-bye was crowding us out. She walked to the desk, her back to me.

She said: "Arcturus, I'm—sorry you've seen me. Seen my family."

I followed her. Then I put a hand on her shoulder. She let it stay.

"Why? Because you're not rich? Because you save your good clothes to make an impression? Do you think I care?"

She didn't respond. Her eyes were dull today. The spark of urgency, of resistance, was gone. I turned her around to face me.

"Listen to me. Maecenas was murdered last night. I know you saw him."

There was no surprise. She searched my face, but didn't find what she was looking for. Despair hung on her beautiful body like a shroud.

"I'm so tired, Ardur. Tired of fighting. Tired of worrying." She sank on the bed.

I sat beside her. I reached over and brushed a stray hair from her neck. She stiffened. A coolness crept between us, and froze me colder than a Vestal's tit. We were two strangers sitting on a bed. And I was running out of patience.

"Do you want my help or not?"

She got a little sharper. "Of course I do. I—I told you so yesterday."

"You said a lot of things yesterday. Were they all true?"

I expected her to get mad. But she answered as if she were really thinking about it.

She said slowly: "Yes. All of them."

"Including the part about needing me?"

It was too hard and too easy to look at the face that turned toward me. Somehow I managed.

It was just one word. She said: "Yes."

I was tasting her hair before I realized she was wrapped around me. I smelled lavender again, and the pressure of her nails in my back felt as good as anything could. We drank each other in, but the thirst wouldn't go away.

After a while, she nestled under my arm. I knew the peace, the leisure of it would end, and I knew once it did I might be sorry. But I didn't care.

"How did you know about me?"

"The women gossip. They wonder why you're not married."

"I'm not the only bachelor in Londinium."

She reached a hand up to feel the growth of beard on my chin. "But you're the best-looking. You should learn to trust women again."

I looked down at her in surprise. "What do you mean?"

"Everyone knows you had a torrid love affair when you were

young and in Rome, and then Agricola's daughter fell in love with you but they married her off to someone more ambitious, and then you just stopped looking."

I didn't know whether to be outraged or amused. "What else do they know?"

She ticked off the points of my biography with her fingers.

"Your mother was killed in the War by Boudicca's army, and your Roman father was already dead—stop it—and you were adopted by an important man—Nero's procurator, I think. And then you studied—Ardur, no, I mean it—and decided to become a *medicus,* which most people find strange—will you *stop?*—but I don't. And everyone knows you've been solving problems for a long time, too. They say you've saved innocent men and helped to punish the guilty. They say the gods favor you."

I had my doubts. Sometimes I wished the goddamned innocent would save themselves. I reluctantly removed my arm and sat upright. I held her hands.

"We need to talk."

She nodded. The spell was over. It was crawling back inside of us, where we'd try to forget about it but wouldn't be able to. We had to be two strangers again.

She squeezed my hands and then let go.

"My—my father doesn't know I saw Maecenas last night."

"I didn't think so. Don't worry—I didn't mention it."

"He'll find out eventually." She rose from the bed, and walked to the small window. The light was getting darker. Her next question surprised me.

"How did he die?" The words blurted out as if she hadn't meant to ask.

I couldn't lie to her. But I also couldn't tell her everything. So I told her what I told her father. "Somebody slit his throat. He was found in the mithraeum."

Her quick blue eyes flashed. With—what? Relief?

"Thank you. That's what we'd heard this morning."

" 'We'? Who told you?"

The pointed question surprised her.

"Rhodri." The dim light illuminated her body, wrapped in a cloth much too rough for its delicacy. Her face told me that she knew that I knew who Rhodri was. But I had to finish the game.

"Who is Rhodri?"

She turned and smiled down at me. It was her father's smile.

"A man who desperately wants to marry me. A native. A troublemaker." There were other questions more pressing, but what the hell.

"And you? Do you want to marry him?"

She fidgeted, turned her back on me, and straightened a wax tablet that Hefin had been writing on.

"I—did. At one time."

"And now?"

"No." It was a simple word, just one, and it was whispered. But my lungs were working again, and this time I didn't kiss her.

"Where is he now?"

I could hear the armor go back on. She wasn't going to tell me everything, either.

"I don't know. In hiding, I suppose." She responded to my raised eyebrows.

"I know he's a suspect. And for good reasons, which will soon be on everyone's lips, if they aren't already. He was here, last night. He threatened to kill the Syrian. And then he followed me—to the inn."

She arched her back slightly, and rubbed her neck.

"Rhodri is innocent, I'm sure of it. I begged him not to go, and I didn't see him follow me, or I would have stopped him. Somehow. He must've gone in after I'd left for home. He's not a bad man. He talks more than he acts."

"He acted last night; he started a fight at Lupo's before he ran up to Maecenas' room."

She nodded with impatience. "Yes, I know. He told me. But he's like a child. His anger flares and burns out and then it's over. He wouldn't—couldn't—have killed the Syrian. Besides, he wouldn't know where the mithraeum is or how to get into it."

But he knew that Maecenas' throat was cut. And he knew he was found there. That meant one of the soldiers talked, or somebody—possibly Rhodri himself—had been around last night to see it. Or it meant Rhodri was guilty. Either way, he was a man to see.

I wondered how many people knew the Syrian was dead. Madoc did, and Rhodri not only knew, but told Gwyna where the body was found and how—apparently—he'd been killed. There were too many people who knew too many things, and I wasn't one of them.

"You still haven't told me why you were on your way to see Maecenas. Without your father's knowledge. I can guess why Rhodri wanted to kill him."

She turned her back on me. A flat irony crept into her voice. She didn't sound like the same woman from a few minutes before.

"It's difficult to explain how hard poverty is—particularly on my father. He's been depending on the—the marriage fee." Her body shook a little, but the words were steady. I waited.

"Maecenas sent me a note yesterday. He arrived earlier than we expected, on the night before, from Dubris. Obviously, I hadn't known he was already in Londinium when we spoke. He sent word to my father through Caelius. My father was—delaying the process as long as possible, and didn't give me the message until I returned from my visit to you."

Somehow, this didn't seem like Urien. He struck me as a

man who would do almost anything for money—and pride.

"After I left your house, I came home. The message was that the Syrian wanted to meet me at the inn. To make sure he was getting his money's worth." I could taste her bitterness.

"He also said that he'd release some of the marriage fee early, if he—if he—if I would sleep with him last night."

I remembered the brief sense of elation I felt when I realized who the corpse was. Now I wouldn't have to feel bad about it.

"Rhodri came to see me. My father told him what happened. Of course, he would never allow me to debase myself."

He'd sold her to the bastard to begin with. I wasn't sure Urien would've stuck at formalities. She turned to face me, and caught at the doubt in my eyes.

"He—would—never—accept that arrangement," she insisted stubbornly. "But we have creditors. We owe money. I can't sell my clothes, because they're the illusion that feeds us. When people don't think you're in trouble, they're more willing to help."

An indisputable truth. *Homo sine pecunia mortis imago.* Maecenas was now a man without money, and he was most definitely the image of death.

"And so, unknown to your father, you left the house to go to Lupo's and see Maecenas. You told Rhodri not to follow, and not to interfere—" She nodded. "And you—you—"

"I didn't sleep with him." Her smile was painful. "That had been my plan. But my courage failed me. I failed." Exhausted, she sank on the bed again, holding her head in her hands.

I fought the urge to hold her. I fought the relief filling my chest like air to a drowning man. The words hurt, but I still said them. "Even if you had—there's no guarantee he would've given you the money."

She looked at my face but didn't see it. Her eyes were muted, and somewhere else.

"There's no time left. Within the week, my father will be called to court. Maecenas was our only hope, and now he's dead."

She spoke softly, flatly. I wondered at the difference between yesterday's impassioned speech and the detached, regretful woman in front of me. She said she'd kill him if he touched her. But she'd apparently still planned on marrying him.

"Gwyna, you said yesterday that you'd kill the man before he—"

"I know what I said." Her eyes snapped, angry and suddenly awake. "I meant it. But my father needs money. I'm all he has, the only one who can help him. And I must think of Hefin, too! I'd do anything—anything!—to save my family."

She'd risen from the bed, her hands clenched into fists. The knuckles were white.

"Even murder?"

She stood frozen, her eyes locked into mine. Pain was there, a fresh, surprised pain, anger, fear and maybe a little admiration: she hadn't thought I'd ask. I hadn't thought so, either.

After a few moments she spoke. Her tongue moistened her dry lips. "Obviously not. How could his death benefit my family?"

I kept going. "What happened last night?"

She looked at me and didn't waiver. "He was already drunk when I arrived. He was disgusting, a sweaty ox, not fit for even that horrid place. He stank of perfume, and played with me as a cat does a mouse."

She shuddered, more in anger and disgust than fear.

"He—he refused to release any money unless he—he 'approved' me. So, first, he ordered me to take off my clothes, like a slave. Then, he said, he'd decide if I was worth—if I was worth bearing his seed."

She didn't seem to hear my teeth grinding.

"I refused, and he taunted me, pawed at me. I—I endured it as long as I could, the insults—his hands on my body, foul and filthy—even through my clothes, I felt them soiling me. He mocked my father, called him names, and boasted that none of us would see even a tenth of what had been agreed upon. I finally understood my debasement would accomplish nothing."

Her jaw set in a grim line as sharp as her words.

"I even begged the bastard for a hundred *sestertii*, a fifth of what he'd promised, told him our honor depended on this money, and he laughed in my face."

Tears of anger didn't soften the hate in her eyes. She turned and looked straight at me, frank and direct.

"He said a pauper's daughter was worth bedding, but not marrying, and he'd have to rethink the entire arrangement."

She broke off for a moment, and wiped her face with her tunic, as if she were washing herself. I felt dirty hearing it. She took a deep breath.

"When I walked out the door, he was unfavorably comparing me to one of the whores he was about to use."

I said: "Did he mention Agricola?"

"Once or twice. He thought he was being sly. Said something about having a new governor soon, one with whom he could do business."

"How did you get the information you brought to me? About Domitian and Maecenas?"

She hesitated.

"Keeping something back won't help your father."

Her eyes flicked doubt and a little irritation at mine, but she continued.

"A few days ago, my father told me the Syrian was a spy. For Domitian. Word has been going about for months that the governor was to be replaced, so I wasn't surprised. And it's difficult to know what one means by 'spy.' Some people might boast about an imperial connection but not really have the ear of the Emperor at all. That sort of thing. The betrothal itself was negotiated about four months ago, rather suddenly, and I assumed this was all bluff, or some gossip my father had heard from Caelius."

"Marcus Caelius Prato? The real owner of Lupo's?"

"Yes." She pronounced it with distaste. "He—takes an interest in my father. It was he who suggested me to Maecenas."

She locked eyes with me. "I knew what Maecenas was—I met him two or three years ago, when my husband was alive, at one of your Roman festivals. I think he had investments here. He leered at me even then, and Idwal—my husband—nearly throttled him. But now—"

"Now you needed money for your family."

She looked away. "Yes. And anyway, I didn't think anything sinister about it—everyone, after all—even Agricola—has spies. But the morning of the day I saw you—yesterday, I suppose, though it seems much longer—Caelius was visiting, and I—" She blushed. "I hid behind the hearth and tried to overhear their conversation."

Throughout the entire humiliating story of Maecenas' behavior, she hadn't reddened. And now she was blushing at some eavesdropping. The woman amazed me.

"What did you hear?"

"Not much," she admitted. "Bits and pieces. But I did catch something about—about a message. Later, after Caelius left, my father told me that Agricola was to be removed as governor and that the Syrian was going to help. How, he didn't specify—he just gave the impression that Maecenas had a job to do, and would do it any way he could."

She tugged at her hands, over and over again. "I was upset. I'll do whatever's necessary for my family, but I won't harm my own country. My father—" She hesitated again. "My father is dying, and he's bitter. He feels cast aside. Ever since my mother died—in childbirth, delivering Hefin—he hasn't been well. It's been slow for him, and painful. Idwal gave him hope. And strength. He knew Hefin would be provided for, and have a father to teach him. But Idwal died, and since then, my family has died, too, a little more every day."

Her hands, still now, dropped to her lap. Sadness lined her face deeper than age ever would. I took her hand in my own and held it.

She looked at me, her eyes warmer, and back down to earth. "My father has heard of you, and spoke of you once or twice. Someone told him you're a friend to the Old Faith. But when I told him I wanted to speak with you, he became agitated, and absolutely forbade it. As soon as he fell asleep, I came to you, anyway."

The old fox hadn't shown any recognition when we talked. And didn't he realize that forbidding his daughter from seeing me—especially when her freedom was about to end—was practically throwing her in my face?

"After I left you, I returned home to find that Maecenas was already here and had sent us his message."

She moved closer. I could smell the skin-sweet dampness between her breasts. She grasped my arm.

"I—I thought I could love Rhodri. When I came to you, I only wanted to warn you. But—I can't love Rhodri now."

Her mouth opened underneath mine, probing and demanding and almost angry. I kissed her harder, and she pulled me down against her. After a few minutes, we drew apart. We both knew it wasn't finished.

She adjusted her tunic and smoothed her hair. I said: "I can help your father."

"How, Ardur? You can't marry me, if that's what you're thinking. You'd be a suspect."

"That isn't actually what I had in mind."

Two bright pink spots appeared in her cheeks, but she met my eyes.

"What, then?"

It was a simple question, and remarkably unemotional under the circumstances.

"Maecenas left money. A lot of it."

"You found it?" She seemed surprised. "Was it a great deal?"

"Yes. Much more than five hundred *sestertii*. In a few days I'll make sure some of this money makes its way to you and your father."

She stared at me as if she were trying to solve a philosophical dilemma. I'd maybe expected a more earthy thank you.

"You can give your creditors my name—"

"No. That would be stupid. Then you're linked to me again." She thought for another moment.

"I'll tell them the money was paid, but that it's tied up in the investigation, waiting for the governor's personal clearance. That should give us some time. Caelius will be able to do something, as well. Though I don't like owing him anything."

The only thing I owed Caelius was pain. I didn't think he'd be as good at taking it as he was about handing it out. I wanted her far away from him. He was as rotten as a fat maggot.

"Say nothing to Caelius. Nothing about me, the money, nothing. No one knows about it except you—that means your father, too. And if you can, spy on him again, but only if it's safe. He's dangerous, especially when he's got nowhere to run. How did he get so close to your father?"

"I'm not sure. But for the last year or so, he's been visiting regularly, and my father treats him almost like a son. I suspect he's been helping to keep creditors at bay, and he's never been less than deferential and polite to me. But I've never liked him."

The thought of Caelius looking at her made my temples hurt.

I stood up to leave before I couldn't. She stood up, too, and pressed herself into me, reassuring me with the weight of her body against mine. Her fingertips sank into the flesh of my arm.

"Be careful, Ardur. I don't want to lose anyone else that I care for."

The grinning skull of Vibius Maecenas was breathing down my neck. I held her at arm's length.

"I have to find Rhodri."

She stiffened, and backed away. It got chilly again.

"If he's innocent I can help him! Running away won't solve anything—I might be the only chance he has. Tell me where he is, Gwyna. I know you know something."

She turned her back. "No. Get out."

"What—"

"I said get out. And we don't need your charity. I'll man-age—something else."

"But—"

"Get—out!" She finally turned to look at me, her eyes flow-ing with tears, her face blurred with pain and anger. "I thought you cared about me—I thought you loved me!"

"I do love you! I'm just trying to—"

"Get out! Get out! Get out!"

She shoved me through the door, and when I stepped outside she shut it with a violent clang that I was sure rang through the shuttered house. From her room, I could hear the sounds of sobbing.

Eleven

The weather outside matched my mood. The sun had teased us on the way here, whispering promises of warm days, lovely sunsets, and happy endings. The sun was a liar. I leaned against the door and grimaced. Not hail, not snow, not even decent sleet. Some ungodly cross of rain and dirt and mud and filth was raining down in sheets, pounding the pocked and rutted streets into submission. My toga would never be the same.

With a groan, I pried myself off of Gwyna's door, and sank into the mud. The cold, liquid dirt squirted between my toes, and the ankle boots gave up their last breath and died. Draco trudged ahead of me through the murk. It was still about two or three hours before sundown, but no one was counting.

The rain froze my toes. I couldn't feel the mud anymore, or even the waterfalls cascading down my back. I couldn't feel anything except what I didn't want to feel, and that was a hell of a lot more uncomfortable than the weather.

She was obviously protecting Rhodri. She must still care for him. But what she said, what she did . . . A donkey and a cart crawling by on all fours flung some of the road in my mouth. It tasted better than what I was thinking. Goddamn it. She wasn't lying. Not completely. There was more to it than that.

The voice said: "Remember Dionysia."

It was a resigned tone, one that said it knew this would happen all along. I hated the tone, and I didn't care much for the voice, either.

"I was eighteen years old! And Dionysia was . . . well, you know what Dionysia was. That doesn't make Gwyna a liar. I know all about using people. I know all about lying."

It whispered this time. "To yourself, maybe. But where women are concerned . . ."

I swatted some mud at it, and a chunk clung to my lobe like an earring. Gwyna was no Dionysia. Or Julia, for that matter. Dionysia was a sophisticate; Julia a spoiled, oversexed child. Gwyna was a native—a Trinovantian!—and she had a family to think of. She was a fiercely loyal woman, loyal to her father, her people, her country—

"Her lover?"

I was getting tired of the argument. Why couldn't I just shut up? Wasn't the weather misery enough? I stepped in a puddle, and tried to drown myself.

I remembered how she felt. How she smelled, how she looked. She was hiding something, but it wasn't about us. She could still be loyal to Agricola. And her father. She could still be in love with me—*and* want to help Rhodri. Maybe she was protecting him in the only way she knew how: by keeping her mouth shut. And maybe I wasn't the only one looking for him.

Even if Rhodri were innocent, he knew something, saw something, and it was something dangerous. Maybe Rhodri had to run. Maybe Rhodri was being set up.

I needed to find him. There was a chance he was guilty, and Gwyna knew it. Maybe her loyalty went that far. But loyalty didn't make her a liar about us. And at that moment, standing in the mud and rain, I didn't give a damn about anything else.

A smile cracked through the mud on my face, and I swam ahead to catch up to Draco. The voice scurried to a dark corner. I had the uneasy feeling we'd be talking again soon.

Home was somewhere up ahead. The rain slacked off as the

weather got colder. The drop in temperature made the mud harder. I felt like one of those trick Silenus statues you crack open to find another statue inside. If I peeled off enough layers, maybe I'd find a cleaner, brighter Arcturus.

I was thinking about not thinking about Gwyna. So I thought about Maecenas. I was wondering who killed him.

Rhodri had a personal motive. But he also had a damn good reason for *not* stealing the papers. All he had to do was wait, and Domitian's orders would do what a few thousand natives couldn't. Any enemy of the governor would've toasted Maecenas and those papers with the finest Aminnian.

Funny how Urien hadn't asked about them. For a man who liked gossip so much, I figured he'd want to know whether he'd be getting a new governor. He was quick enough to point out that the governor's friends and allies were the strongest suspects. But he never asked if the papers were found or delivered.

And what about the mithraeum? The murder took place on the New Year. And the Syrian was trussed with a native knot. And Rhodri and Madoc both knew a lot more than innocent men should. I'd like to find out how.

Maybe the Christians did it, whoever they were, wherever they were. Maybe they wanted the Romans and natives to start killing each other again. But why take the papers? Isn't the *numen* you know better than the *numen* you don't know?

And then there was Caelius. I'd like it to be him. He'd told Maecenas about Gwyna, and had acted as Urien's broker. But why would he kill the Syrian or steal the papers? And why wouldn't he—or anyone else—have stolen the money?

I chewed my muddy lip. There was a personal motive to kill Maecenas, and political motives to steal the papers, but not by the same people. Maybe we were dealing, as Bilicho thought, with multiple crimes. A murdered man, a stolen document (but not stolen money?), and a desecrated temple?

Then I was home.

Nothing looked as good as my door. Maybe not quite nothing. I needed a warm fire and clean clothes, surrounded by a peaceful household of order and harmony. When Draco pushed on the door, it opened. Something was wrong.

I could see his jaw set, as if a sculptor were making final adjustments to a clay mold. He fumbled through the dripping wool to his old *gladius,* and removed it. He motioned for me to stay behind him, but as he entered the waiting room I pushed him aside. The sound of barking was coming from the *triclinium.*

I sloshed quickly through the hall, and paused in the doorway, the drip-drip-drip of the unbearably heavy toga dropping in rhythm with the labored breaths of Draco, behind me.

The dining room was in an uproar. Velox and Ludens were running around the couches, nearly tripping Brutius, Coir and Venutius, and barking at one of Fera's kittens, which was contemplating a tapestry of Alexandria in the corner. In the center of it all was Bilicho, propped awkwardly on a couch, with a too large cloth around his head that had too much blood on it.

I plowed through the slaves.

"Venutius, bring some warm water. Brutius, get my surgical bag from the examination room. Coir, go with him to make sure he finds it."

I turned to Draco, who stood in the middle of the floor, huge, wet, and confused. "Change your clothes."

The puppies and the kittens looked at me, waiting for orders. "You—be quiet." Then I looked down at Bilicho, who was faintly smiling.

"Shut up while I look at your head." He tried to nod, and grimaced in pain. "And don't move, damn you!"

Coir ran up with the bag. "Did you bandage Bilicho?"

She nodded. "Brutius and Venutius argued with me."

"You did a good job. But I need to cut this off, and it's going to start bleeding again. Go out to the shed with Brutius—Brutius, take out the animals—and bring me some of those fat oak leaves—you know the kind, the ones the beetles lay eggs in."

By now Venutius had arrived with a large pot of water. "Take that back to the kitchen and pour some of the water into a shallow dish, Venutius, something like a *kylix*. I can't use a cauldron's worth."

I leaned over Bilicho and studied his eyes.

"You've got a concussion. A bad one. I don't know whether your head is split open or not."

"It's not. I felt it."

"I told you not to talk, Bilicho." I opened the bag and removed one of my small knives and started cutting through the cloth wound inexpertly around his head. It was one of Draco's old cloaks.

Coir and Brutius came in, looking only faintly damp. The rain must've stopped. Typical. She was holding the oak leaves.

"Get me a mortar and pestle from the examination room."

Brutius looked at me eagerly. I told him to go help Draco change his clothes.

Bilicho grunted. "A lot of fuss."

"Shut up."

The makeshift bandage was now off, and I took a closer look at his head. His hair was still damp, with rain and clotted blood. A blow from behind, but not with something sharp—a large, tender bump, and purpled, puckered skin, but no cut. I felt around the area of the blow. Bilicho stayed still, but I knew he would, no matter how much it hurt.

"No fracture so far. But I've got to see what's making you bleed." Coir came back with the mortar at the same time that Venutius arrived with an old black *kylix* full of hot water. After setting both on the low table closest to Bilicho, they stood off to the side, anxiously looking on. Brutius and Draco, freshly dressed but still wet, joined them.

"Coir, get me some flax. This will hurt, Bilicho."

The blood was thick and clotted on his left side, right above his temple. That was good, since a blow to the temple itself sometimes meant unconsciousness and death, unless it was opened up, which was tricky business. I took out a thin pair of forceps and a short probe, and carefully, tediously, tugged at the bandage where it was glued with Bilicho's blood.

Coir appeared at my side, and handed me some squares of flax. I dunked one in the hot water, and, showing it to Bilicho so he could prepare himself, laid it on the cut. He made no sound, but his body stiffened all over.

I straightened up. My sodden toga was in the way. "Help me out of this."

Brutius and Coir lifted and heaved, and between all three of us, we got it off. My undertunic was wet, but not so bulky. The hot cloth on Bilicho's head had drawn some fresh blood. I took up the forceps again.

"I'm taking off the bandage now." I tugged a little harder from first one corner, then another. With one quick, decisive pull, I removed it completely. He shuddered.

"Heat up some wine, Venutius. Coir, I should have a little willow bark left in the drying shed. Give a handful to Venutius to add to the wine. And bring a needle and thread from my bag."

The wound was visible, now that the blood was flowing again. The lips were jagged, and heavily swollen, and a large bump— the equal of the one on the back of his head—rose underneath it. With the forceps, I delicately pried it open. I didn't see any brain or other tissue, but I had to make sure.

"Hold on to something, Bilicho."

His hand crept out of the coverlet Coir or one of the others had thrown over him, and gripped the edge of the couch. I inserted the probe into the wound, and felt the bump with my fingertips. Bilicho was trying not to bite his tongue too hard. The probe was coming up against skull. He needed stitches, but at least his head wasn't fractured. I took another flax bandage, dipped it in the hot water, and reapplied it.

"I have to stop the bleeding, clean it out, and sew you up. You don't have a fracture."

Bilicho's pupils were dilated and far away, but he still grinned.

I turned toward the oak leaves. Bruising them drew out a squirt or two of a thin, blackish liquid. I picked up the flax bandage I'd first placed on Bilicho's head and cleaned my hands with it. Then I bruised the leaves some more, until I had a thick black and green paste. I took another piece of flax and soaked it, and gently pressed down on the cloth on Bilicho's head before taking it off. Thanks to the rain, there wasn't much to clean.

Venutius came in on tiptoe with a warm cup of wine and willow. The flax was soaked through. I scooped up the rest of the paste with it and tamped it around the wound, before covering everything with my last piece of dry cloth. I turned to Coir, who was standing beside me.

"Leave the needle and thread here. I'll stitch it later. Venutius, Bilicho will need some broth—chicken, goose, whatever's on hand. Put some cabbage in it."

I stood up and stretched, and saw the worry still lining their faces.

I said: "He'll be fine."

Brutius smiled, and stepped outside to bring in a log for the fire. Coir hesitantly approached me with a dry tunic. I let the soaking one I was in fall to the ground, and gave the grinning patient a severe look. "Don't even think about talking."

When I was done, I looked around. The living room was how

I'd pictured it from the outside, when I stood in the rain, dripping and drowning.

I let Bilicho talk a few hours later, after I'd stitched him up and he'd had enough wine. Draco was standing guard by the door. Finding it open had bothered him, and finding Bilicho hurt had bothered him even more. Venutius tied his seasoning hand behind his back when he made the broth. And the patient was trying to pretend that nothing had happened.

"Why can't I eat real food?"

"You know why. There's a risk of fever—a big risk."

He grunted. "I'll be fine in the morning."

"You will not be fine in the morning. You're staying in bed for at least two days."

He glared at me.

I grinned. "The evil eye won't do you a damn bit of good. Now tell me what happened—and make it quick."

He adjusted his position on the couch. "I was knocked on the head."

I made a face at him.

"All right, all right."

He settled in again, until he was as comfortable as he could be. Then he took a minute to get it in order. "I was at the marketplace, asking questions about Rhodri. Remember him? Well, I found out a few things. He's the subject of gossip, these days, and you know Londinium—tongues wag faster than a two-*sestertii* whore's. Luckily." He winced. "Or maybe not so luckily."

"Anyway, he owns a cattle farm near Camulodunum—your home town—and comes into the city to buy and sell, stir up trouble against the Romans, and take a poke at Gwyna. Not that he's ever succeeded in that," he added hastily. "But everyone knows he's been lusting after her like a dog in heat."

"Go on."

"So cattle is where and how he gets his money. While he's in Londinium, he stays in a small house on the outskirts, across the river near the bridge. Naturally, after learning all this, I felt compelled to find it, and hopefully Rhodri, too."

"So you went across the bridge? That's a rough area."

"Yeah. In more ways than one. I found his district, all right, thanks to a honey merchant. You might want to try his honey for the wound dressings—it tasted good, anyway."

"What happened then?"

"I made it across, but only because I took off my freedman's ring. The whole place is very unhappy with us. You should see some of the graffiti."

I frowned. "I've never had a patient from there—they wouldn't trust a Roman, even if he's half native. But it's a poor neighborhood, and their numbers keep shrinking."

"Not fast enough to save my head. I found a tavern near Rhodri's house—which is next to an oak grove, by the way, very handy if he happens to be worshipping the Old Ways."

"And?"

"Well, I walked in, and ordered some mead—no sissy Roman wine, remember—and people were friendly enough. But cautious."

"Did you see anyone from last night?"

"Not that I could be sure of. There were two that looked familiar—rough types, leather aprons, maybe tanners or something. It was dark, like all those places, and darker than most, even Lupo's." He grinned. "At least the food was good."

"Then don't complain about the broth."

He grimaced at the empty bowl, and continued. "Anyway, once I started asking about Rhodri—and not even about Rhodri, kind of around Rhodri—they clammed up tight. Couldn't get a thing out of anyone. So I left, and decided to prowl around his house myself."

"You should've gone home to get Brutius. Or waited for me."

"Yeah, I know. But I was on his trail, Arcturus, and I just had one of those feelings that he was there, that he hadn't left town."

"So then what?"

"What you see on my head. I left the tavern, strolled over toward Rhodri's house—it's very countrified out there—and walked around it."

"What does it look like?"

"Not much. Wooden farmhouse. Probably about fifteen years old."

"Any sign of life?"

"I found some horse tracks, fresh, on the road in. I think he was there."

"If he wasn't, I don't see the point of knocking you out. How did it happen?"

"I rounded a corner. I thought I was being quiet. I heard voices from the oak grove. Then a crashing pain on the back of my head, and I must've fallen and hit myself on a flagstone—I was close to the house by that time. Next thing I knew I woke up on the bit of road leading back to the bridge and Londinium proper. And it was raining. Hard."

"They could've killed you."

"I know. I don't think Rhodri's guilty of murder, if Rhodri or one of his friends gave me this."

"Maybe." We were silent for a while. Then I told him what happened to me.

"So we've got three crimes now?"

"Unless we can think of something to tie them all together. It just doesn't make sense. Why was Maecenas clutching a document he hadn't delivered? Why wasn't the money stolen? How did Madoc and Rhodri and everyone at the whorehouse know he was killed?" I shook my head.

"I've got more questions than a Greek philosopher, and they're just as useless. Maybe someone from Agricola's inner circle did murder the Syrian. Maybe I did. Who the hell knows?"

"What do we do next?"

"You stay in bed. People are going to a lot of trouble to keep me from finding Rhodri, so that's where we start. I don't think he's guilty, at least of murder. But he knows too much—and it's something ugly."

Caelius' face flashed into my mind. I felt the stubble on my chin and frowned. "I'll have to see Agricola first. We don't have much time. Maecenas was a lackey, but a lackey for the Emperor. And what he was carrying—wars have been started over less. Then Rhodri next. I'm sure he's left town by now, maybe returned to Camulodunum. I still have friends there— you remember my father's freedmen, the ones who paid for his tombstone?"

"Favonius, you mean? Your father the centurion?"

"Yeah. Verecundus and Narcissus. I gave them one of Pyxis' puppies a couple of months ago, when Verecundus was in town on business. I can talk to them, they might know the local gossip."

"What about Caelius?"

I wanted the next time I saw Caelius to be the last time I saw Caelius. He was too poisonous to handle too often. And I needed information first.

"As soon as I talk to the governor, I'll leave for Camulodunum and look for Rhodri. I should be back in four days. That'll give you one or two days to find out what you can. Chase any leads. Find any connections between Caelius, Maecenas, Urien. And keep an eye on the whores."

I didn't want to meet his eyes. "One other thing. I want to know who Urien owes, and I want to pay off his debts."

Bilicho raised his eyebrows at me, then scowled in pain.

"Arcturus—"

"I know what you're thinking. Yes, I know she's lying or at least keeping something from me. And I don't care."

He let out a groan. "I hope you know what you're doing."

I hoped so, too, but I wasn't going to tell him that. A loud bang made us jump, and Bilicho grimaced. He started to get up, but lay back down after I shot him a nasty look and stood up myself. Draco came running into the room, agitated.

"It's the man from last night. He's—"

"—Right behind you. Hello, Favonianus."

"Hello, Avitus. Can I expect a visit from you every night from now on?"

He didn't respond. "What happened to him?"

I rolled my eyes. "Got drunk again. Fell down and hit his head. I'm thinking of sending him back to work in a mine."

"You freed him."

"Yes. But he just can't seem to adjust." I stood in between Avitus and Bilicho, so that the *beneficarius* couldn't look at him too closely. "So what brings you here tonight?"

The lines on his face were deep, and there was a weariness in Avitus that I'd never seen before. His cloak and boots were even muddier than last night. "Agricola wants you. Now."

I reached for my bag, which was still next to Bilicho. "Should I bring—"

"No. It's not the kind of healing we need."

I straightened up and looked at him. "What's going on, Avitus?"

The *beneficarius* sighed. The weight of his exhaustion—and more than exhaustion, despair—was crushing him to the floor like a midget with a millstone.

"Just come with me, Arcturus. Leave your bag. Leave your slaves. Leave your drunken, sore-headed freedman. Just come with me."

Avitus called me Arcturus. It was unlike him to unbend so far. But it was also unlike him to look so much like a tired old man. I whispered to Bilicho to get some sleep. He gave me a look that said to be careful.

Draco brought me my warmest cloak and thickest boots. I told him to stay awake—Bilicho's life might depend upon it. He nodded, wide-eyed.

When we left the house, instead of turning left toward the palace, Avitus turned right.

"Isn't Agricola—?"

"Just follow me."

The *beneficarius* was unusually taciturn, even for him. The icy mud crackled as we walked, and it all started to feel like a bad dream that wakes you up every night. We were taking the same road as the night before.

We passed Lupo's, but no drunk was singing and no Galla appeared in the window. The lights were on, but it was quiet. By taking the same path, Avitus was trying to tell me something, prepare me for something, I was sure of it.

I saw the answer when we reached the meadow with the mithraeum. There, standing in a circle, were Agricola and some of his highest ranking officers. And there, on the torn, muddy ground that last night opened up to reveal the mystery within, was the naked body of Vibius Maecenas.

TWELVE

Agricola was not happy. He stood over Maecenas—and whatever he'd done, I was beginning to feel sorry for the poor bastard—like the Colossus of Rhodes. He had a look I'd seen before, but not very often.

As my eyes adjusted, I glanced around. No one greeted me; no one even dared to shuffle. I saw the unmistakable, burly shape of Lucius Antonius Saturninus, Agricola's *quaestor,* his brown eyes gleaming from beneath furry eyebrows, his mouth pinched uncharacteristically tight beneath his thick beard. I caught a glimpse of one of the governor's top *speculatores,* a man he used often as an executioner and whose name I never remembered. I saw the short, swarthy figure of Agricola's *princeps praetorii,* Quintus Claudius Corvus, the governor's tough head of staff. Farther back, I thought I could see Arian, and I wondered if he'd wonder if I would remember his name. I squirmed a little, feeling the grey-green eyes of Publius Junius Meditor on my back. I turned around and grinned at him. My charm didn't impress him. It never did. Serenus was by his side. So somebody had finally called in the *praefectus vigilium*—or maybe he was standing in the mud because someone had lost a dinner napkin?

Agricola grunted, and anyone who had been thinking of slouching stood up straighter. "Look at the body."

I assumed he was talking to me, but didn't wait to find out. Agricola was a sociable man—most successful politicians are.

Romans don't trust people who creep off by themselves too much. Just one of the reasons no one liked Domitian. But the governor wasn't going to waste time or words tonight. Tonight he had a problem, and I was going to have the very unpleasant experience of telling him the extent of that problem.

I knelt in the moist ground by the Syrian's side. A few hours in the earth had done nothing to improve his appearance. The cold weather was holding off some of the smell, and his naked limbs were as stiff as a mother-in-law. His head and what was left of his neck were beginning to get a little soft. They were suffused with the ugly green-red of rot, though it hadn't yet spread all the way down his face. Also due to the cold. I'd wished for a chance to look at him again. Be careful what you wish for, Arcturus.

I tucked my hands into the dirt underneath him and heaved. Agricola stood back; Avitus blended into the darkness by his side. Everyone stepped away a few inches—bad luck to touch a corpse. Except for a *medicus*, of course. I was used to bad luck. Serenus was craning his neck forward, in imitation of a doctor.

I looked up at him. "I could use some help. That's why you're here, isn't it?" He looked first at Meditor, who looked at Agricola, who nodded. Meanwhile, I was propping up a very fat, very dead, and very naked Syrian all by myself, and not getting any happier about it. "Hurry the hell up; he's heavy."

Serenus knelt beside me and together we rolled him over. I could finally get a look at his back, unhindered by clothes and circumstance. Most of the men stepped back a little further. Romans were good at all kinds of killing, but they got a little squeamish around decaying corpses. Especially ones that used to be buried. Agricola stared down at us, his face immobile.

A thin line of white stood out against the pocked grey skin of his back. I bent over it. Yes. What I'd been looking for, what I thought I should find. A knife-wound, a smooth, hard, sharp thrust of a professional killer, right through the heart. Minimum fuss, minimum blood. Serenus looked it over, too.

"You think maybe a *pugio?*"

I nodded. A legionary dagger would work. "Sure. Or something equally short, sharp and not too thick. This is what killed him."

Serenus arched his eyebrows in surprise. "Not the throat?"

I squinted up at Avitus. "No."

I wasn't sure how much he'd told Agricola about last night, and how much everyone else knew. Serenus stood up, his imagination exhausted for the evening. I pored over Maecenas for what I hoped was the last time, determined not to miss anything else, front or back. The fact that he was clean, of course, meant that he'd been dug up and laid out here before the rainstorm or during it. Probably late last night, right before dawn.

The corpse was uncooperative. It couldn't tell me anything I didn't already know. Past time to put it to sleep. I stood up slowly, wondering how my knees got older than the rest of me. I looked Agricola in the eye. "I've seen enough. You can bury him."

The general nodded, a massive head on a bullish neck, looking much like his friend, *divus* Vespasian. "Avitus, take a few trusted men and bury him." He glowered. "Deep." Avitus slunk off. I saw him gesture to Arian and another soldier. "Saturninus, Meditor—we talk at the palace. Two hours." He turned to face his men.

"My brothers—my sons—a tragedy has befallen our temple. But that does not lessen the duty we owe to each other, to our god, and to Rome. Do not discuss what happened tonight. We will discover who sent this pollution upon us, and why, and gossip will only hinder our efforts.

"We cannot celebrate tonight. But we will cleanse the temple, and practice the rites, and our new brothers will be made one. This I swear, as *legatus*, as *pater*, as Agricola. And soon we shall build a new temple, one above the ground for all to see, but where the secrets of the god are forever safe. This also I swear. Go, now, and wait for the purification. You will be called when it is time. And as always, find comfort in the redemption, the blood shed by our master and god. *Ad astra in aeternum! Mors ianua vitae! Mithras—Mithras regnet!*"

The speech, as always, fired up his troops. They were friends and subordinates, but mostly soldiers from the nine hundred or so *singulares* living at the nearby fort, handpicked legionaries who served as the governor's bodyguard, men from every legion in Britain. They'd go back to their families, in Eburacum or Deva, and tell them about the night Agricola stood over a dead man and was inspired by their god. Such was the general's gift of oratory. Another necessary talent—though Domitian preferred the nimble tongue of flattery to the golden tongue of rhetoric.

The men began to disperse, fading into the clear, dark night like so many shadows. Avitus and his helpers heaved the Syrian off the ground and carried him away, presumably to another spot. The governor turned to me.

"Arcturus. Come to the palace in two hours." His mud-brown eyes, as dark as the earth beneath his feet, burned into mine. "Be prepared to tell me what you know. All of it." He turned to Saturninus and the *speculator*, who were both waiting for him, apparently for some temple purification ceremony.

Well, I'd been told. That didn't mean I'd listen.

My relationship with Agricola was complicated. I had time to think about it on the walk back home. I could check in on Bilicho before going to the palace, and wash my hands. I still had the dead man's skin under my fingernails.

The governor was ten years older than I was, but it seemed more like twenty. We had a lot in common: fathers who had been provincial-born procurators, both appointed from the Equestrian to the Senatorial class by the Emperor. I used my purple stripe to impress the denizens of a whorehouse—he'd used his to advance to the highest offices in the Empire. Agricola knew I had no interest in politics. One of the reasons he'd married off Julia to another man. His wife Domitia had never forgiven me for her daughter. Nothing serious had happened between us, though Claudia tried like hell to get me into bed with her, and I enjoyed the trying.

Agricola's mother was murdered by Otho's thugs when he was an adult. But he knew, a little, how it felt. He liked a good story, either in a bar or a book, and was one of the most affably ferocious men I'd ever met. Genial, generous and devoted to his family, he was also ruthless, ambitious and obsessed. He was a perfect soldier, but saw war as a necessary evil. He was honest, except when he had to not be. And he was optimistic to a fault.

The wind was cold, and I rubbed my nose to keep it from freezing. He'd come through it all right—Agricola knew what the system was like. He'd been a favorite of Vespasian's, an *amicus* of Titus', and now was a "friendly advisor" to Domitian. Agricola was careful. He couldn't help be everything Domitian was not. But he didn't have to let Domitian know he knew it.

I'd met the Emperor just once. Even then he was more pedant than scholar. And he never laughed. Vespasian was a garrulous old sod who never minded a good joke, even at his own expense. But his slight, bald, correct-to-the-letter son believed in his own sanctity too much. He wasn't much of a god, and still less of a man.

The incest rumors gave him a certain cachet among certain parties—and made it easy for everybody else to hate him. But there were plenty of real reasons, without inventing the same old bedtime stories about him and his niece. His eunuch he kept around for appearances. The simple truth was that Domitian didn't like sex. What was more, he didn't trust anyone who did. No wonder he saw conspiracies around every corner.

I grinned, thinking about Saturninus. He'd always nursed a soft spot for the Empress Domitia. Maybe because he knew where to find hers, if half the stories were true. But the soldier in him despised her husband, and never more so than now, with Domitian calling himself "Germanicus" after roughing up some little tribe on the Rhenus. The triumph cost the Emperor more than he made for the treasury. And he left a weakened Ninth legion for Agricola, who fortunately could do more with less than any other general in the Empire.

And now Domitian wanted to recall his most successful *legatus*. And I'd have to explain to the general—my friend, my patron, a man I'd known for years, who'd known my adopted father, Classicianus, and was one of the few on the ex-governor's staff not to deride him, a man whom I respected and admired and sometimes disagreed with, whose wounds I staunched and whose illnesses I treated—I'd have to explain to this man what the hell a naked Syrian was doing on top of his temple. It was going to be another long night.

THIRTEEN

When I reached the house, Draco was standing guard, looking grim. He'd watched over Bilicho carefully, and now the patient was sleeping the sleep of the innocent. I checked on him. His head felt cool, not warm, and his breath eased out in rough, tranquil snores. He'd be fine.

I put on a new mantle, and padded into the kitchen. When I'd washed off Maecenas, I told Draco to wait up for me, and to look after Bilicho. Everyone else was asleep. Someday I'd sleep again, too.

The walk to the palace was short and cold. I was a little early, and decided to take the long way, to the street-side, formal entrance rather than the riverfront. Most of the byways and alleys in Londinium were gravel or hard dirt, but the riverfront, along the quays, was paved for carts, and the streets around the major Roman arteries—the palace, the forum, the bath, the fort, a couple of temples—were hard cobblestone. It was the first firm ground I'd stood on in awhile. And there it was. The only sign of activity was a double-helping of guards at the gate—and they were unusually alert.

This entrance was about as restrained as Nero's Golden House. Even compared with the river side, the formal entryway made you want to piss in your pants.

I gazed at the multicolored marble thoughtfully. The standing stone still bothered me. Agricola had brought up a monolith from a native shrine outside Londinium, and used it to decorate the entrance courtyard. It was more tasteful than the Colossus in Rome, but so were the Egyptian pyramids. Placing the stone there would only remind people of what they'd lost, and no one needed any reminders. It wasn't the first time or the last time I disagreed with the governor.

The palace, like most things official and Roman, was huge. It housed Agricola, his family, his staff, guests, friends, visitors, messengers, all the business of the Empire except for that of the procurator, who enjoyed his own, slightly more livable, slightly less ornamental palatial home directly to the east. It was really three palaces in one—formal meeting rooms on the first terrace, state rooms, business rooms, and garden rooms on the middle terrace, and all the mundaneness of real life on the third level, closest to the river.

The guards at the gate expected me. One nodded, and led me through rooms with gold, rooms with silver, rooms with garden paintings, until we reached the massive garden courtyard on the second level. Even in December, violets made a lush, perfumed carpet against the brushy yellow gorse. There were fish swimming in the big pool, despite the river next door. Romans always figured they could improve nature, given enough time and money. They'd piped in 50,000 *amphorae* of fresh water, just to prove it.

More guards were waiting, and a sandy-haired one detached himself from the rest. He led me into the smaller, more human section. We wound our way through the smoky, yellow-lit halls. I could feel the warmth of the floor through my shoes.

The *singular* finally came to a broad door I recognized as the entrance to the governor's study. It was here he liked to compose his letters, play a few games of dice or *latrunculi*, and maybe even relax, preferably with a cup of good wine. I enjoyed a good game of *latrunculi* myself.

The soldier knocked, and a gruff voice answered. I stepped

into the room. None of us were here to play tonight.

"*Salve,* Arcturus. Come in." He was leaning back in a basket chair, looking like the proverbial farmer his father had named him for. Agricola did what he could to recall the Cincinnatus ideal of the plain, simple man of the earth who serves his country—and his Emperor. Cincinnatus never had to deal with one of those.

"*Salvete* yourselves, gentlemen." I was early but apparently the last to arrive. Saturninus was perched on a folding chair, about as comfortable as an elephant on a footstool, Avitus was hovering near Agricola, and Meditor was trying to thaw out his brain in front of the fire. I wished him luck.

I understood why Agricola had insisted on forming a *vigiles* detachment. It was unusual—most provincial capitals lived happily enough without one, but he was campaigning far from home, and wanted the natives to get used to Roman bureaucracy. He encouraged them to turn to the *vigiles* instead of their own system of justice, and since he'd tried to eradicate that system along with Mona, he needed to replace it with something.

The tribal council was there, of course, but for the frequent tavern brawls and occasional homicides, the *vigiles* were handy in an emergency. Londinium was too wet to worry about fires, so they mostly just nosed around looking for trouble, and made some up if they were running short.

For reasons known only to him, he chose as their *praefectus* the one man in town less imaginative than Serenus. Publius Junius Meditor had a few ideas in his head, none of them nice, and once they got in they enjoyed the room so much they decided to stay indefinitely. He was plodding, deliberate, and as suspicious as a rich woman with a cough. He hated me, and I was glad to return the favor. Sometimes I think Agricola kept him on just to annoy me.

Meditor was standing in front of the fire with his legs apart.

He was about as impressive as a bald, bowlegged idiot could be. I ignored him and addressed the governor.

"How is your son?"

Agricola's boy was always a worry—he'd been born two weeks too early.

"Well, thank you, Arcturus. Domitia is feeding him that tonic you prescribed, and he's been stronger of late."

I nodded, pleased. Domitia didn't always appreciate my advice.

Saturninus shifted his bulky frame. "We're all here, so let's get on with it," he growled. "I for one have a warm bed waiting for me."

"Whose?" I asked, innocently.

Saturninus grinned, his wolfish teeth showing through his beard. "Wouldn't you like to know, Arcturus."

Agricola moved a little finger. There was an immediate silence.

"Gentlemen, you know why you're here. Two of you—Meditor and Arcturus—are not members of the temple, and I ask you both not to divulge any information about our worship. We must assess this threat, for threat, I fear, it is."

Unless he was drunk or angry or on campaign, he talked like someone out of Livius. Agricola hungered for a place in the history books—and preferably not as a victim of imperial enmity. Unfortunately for the general, the era of the self-made man was over. He sounded about a hundred years too late.

"Who found the body?"

Meditor stirred in irritation. Maybe something had bitten him. And then crawled off and died. "The governor is asking the questions, Favonianus."

I grinned at him nastily. "The governor, Meditor, may not know the questions to ask."

Avitus spoke up. "The senior officers of the temple. The

governor, Saturninus, Marcus Tettius Felix, the *speculator*, and I."

Felix—how could I forget an executioner named Felix?

"What time?"

"Dusk."

"Have his clothes been found?"

"They were wadded up and thrown back in the grave where we buried him." Avitus cleared his throat, and glanced nervously at Agricola. "The first time."

"Who called in Meditor and Serenus?"

Agricola was getting impatient. "I did, Arcturus. Our men were waiting for us, we couldn't continue with the ceremony, and trying to hush this up would only make it worse." He turned slightly toward Avitus. "Avitus told us about the night before. Secrecy won't do a damn bit of good. If someone's playing games with me, I want him to know I know about it."

"You don't have to worry about advertisement with Meditor on the case."

The *praefectus* grew red. "Look here, Favonianus—"

I continued like he wasn't there. It wasn't too difficult. "I'm trying to find out, gentlemen, who knows what and how much, and how much of what I tell you—and yes, I've got some information about the Syrian, and he is a threat, Governor, even more so dead than alive—how much of what I say will be out in the streets before midday."

The firelight gleamed on Saturninus' teeth. He didn't like Meditor, either. Agricola's mouth twitched. I knew how to talk to him, how to snap him out of his governor-speech. I much preferred to deal with the general.

"This is a confidential and private conference. All of you are here because I think you need to be. Nothing—I mean, nothing—will be public knowledge."

I shook my head. "No offense, Governor, but who is in charge of this investigation? Avitus, Meditor or me?"

Agricola leaned back in his chair and studied me, frowning, his brow furrowed.

"What does that have to do with anything, Arcturus? I don't give a good goddamn who is in charge of it, as long as it's over, done and our temple is back to normal."

"Begging your pardon, sir, but it's more complicated than your temple." I felt their eyes on me, Meditor's screwed up in suspicion.

"I've been working since last night on this. And keeping things quiet is about the only advantage I have. I can't risk Meditor or his men sniffing around, tramping on witnesses and stirring up shit until Londinium stinks with it."

Meditor exploded. "Just who the hell do you think—"

"Easy, Junius," Agricola interrupted him. "I want the *vigiles* to take root in Londinium, but your men aren't exactly known for their subtlety."

The governor turned toward me. "All right, Arcturus," he said slowly. "As of this moment you're in charge of solving this . . . whatever it is. But I want results. And I want them quickly. And the time for you to tell us what you know is now."

I didn't argue. "The naked man was a Syrian by the name of Vibius Maecenas. He was a freedman of Caesar's, and was sent out here with an imperial document for you."

The *beneficarius* was straining forward, two bright spots in his cheeks. He knew I'd kept something back, and he wasn't happy about it. "How do you know?" he asked.

"I found a signet ring with his initials, and a fragment of a document in his palm. I didn't tell you about it last night, Avitus, because I wanted time to confirm the facts."

His eyes were little slits of anger. "Initials aren't the same as a full name."

"Let me finish. There was no seal box on the document, but

what was left of it looked like an official dispatch. No cord, either, someone had opened it and read it—at the very least Maecenas, since it was torn out of his hand. I recognized the initials because someone came to me yesterday afternoon to warn me that Maecenas was arriving. To set you up, Governor."

Agricola grasped the arms of his chair. "What? I don't believe it!" Saturninus started muttering under his breath, and Meditor backed against the hearth.

I held up a hand. "I wasn't sure whether I believed it or not, either. But I talked to a few people, people who knew Maecenas, and even people in the inn where he was staying, and there was a rumor—apparently fed by Maecenas himself—that the papers were orders for you to step down."

Agricola's ruddy face turned white. His greatest fear. "Orders? To leave?"

"The little bastard! Of course he wants to get rid of the governor—no stomach for a real soldier—just an ass for every long prick in the Empire!" Saturninus roared like a rampaging bear, and his hands were grasping air, searching for something to break.

Meditor was quiet. It wouldn't take him long to find out who had called on me and in what inn Maecenas had stayed. And Agricola putting me in charge would give me about a five minute headstart before the *vigiles* started to make my life miserable and make the mystery of Maecenas impossible to solve. Careful couldn't begin to describe what I had to be.

"The Syrian's behavior wasn't exactly routine. He arrived the night before last, from Dubris. He never showed at the palace?"

Agricola shook his head. "My secretaries would've informed me immediately if a messenger from the Emperor were here. And my spies should've told me days ago." He shot a glance at Avitus, his normally generous lips thin and tight.

"Maecenas was killed either in his rooms or on his way to the temple. He was stabbed in the back, probably with a *pugio* or something similar, by someone who knew where to stab and had the strength to do it right. I don't know yet whether the murderer is the same person who took the papers, or the same person who stuck him on top of your altar. Or dug him up before dawn."

I looked into Agricola's eyes and held them up. "If word gets out about why he was here and how he died, all kinds of rumors will start to fly, and it will only be a matter of time before they get to the Emperor's ears. His informers are always hungry, aren't they?"

Agricola nodded slowly. The knots and blisters on his hardened, soldier's hands stood out, red and raw, and he clenched the basket chair again.

"We have about seven days. I'll need to get an answer out for the Emperor by the New Year, on the fastest ship we've got. Avitus, find out about the Syrian and why no one saw this coming. The last message I received from the Emperor was a pleasant one, right before Saturnalia. He wanted to know how my plans for spring were progressing. Last I heard—" he again looked at Avitus "—he was still quite happy over his triumph, and was thinking of renaming one of the months 'Germanicus.' "

Saturninus snorted. "Exiled Domitia because she won't moan when she's—"

"Be still." Agricola slowly unclenched his fingers from the chair and rubbed the back of his neck. "I have no reason to think Domitian thinks ill of me. I've heard no rumors, received no reports. He craves salutations and glory, and I've promised to give them to him."

He looked at me. "If this Syrian is who you say he is, I have to explain to the Emperor why he was killed, no matter what news he was bringing me." His gaze covered everyone in turn. "If we don't handle this properly, I'm facing exile or death."

Agricola's words—low, quiet, emotionless—froze any warmth in the room. "Saturninus, call up Priscus from wherever he is. I want him here—he should know what's going on."

Iavolenus Priscus was Agricola's *legatus iuridicus*—appointed by Domitian, but a loyal and honest friend, and damn good lawyer. He was on a trial circuit listening to important legal cases around the province, something the governor usually did, but had opted out of the last two years to be with his wife and supervise all the construction in the town he'd made the provincial capital. Priscus' sense of humor was something I missed.

Meditor spoke, his voice as dry as dead leaves. "Arcturus hasn't told us who warned him about the man, or why."

All eyes turned to me. "How astute of you, Meditor. And here I thought your father named you as a joke. I'm getting tired of standing. Governor, do you mind?"

Agricola shook his head, and I pushed myself up on his desk. "A native told me about Maecenas, but the Syrian was apparently best known to a citizen in Londinium, the man who owns the inn at which he was staying."

"And?" Meditor prodded.

"And nothing. You know my methods, and I know yours. Avitus came to get me last night because I can keep my mouth shut and I'm discreet. Do you know what discreet means, Meditor? It means minding your own goddamn business."

Meditor got red again, and Avitus was almost as angry at me. "You know how to keep your mouth shut, all right. And your freedman was on the spot, too—am I supposed to believe that was a coincidence, that little act you put on?"

I looked him in the face. "Believe what you want, Avitus. But don't forget we're fighting for the same thing. The governor. I know these people, I know how to talk to them. They talk to me, because I'm a *medicus*, because I'm half-native, because I'm neither one thing nor the other, and sometimes that pays off."

"Like it paid off with that *eques* this afternoon?" Meditor asked it like he'd won a prize. I knew he was holding something in reserve.

I stood up again, and crossed over to him. "I'm glad the *praefectus* of the *vigiles* has so little work to do that he follows the governor's doctor around. Next time, show your face."

His bald head turned bright pink. "I wasn't there—one of my men mentioned he saw you. He thought there was going to be a fight. Don't wear your toga if you want to be inconspicuous."

I took one step closer. "You're about as inconspicuous as a eunuch in a *frigidarium*. Keep away from me, Meditor."

He turned toward Agricola, who was still lost in thought. "Governor—"

The general looked up sharply. "Stop whining, Junius. Arcturus, you know the deadline. It's imperative we find out why this Maecenas was here and who killed him, so that we can determine how to respond to the Emperor." His brown eyes searched mine. "My life is in your hands. Not for the first time, but I'd damn sure rather take a spear in the stomach than this. I hope you have some leads."

"I do. I may be out of town for a few days, but I'll have some answers for you before the New Year." Both Avitus' and Meditor's ears pricked up.

"Sooner, if possible. And I think you should speak to the procurator. If this Syrian was an imperial messenger, one of Domitian's freedmen, he may know of him. He sees the Emperor more than I do."

Agricola didn't have to tell me to be careful with Sallustius. The procurator had a direct link to Caesar, and we both knew the kind of power they could wield—our fathers had been promoted that way.

Numerius Sallustius Lucullus was a dapper little man, and

an unlikely inventor of weaponry. He'd always been nice to me. In fact, I'd never met anyone who disliked him, a rare trait for the Emperor's provincial money-man and tax collector. But then again, he wasn't the kind of man anyone really noticed. His rank was his most unusual feature. Most of the time the procurator's office was occupied by equestrians—like my adopted father, or Agricola's father—but Lucullus was a senator. Domitian enjoyed trite humiliations. Lucullus, for his part, seemed oblivious.

"Right away, sir," I said.

Agricola stood up slowly. He looked older than he did an hour ago. "Well, gentlemen—I needn't tell you to keep your mouths shut. Put aside any differences and help each other. Publicly, this was a robbery and an attempt to harm the temple, not me. In the next few days, I'll start to plan for another temple site, but meanwhile, we carry on.

"Someone in our brotherhood is involved in this—even if it is unwittingly, by talking to a tent mate or a friend in a tavern. Avitus, I leave that for you to investigate. Assign some of your men to the task, and learn all you can about Maecenas.

"Saturninus, send word to Priscus to join us. We need to discuss strategy. And we may have to get word to one or two of the legion commanders to stay on alert."

So Agricola was considering the possibility of a civil war. Nothing like a little pressure, Arcturus.

"Junius, provide any and all help to Arcturus. Stay out of his way. Share your information, and above all, do nothing unless you hear from me personally. No arrests, nothing."

Meditor wasn't happy, but he nodded. He at least recognized the magnitude of what we were dealing with. I knew he'd still shadow me, but I also knew his men weren't very good at it.

"Arcturus, you know the urgency. Make haste. Stay in close contact with me. And I think it would be a good idea if you became a member of the temple. That all right with you?"

I nodded. It would give me a chance to get close.

"Good. We'll conduct the ceremony in a few days. Saturninus will prepare you for it. Don't let me down, son. More lives than mine are riding on what you find out."

Civil war, even. Romans and Britons. Legions and other legions. One fat, nasty Syrian could make a big difference to a lot of people.

We all got up to leave. I lingered behind, Avitus and Meditor both giving me looks on the way out. They wanted to grab the governor's ear, but I wasn't letting go of it.

"General—Agricola—have you heard anything about Christians? Here, or in Rome? Any campaigns by Domitian to root them out?"

He scratched his chin, then shook his grizzled head. "Nothing out of the ordinary. I've heard a few stories about arena kills, but nothing in particular that Domitian is doing. He's more interested in taxes than god. Why?"

"I know the arena stories myself. Seems I've heard Domitian compared to Nero, but now I don't know where I heard it."

I watched his jaw muscles move in and out. "Rumors. How I hate the rumors that fly around this place, that fly around the Emperor's palaces, that fly around Rome. Damned nonsense, most of them."

I nodded my head and started to leave, but turned back. "One more thing, sir."

His face told me to hurry.

"There's an old man—an ally of Rome. A Trinovantian warlord, name of Urien. He was decorated by Claudius. He's dying, now, and feels abandoned, alone. It would mean a lot if you went to see him."

Agricola's eyes raked over me. "Does this have something to do with the Syrian?"

I hesitated. "Yes, it does. What, I'm not sure. But Urien knew about Maecenas. I think you might be able to find out more about how yourself."

"So you'd have me do your job in addition to mine?"

"No, Governor. I'd have you pay your respects to a man who deserves them."

His mouth twitched a little. "All right, Arcturus. I'll find the time somehow. Is that all?"

I looked around the room and moved a little closer. "No. I found some money on the Syrian, the new money Domitian just issued. Gold *aurei*. Too much money for Britannia."

He looked startled. "But if you found it—"

"Yes. It wasn't stolen—originally. I think he was dug up again because someone's looking for that money. Either to spend it—"

"—or to hide it. I take your meaning." Agricola was nobody's fool. He knew how difficult it would be to use the cash. Gold left a trail even a blind man could follow, given enough time. I hoped this blind man could do it in a week. "Very well. No one need know."

My stomach dropped a little. I couldn't tell the general that I'd already told Urien's daughter. "One of the leads I'll be following up. And some of the money was owed to Urien, so when—"

"—If I'm still governor, I'll see the man gets paid. Go home and get some rest, Arcturus. I need you at your best." His eyelids drooped beneath the shaggy brows.

"Good night, sir. You'll hear from me soon. *Vale.*"

He grunted, and closed the door behind me. No guard waited for me; luckily, I already knew the way out.

FOURTEEN

I was dreaming of Camulodunum—green and yellow with buttercups and narcissus and daisies in the springtime. Blood began to drip down the petals, and splashed against the elms. I asked the Syrian, who was trying to saw off the rest of his head, if he knew how to stop it. He nodded, and the head came off and rolled at my feet. I picked it up, and my hands were useless, soft and swollen with decay. Then it turned into Agricola's head, and then my eyes opened.

I sat straight up. The dark room was suffocating. I shook my own head to clear it, gingerly checking my neck to make sure it was still attached.

When I walked out of the room, the house was still and cold. Before dawn, then. Good. I'd need to be at the procurator's at dawn. My house shoes made a comforting skidding sound on the floor, as I walked through the hallway to Draco's room. I'd sent him to bed when I got home last night, and hadn't bothered to wake up Brutius for door duty. I opened the door, and the squeak of the hinges was enough to make him jump.

"Master?"

"Yes, Draco. Wake up Venutius and Brutius, and have Brutius heat up the *caldarium* for me."

I could just barely make out his form springing from the bed. "How is Bilicho?"

"I don't know yet. I'm going to check right now." I left him fumbling in the dark for a robe. I was seeing qualities in Draco

139

I didn't know existed.

I walked back through the hallway, passed my room, and carefully swung Bilicho's door a few inches. I could hear his breathing: it was regular, even, and untroubled. I'd wait until I lit a lamp before I looked him over. I opened Coir's door, and made my way to the side of her bed. Before I could wake her, she sat up, shaking.

"I'm sorry. I didn't mean to scare you."

I could hear the sounds of Brutius lighting the furnace, and Venutius clanging a pot. No roosters yet. Did I even go to sleep last night?

"What would you like, Master?"

She let out a deep breath, rubbed her eyes and yawned, her short hair sticking out all over. I smiled. "Some light. I need to see Bilicho."

It only took a few minutes for the household to seem like it had never slept, like there was never a night at all. I smelled oat porridge from the kitchen, and started to feel some warmth beneath my feet. I could hear the dogs barking outside, waiting for Brutius to put down their food. Draco was whistling, while he lit the fire in the *triclinium,* and I watched a grumbling Bilicho still propped up in bed.

He was better. No sign of fever, and his pupils were normal. Best of all—he was complaining.

"I'm fine. Let me up! I can't do a damn thing lying here."

"One more day's rest, Bilicho. Two would be better. I'll compromise that far—and only that far."

He glared at me. "My doctor thinks he's my mother."

"You had a mother?"

We grinned at each other.

"All right. Can I at least go lie down on the couch in the dining room?"

I helped him up. I could tell he was still sore and dizzy. He'd need another draught to relieve the pain and help him sleep. By the time we got to the *triclinium*, Draco had built a steady fire, and Venutius was serving porridge with honey for breakfast. The oats wouldn't hurt Bilicho, but even he had to admit he wasn't very hungry. So while I ate, I told him about last night.

"So the upshot is that Meditor—who's always hated your guts—will be making your life as miserable as only he can, and Avitus is also on your back. This is what happens when I'm out of commission."

"You don't get all the credit. Avitus is pissed off because I kept my mouth shut about Maecenas. And Meditor is—well, you know what Meditor is."

Bilicho started to nod, and then winced. "Yeah. Luckily for him his ass isn't as narrow as his brain, or he wouldn't be able to shit. So what happens now?"

"After I make up a tonic for you and take a quick bath, I'm going to see the procurator. He might've known Maecenas, or maybe he heard something. And Agricola asked me to. I'll leave for Camulodunum tomorrow."

"Makes sense." He shot a glance at me while I finished the apple preserves. "So you think Rhodri dug him up?"

"Uh-huh. Probably Rhodri and Madoc. Sometime before dawn yesterday. And when they couldn't find the money, Madoc went to Lupo's to find out what happened. Then he followed me, to figure out what I knew, and what I was doing, and maybe to give me some friendly—or even unfriendly, it's hard to tell these days—advice. They had even more reason to knock you on the head, if Rhodri had unburied a corpse a few hours before and left it on top of the mithraeum. I'd want to get the hell out of town, too."

"They didn't need to leave him on top the temple. That's just pure spite."

"Maybe. Maybe it's also a warning."

"What do you mean?"

I rubbed my neck. "I think the killer is after Rhodri and Rhodri knows it. If he exposes the body, word gets out, and that means the *vigiles,* the *beneficarii,* everyone will be after the killer."

Bilicho wrinkled his forehead for a minute. "But what if everyone thinks Rhodri's the killer?"

My mouth felt a little tight. "They will. As soon as Meditor finds out about that brawl. It was a desperate move—like the sacrifice squeeze in *latrunculi.* But apparently Rhodri and Madoc feel they stand a better chance of survival if the murder is brought into the open—because maybe it will bring the murderer into the open."

"That is desperate." He felt the back of his head, tenderly. "I won't hold this against them."

"Your bump on the head and the Syrian's return visit last night are what convinced me that Rhodri's innocent. But his only chance is if I find him or the murderer before either Meditor's men or the murderer himself."

"So how many crimes now?"

"I don't know. I think the murderer is the same person who laid out Maecenas like a roast pig. But I don't know whether he took the papers, or Rhodri did. Or even someone else. We can figure out why someone would want to dig up Maecenas, but I still don't know why someone killed him. Unless it was to protect Agricola, which doesn't make sense. Nothing much does."

I stood up. I could tell what Bilicho was thinking, and what he was about to ask, and I didn't want to talk about it. "I'll make your drink. Burnet and valerian, I think."

He lowered his lids and said nothing. I called Coir to help me, and my back felt relieved when it couldn't feel Bilicho's eyes on it.

★ ★ ★ ★ ★

By the time I finished bathing, he was asleep. The valerian would keep him out for hours.

I felt cleaner, but not as clean as I'd like. My mind flitted over the last two days, searching for a way out or a way in—I wasn't sure which. What I needed was less thought and more action. I had too much to think about to think about it.

It was a little after dawn when I headed for the procurator's house. For once, it looked like the rain might be pouring on someone else, and some sun trickled over the muddy streets. Still icy, still Londinium.

I'd left Draco behind. With Meditor and his boys on my tail, I needed to be inconspicuous, which was hard enough for one tall man. At least I could trust Mollius. I'd helped him get the assignment with the *vigiles*. Meditor wouldn't give his men anything like the truth, and he'd probably try to make something up about me. But whatever scent he was on, Mollius would let me know. If I couldn't stay one step ahead of Meditor, someone should slit my throat.

I passed the governor's house, and saw the long line of hangers-on, dull and shuffling, waiting for the governor's handouts. Some Roman, some native, all needing something that they probably wouldn't get. Sure, maybe some money, some food, maybe a pardon in a court case, but everyone wanted a favor, and Agricola carried the patronage of every man, woman and child in Britannia on his back.

One or two were pitchmen, the kind that helped themselves, but needed a little encouragement in coin. "I've got a sure-fire investment scheme, sir—only take a minute of your time—" the story ran. Or "I've got *silphium,* slaves and the best Falernian loaded on my ship, and if you'd like to invest in bringing her to port—" There were other versions, all of them smelled. God, Arcturus, you're depressing this morning. Don't start that again.

Only stupid people never get depressed. Stupidity acts like a shield, one not even a *pilum* can penetrate. Sometimes I could use a shield that thick.

The man following me slowed down when I did. He was a little more skilled than Meditor's usual recruit. He was wearing what was supposed to be a nondescript brown mantle, but the stiff way he wore it and his uneven rate of walking—first fast, then stop, then fast again, then slow—told the story. Avitus wouldn't bother to have me tailed—he had too many other things to do, and he knew in his gut that I was trying to help in my own irritating way. That made him one of Meditor's.

I started to whistle an obnoxious tavern tune, and slowed to a stroll, to get a better look at the pack waiting on Agricola's doorstep. The *salutatio* was a time-honored tradition, and the Romans never met a tradition they didn't like.

Some were there as the general's clients—members of conquered tribes seeking protection, or help, or a post on the tribal council. Some were citizens, clambering for a position nearer the top of the ladder, or some other kind of recognition from the closest person to the Emperor they'd ever meet. Some were tourists, or merchants from Rome or Gaul, whose rank demanded time with the governor. And the others—the others were just prowling around, trying to pick up a bite, slinking in between the likely takers, hoping someone would be stupid enough to buy what they were selling. Somehow, it all made me feel better. So I sped up, and so did the footsteps behind me.

The procurator's house was to the east of the palace, terraced on two levels, not three, and, just as without the governor the procurator would be the top, without the palace, the house would be much more than it was. Unfortunately, its own ostentation would always suffer in comparison to the governor's little shack, but that was the procurator's life for you. For an equestrian, it was the Palatine Hill. For a senator—well, it was best not to be the sensitive type under Domitian.

The men waiting to see Lucullus were appropriately more hungry than those waiting for the governor. Tax problems, most likely. And some people thought it quite the bright idea to bypass Agricola and go to the man who reported directly to the Emperor. Ambition and appetite ran approximately neck and neck, until they'd get tangled in each other's feet and take a nasty fall. From the looks of the procurator's morning callers, most weren't getting back up.

Big Feet took up a post by a nearby temple—as luck would have it, the Temple of Fortuna. He'd need all the *fortuna* he could get if he wanted to follow me around. I walked through the crowd, collecting some dirty looks, and up to the guard, who was burly and bored, and busy cleaning his fingernails with a knife.

"Julius Alpinus Classicianus Favonianus." One thing about my name—you can't say it with a stammer. I lowered my voice. "Agricola sent me. It's urgent."

He stopped slicing fingernail long enough to look up at me with a tired expression. "Wait here."

So I waited, and I could feel the crowd getting more hostile. I turned toward them, a confident grin plastered on my face. It's harder to spit on someone who's looking at you. Big Feet, in the distance, was watching but trying to pretend that he wasn't. Fortunately, the bored tramp of little legionnaire's feet came to my rescue, and without a word or glance to the throng at the steps he ushered me in the house.

House didn't really describe the place, though it's where Lucullus ate, slept and dreamt of new things to tax. It felt more like a law office, a large, basilica-type building, two floors, two levels, and very formal. A large bust of Domitian was the first thing that greeted me.

There's one thing I really admire about Roman sculpture—it

doesn't lie. It stretches the truth, all right—that hideous statue of my Aunt Pervinca made when she was fifty-five gave her the nude body of a Greek nymph—but even that statue, a tribute to a blind old woman's vanity, put a fifty-five-year-old, wigged and whiskered head on top the body. I always suspected the slaves covered the face with a sack when she wasn't looking.

So there was Domitian, bald and chinless, spiteful and suspicious, as real as he ever was. I nodded at the Emperor and kept walking. The guard never looked behind, but plodded his way to a large reception room on the ground floor of the first terrace.

I could feel the buzz of scribal business before I walked in. Sitting at a desk was Numerius Sallustius Lucullus, with about three or four—I lost count from the blur—scribes and secretaries hovering and diving, like flies around a choice pile of house slops.

"By the balls of Mars—"

I jumped. Lucullus looked up, smiled, and apologized. "Sorry, Arcturus. Some records have been misplaced, and I need them for an assessment this morning. What can I do for you?"

My eyes were still trying to follow the scribes. "Thank you, sir. It's a private matter—"

A shadow of recognition crossed his face. "Of course. Leave us."

The buzzing stopped, and the group fled the room, wax tablets, papyri and abaci and all. He motioned for me to sit down at a chair in front of his desk. Lucullus was an amiable little man—nothing much to look at, so ordinary that he was hard to describe. He was grey and brown in about equal measure, and pleasant company—if you didn't mind the stench of failure that draped him like a too-big toga. He didn't seem to be aware of it. We all have our blind spots.

He lowered his voice. "I received word from Agricola this

morning that you are investigating a murder. Is it true what I heard? That the dead man is Vibius Maecenas?"

I leaned back a little in the chair and crossed my legs. I wasn't sure how much Agricola told Lucullus, and I wasn't about to add interest to the total.

"Apparently. Do you know him?"

"A little. I've seen him at the palace—mostly in Rome, not in Alba." His fingers nervously drummed a beat on his desk, and he picked up a stylus to have something to fidget with.

"The message didn't say much—just that someone robbed and murdered him and polluted the mithraeum. Is that what happened?"

I nodded. The little man looked happier with a stylus in his hand. Numbers must comfort him. "The governor wants the crime cleared up as soon as possible, and naturally he's concerned about the temple."

A sad smile crossed his face. "Yes. I'm not a member myself, you understand. The temple is really for men in the legions." His face brightened again. "Have you seen my new kind of *pilum?* I've invented a tip that allows for longer throws and yet won't come out once it strikes."

I'd heard about the procurator's hobby. He attended every triumph, every procession, read Julius Caesar incessantly, studied Alexander's letters, and collected maps of historic campaigns. But still he wasn't a general. He'd served as *quaestor* in Maecedonia, not exactly a hotbed of action these days, and never had a chance to conquer anybody. So he invented weapons, and tinkered with armor, and got a pat on the head from Agricola now and then and was appointed the tax-collector and paymaster of Britannia by Domitian. At least it kept him in *pila.*

I tried to look enthusiastic. "That's wonderful, sir. More efficient weaponry means saved lives." Not just Roman lives, but I didn't add that much.

He nodded energetically. "That's what I've always felt." He paused, and started tapping on the desk with the stylus. "So how can I help you?" he asked, a little more formal than before.

"Well, to begin with, what kind of man was Maecenas? What did he do for the Emperor?"

He thought for a minute. "Now, I didn't know him well, you understand. But I think he was one of Caesar's freedmen, a sometime secretary and sometime messenger. As I said, I saw him in Rome. And of course, he's been in Britannia a few times—somehow, I seem to recall he had an interest in a silver mine here. Moderately well-off, I should think. Syrian by birth."

"Do you know why he was in Londinium?"

"No, I really can't say. Business, probably. He struck me as a somewhat greedy fellow."

"You haven't heard anything about a marriage?"

He smiled, laid down the stylus, and rubbed his eyes. "My dear Arcturus. If I paid attention to every vulgar rumor that crosses my path, I should be unable to do my job. Bad things, rumors. I try to avoid them."

I smiled in return. "For the sake of my inquiry, sir, I'd appreciate it if you'd try to remember any you've heard recently."

His mouth twitched, a little petulantly. "Oh, very well. Rumor is the lowest form of information, you know—completely untrustworthy. Let's see—I seem to recall someone telling me something about Vibius marrying a native girl. I wasn't sure when or where or whom, because, as I've said, I wasn't paying attention. That's all, I'm afraid."

"Nothing else? Nothing about a message, for instance?"

On the last word, he stared at me, and sucked his teeth a little. "Garbage. Nothing but garbage," he snapped. "You should know better than to listen to them. There was talk at the triumph for the Emperor, and I refused to hear it then, and I refuse to hear it now. Garbage."

"Garbage that maybe killed Maecenas," I said softly.

Lucullus pinched his face up tight and suddenly didn't look as nice. "I don't like this, it does no credit to the governor or the Emperor. Or to you, I might add."

"I'm willing to get dirty. That's why I'm here."

He clenched his jaw, and stared at me. I held his eyes, and he finally caved in. "All right. It goes against my principles, but if it helps the governor . . ."

"It will," I assured him.

His brow knit in memory. "There was a rumor going about at the triumph—I don't remember who tried to tell me—and I immediately dismissed it as the sort of bilge sparked by jealousy, and afterward I didn't hear any more about it, thank goodness. The rumor was that a messenger would be coming to Britannia with imperial orders for Agricola to step down. I don't think Maecenas was mentioned personally, but I seem to remember he was present when I heard this, and in an uncommonly good mood. Until I told them all what I thought."

He frowned, and his mouth dug ditches down to his chin. "But that can't be true. Domitian thinks very highly of Agricola, he's told me so on numerous occasions. He knows the governor is about to conquer the rest of the province, and believe me, he wants it. And Maecenas was robbed, wasn't he? Was he supposed to have a lot of money on him?"

Never discuss money with a procurator. I laughed. It sounded a little hollow to my ears. "What's a lot of money in Britannia? They'll slit your throat for a night on the town these days."

He looked at me closely, like I didn't add up. But it seemed to pacify him. "All too true." He put down the stylus with finality. "Well, Arcturus—"

I rose. "Thank you, sir. I really appreciate you telling me what you've heard. Good luck with your records."

"Thank you. And do come back for the *pilum* demonstration."

"I will." At the door I turned back to face him. "I almost forgot—just one more thing, sir—"

He'd already started to unfold a tablet full of calculations. "Yes, what is it?" he demanded impatiently, not looking up from the book.

"Do you know a Marcus Caelius Prato?" A pause lingered in the air between us like a bad odor. I waited for it to clear. The procurator was still hunched over his tablet, and hadn't said anything.

"Caelius—"

"I heard you the first time. I'm trying to remember. Seems to me I've heard that name in conjunction with a business here in Londinium." He finally looked up, and scratched his chin. "Something unsavory, as I recall. Wait—I do remember. Prato, you said? There was a Prato mentioned in that last rumor I told you about, the one about the message. Don't know whether it was Caelius Prato or not. Is that all?"

"Yes sir, and thank you again."

The siren call of mathematics lured him back, and he barely grunted in reply. I opened the door, to find the pack of scribes and assistants waiting anxiously. "He's all yours," I said with a bow, and turned to walk down the long hallway.

As I passed Domitian, the bored guard was leading in a soldier. The man—a legionary—stared at me. His eyes were an unusual brown-green, and glowed with something I couldn't see. Someone I operated on? I couldn't remember. Probably a temple member, who recognized me from last night. He was wearing a green scarf with a thick red *sagum* held in place with a fancy gold pin—looked like the shape of Apollo. Maybe he was one of Avitus' men. If he was part of the mithraeum, I'd soon meet him. Saturninus would have to prepare me for the initiation when I got back from Camulodunum. But meanwhile, I had real work to do.

Big Feet was waiting for me. He sprang up from the steps of the temple when he saw me—they must've been cold, and he wasn't wearing trousers. I smiled a little, and threaded my way through the rest of the pack, their numbers dwindling with their hopes.

I walked out in the street, and meandered northeast. I thought I'd pass the Forum on my way—where? I was improvising, and I didn't like the tune. I needed to find Rhodri. That was the one refrain that kept playing over and over, and I was getting tired of hearing it.

Too late to start for Camulodunum now. I could swing by Lupo's, and just observe the place—maybe take a look in on the whores. Then go home and check Bilicho, and send a message to Saturninus and find out when this initiation was supposed to take place. And I could look up Mollius, see what the *vigiles* knew. Head for the palace and tell Agricola I was leaving tomorrow. Maybe Avitus discovered something. Maybe Meditor had an epiphany and killed himself.

It all sounded good, particularly the part about not seeing Gwyna. I was resolutely pushing her out of my head. If Meditor somehow discovered my interest in her, he'd be first in line at the crucifixion. I'd left out any private motives for the murder last night—better for Rhodri's chances, and better for me. Even if Vibius was killed for personal reasons, he was here as the Emperor's agent. That made everything political.

The streets were beginning to get crowded, and I could see a throng at the market in the Forum. Big Feet almost lost me in the crowd a few times, but I waited for him. I wriggled my way past the turnips and cabbages and homemade beer and pots and pans to the *rostra*, the site of official speeches and official boredom.

The *rostra* hadn't really meant anything since Cicero had his hands and tongue nailed to the one in Rome a long, long time ago. But the Romans held on to the illusion that public speaking was free and put a *rostra* in every forum in every city in the Empire.

It was a good place to advertise. There was a gladiator show today, featuring some half-naked women from Carthage. They were probably fat, forty, drunk and from Gaul. Also on the bill was a live Thracian—always more exciting than a dead one—and a few dwarfs. Slave children the promoter bought, probably. As long as the crowd got some blood, they wouldn't care even if they knew the difference.

I planned a little. I'd avoid the northeast—people would be heading out for good seats. Maybe that's why it was so crowded. Games ate into tavern and brothel business, but afterward they doubled it. Lupo's should be quiet right now.

Someone was trying to sell some family jewels—no doubt stolen—and someone else had scratched a rough drawing of certain sexual positions in very flattering proportions. Beneath it was a curse, apparently on the artist. Then an exhortation to bet on Maximus in the races, with odds given below. Above it all was an official announcement. "Wanted: Information pertaining to the robbery and murder of Vibius Maecenas, a Syrian merchant. See Publius Junius Meditor at the Basilica Claudia in the Forum." Listing "robbery" first was Agricola's idea—too subtle for Meditor. So that's how they were going to play it—robbery and murder of a foreign merchant.

I yawned, and glanced back. Big Feet was trying to ignore a man selling decorated banqueting pots and dinnerware. From what I could see, the pictures on them looked the same as the drawing on the *rostra*. Maybe he was the Zeuxis of the three-foot prick.

I squared my shoulders and plunged into the crowd, headed

straight for Big Feet. He was waving the potter away in a panic, his eyes getting bigger by the moment. I didn't look over, but threaded my way through so that I would brush up against him. I could feel him hold his breath. He let it out as soon as I passed, but nearly fell into a large *krater* when I pinned his arm behind his back. I pretended to look over his shoulder and admire the handiwork.

I whispered in his ear: "Run home and tell Meditor to stop wasting your time. There's a murderer on the loose."

He didn't say anything, but I could hear a squeal rising up in his chest. What had Meditor told him about me?

"And I'm not it. I'm a *medicus,* a simple *medicus.* And I'd drink some peppermint and anise, if I were you—that's quite a wheeze you've got."

My fingers tightened on his wrist. "Don't follow me anymore. Next time you try to be inconspicuous, leave your gold *fibula* at home. They don't give those out with the grain dole." I relaxed my grip, and I thought he'd fall. Without a backward glance, he fumbled his way through the shoppers and headed for the basilica behind the forum, where Meditor had his office.

The potter was looking at me with curiosity and irritation. His teeth were yellow from chewing caraway seeds, and he belched a few times as an added incentive to stick around. I hurriedly bought a water jug with Jupiter and Danae—at least I think it was supposed to be Danae, you never could tell with potters, they always seemed to mix the stories up—and left. I tried to melt into the crowd but it wasn't hot enough, so I skirted around the edges and headed west for Lupo's.

The crowds thinned considerably. Most of the city would pour into the amphitheater, leaving it nice and empty for me. Some shops along the way—increasingly shabby, as I headed westward—posted closed signs because of the show. I could see the rear of Lupo's in front of me, the side with the door exiting into the mews, when I noticed a wagon pulled up next to it. I doubled my pace. Lupo was coming out of the back door, talking to a wiry, thin man, as lean and mean as a miser's purse. The big man looked surprisingly small. As I got closer, I saw why. The pot slipped out of my fingers and broke on the hard, muddy ground, but I didn't hear it shatter. The wagon was an undertaker's cart, and in the cart—I reached it, out of breath, not able to breathe—was the dead and broken body of Galla. She'd been beaten to death.

FIFTEEN

The nausea came over me suddenly. I turned my back to Lupo and the undertaker, and vomited in the mud as quietly as I could. I never got sick in the hospital, but then again I didn't usually feel responsible for killing my patients.

There were a few other people standing around. A couple of whores, the blonde I'd seen the day before, looking bored. One who must've been kept on for men with mother fixations. Pigeon-Chest was lurking farther back on the side of the building. I didn't think he'd recognize me without my toga, and with vomit on my breath. Lupo wasn't paying attention: he was arguing with the undertaker.

"You don't got enough for a fire. Y'r lucky I can bury her for this. Ya want a mourner, too? That'll cost you thirty *sestertii*. Music's the same price, as long as you like a pipe. Why you want to buy a procession, anyway? She's just a whore!"

I could see the muscle under Lupo's tunic quiver. He was facing the undertaker, and the lean man started to back up. "Don't get hasty, I'm not saying nothin', you do whatever you want, I'm just tryin' to save you some trouble."

The big man's hulking frame suddenly shuddered and collapsed, like a blown-up pig's bladder kids like to kick in the streets. He turned around, and there was a dark red rim around his one eye. They started to walk toward the cart, where I was standing. I hadn't looked in again—I knew I'd have to, but not just yet.

"You. Undertaker."

Surprised, the skinny man looked me over, wondering how I got there and why I cared. The blonde eyed me curiously, and the old lady just sobbed into a filthy handkerchief. Lupo hadn't noticed me yet. He was staring at Galla's body.

I took out a pouch, and that was enough to capture the full attention of the undertaker. I said: "Here's seven *denarii*. I want a lyre, a pipe, a dance, and a full ceremony at the gravesite. A pyre, if that's what she wanted. And a marker—stone. Standard bereavement." The undertaker licked his lips in excitement.

"And a full *cena novendialis*. I'll be there for it, you cheap bastard, and I want the best your small-time service offers, so don't start figuring out how to cheat the dead just yet."

His hand stretched out for the money, and Lupo finally caught on. "Now, don't be hasty, I got some good people in line, if you wanna waste your money on a slave, who am I to—"

He moved quickly for such a large man. The fingers around the undertaker's throat weren't quite as fat as sewer pipes. I said: "He's not worth your time, Lupo. It won't bring her back. Let him go."

Pigeon-Chest had moved closer by now, and both women had stopped crying, staring at me, puzzled. The undertaker staggered, and lurched against the wall, his breath coming back in hard gasps. I heard some footsteps behind me, and turned and saw a short, squat middle-aged man wearing a cobbler's apron. He looked agitated and out-of-breath.

"Is it true? Is Galla . . ." We led him to the cart with our eyes—we couldn't help it. He took some slow, delicate footsteps for such a paunchy build, and peered over the edge. The tired white cart horse stomped, and for a second all any of us could hear was the swish of its tail.

He didn't make a sound. His body stiffened, and his paunch shook a little, and then he faced us. There was a fire in his eyes and flabby cheeks.

"Who? Customer?"

Lupo studied him soberly, his one eye still red and raw. He slowly shook his head. That meant it was Caelius. Of course. I'd been so worried, so hoping that she would come find me. And Caelius could do whatever he wanted—she was his slave, his property, and it was his—monetary—loss.

The fat man wheezed a little, and stood up straighter. He looked around, reality starting to hit him, and I suddenly remembered where I'd seen him. He was the drunk, the one who sang the song about Galla two nights ago when Maecenas was murdered. He'd been one of her "reg-u-lars." His eyes were a little piggish, but not stupid, and they were starting to panic. The undertaker was rubbing his neck theatrically, but nobody paid attention.

The cobbler whispered: "She told me—she told me—"

Lupo and I looked at each other. I moved him off toward the other side of the alley, away from what was left of Galla in the cart, and away from what was left of the people standing around. Lupo lumbered toward the undertaker, who blanched.

"When did you see her last?"

He was still in shock. "Last night. She was drunk. She was always drunk, lately. But I still—I still—"

"I know. Listen. Galla knew something about a murder. That's why she was killed. Did she tell you?"

He pulled away from me, the slits of his eyes popping open in alarm. "Who are you? What do you want from me?"

"I am—was—a friend of Galla's. I'm investigating a murder for the governor. I'd like to find a way to punish the man responsible for this one. Use your head. If he killed Galla, it was because he was involved with another crime, a crime he could pay the price for."

His eyes darted nervously across my face, behind my back

and through the streets, now getting a full dose of sunlight splayed against the buildings, and back toward Lupo. "If I tell you—if I keep my mouth shut—"

"If you keep your mouth shut you can still be killed. Galla was a slave, he can do what he wants. But you really think he'll stop here? He's found out by now from the other whores who she's been seeing—who might know something."

He started breathing harder, and sucked in his gut. "What can I do?" The words came out in a whistle. "I got a wife, three kids, a shop that don't make much."

"You won't need to make much if you're dead. Who's gonna take care of your family? Come on, tell me. It's your best chance. It's your only chance."

He looked around again, his eyes rolling a little, some spittle on his lips. He'd tell me now, or never. His voice dropped to a whispered rattle.

"She said—she said—she said she heard a squeal that night. Like a pig. Somewhere outside in the alley. And she poked her head outside and saw two men on horseback. One was a soldier. One of the horses was pulling a little cart." He turned involuntarily toward the undertaker's, and swallowed. "Not as big as that one. She couldn't tell who they were, because it was dark outside, and they were up the street some, not right in front of the door."

He didn't know he'd grasped my arm. "She didn't think nothin' of it. Until later. Then she figures maybe they had something to do with the murder—the one that everybody's talking about, the one with the sign in the forum. Said she was gonna start charging more, 'cause she was so valuable." His voice started to crack. "And then she—she—"

"When did she tell you this?"

"Last night. I thought she was just talkin', like she always did. Galla liked to brag, but she was always good for a laugh."

His eyes were round, and he suddenly sucked in a sob. "Not anymore."

"Would she have recognized the men?"

He shook his head. "I don't think so. She said it was dark, she couldn't see the faces. But she could tell one was a soldier from the clothes he was wearin'." I was silent for a moment, and the fat man squeezed my arm.

"What happens to me now? What do I do? Can you help me?"

I didn't much like my chances for helping anybody anymore.

"You need to get out of town. Fast. Close the shop for a few days, take the family, and go. You got a place?"

He nodded, numbly. "West. Over in Durnovaria. My wife's from one of the tribes there. We could stay with her folks, for awhile, if I explain it right."

"Go. Now. Don't wait for tonight. Shop near here?"

He gestured with his head down the street I'd just walked. His hand dropped from my arm. He'd have to think of a good story to tell his wife.

I reached into my pouch and took out another couple of *denarii*. "Here."

He took the money, not really seeing it. I grabbed his shoulders. "Get out of town. You're a freedman, aren't you? Then go. That fat used to be muscle. Use it, and move!"

His eyes darted up into mine, alarmed, scared, but finally fully seeing me. Without a word, he brushed my hands off, and scurried down the bright street.

The others watched us from the other side. The undertaker was bored—he had other bodies to deliver. "Can I go now?" he whined to Lupo.

Lupo walked to the cart and I met him there. The horse was stomping again, and I stroked its scarred flank. I could look at her now.

Her neck had been broken, but before that she'd been beaten. Sometime before dawn, probably about when I woke up. Caelius had used a stick. Didn't want to get his hands dirty. If only she'd come to me, when she pretended to be Stricta . . . Stricta! If Caelius had done this to Galla for what she knew—

"Lupo—where's Stricta?"

The giant looked at me steadily with the one, large eye. The undertaker whined a little more. "I got other calls t'make, y'know?"

Lupo took my arm and nearly lifted me off the ground as we moved away from the others. He tried to whisper. "She gone. This morning. Heard—heard—"

"I know. That means he'll be looking for her. And he'll do worse."

Lupo nodded dumbly. "Wanted to stop him. He said he'd send me to mines. Don't care. Then he said blame me. For this."

Understanding struck me like one of Caelius' whips. The welt would be there for a long time.

"You're a slave, aren't you?"

He nodded again in misery. "Sometimes I forget. Try to help. Try to protect. Do what he say."

So Caelius used Lupo as a front, but the big man was his slave. Power of life and death. And power was how Caelius got his kicks.

"Lupo—where did she go?"

"Don't know. She wore green cloak. Only one she has."

My mouth twisted into what passed for a smile.

"You watched her leave, didn't you?"

His eye met mine, and he nodded, his features hardening into crags. "Try to help."

"How did she get away?"

"Drug. Drug a man. When Galla—when Galla—"

160

"She drugged a customer and escaped when Caelius was beating Galla."

His bowed head confirmed it. If Caelius tried to pin the murder on Lupo, all of the slaves could be executed. But then he'd have to admit Lupo was a slave. Maybe that was enough to protect him and the others. For now. And Caelius would figure no one would give a damn about what happened to a whore— especially one he had the legal right to kill.

"You don't know where she went?"

"No. She said safe place. Like home."

I looked up quickly. "She said 'like home'? Are you sure?"

He nodded again. "Thanks, Lupo." I turned to leave, and he grabbed my arm.

"You no stay? No stay for Galla?"

I shook my head. "Make sure he builds a hot enough pyre."

He dropped his hands into huge fists by his side, and walked back to the undertaker. Pigeon-Chest was there now, staring at me, his face tight with the strain of memory. They formed a procession, the two whores, Pigeon-Chest, and the giant man, to follow the undertaker to his business, where he'd dress the body and line up the musicians and dancer. Then they'd head out to the western edge of town, and light a fire, and say good-bye to Galla, and toast her with her favorite wine, and share some food, and send her off to the land of the shades with one final drink. When I looked back, Lupo was lumbering behind the cart, and I could swear I saw a tear ooze out from the patch on his missing eye.

SIXTEEN

"Like home," he'd said. Like home. Only one place in Londinium qualified as like home—The Temple of Isis. I'd look for Stricta there. Lupo wouldn't tell anyone else. Caelius could torture him if he wanted, but I doubted that he'd try. Lupo might forget himself again and pay Caelius what he deserved.

Galla's face hovered before my eyes for a few seconds, until what it was this morning faded in on top. Fatal memory. Two men, a soldier and another. A cart. A pig squeal. That proved the mithraeum set-up was planned. It was pig blood on the altar, and the cart was for hauling Maecenas' body.

But why would Caelius kill Maecenas? Was it the silver mine Lucullus mentioned, or some other dirty business? Why the mithraeum? Too many questions, and none of them came close to helping me forget what I kept seeing. I walked southeast in a hurry. The *Iseum* was near the big bridge across the river, where Bilicho had woken up to a headache.

She was a gentle goddess in an ungentle world. I'd seen one of the big processions in Rome, the priests with the shaved heads and the spotless white robes, the *sistra,* the buckets full of the sacred Nile water, the palms, the lanterns, the gold breast full of milk. Isis was a suffering goddess. She understood what pain was like, and knew all about death, and didn't care for it much. She made Egypt the grain center of Rome, because her tears flooded the banks of the Nile every year. And she'd saved her husband, Osiris, and brought him back from the underworld.

I guess she promised to do that for her followers, too. She was like Demeter at Eleusis, but not as exclusive. She helped those who needed help, so she helped everybody.

We wanted our gods to be kind—unless we wanted them to be cruel to someone else. We were Romans, after all: god was always on our side. But Isis took in the lame, the blind, the sick and the dying. She offered them hope, if not healing. I liked her. And since I didn't really believe in much—I'd seen too many gods toppled in my life—liking was as close to worshipping as I ever came. I paid my taxes, and made the public gestures. But I still felt more at home in a grove of trees than a stone temple.

In a few days I'd be in that suffocating dirt hole where Mithras would reveal himself. Another of the savior gods. Promising life after death was fashionable among deities. I didn't mind going through the motions if it helped me solve this murder. These murders.

Stricta could hide in the *Iseum*. They'd give her sanctuary. Not even Caelius could walk into the temple and do what he pleased. Hell, not even Agricola would do that, at least without his guards. Those Egyptian priests were a burly bunch, and Caelius was a coward without his bully stick.

I made my legs walk faster. I didn't want to think about Caelius. I liked problems I could solve. The law didn't recognize Caelius as a murderer. I couldn't help that. Couldn't help Galla now. I could only chase shadows, hunt whispers, pump procurators for rumors, as impotent as the Emperor without his Empire. Goddamn it. Goddamn Caelius. Goddamn Maecenas. Goddamn me.

The temple loomed up in front, a modest affair. I was glad to see it. Concentrate. I swallowed, stopped breathing so hard, stopped shaking so much. Must be a festival today—I could hear women ululating from within, a kind of ecstatic but painful moan. A cloud of incense curled out into the brisk air, swelled and grew thin, then dispersed to the sky. I walked up the rough stone steps, pretending to admire the carving on the columns. The outer door was open, the middle door was shut. The members, the initiated ones, were behind the middle door, or maybe the door after that, in front of the holy of holies, chanting the pain of life.

The temple was more Roman than Egyptian, and the man in white who came to greet me looked like he was from Hispania, but he spoke Greek. I stood in a wide, hospitable chamber, rugs on the floor, a small niche with a marble statue of Isis wearing the moon's crescent, a clean wooden roof above me, with two doors leading out, one directly in front, the middle door, and one to my right. It was probably like a labyrinth inside. You had to be initiated to know how to get in or get out.

Unlike Roman temples, it wasn't all facing front, it wasn't a big long room with steps and inner chambers and columns everywhere, and it didn't have a gloriously large front altar. But it was still built east to west, and the columns it did have were Roman style, Roman marble, though the temple itself was painted brick and wood. A hybrid, like most things in Britannia.

The smoke was unfolding from a small altar in this room, a public one for non-initiates to leave offerings or pay their respects. The incense was high-quality frankincense.

I said in Greek: "Greetings, friend, and son of Isis. I come in peace."

The bald man nodded, and raised an eyebrow. Most of his believers wouldn't speak Greek. To maintain purity, he'd open with that language, and then quickly switch to Latin. But Stricta would speak Greek, and I was, too. His sunken eyes, fathomless, roamed my face. He was a big man for his height and well-muscled. He could've been an infantryman or a eunuch. I didn't plan to ask him which.

"You wish to make an offering to the goddess?" he asked courteously.

I pulled out my pouch again, and took out my second-to-the-last *denarius*. "Alas, my troubles have overflowed this day like the waters of the Nile—I did not have time to purchase an offering, and hope that The Mother of Us All will be content with a base gift."

The wails built into a crescendo, and the door on the right opened. A procession of women with cloaks covering their heads emerged from an inner room, now moaning softly. The one in front carried a small, crude wooden statue of Isis with cow's horns suckling Horus. She opened the back door, and the others—about twenty in all—followed.

The priest interposed himself between me and the view, and deftly plucked the *denarius* from my palm. "Your gift is a generous one," he said in an undertone. "The goddess shines love upon all of her children, but this day is her son's birthday, and she looks with especial favor upon those who pay him tribute."

Horus' birthday. Stricta must have been planning her escape for some time, since she had the drugs ready. Or maybe she was going to take them herself, and Caelius' crime changed her mind. Horus' birthday. That explained the moaning, at least.

I bowed my head, and took hold of the priest's white sleeve. It wasn't as immaculate as the one I saw in Rome, but neither was I.

"Childbirth is painful for women. Many die."

He looked at me warily, and pried my fingers from his cuff. "Yes, but Isis will bring them eternal life."

"The Goddess With Many Names will protect all who are in pain, I know. But there are some within who may need a doctor."

This time he took hold of my wrist. His grip was not gentle. "Who are you? You speak Greek, but are not Greek and not of

165

this temple."

"I am a healer. The doctor whom even Isis may need."

His grip tightened, and his breath felt hot on my face. "You answer questions with riddles. What do you want?"

I flung my arm suddenly, and took him off-guard. He reached inside his robe, and held something there, ready. I smiled.

"No, brother, you don't understand. I am a friend. I am a *iatros*. My name is Arcturus. I have a message for one within, who today has given birth to both grief and freedom. When she is ready, when she is able, I need her help. She can save lives. She can punish the evil. Send word when she can talk."

His eyes bored into mine, intense, emotionless. Not a flicker. But he dropped his hand back to his side, and opened his palm to look at the *denarius*. Then, without a word, and without a backward glance, he turned around and walked through the rear door, the hem of his white robe grey and dirty, dragging in the dust.

The third woman in the procession had been in a green cloak.

Keep busy. Keep walking. Stricta was safe, for now. Caelius would look for her himself—he wouldn't want the involvement of a *fugitivarius,* even if he could find one, unemployed and waiting for him, in Londinium. The priests would give her sanctuary, hide her well. But she couldn't stay there indefinitely. Another problem; maybe one I could solve.

Where was I going? I watched my feet step, toe to heel, one after another, like a captive led in a triumph. The sun was going away again, the clouds were coming, and I didn't know what to do. The squish of icy mud played harmony to my breath—in, out, in, out. This morning I made a plan. This morning seemed too long ago for memory.

I was heading east again, toward the river and some warehouses. Mollius lived there. Maybe I could find him. He could tell me what the story was with the *vigiles,* if they knew anything yet. Maybe he could tell me if I knew anything.

I turned right at the next corner. There were a couple of ships at the dock, unloading grain, wine, *garum.* Food for the army. The sailors were loud—sailors were always loud. Romans didn't like the sea, too much. Maybe being out there, on the wine-dark waves, they got a little drunk on loneliness. They yelled so they could hear themselves breathing. I skirted around the men in dirty tunics, yesterday's dinner rubbed on their fronts, grunting as they unloaded barrels and *amphorae.*

Mollius' *insula* was on this street somewhere. At least he lived on the first floor, above a baker, and with running water. The top three stories had no such luck. I spotted the building, a mud and timber affair badly in need of another whitewash.

A couple of grifters lounged against the wall. They must not be too good at grifting or they'd be at the gladiator show with everyone else. They looked at me, too bored to make a pitch, or maybe they didn't like my size. One took out a couple of dice from a pouch with patches on it, and they both crouched in the mud, tossing the dice, half-heartedly asking a god for benediction.

I walked past the shops, past the small bakery stall and felt the heat from its oven. A woman was haggling over a price inside, the baker was ignoring her. I walked in through the doorway, into a run-down courtyard with a small well lacking a cover. The wail of a baby startled me, and sparked a couple of others to wail back, like the howls of hungry wolves. The walls were as thin as a debtor's excuses. I could hear sobbing in one, a man shouting in another. The first baby abruptly stopped, and the others followed. Maybe its mother shoved a dirty rag into its mouth. It was that kind of place.

I climbed the stair, and tried not to make the wood scream too much while I clutched the wobbly banister. I hoped Mollius was in. Third door on the right. No sound from his neighbors. The Esquiline of *insula* floors, I guess. The door was spindly, and shook dramatically when I knocked. I knocked again. A head covered in a grey rag, looking like it wiped dishes, from two doors down on the left, poked out, saw me, and poked back in again. I tried one more time, and gave up. The winter daylight hours were running by me, and I needed to get home to Bilicho, get word to Agricola. Figure out when and how to tackle Caelius.

I made it down the stairway again, and my stomach growled. I didn't feel like eating, but it was empty and cold, and the least I could do for it was buy it something to gnaw on. One of the stalls on the ground floor was a small tavern. The grifters were gone, dice and all, when I came out into the bankside air.

The sailors were singing, now, something rough and rude about girls with tits like wine jars. I turned right, and three shops down was the tavern. Mollius was sitting on a low stool, a large cup as close to his hand as an overprotective bodyguard.

Mollius drank too much. That's one reason he lived here, even though he made a decent living as a *vigil*. The second reason was that he also gambled too much. And maybe he did both because he'd been hurt in the army, and the ache of the mangled leg never went away.

Instead of mustering him out, someone—I forget who— recommended him for the *vigiles* company that Agricola formed. I seconded the nomination, to the governor himself. It kept him in wine and winnings, and occasionally, women. It also kept him drunk and poor, and living in a shithole. Mollius didn't seem to notice, or care. And still he was cleaner than Meditor.

I squeezed in beside him, and he looked at me without recognition, his eyes rheumy. A large-bodied, blue-black fly buzzed heavily around us, finally landing on a half-eaten plate of fried pork bellies and cabbage. I watched it rub its legs together. Even it wanted to wash before it ate what was on the plate.

"Mollius. I've been looking for you."

He squinted hard. "Ah—Arcturus. Glad to see you. Thought you'd be comin' t'see me. Din't recognize you. Been awhile."

I'd seen him drunker. He grasped the cup lovingly, and swigged a shot of beer, dark with malt. Maybe the drink kept the smell of the food from getting to him. A woman with straggly grey hair chained up but trying to escape came over with intention. I was occupying one of the few stools in the place. I checked my pouch. Only one *denarius* left. A glint of gold caught my eye, and I remembered I hadn't taken out that bit of pin I found in Maecenas' room. Just like this case. Every time I thought about going straight ahead, something shoved me sideways. I pushed it back down in the seam, and extracted the coin.

"How much for a beer and some bread?"

"Two *as*es for the bread, three for the beer." She leered at me a little. "I ain't seen you 'round here before."

"Just visiting. Change for a *denarius?*"

She got a little red in the face. "Do I look like a bank?"

Mollius was watching me in amusement. He started to shake a little, but it was only suppressed laughter. He fumbled around in his blood-brown cloak, and pulled out a pouch. He counted out five *as*es, and the woman, glaring at me, scooped them up like a pelican gulping a sea bass.

"My treat, Arcturus. You're in the wrong neighborhood. Now—what was I going to tell you?" He was trying to speak more clearly, and he seemed to shake off some of the stupor.

"I came to you about a murder."

He eyes wrinkled up at me from beneath a ginger-haired eyebrow. "You kill somebody?"

"Go ahead and laugh, Mollius. Meditor's on my ass. Set one

of his men on me today. I'm investigating a murder for the governor, and you know what Meditor's like."

"I do, indeed. A rat in a hole, is Meditor. But a rat is a smart animal." He hunched over the counter closer to me, and gestured with his eyes for me to do the same. I shoved the plate—the fly was still feasting—out of the way and leaned in, my elbows on the scarred wood.

"The Maecenas murder, right?" he murmured. "He called us together late last night. Told us you were involved, you were covering up something."

My face got tight. "The bastard. I'm involved, all right, but not like he'd like it. What's he know?"

"I got off duty about an hour and a half ago. I was waiting for a friend of mine when Meditor came in, very excited. He called us back in, had one of the men run out to find the rest, and told us he had the murderer."

"What? In custody?"

Mollius shook his head and leaned closer. The grey-haired woman flounced by and threw a plate of warm bread by me, and without taking her bloodshot eyes from my face, drew me a *hemina* of beer, and threw that at me, too.

"You really know how to make friends, Arcturus." Mollius chuckled, and shook some more. "Nobody is in custody. But he had us track where Maecenas was staying, and somebody squawked about a fight that night, so he's looking for a native named Rhodri. He thinks it's all a plot of the Brits."

Meditor was nothing if not predictable. "What's he going to do?"

Mollius tore off a piece of the bread, and downed a gulp of the beer. "What do you think he's going to do? Find him, arrest him, and kill the poor bastard. Meanwhile, we're supposed to really put the screw to the natives. He's trying to convince Agricola right now to chop down all the oak groves around Londinium. And he wants a curfew. Meditor doesn't give a shit if he hounds the innocent, as long as he can hound somebody."

I bit so hard on my lip that it hurt. "I don't think Rhodri's guilty. And making trouble for the Brits is cruel and stupid."

"That's Meditor." He took another drink of the beer. "You mind?"

I shook my head. My stomach would wait for better things. "Agricola won't do it. He's trying to win them over, not punish them." I don't know whether I was attempting to convince myself or Mollius.

The *vigil* snorted. "He'll do whatever is best for Rome. And that translates into whatever is best for him. And even if he doesn't let Meditor go all the way, some of the men will. They've been itching to get at 'the troublemakers' as they call them."

He turned to look at me, his worn and tired face suddenly earnest. "Listen, Arcturus. I'm nothing. An old soldier. I've killed a lot of men, because I didn't have a choice. I do now. But Meditor and his boys will harass every hut from here to the coast if they get a chance. If you know where that boy is, find him. And if you know he's innocent, you'd best be prepared to have proof."

"Thanks, Mollius." I laid the *denarius* on the bar. "Keep the change."

His mouth curved wryly. "I'll just lose it on a bet." His hand reluctantly caressed the coin before he picked it up. "Thanks."

I leaned in close again. "Did Meditor say anything about a Marcus Caelius Prato?"

He wrinkled his brow for a minute, then shook his head. "Not that I've heard. Why? How's he figure?"

"He's the real owner of Lupo's—the place where Maecenas was staying."

His thick eyebrows arched in surprise. "Want me to find out about him for you?"

I looked my gratitude. "Very much." I lowered my voice still further. "He murdered one of his slaves today. A prostitute. Beat her to death."

A spasm of pain and disgust crossed Mollius' worn face. He lowered his eyes, and groped for the cup. His head tilted back, and back again, as he drained it, and laid it with a thump on the bar. "Don't consider it a favor. I'll do what I can."

The beer was starting to take him again. "Goddamn *pietas*, you know? Agricola kills the natives, the natives kill someone else, some prick kills a whore—all *pietas*."

He stared at me, his eyes watery and blind. "It's not just a Roman thing, y'know. Not just Virgil and Aeneas and all that literary, legendary crap. Everybody's got a little *pietas*. It's a fancy name for what it means to do what you think you have to do, for your country, your god, your wife, your kids, your miserable shitty little life, no matter who gets in the way and who it hurts. No, my friend—everybody's got a little *pietas*."

I left him on the stool, muttering to himself. The fly and I escaped together.

Seventeen

I walked along the quays and the docks on the way home, past the palaces, large and small, brooding over the river—their inhabitants and visitors still scurrying like ants, though the sun had withdrawn its favors and darkness was around the corner. I didn't think, didn't talk, didn't whistle, just walked. No one followed me. I followed myself.

When I opened the door, Draco and Brutius greeted me.

"How's Bilicho?"

"He's very well, Master, Coir's been with him all day." Draco answered promptly. Brutius cleared his throat.

"What is it? What happened?"

"Nothing to do with *Dominus* Bilicho. He's been awake for hours. There's someone else to see you."

I started walking toward the *triclinium*. "Where?"

"No, Master, not there." This time it was Brutius. "Your examination room."

I didn't need to ask who. Avitus, again, I was sure of it. He must've wanted to see me personally, and to keep it quiet, which is why Brutius and Draco were so nervous and why they put him in there. I walked fast, fully prepared to face the *beneficarius,* and found myself facing Gwyna.

The switch didn't bother me much. She was dressed somewhere in between her campaign uniform and the plain tunic I'd kissed her in. She turned with a genuine-looking smile of relief, and came toward me, her hands outstretched.

She grabbed my arms and got closer. "Thank God you're all right. I came as soon as I could."

I stared down at her, and disengaged myself. "You run as hot and cold as a *thermae*. Last time I saw you was yesterday. You shoved me out the door, remember? What's wrong, Gwyna? You need something?"

The blue didn't snap this time. She held up her head, and returned my stare, some pain making fine lines around her eyes.

"I deserve that. I'm sorry."

I chewed my cheek a little. After we both shuffled our feet and smoothed our hair, I motioned for her to sit in one of the two chairs I pulled up near the brazier. I sat in the other. I looked at her until her face turned red.

"Don't stare at me."

"Why not? I've come close to doing a hell of a lot more."

She jumped up angry, and headed for the door. Then she stopped and turned around, slowly, deliberately, walked to the chair where I was still sitting, and slapped me across the face. Twice. She was strong for her size. Then, still slowly, still deliberately, she lowered herself back in the chair, her eyes black-hot and her lips curved into a challenge.

I rubbed my cheek, and chewed it some more. Then I leaned over, grabbed her arms, picked her up and pulled her into my lap, the chair squeaking beneath the two of us. She fought me with her mouth, pulling my hair and scratching my back and the match was about even. She might even have been winning a little.

I broke it off, finally, needing to breathe. Her breath was warm and on my neck and her hand stroked my face.

"You need a shave."

"Did you come all the way out here to tell me that?"

She pushed herself up from my chest to look at me. "I came here to thank you. And to tell you. Everything."

Her hands were doing their best to keep me from paying any attention. I picked her up again, while she protested, and placed her, more gently this time, back in her chair.

"You can thank me later. And for what?"

She leaned forward. "Agricola came to see my father today. It made him happy—happier than I've seen him in a long time. They talked about Claudius and the wars, when my father was young. The governor gave him a ring. It helped him—helped him heal, just for this one day. I know it was because of you, and I . . . I thank you, Ardur."

I rubbed my neck. "Thank the governor." I looked up. "But not like that."

She grabbed my hand and held it to her lips. Her eyes wouldn't let go. The words rushed out of her, and they sounded true. And felt good enough for me not to care if they weren't.

"When I thought I'd lost you, I felt like I was dying, too." She gave me a crooked smile. "The games we play. My family has always been too proud. I was going to tell you everything. Even—even if it meant you'd stop wanting me. And then you sent the governor. And I knew you still cared, and I hoped you would even after I told you."

"Told me what?"

She watched me for a moment. "Your hands are shaking. What's wrong, Ardur? What happened?"

I held my palms together. "There was another murder today. Caelius beat one of his prostitutes to death because she knew something about Maecenas' murder."

She paled, her blonde hair glinting copper in the red hue of the brazier. "Caelius . . . he's consolidated our debts. My father told me today. I—I think he wants to marry me."

I jumped up and pulled her to me, holding her tight enough to hurt, my arms locked around her, my lips in her hair.

"Tell me what you know, Gwyna. About Rhodri. About

175

everything."

She pinched my arm to make me move it and adjusted her *palla*. We both sat down. My hands started shaking again.

"A *vigil* came today, after the governor. He was looking for Rhodri, asking questions about Maecenas. I told him about the marriage contract—I had to. Nothing else. I didn't mention you, though your name came up. He wanted to see if I knew you."

She answered the alarm in my face. "I wasn't followed here. I'm not a fool. I know you sent your man out after me that day. I recognized him in the tavern."

I smiled a little. Bilicho would be devastated. She swallowed, and licked her lips. The next part would be harder.

"I've been protecting Rhodri. If I told you where he went, I was afraid someone else would find him first. The *vigiles* won't believe his story, and he won't tell it all because it involves me."

"Go on."

"Yesterday I hoped you'd forget him, let him escape to the north or to Gaul. Today I want you to find him. You're his only chance. I see that now." She looked at the floor and her fingers grasped the chair arms until her knuckles turned white. "I'm the reason he's in danger."

"What made you change your mind?"

"I told you. After you left I was miserable. I knew you were right. And then this morning—"

"This morning you and Rhodri were both in danger. From the *vigiles,* from Caelius. So you came to me for protection."

She leaned forward and half-rose, her mouth twisted into a scar. "What do you mean? I told you how I feel. I—I love you. I'm not a liar."

"You've been doing an awful lot of it for someone who isn't."

She sank back into the chair. Her voice was heavy, and her eyes tightened into bright blue slits, blinding me like a ray of sun in a dark cave.

"Think what you want. I've always told you the truth, as much as I could. And when I'm through, you can tell me to go to hell, if that's what you want. I've done what I've done to protect my family. What do you care about, Ardur? Is everything tainted for you? Is everything ugly and dead?"

Camulodunum, twenty-three years ago. A little boy, frozen to the ground, hiding in the woods, watching while his mother was cut down like last year's chaff. I couldn't move, then, couldn't think. Twenty-three years ago. Why was I still paralyzed?

The voice whispered, "If not now, when, Arcturus?"

I stared at the woman in front of me, who blended into my mother's face.

Keep waiting, Arcturus, keep in the shadows. Wait until you're crawling with worms, a skinny undertaker bargaining for what kind of wine to pour on your shade. Or wait until you can smell the burning fat and hear it sizzle. Go ahead and wait. Because if not now, when, Arcturus? When?

I walked to her chair. Her eyes met mine. There was no guile in them.

"I love you, Gwyna. Whatever you've done, whatever you'll do." I didn't need to kiss her. I fell back in the chair. My hands were still.

She cleared her throat. A lifetime came and went.

I said: "Tell me."

It came out fast. "When I first learned about Maecenas, I planned to kill the both of us. I'd give him a warm, sweet drink with enough yew bark to kill him. No one could prove it was poison—yew acts slowly, as you know. He wasn't a well man, and he was a drunkard. So I felt safe."

She leaned forward and put her hands on my knees, like a suppliant. "There was something quicker for myself. My father and brother would have enough money to live. That was my plan."

"And what happened?"

She looked away, but turned back to face me. Her cheeks were flushed, almost feverish.

"Rhodri convinced me not to. I told you I thought I was in love with him. It would be better to say that I wanted to be in love with him. He's one of my people, and knew my husband. He's like a little boy, and I'm fond of him, and I persuaded myself that I could love him. It was easier than persuading myself to die." Her shoulders shook. My lovely, lovely, so-alive Gwyna.

"So what was his idea?"

"He thought it would be better if I just drugged the Syrian enough to make him sleep, and he'd come in later and steal the money, and then I wouldn't have to go through with the—the marriage. Maecenas wouldn't be able to prove anything, or find Rhodri, and eventually he'd have to leave and go back to Rome.

"So when we got word that he was at Caelius', Rhodri came that night and made the preparations. My father didn't want to let him in the house. He knew Rhodri still loved me. But Rhodri had already made plans, and some of his men agreed to help him. All of them except Madoc thought it was just an excuse to fight the Romans."

"I've met Madoc. He's a priest, isn't he?"

She nodded. "Rhodri is as well. There are so few left, the *Druvids* are now both wise men and soldiers. But you must know that. He leads many men and women who are unhappy and poor and blame the Romans."

I grunted. "There are quite a few unhappy and poor Romans, too. I don't say Rhodri or any native doesn't have reasons for resentment, but he doesn't look like Rome's hurt him much."

"He's a stubborn man." She squeezed my knee. "In many

ways, like you."

I asked: "What happened that night?"

"Everything that I told you before. The Syrian mocked me, pawed at me. But I stayed long enough to see him drink. He took a few sips, and I urged him to finish it, told him it would help him be a—a husband to me." She avoided my eyes. Her neck was taut, and she held herself steady on the edge of the chair.

"He had half a cup by the time I left. And I was afraid that I'd killed him." The words came out simply, without emotion.

That explained the slightly sweet odor I caught that night, and Maecenas' sluggish blood. I chewed my cheek again. The *pugio* was meant to kill him. Intention was enough. I looked at her.

"You didn't. He was stabbed in the back."

She nodded, relieved all over again. "The *vigil* told us. And you'd told me about his throat, and the mithraeum, and I knew something terrible—someone terrible—had interfered with Rhodri's plan and had killed the Syrian." She shook her head.

"He didn't want to tell me anything when he came the next morning. Except to say that he'd waited by the temple with Madoc, and they saw where the body was buried, and they dug him up but didn't find the gold."

She looked at me again. "I was so thankful when you told me you had it—one less thing they could find to hang him with. But poor Rhodri—he wouldn't tell me what went wrong. He was supposed to run upstairs, grab the money pouch, and run out the back. He must not have had time to get to Maecenas or the pouch, and I suppose he and Madoc followed the murderer to the temple, trying to find the money for me. He was shaking when I saw him last, white and shaking and terrified."

"He's brave."

"Yes, he is." She hesitated. "And part of me wishes I could

love him, because he's a good man and he's sacrificed everything for me." She held my eyes and didn't blink. I hoped she'd always look at me like that.

"But all I could do was protect him, keep his secrets. Our secrets. I hope you understand that now, and forgive me. Forgive me for lying. Forgive me for not loving Rhodri. Forgive me for loving you."

My mouth was dry, as I stared at her. "I think I can manage."

"He knows I have feelings for you. In the meeting we had before you came, I mentioned you. He's jealous, Ardur."

"So am I. Where is he?"

This time, she said: "He told me Camulodunum. He has a farm, and there is a stronghold of the Old Faith in the forest nearby."

"I'll leave tomorrow morning. The *vigiles* are hunting him because they think he's guilty. And while they're at it they plan to make life miserable for the natives in this town. Be careful while I'm gone. Draco will keep an eye on you."

I looked down at her until it hurt too much not to hold her. And then I remembered the shadow.

"When did you find out about Caelius?"

"This afternoon, after the *vigil* left. He sent a message to my father. I came to you right after."

An anger sharper than anything I'd ever known rose up in my throat until I thought it would cut me like Maecenas. "I'll kill him myself before he looks at you again."

She lifted her head and stroked my jaw. "My Ardur. You are not a Roman."

"No, my love." I looked down at her, and Galla's battered face blended over hers. "Romans hate, too."

We were quiet for a time.

And then she shifted her weight and swallowed hard and said: "I've got to tell you something."

"What?"

She stood up, and was still for a moment. I could feel her will herself to look at me. I stood, too, and waited. She came to me, tentative, and touched my hand, to make sure I was still there. I wasn't sure.

"I didn't care if the Syrian did die. I was frightened, but only of being caught. I would've killed him if the murderer hadn't. There was more than enough poison. He would've died in his sleep."

I didn't keep it from her. "I know."

"And that doesn't bother you? Doesn't make you hate me?"

I brushed a stray lock of blonde from her forehead. Her cheeks were flushed, her eyes pinpoints of blue, and she was breathing hard. She avoided looking at me again. I turned her face toward mine. Her lips parted, and again I drowned, dying, living, I couldn't tell which and I didn't care.

I tasted her skin and held her face between my palms. "We're all killers, Gywna. Every one of us. We scratch out a life on a marble brick and wonder how our fingertips get bloody."

I dropped my hands to her shoulders. I wasn't talking to just her anymore. "Murder's got a lot of names. In war, it's called being a hero. The poor bastards in the arena aren't killed, they're executed. And if I run a knife across Caelius' windpipe, I'm a criminal, too. Because what he did to Galla wasn't a crime."

Her shoulders were shaking. So were mine. "You learn to live with it. The anger and the hate and the cold right alongside everything else. It's all related, like those incestuous gods we pretend to believe in. Love and hate. Two sides of the same worthless coin, the one we pay Charon to ferry us over, the price of being human. But it's all we've got. We're all we've got."

She stroked my jaw again, and nestled in my lap, and my throat constricted, and to my surprise I felt tears on my face.

EIGHTEEN

Bilicho and I sat up talking that evening. I'd be tired tomorrow, starting out before dawn for Camulodunum. We looked at the papyrus fragment again; I finally dug out the piece of *fibula* I'd found in Maecenas' room. And we looked at the money. The money worried me.

Bilicho asked: "Are you sure you want to leave? Seems to me we should pay a visit to Caelius."

I could feel my mouth tighten up again, along with my stomach. "We need more information, Bilicho. When I see Caelius, I want it to be for the last time. And I owe it to Rhodri."

"And you promised Claudia."

I looked up at him. "Gwyna. But even if I hadn't, I'd need to find him."

An awkward silence fumbled in for a drink. I sipped my *mulsum,* and waited.

I'd led in Gwyna earlier, and made everything obvious. I told him we were going to get married. Bilicho's smile had slipped off his face so fast I didn't have time to catch it. He looked around the room as if I'd said I was knocking down the house.

The shock wasn't the best for him. Hell, it wasn't the best thing for me, either, but everything was moving too fast and if I didn't reach out and grab something I'd get dizzy and fall down. And maybe not get up again.

He reddened, and sipped his own cup. I'd made some more burnet drink, mixed with some *defructum* from last season, clover honey and a dash of valerian. He'd be out roaming the streets tomorrow, pretending to be back to normal. We all would.

"He can probably tell us more about the two men and the cart. What Galla knew that killed her." He paused, and scratched his ear, and the brown eyes that met mine were creased with worry and a strange hesitation. "Are you sure—really sure—that Stricta . . . that she'll be safe?"

"As safe there as she would be here. But check on the temple. Draco will be watching Gwyna's house, too, so he won't be too far if you need him."

Bilicho leaned back on the couch and stared at the ceiling. "I know what to do. And I'll talk to the money men, throw some lines out about Christians, silver mines, Urien's debts. Track that bastard Caelius. Talk to Mollius. Avoid Meditor like the plague he is. And I'll try not to get knocked on the head again. I've got my reputation to consider."

He grinned like it was yesterday. But his face loosened, grew somber again. Dark lines fell across his forehead, and he looked older than I remembered.

"I know how serious this is, Arcturus. Agricola doesn't know whether to fight or run, whether to pound the natives in the ground or cut their chains off. You know I'm a simple man. I don't have it in me to worry so much about the big things, the big people. Somehow, they come through it, if not in this life, then in the next. It's you I'm worried about, you and—" He swallowed. "—Stricta and Coir and Brutius and Draco and this house and—"

"Bilicho. Nothing is going to change between us. You're my best friend. You'll always be my best friend, my right arm, and the thorn in my foot. I love Gwyna—she loves me. You'll come to know her, to understand. And maybe—just maybe—you'll fall in love one day. I pity the woman."

His eyes were as warm and brown as a swig of ale on a hot

summer's day. The old Bilicho. He threw his head back and laughed until his head ached again, and for some unaccountable reason, he blushed.

Camulodunum was sixty-five miles away, by a good Roman road, but it would still take me a day and a half with a fast horse and no rest. The horse I borrowed from Agricola's stables. The lack of rest I already owned.

She was a good grey mare, a little heavy in the flanks, about fifteen hands high. I loaded her lightly, with Brutius' help, packing only a rug and a blanket, a water skin, a wine skin, and some hardboiled eggs and dates. She was a courier's horse, used to traveling long distances, and knew how to pace herself.

The mare was the only good thing I'd brought out of the meeting with Agricola the night before. After watching Bilicho drift off to sleep, I walked to the palace in a hurry. I was by myself again, inhaling air that cut my lungs and knotted my insides like a first love's first good-bye.

I didn't want to be alone. I wanted to be with Gwyna, and forget why I was walking so late, forget my friends, forget my house, forget my patron, forget myself, and most of all forget Caelius. My leg itched where the blood was pumping. I could taste his blood, see myself twisting his head until I heard his neck crack. I didn't like how much I liked the sound.

Meditor smirked when I passed him on the steps to the back entrance, past the guards who waved me in. His shallow, stupid, gloating helped cool my head: I grinned in his face. He reddened, his eyes screwing into sow-like slits that bore into my back like termites in a fallen oak. My shoulder blades twitched, but I kept walking.

I understood the reason for the smirk when I reached Agricola. He was in his study, pacing, Avitus at attention in front of the fire, as if the governor had forgotten to take him out of the kennel. Priscus hadn't arrived yet, and Saturninus was probably in a tavern, imitating the drinking and whoring habits of another general named Antonius—*praenomen* Marcus.

Agricola was uncharacteristically nervous, his hands clutching his tunic, his face haggard and etched in worry. The governor looked like an old man. The general was nowhere to be seen.

He jumped when he saw me. "Yes—Arcturus. Any news? Have you found the native yet?"

I didn't say anything, but looked over at Avitus. He wouldn't meet my eyes. One of the logs snapped in the blaze, but there was no warmth in the room.

"What has Meditor told you?"

Agricola stopped pacing for a moment, and frowned at me. "More than you have. This Rhodri is a troublemaker, he started a fight, was seen running upstairs, and that's the last time anyone saw the Syrian. It seems obvious."

"Maybe to Meditor. I'm not saying that Rhodri wasn't involved in something. But it wasn't murder."

Agricola took a step toward me. His brown eyes, normally warm and frank, were filled with anger, panic and something I'd never seen before. Maybe I'd just never noticed it. Contempt.

"Listen, son. I know you like to help your people as much as you can. But we don't have time for coddling. You haven't given me one damn reason or explanation why we shouldn't follow the only lead we have. Goddamn it, Arcturus, this is the Emperor we're talking about! And possible war!"

I rose to my full height, something I rarely did around him. "If you follow Meditor's advice and start undoing every decent thing you've done for these people, you'll be making a war, not preventing one."

He stared at me, breathing heavily, and after a few moments started to pace again. "Meditor thinks this is a crime by insurgents. Leftovers from Mona. We need to come down hard on them. Maybe we've been too soft."

"Why would insurgents do you the favor of killing a man who was bringing you bad news? Not even your wife loves you that much."

I watched the words strike his face like a closed fist, and wished them back too late. Agricola turned red, and the muscles around his mouth twitched while he stared at me. Where were my political instincts this evening? Buried with Galla?

Avitus shifted his weight, his mouth open in shock. The insult had at least braced the old man. His voice was guttural, a low growl.

"It's late, so I'll overlook the rudeness, Arcturus. I put you in charge of this—so far, you've told me nothing, given me nothing except complaints and laments for your mistreated natives. Meditor has brought me a name, one I could put before Domitian as an excuse for not responding to a message I can't admit I know the contents of. You've brought me nothing but warnings."

Anger closed my throat, but the words pushed through anyway. "You want a name, general? I'll give you one. Marcus Caelius Prato. A Roman. He's the owner of the whorehouse where the Syrian was killed. He told one of his whores to advertise that she was with the Syrian all night, until Maecenas supposedly skipped town and forgot his bill on the way to some other inconvenient little city. All lies. Meditor's right about one thing. The murder took place at the whorehouse. And one of the whores, who knew just a little bit about it, was murdered last night or early this morning, by Caelius. She was beaten to death. He's also consolidated the debts of the man you visited this morning, and wants to marry his daughter—the same woman Maecenas was going to marry. So who looks more guilty, general? The native or the Roman?"

Fear crawled back behind Agricola's eyes. It was a hell of a lot easier to make it a native. The cracks in the general's soul were showing. Funny, I'd never noticed them before. Not even at Mona.

"If the whore was a slave—"

"She was. But she was killed for what she knew. Rhodri was planning to rob the Syrian, not murder him. It's Caelius that can lead us to the truth."

He sighed and collapsed, suddenly, like an autumn leaf let down by the wind. "What do you suggest? That I arrest a Roman citizen?"

"No. I want to deal with Caelius in my own way. There were two men involved in the murder, according to what the whore knew. Caelius wasn't either of the men, but he'll know at least one, a soldier, a legionnaire. That could also explain the mithraeum connection. The bastard is as oily and slippery as a day-old cod. He'll squirm his way out of the country if we're not careful."

I scratched my chin, feeling the growth of beard. It would grow some more before I could shave again. "Rhodri didn't kill Maecenas, and I don't believe he knows anything about the message. But he's in danger from the real murderer, and he needs to be approached with caution. I'm riding to Camulodunum tomorrow to find him. I'll need a horse."

He was now sitting down in a basket chair, and Avitus had moved away from the fire to stand by him. The general waved a grey hand. "Take one of the courier horses. What if he's not in Camulodunum? What about Meditor?"

"All I ask, Governor, is that if Meditor finds him before I do, he is to take him alive and unharmed. And don't make a bad situation worse by stirring up a hornet's nest with the natives. Your kindness has tamed them, not your sword. As your visit this morning should've reminded you."

Agricola smiled, a small, tight, tired smile. "I forgive you lecturing me like a schoolboy because you're a doctor and you're used to it. I did enjoy the visit with Urien, and the fact that I went at all should tell you how much I value your advice, especially on native matters. But time is a luxury I can ill afford, Arcturus. I'll do what is best for Rome."

Mollius' face flashed into my mind. *Pietas.* I was tired, too, tired beyond caring, tired beyond feeling. I wanted to go home, forget this frightened old politician warming himself with a cold fire, forget what I owed him, and what I felt for him.

Avitus finally spoke. "Anything else, Favonianus?"

I wrapped my cloak about me tighter, the room chilly, as if a gust had blown through the crevices. "I'll be back in four days. When is the initiation?"

"Antonius will fetch you when you return. He'll lead you through a rehearsal first."

"Avitus—do you know any Christians among the men at the fort?"

The *beneficarius* arched an eyebrow. "Christians? No. Not that I've heard. I'm not sure I'd know what one was even if I saw one. Why?"

I shook my head. "I'm not sure."

Agricola rose, his paternal benevolence reassumed. "Be careful, son. Chasing shadows can be dangerous."

I turned to face him as I went through the door. "Not as dangerous as chasing glory." I bowed and left him there.

It was dark when I left for Camulodunum, but the kind I could see through. More bad dreams that night. Screams and cries, the whistle of a blade before it strikes flesh, Gwyna bearing a child that turned into Galla's battered face. I never told anyone but Bilicho about my dreams. Some people swore by them, claimed they knew how to interpret them to tell the future. I knew better. Mine could tell the past.

The grey mare was alert, her ears pricked forward, her shod hooves sure and steady on the cobbled streets. The echo rang against the muddy buildings, the businesses that followed the Romans like egrets after cattle. The egrets were better at keeping the flies away.

I called her Nimbus, because she looked like a rain cloud, and we'd have to be lucky not to run into any on the trip. I breathed in, trying to catch a whiff of country air. Maybe it would clear my head.

Londinium was thinning out. I passed the amphitheater, and wondered how the betting had gone yesterday. Some people loved the games, and I never understood why. Maybe power: power over life and death. That's a power I sometimes thought I had, and never wanted. It wasn't real.

The hoof rings grew infrequent, and fell into the choppy, comforting sound of churned-up mud. The road was starting to decay a little. Scratch the Roman surface with a fingernail and you uncover British dirt. That described just about everything in Britannia.

I abruptly reined Nimbus toward the north; she questioned me, her nose flaring. The road to Camulodunum was to the northeast. But we were outside the cemetery, and there was someone I wanted to see.

I passed the larger monuments, the ones offering dire curses on anyone who might disturb the peace of the dead, the shades and the shadows competing for attention just as much as they did in the upper world. "Look, stranger!" one called. "This is the grave of a good baker." "Hearken, you who walk by," another one shrieked. "I was a Senator's daughter." All the wives were good women who worked wool; all the husbands were faithful and kind. Funny how death makes everyone perfect.

I needed to talk. I didn't recognize myself. Too much had happened. I'd found Gwyna, lost Agricola, and misplaced my reason. Stricta was safe, at least for now, but Galla was dead. Caelius was free. My teeth were grinding again, so I held my jaw with my left hand and rubbed the muscles. Mollius was the cynic, not me. I was a healer. A problem-solver. A Roman. A native. A man with too many names and not enough time.

We threaded our way along the path until I found it. My adopted father's gravestone, erected seventeen years ago by his wife, Julia Pacata, who had the wisdom to never call herself my mother. I was sixteen; he'd been made a senator the previous year by Nero, who'd at least had enough decency to appreciate him.

The usual description, detailing his accomplishments, inscribed the monument. It was one of the largest in the cemetery. Julia mourned for three years, and then followed him below. I dismounted, Nimbus watching me with curiosity, her soft nose reaching out to smell my side. I placed a hand on the stone, and followed the carved letters with my finger.

My adopted father understood. He'd taught me to be wise, to be pragmatic, but to never forget compassion. He taught me to survive and succeed in an environment I was never really a part of. He helped me see how people fought, how they feared, how they scrambled and clawed and gave birth and died and started all over again.

I hated so much then, and didn't know where to start. The natives that killed my mother? But she was a native. The Romans that caused the war? But my father was a Roman, and my adopted father was one by choice. He tried to teach me to take the best from each, but to understand that Rome was the present, past and future. Rome was the sun, and God knows Britannia could use it.

He told me, once, on the day I received my *toga praetexta*, that I needed to learn to see people as they are, not as I wanted or feared them to be. I'd forgotten that. I'd almost forgotten how.

I could hear Nimbus eating some of the tall grass around the grave. The rough stone felt good. It was wearing thin in a few places: I'd have to hire a stonecutter to renew the inscription.

I climbed back on the mare, who snatched a final mouthful of grass before lifting her head. I turned her to the east, and struck the road to Camulodunum, passing the hills, fertile with rain, the forests, the creeks, the rivers and the vales until we couldn't ride any more.

We stopped to rest, briefly, while she ate and drank in the afternoon—the sky told me it was after midday. My senses cleared; my thoughts got sharper. I could see the silver flash of trout in the stream, hear the scream of the eagle, the rustle of the hare.

I passed travelers who paid little attention to the man on the grey horse, soldiers who marched a steady beat along the well-paved, well-drained gift from Rome. Couriers passed me at a gallop, and farmers with carts passed me at a crawl. But as the night fell and tumbled in the darkness, we'd covered forty-two miles before we came to an inn, where we lodged, comfortable and warm, Nimbus in a hay-filled stall, I in a snug room, my belly full of ale and cheese and ham, and warm, sweet wine cakes. I didn't dream at all that night.

Nineteen

I woke up before the roosters. Two long night hours of sleep after a hard journey weren't enough, but the pain in my legs helped keep me awake. I didn't want the landlord to wonder why I was in such a hurry. At this hour, he wasn't wondering about much other than how to wrap his fat hands around a barmaid. I could hear snores and the sound of jowls making sleepy, smacking noises, when I crawled downstairs. He'd served a large party of farmers last night, boisterous, bawdy and bragging about a local whore they'd bought the day before. Today they'd creep home to be greeted by wives waving a skillet in one hand and a poker in the other. Women ran farms: men just talked a lot.

There was a breeze blowing through the stalls, warm, western, carrying some moisture with it, a little heavy in a good way, like a thin blanket on a hot night. I sniffed. Straw and hay and horse manure. They were good smells, smells I missed in Londinium: I missed horses, I missed the clean feel of dirt in my skin. I missed the country.

I heard a shuffle; Nimbus was awake, and after I stepped on his foot so was the groom.

An over-generous tip made him move a little faster. I packed the cheese and bread I'd bought from the inn-keeper yesterday, and we rode out into the night, Nimbus ready for a new journey, her master not quite.

The road was silent. No creak of wheels, no gentle, resigned snorts from tired horses. No sound, no lights, of anything but us. I liked it that way. I couldn't see much in what little moonlight made its way through the clouds. By dawn, it would be grey, and even in the dark, that's how it felt. But it was a good grey, a peaceful grey, the grey of green trees and foot-high grass, the grey of life.

We climbed over one hill, descended into a valley. The wind slapped my face from the southeast, and I could smell a storm on it, somewhere out at sea. Then we climbed again, more trees, shielding the wind, arching over the road, protecting us.

Once in a while, a small road branched from the main one, leading to a shrine, or a small settlement. The countryside was filling up, but there was still plenty of room. Sometimes Nimbus slowed, her ears pricked toward the side of the road, catching the sight or scent of an animal. Small yellow or red eyes would blink at us slowly, and then close, climb a tree or dig into a burrow, and live a lifetime before seeing another human.

I had so little time. I was used to pressure: doctors, at least the ones who give a damn, are never far away from it. But this was more than a spearhead in the back, more than one man's life or a robbery that went wrong. The weight of civil war was crushing me to the ground, and I'd have to run far and fast enough to get out from under it. My leg twitched, and I bent down to rub it. I didn't have time for pain.

I straightened up and looked down the dark road, and saw Agricola's grizzled face. I'd been hard on the governor, maybe too hard. As popular as he was, the legions often preferred the man who paid them—and Domitian increased the base pay to three hundred *denarii* just a few months ago. If it came to a show of loyalty, Agricola wouldn't carry the support of every soldier in Britannia. It wouldn't come to that. It couldn't come to that.

I shook my head. The fog inside it and the black around me

weren't going away. I couldn't let Meditor sacrifice the natives, either. At least not without a fight. The governor was hungry for the history books, yes, but there were plenty of great generals in Rome's history, and not many great peacemakers. I said a small prayer to Silvanus that Agricola would be one of them. I didn't believe much in prayers, but it couldn't hurt.

We'd traveled twenty miles by midday, and I was already sick of my own thoughts. Nimbus wouldn't talk to me, and I couldn't afford company, so my mind treaded the same ground until it got stuck in a ditch and couldn't find its way out.

I wrenched it up and put it back on firmer ground and somehow it threw Mollius in my face. Mollius? Why Mollius? Sure, he drank. Why not? People drank too much for two reasons: they were either very happy or very miserable, and I didn't know many happy people. I'd worry about Mollius later.

Gwyna? The know-it-all voice that had harangued me a couple of days ago was sullen and hiding in a corner. At the moment, I wouldn't even mind having a conversation with it. But if I started thinking about Gwyna, I could just pin a sign on my back that said "idiot." I wouldn't be good for anything else.

A weedy dirt track on the left looked familiar. We were approaching the main Roman cemetery just a few miles from Camulodunum proper. Nobody, not even Romans, referred to the town as the "Colonia Claudia Victricensis." Boudicca's victory on the same site—in the Temple of Claudius itself!—guaranteed that.

I grinned, remembering the reparations to the giant bronze statue of the deified Claudius, after the rebels tore off the original head and threw it in the river. I was back from my first trip to Rome with Classicianus, a new son for a new father. Nero had just made him a procurator. I was eleven.

We were at the ceremony, and I was ready to be full of Roman pride and native awe. But Claudius' head was two sizes too small. It made him look like the moron some said he pretended to be. Nero, had he known, would've enjoyed the joke—and when Vespasian came to power, it was fashionable to ridicule some of Augustus' bizarre family. So there he sat still, all golden, his Julian lock parted over his forehead, trying desperately to fit in as a god with a shrunken head. So much for awe.

I reined Nimbus, and turned toward the left. From here to the main gate of the town, the road from Londinium was lined with grave markers. I'd had enough of cemeteries yesterday, but there was one grave here I needed to see. I couldn't visit one father without the other.

Marcus Favonius Facilis. There he was. The paint was still holding up—he looked almost life-like. At some point, the carving became my memory. I'd spent more years with it than with my father.

He lived with my mother when he was in the XX Legion, stationed at the fort which would become the Roman colony of Camulodunum. When the governor pulled the Legion out, the *colonia* was born. In a burst of typical Roman overconfidence, they filled in the defensive ditches and built a thriving, wealthy city out of the fortress architecture.

I remember, when I was very young, my father pointing out which buildings had been barracks, which had been storage rooms, when we walked through Camulodunum. In those days, Claudius had the right-size head.

He left with the Legion, and wasn't discharged until a.u.c. 811. I didn't see him again until I was eight years old. Marcus Favonius Facilis. I picked off some moss that had grown over two of the letters.

He was a smart man, and lived up to his name—everything came easily to him. He purchased an old farmstead from a veteran who was moving back to Italy, and found a bargain. It was bottom land, with a nice slope rising up to a hill, just in front of a forest, and the house looked over the land with pleasure. He moved my mother and me out of the little round hut we'd been sharing with another family. It was home.

Everything came easily to my father. Even death. There was nothing my mother could do, but at least there wasn't pain. I'd known him for a little over a year. I didn't understand that my parents weren't considered married until later, when I went to Rome with Classicianus, and some people called me a "little British bastard." Some said it fondly, some said it condescendingly. I wasn't sure which part was supposed to be the insult. No one said anything at all after Classicianus adopted me.

Marriage was not a privilege for the legionary, unless he was an *equites* and an officer. My father was made both when he achieved the rank of centurion, right before he retired. He could've continued in the army, could've left us behind, but he wanted to farm. Love is not something even Rome could control, and most men had "unofficial" families somewhere. Not all of them returned to make them official. I turned from the stone, from his painted picture, and looked at the view. His view. The bare tree limbs would be green again, the flat meadows slow and heavy with grain. Spring would come. The farmer's favorite season.

He'd had such grand plans—he wanted to grow vines, make wine, have a real, thriving farm. I was glad he died before they burned the fields: the fields where my mother lied buried. I shrugged off memory, and took some wine and poured it for him. I couldn't afford to linger. I had no time.

Nimbus and I—at least, Nimbus—drew appreciative looks when we walked through the giant triumphal arch that served as the western gate into Camulodunum. In a year or two it would join the walls that were almost finished, strong, high defensive walls around a prosperous farming town. Too little, twenty years too late.

At least Boudicca had evened the score for the natives. Camulodunum didn't symbolize "Roman tyranny" as it used to—in fact, it seemed more Roman than Londinium, thanks to the veterans, two decades of enforced cooperation, and—most of all—money.

The largest theater in Britannia coaxed the rich out of all the cities within a two- or three-day ride. There was even a modest circus south of the town, a solid financial and social investment, since horse-breeding was a passion for all the tribes. Druids rubbed elbows with investors from Gaul and Cyrenica, and everyone was so damn cosmopolitan it was hard to find an honest face.

I nodded a few times at passers-by, most more interested in where I'd found the grey mare than what I was wearing, and headed straight for Narcissus and Verecundus. They lived in a small, comfortable town house near the Temple and the forum, on the east end of town.

My father freed them a few years before he retired, and they'd gone into the import/export business. Nothing ostentatious, but they'd made enough to live well and without worry.

When he died, my mother was left with practically nothing; my father's fortune had gone into the land and rotting root stocks of vines from Gaul. So they purchased the gravestone, and paid for an excellent carving, fully painted and inscribed. They'd been in Gaul when the fighting broke out, but came back, and helped rebuild the town, keeping their investments in the area.

They loved one another. Somewhat unusual. Love always is.

We arrived at the house, and I dismounted and knocked on the door, holding Nimbus' reins in my hand. She'd be entered in the fifth race if I didn't keep an eye on her.

An old woman answered the door, her hair the mottled color of week-old straw. She hesitated, then leaned forward, squinting slightly, and suddenly a smile made her look ten years younger as she threw her arms around me.

"It's you, is it? Arcturus! It's been too long since you've visited. Come in, come in—they're here, no mistake, and they'll be so glad!"

"I can't just yet, Dilys. Unless you want me to bring my horse with me."

"I'll get someone. Don't leave!"

I grinned, and stroked Nimbus' nose when she shoved it in my side. Another head popped through the door, a red, freckled face of a young boy of thirteen.

"I'll take him to the stables, sir, if you like."

"No thanks, Nye, I can't stay long. Can you hold him for me?"

His eyes glowed at the thought of getting close to Nimbus. She looked at him a little doubtfully, but I whispered in her ear and handed him the reins. "Hold tight, now. She's ridden far and will have to again."

Nye nodded, and I glanced back as I entered the house, Dilys holding the door for me. He was gazing at Nimbus with the unmistakable, open-mouthed look of horse-love on his face. I laughed, and heard a dog barking from inside.

"Is that—"

"Yes, it's the one you gave us, and a more feisty little thing I've yet to find. Play, play, play, all the time. Lucky for the gentlemen, we have Nye to take it out of her."

Dilys and Nye weren't slaves—they were native servants, hired by Verecundus and Narcissus to run the household. But Dilys never referred to them as anything but "the gentlemen."

She ushered me into the dining room with an air of pride.

Chances were that they'd be eating, whatever time of day I happened to come by. Narcissus in particular loved a good meal, and—though at least fifty—had managed to somehow maintain a trim figure, and his dark, boyish good looks.

Verecundus was red-nosed, jolly, a little thick around the middle, and a one-time gladiator. He enjoyed more simple pleasures—beer, bread and pork, in that order. He humored Narcissus, but ate plebeian style whenever the latter wasn't looking.

They both rose to greet me, Narcissus with his typical elegance, Verecundus in a hug that nearly fused my lungs together.

"Arcturus! How good of you to come! Sit down and eat with us!"

Pyxis' puppy was as fat as a calf. She must've been devouring table scraps on a regular basis. She sniffed my leg suspiciously, then decided I wasn't worth her time and effort and turned back toward Narcissus, cadging for a snack.

"What's her name?"

"Fames."

"Appropriate, as always. Are you enjoying her company?"

"As much as she's enjoying our dining habits. Come, Arcturus, sit, tell us why you've come—I can see you're not just here on a social call."

Narcissus was always astute. He'd been my father's secretary and bookkeeper, and he had an excellent financial brain. I smiled, and sank into one of the plushly stuffed chairs.

"It's nice and soft, isn't it?" Verecundus asked eagerly. "Stuffed with chicken and duck feathers. Very comfortable."

"Yes, it is. Though my ass isn't in much of a position to enjoy it, as I just left Londinium yesterday morning."

"What? Why the hurry? What's wrong?"

"Plenty, but nothing for you to worry about. I'm working for

Agricola, on an important case, and I've got to find a native, a townsman by the name of Rhodri—and now wouldn't be too soon."

Verecundus knotted his thick red-gray brows together in thought. "Rhodri. Rhodri. Can you recall anyone by that name, Narcissus?"

Narcissus sat up on the couch where he'd been reclining. "Yes, I can. He's a horse-trader and cattle farmer. I've looked at a couple of his horses. Not for a bet, Verecundus," he added hastily. His one weakness. There was a bookmaker inside every bookkeeper.

"Arcturus—are you sure this doesn't affect us somehow?"

His eyes were deep and brown, and spoke about things I understood without mentioning. Domitian's new bedroom laws had frightened him. Romans frowned on men who had sex with other men, particularly men of equal rank. And, though relatively wealthy and locally popular, Narcissus tended to worry about it.

Gentlemen could pound the back ends of as many slaves as they'd like—as long as they were content with being on top. But men who liked the other side—especially high-ranking men— that bothered Rome. Seems you couldn't be ready to use your sword if you liked someone else's stuck up your ass. Even all the emperors everybody claimed to hate—Nero, Tiberius, Caligula—all were supposed to enjoy playing the little Roman wife. Of course, it was "common knowledge" only after they were dead.

Flings were all right, especially with boys who looked like girls, but relationships were unusual, and could be dangerous. Adult men . . . men who stayed together like a married couple . . . even in Camulodunum, Narcissus was afraid.

I smiled at him. He and Verecundus were freedmen. Still citizens, but only the lowest rung. And that bothered Rome much, much less, and local people not at all.

"Doesn't affect you at all. It might mean civil war, but nothing more personal than that."

He looked relieved, but raised an eyebrow. "I'll hope for the best. I take it you want to find Rhodri now. His house and land are to the north of town, near a sacred grove. He's a Druid, you know."

"I know. How do I get there?"

"Let's see . . . go straight on, and exit through the eastern gate. Then turn left, and follow the road north-northwest, until you find two roads, one on the right, one on the left. The one on the left leads to the grove—still active, from what I hear. The one on the right—Rhodri's farm."

"Thanks. I promise I'll stay longer next time. And invite you to my wedding?"

Verecundus nearly spit out his wine and stood up to hug me again. "Wedding? Who? When?"

"A native woman. A widow."

Narcissus raised his eyebrow again. "A widow? After you for your money, Arcturus?"

I grinned at him. "My other attributes."

Narcissus threw his head back and laughed so hard he nearly choked on his peacock wing. Verecundus filled my hands with fish roe, a duck egg, and a couple of radishes pickled in *garum*. I thanked him profusely, handed the food back to Nye along with a *sestertius*, kissed Dilys on the cheek, and headed up the street, into the quickly fleeing sunlight. Rhodri was next.

TWENTY

The streets were crowded with soldiers, farmers, traders, and slaves, all trying to squeeze out a few more drops of warmth and daylight. It dribbled from the sky like wine from an empty skin. I was running out of time.

I passed Claudius' gaudy temple, showing off more colors of marble than Agricola's palace. I grinned to myself, thinking of the statue inside. There were a few soldiers by the steps, obviously new arrivals, probably en route to a Legion somewhere. You could always spot a newcomer by his shiny red knees. Men who lived through a winter conquered their legionary distaste for "sissy" trousers. The recruits looked as out of place as Numa at a Bacchanal.

Nimbus and I continued past the enormous temple, avoiding the hawkers of spurious goods, pots that wouldn't hold water, bridles that would snap before you got them on the horse's head. Some men tried to blend into the shadows, their furtive eyes scanning the afternoon crowds for a purse, a play, or a tip. It must be a racing day—Camulodunum was usually more well-bred than this.

We crossed through the eastern arch, a less ostentatious and more effective gate, and turned left, toward the north. It was quiet, and I urged the mare forward. The warmth was fading fast. This road wasn't as well-traveled as the Londinium route, and I hadn't met anyone coming or going. The quiet was starting to get to me.

A grassy track led to the right, toward Rhodri's house. He couldn't be that stupid, but I had to check anyway. Trees on either side watched me, as we turned and rode toward the farmstead. It was sturdy and well-built. The sound of no sound at all was deafening.

I nudged Nimbus closer to the house, my back stiff from tension. I loosened the scabbard of the *gladius* tied to my saddle. Nimbus sniffed the air like an elegant greyhound, and carefully picked her way, ears alert and listening, toward the house. We rode cautiously around it.

The main house was a small, one-wing villa, with smaller, separate buildings for different functions—storage, threshing, feed, livestock. There was a back entrance, and it was ajar. I nudged Nimbus in the ribs again, and took out my sword. Without getting out of the saddle, I leaned down and to my right, and managed to use the *gladius* to open it a little wider.

The inside was a mess. Whoever had been here had left in a hurry, or someone else had come and searched—and had made an obvious job of it. There were clothes on the floor, ledger tablets, some broken crockery. A sparrow landed on the door, and cocked its head at me, its bright eye inquisitive and curious. I straightened my sore back, while it cheeped at me.

I opened a bag on my other side, and took out a bit of bread and tossed it on the ground. It cocked its head the other way, cheeped some more, and flew away. Maybe it was trying to tell me something.

I rode again around the outbuildings, checking to make sure there weren't cattle needing feed. No livestock. Rhodri had either sold everything, or—more likely—had a neighbor looking after his herds. There was nothing here for me except trouble, and I had enough of that at home.

I pulled Nimbus back toward the road, and urged her to a gallop. Light was starting to fail: long shadows were creeping from beneath the trees, and the thick line of green marking the river was deepening into black.

Where the hell could he be? The shrine? It seemed natural. Someone would know where he was. But they might not want to tell me. I was still holding the *gladius* with my right hand, and its heft wasn't much comfort.

I slowed Nimbus to a canter and then to a walk, as we crossed the main road and started down the other track. This was better traveled. Wheel marks were still scratched in the drying mud of a few days ago. The trees on this side of the road were old and thick and full of thought. They loomed over me like maiden aunts over a newborn baby.

The road turned twice, and wound steadily uphill. The trees made it too dark to tell what time it was. When I saw the opening of the grove, the lush, green clearing up ahead on the peak of a small slope, I was hoping it wasn't too late.

It was filled with a listening quiet. No birdsong. Not even the trees whispered. A faded memory of long-ago magic clung to it like a forgotten lover.

Some statues ringed the glen, rough-hewn stone with a bluish hue. They looked like they came from Mona. At the front was a stone altar, and two stone pillars, hollowed out laboriously, each with two niches. Inside each niche was a human skull. Near the altar was a well, crowned with mistletoe and ivy. And next to the well, staring at me, was a huge, bearded man.

He didn't say anything, but his eyes never left my face. I very carefully replaced my *gladius* in its sheath. Then, at a respectful distance from the altar, I dismounted. Nimbus started to tear at the lush grass. I hoped this particular grove didn't consider the grass holy.

The man, dressed in a rough tunic, came forward. He looked at me like I owed him money. I waited for him. I was taller, but he was thicker. His fists were small hams, and the knuckles were callused and knobby, as if they'd seen plenty of action.

He stopped about two feet away from me. Then, very deliberately, he looked me over. Even in the long shadows, I could see the corners of his mouth disappear, and his eyes get very hard.

His first words were: "What do you want here, Roman?"

He spoke Latin, but hadn't heard about the last twenty years. I replied in my mother's tongue. "I was born in Camulodunum. I know the truth."

He looked surprised. "And what is the truth?"

"That men die, but the soul lives on."

"And who decides when men die?"

"The gods."

"And how do we know what the gods want?"

"From sacrifice and the stars."

He paused, and looked a bit disappointed. My understanding some Druidic rite made it a little harder to punch me in the face. Harder, but not impossible.

"You speak well," he admitted grudgingly. "Are you here to worship?"

I answered carefully, smelling a trap. "The time for worship is after the time of understanding." I pointed upward. "I came because I seek a brother."

His eyes widened, and gleamed more brightly. "Who?"

It was now or never. I tightened my stomach, expecting a blow, and tried to relax my arms and legs. "I am seeking Rhodri. I want to help him."

"Rhodri? He's not here. Why do you look for him?" He took a step closer, and I could feel his breath blowing heat against my face.

"Because he is in danger from Rome. He knows something that makes him wanted by men who want him dead."

He stepped closer again. He smelled like pork. "And how do

I know you are not one of those men?"

I was getting tired of it all, and the light was nearly gone. "Because I said so, and I didn't ride all goddamn night and day to put up with this."

I caught a gleam of shining teeth right before I caught one of the fists in my stomach. His muscles were heavy but quick. Luckily, I'd braced myself, and I bent over, pretending to be in more pain than I was, though that wasn't too hard at the moment.

He was winding up for a punch on the back of my neck when I surprised him by grabbing his knees, throwing him off-balance to the ground. I landed on top, and got in a partially effective right uppercut to his jaw before he got the knife out. He slashed at my left shoulder and I dodged, grunting, trying to pin down his left hand, the knife hand, before he could connect.

I managed to pin his left, but he wriggled free on the right, and with a neat move crushed me to the ground, where I was still holding down the weapon. Then he started to pummel my back, right by the kidneys, and got in one or two blows that made me wince and grit my teeth before I could let go of his left completely and stand up. We faced each other warily, breathing hard, two gladiators without a crowd.

I could still see the shine of his knife and his teeth. He must enjoy this sort of thing.

"I'm here to help Rhodri, goddamn it! Just tell him Arcturus came, and he'll see me."

"I'll do better. I'll show him your dead body."

He made a sudden lunge, and I jumped back in time to avoid it, but a tree root caught my foot and I stumbled. He was on me in a flash, with a hammy fist clenched around my throat.

I dug my fingers into the soft part of his elbow, which wasn't as soft as I hoped, but soft enough to make him his relax his grip a little. With his right hand, he slapped me across the face, hard enough to leave a mark, and the sting brought tears to my eyes.

Before he could do it again, this time with a closed fist, I used an old trick I'd learned from an acrobat, and threw myself to the ground. He went with me, but on the way down let go of my throat.

I got up before he did, and kicked him as hard as I could in the stomach. He doubled over on his knees, and I didn't see his teeth gleam. I took a few steps backward in a hurry to where Nimbus was watching in between mouthfuls of grass. I took out the *gladius,* and walked back over, where he was standing up, holding on to his gut.

I pointed the sword at him. "See a healer if you spit up any blood. Otherwise you'll be all right in a few weeks. I tried to aim for the ribs."

He looked up at me, but didn't say anything. "I know what I'm talking about. I'm a *meddygon.*"

He grunted, and spit. "I know who you are. I was told to watch out for you."

I was still breathing hard. "By Rhodri? For what? To kill me?"

He grinned, a little sadly. "No, that was my idea. The message said to keep you here as long as I could, and I figured if I couldn't kill you I could make it so you couldn't travel. I probably wouldn't have really killed you," he added as an afterthought.

"Listen, you—"

"My name is Lugh. I'm a blacksmith."

That explained the hands. I hurt all over, in places I'd forgotten about. Anger made my *gladius* shake.

"I don't have time to pound any sense in you. It would take too goddamn long. I need to find Rhodri, and fast, for his own goddamn good, even if you're both too stubborn to realize it."

He straightened up a little more, and spit again. He searched my face. I lowered the *gladius.* A little. Finally, he nodded.

"Rhodri doesn't like you. Maybe he has his reasons." I didn't say anything to that. "But I believe you. You could've killed me."

"Rhodri or his men could've killed my freedman back in Londinium. That's one reason I'm here. I think he's innocent of a crime the Romans are chasing him for."

Lugh nodded. It was starting to make sense for him. "You don't like one another. But you both want justice. He is a Druid, and you know some of the ritual. But the other men after him—maybe after you, too—want blood."

He held his hands out, palms up. "Put away your sword. I'll tell you about Rhodri. If he's angry with me, he can fight you." He grinned.

I put the *gladius* back in the scabbard and took down the skin of wine on my saddle and offered some to him. He drank about half of it in one toss, and returned it to me gratefully. I swallowed a mouthful. It still tasted of the warmth of the day.

Lugh regarded me steadily. "Rhodri is still in Londinium."

My face fell to the ground, and almost took me with it.

"He told his woman"—he paused, and I wasn't sure how much he knew, but suspected he knew more than I liked "—that he was coming here, but all along planned to stay in Londinium and wait things out. That's why I was supposed to delay you. There's a hut in the back of the grove. I've been here for two days, waiting for you."

Wordlessly, I offered the wine skin again. He finished it. I stroked Nimbus' flanks. I hoped she had it in her.

The blacksmith wiped his mouth with the back of his hand. "So what do you do now?"

"Now I go back to Londinium, and hope I can get to Rhodri before the *vigiles* do. He's a brave man but very stupid."

Lugh laughed. "I was thinking the same thing about you."

I smiled sourly at him. It was going to be a long, painful journey, made more painful by my swollen face and bruised, throbbing back. I mounted Nimbus, who looked surprised that we weren't sleeping in the grove for the evening.

Lugh looked up at me, and fished something out of a pouch in his tunic. The pouch smelled strongly of sweat, iron and beer. He took out a small egg-shaped thing and handed it to me.

"Take this. It's one of the tokens we use. If Rhodri sees it, he'll talk to you."

"Thanks. Don't forget to wrap your ribs." I put the egg-thing—it was an *anguinum,* a magic token for the Druids—in my own pouch.

Lugh winced, and said: "Now that I can go home, my woman will look after me. She's by way of being a good healer. And a little mead will take the pain away. Remember that for the ride back."

I grunted. "We'll have to ride all night."

He patted Nimbus' neck appreciatively. "There's a good stream, with a little glen about thirty miles before Londinium, right off the road on the right. It's about five miles west of Aeron's inn—the one where the natives stay."

"Thanks. Be seeing you."

He waved, and faded into the darkness. Nimbus and I were alone, with the dark, pain, and panic as our only companions. How could I have been so stupid?

Twenty-One

I looked forward to a long night of beating myself up, until I remembered that Lugh had already done it. But even that wasn't enough. There's no companion more loyal than self-reproach. It stays with you through danger, through discomfort, even through sixty-three miles of pain and trouble. And if you try to drown it out—with wine, or a song, or even a little sleep—it's still there, smiling at you, blowing kisses.

God, I was tired. Eventually, I was even too tired for it. It moved on to fresher meat in a tavern or some small villa, or maybe even in a palace or basilica. You never know.

By this time, my ass was numb, and Nimbus had slowed to a listless walk, the bounce gone from her step, her hooves stumbling on a stone now and then. The never-ending darkness of the next corner swallowed up her equine optimism like a fat man with a honey cake. I'd lost the human variety about twenty miles ago, and there wasn't much there to begin with. Time just lurched along, while the night kept belching out black.

A blanket of fog threw itself over us. Nimbus' thick hair plucked and gathered the beads of water, keeping her skin safe and dry. My cloak took them all in and dug out a small pond, then emptied it on my tunic and started over. After ten hours, I felt like a pickled herring. I smelled even worse. Thanks to Lugh, my kidneys couldn't hold water well, either.

I touched my cheek and didn't recognize it. My face would some day shrink down to normal size. I'd look human again.

Meanwhile, I'd try not to scare anybody. I hoped I wasn't dead, but I couldn't really remember.

Domitian was up ahead on a gold horse. His head was too small, and he was with Claudius and Vespasian, and Agricola was leading him on foot. Then there was just Domitian's head in Lucullus' palace, and suddenly it split into three heads. All of them started to talk to me. I thought it was urgent until one of the heads began to sing a tavern song about Julia's throat muscles, and then my beard itched, and then I woke up and almost fell off.

Luckily, Nimbus knew where home was, and where those oats were that I'd promised her. I looked around, a little less thick. We must've passed the tavern Lugh mentioned while I was asleep. After a few more milestones, I heard a faint burble in the distance. The stream and the glen. We'd be safe there. And we were halfway home.

We turned, and found the place—a little meadow as snug as my own bed. I led Nimbus to the creek and refilled the skins, while a rabbit or a fox rustled in the brush upstream. Old elms and oaks and a few yew and some ancient willows lined the banks and surrounded us.

I staked out the mare. After snatching a few mouthfuls of grass, she carefully bent her legs in the intricate bow horses do when they lie down for the night. I was as comfortable as the pain allowed. I told myself to wake up in two hours, and secretly hoped I wouldn't listen.

I opened my eyes and wondered why the bed was so hard. Military training kept me to the schedule: it was just a little over two hours later, and still dark, though there was a faint suggestion of hope from the east. Nimbus was lying down, her head stretched out on the grass, her tired legs slightly bent under her. I hated to wake her.

I dug around in my saddle bag for a handful of grain. I always packed a little as an extra treat for the horse, and I'd been saving this for when she really needed it.

She raised her head and stared when I stood up, watching me, trying to anticipate what she should do next. I held out a mouthful of barley, the last I had, and she nickered softly, her downy nose quivering in my hand. It was gone too soon, and we needed to be, too. She stood up, tired and with regret, but without me asking. I saddled her and somehow rolled myself on, my back still tender and sore, my face maybe a little more human.

We both felt better after sleep. The breeze was at our backs, which helped our spirits, though it wouldn't do much for anyone downwind. We weren't night creatures, horses and men. We were meant for the sun, or at least the grey haze of day.

I tried to empty my mind and found there wasn't much left. So I looked ahead. Maybe the world was still here: maybe I was still a part of it. The rain had stopped. The sun was thin from a winter diet, but still out and trying. Like me.

So I'd taken a wrong turn. So I didn't have time for mistakes. I'd still find Rhodri before Meditor. And when I did, I'd show him the *anguinum*—it might make a difference. And there was home ahead, home and a little warm food, and Bilicho, and comfort. And Gywna.

I made it to Londinium an hour before sunset. I dropped off Nimbus at the palace stable, and sent a message to Agricola. I rubbed the mare down, and walked her and watered her. Then I told the groom to feed her a little at a time. No riding for two weeks. She shoved her head against me and scratched it on my chest.

He nodded at me. He was a bowlegged man of indeterminate age, but I could see in his face that he knew horses. I stroked her neck. I figured I'd ask Agricola if I could buy her. You don't

212

go through what we'd just gone through and then just say good-bye.

I limped home, my lower back stiff, my side aching, my face unrecognizable, with a dark beard and black eye and swollen cheek. People avoided me.

No one answered when I knocked on the door. I got irritated, then worried. Where the hell were they? I tried to open it, and it was unbolted. What the hell kind of safety was this?

I stepped in and almost started yelling, but choked instead. Strange voices. Strange people, strange, upset people, in my house. What the hell was going on? I thought I heard Gwyna—but she was supposed to be safe at home. Why would she be here? Nobody even expected me until tomorrow. Another female voice murmured, lower than hers, with an exotic accent. What in goddamn hell was happening? Then I heard Coir, and Draco's Germanic Latin, and above it all Bilicho, Bilicho sounding agitated and a little angry and maybe even a little out of control. Bilicho?

I hurried into the examination room and almost tripped over Brutius. He was lurking by the hallway door, and after the few minutes his mind took to register that the smelly, ugly stranger was his master, he was overjoyed to see me.

"Brutius—what in the bloody hell of Orcus is going on?"

"Oh, Master—so much has happened, and what with three women and a child in the house—"

"What?" My already swollen head nearly exploded. "Who? When? Why?"

"Caelius tried to beat up Draco and steal your lady. She came last night, and brought the child, who keeps disappearing. Oh, and before her another woman, a foreigner from Egypt, I think."

"Stricta?" I felt dizzy. I leaned against the table.

"I think that's her name. Master Bilicho invited her, maybe.

She's staying with him, and Coir moved into Draco's room, and your lady doesn't like Coir, and Coir has been very unhelpful, and no one can find the child. And just now that other man was here—the *vigil?*"

"Meditor? Was he the bald one?"

"No, the other. The one that always smells like drink."

"Mollius. What did he say?"

Brutius leaned closer to me. "That's what they're fighting about now, Master. He came to tell us there's a curfew on the natives in Londinium, and that the soldiers have caught—what was his name—"

"Rhodri?" I sat on the table, and thought about crawling under it.

"Yes, that was it. And as soon as he left, everyone started to argue about what to do next, and then Coir wouldn't look for the little boy, and it turned into a row."

I could still hear the voices, though they sounded less like a barnyard.

"Thanks, Brutius. I think I understand." I didn't.

Brutius' brown, honest face fell a little. "I left out the most important thing, Master. The night before last—the night you left. Someone tried to get in the house."

I grabbed his arm. "What? How?"

"Over the wall. Draco wasn't here, only Bilicho, and he was sleeping very hard, on account of his head and all." He cleared his throat. "Pyxis stopped him. She barked, and woke me up, and she must've attacked him, but he kicked at her. Hard."

"Is she—"

"She's not dead, Master, but she's not well. You need to look at her." His face was drawn.

"Let's go see her. Come help me."

I hurried as fast as my legs would let me out the front door to the back of the house. Brutius gave me a boost over the wall, and then climbed over himself. The puppies clambered all over me. He'd left the kennel door open.

Pyxis was up, and wagged her tail and smiled, but walked very stiffly, limping, when she came to greet me. I told Brutius to go to the workshop and get the lamp.

I led her inside, and made her lie down on some straw. She looked at me curiously. She knew she wasn't pregnant, and couldn't figure out why I was there if not to help deliver babies. Brutius ran up with the lamp, and holding her head with one hand, I checked her gums with the other. No sign of bleeding inside. Her breathing was normal. I stretched her out on the straw, and gently put two fingers behind her hind leg, right at the point where it met her trunk. I waited a moment and counted. Her pulse seemed all right.

"Has she been eating?"

Brutius shook his head. "Not as much as usual."

I gathered some skin at her nape, and plucked it. It didn't snap into place as fast as it should.

"She needs water. You'll have to make her drink it if she refuses."

He nodded. Brutius would drink it himself if it helped.

She was lying with the sore side facing up. I started with her head, and looked for a cut or puncture. The bastard probably had a knife. I didn't find anything, but when I got to the leg, she flinched.

I asked Brutius to hold her head, and very carefully felt all the little bones from her hip to her toes. Nothing was broken. But when I laid a flat palm on the muscled area of her flank, it felt like my cheek—hot, swollen and sore.

I patted her head and stood up. She pulled herself up slowly, and was reluctant to put weight on that side, but was still able to do it. She sniffed my clothes, trying to find out why I'd been on a horse for so long.

"She's all right. It's a painful muscle strain, maybe even a small tear. She hasn't been eating and drinking well because of the pain, probably, and we need to make it easier on her. Keep the puppies away from her for a week, and hand feed her chicken with oats. I'll make her something for the pain, too, something that'll help her sleep. Put her water bowl up a little higher, so it's easier for her to reach it without bending. You might have to pour her some from a skin when you feed her. She'll need a warm compress on her flank every day, too—help keep the swelling down." I squeezed his hand. "She'll be all right, Brutius. She's a good, strong, healthy dog."

His eyes filled with tears and he said simply: "I was worried."

My misshapen face tried to smile. "Now what's this about a disappearing little boy?"

Out of the darkness of the corner of the kennel, something stirred. Brutius' eyes got big, but I gestured for him to remain still. Something was crawling toward Pyxis, something about ten years old. The lamp sputtered, and when it found its flame again, Hefin was crouched near the dog, staring at me.

"I didn't disappear. I was watching the dog."

"You like Pyxis?"

He nodded. "I like animals better than people."

"I do too, as a rule. But you're worrying your sister."

He stuck his lower lip out. "She doesn't care about me anymore."

"That's not true, and you know it. It's safer here, for both of you. There's a curfew now."

"Well—" He looked at me doubtfully. "You look different."

"I ran into a tree. Now, Hefin—I need your help."

"You need *my* help?"

"Yeah. I figure you might make a good healer—you stayed with Pyxis while she was hurt. Brutius here needs an assistant to help look after her. Think you can do it?"

He nodded solemnly. "I'd like to." He turned his head away and said it to the kennel wall. "It feels better when you're here."

I smiled a little.

"All right. Run in to your sister, but don't tell anyone I'm home yet. It's our secret."

He flashed a smile, and ran like a small blond lightning bolt through the kitchen door and into the house.

"One problem solved. Keep an eye on him. He's in your charge." Doubt dug into Brutius' face, as he looked toward the kitchen. I grinned. "Don't worry. Children are a lot like animals."

Brutius grinned back. "Thank you, Master. Do you want to go in?"

Rhodri was in a dark hole by now, and the curfew would be causing fights. Everything I'd tried to prevent had happened, anyway, and I was exhausted, sore, hungry and numb. I wished I could sleep in the kennel.

I told him: "Have Venutius make me something to eat— something warm and good. Not pork."

A loud purr interrupted me. Fera was rubbing against my legs. One of her balls of fluff was mewing loudly at Brutius. I picked it up, and it started licking my hand with a scratchy pink tongue.

"They're still in the *triclinium?*"

"If they haven't gone on about something else."

"I'd like to eat a little in the kitchen before I see anybody."

Brutius nodded, and went ahead of me. I made my way through the herb garden, and into the kitchen, where Venutius was already bustling, preparing something for my supper. His expression was as impassive as it always was, and he didn't even blink at my face, though he eyed the kitten I was still holding with distaste.

I handed her to Brutius. "Give her some cream. Give 'em all

some cream." I yawned. How long had I been awake in the last three days?

Venutius poured me some wine, and pulled a large bowl of chicken soup out of his sleeve. Just what I wanted. The broth was thick and rich with barley and turnips, even a few carrots, while big pieces of chicken meat floated away from the bones as I stirred. I ate standing up, leaning against the larder. I could feel every bite. It was good to be home.

In the dining room, voices dropped to a conversational tone. I caught Gwyna's voice, sometimes sharp, sometimes purring, like the kitten at my feet. I heard her send Hefin to bed. I guess she was using Coir's room, and Coir was sleeping with Draco. Draco? Time to talk and find out what the hell was going on.

I wiped my mouth on my sleeve, and told Venutius to announce me. He lifted an eyebrow, and with all the brio typical of cooks, pulled two iron pots down from the wall and walked into the *triclinium*. He struck a theatrical pose, clanged the pots together loudly, and in a stentorian voice proclaimed: "The Master"—dramatic pause—"is in."

I followed on his heels. Everyone reacted differently. Bilicho turned red, and avoided my eyes, Draco stood a little taller, Gwyna gave me a dazzling smile which turned to a frown when she saw my bruises. Coir retreated to Draco's side, and grasped his hand. Stricta was nowhere to be seen.

The voices started up again, all at once, and I put out a hand to hold them off.

"I'm dead on my feet, and was nearly dead in Camulodunum." Gwyna started toward me, but I waved her back, and she reddened.

"I'm all right. I got here as soon as I could. I found out I'd been an idiot, and Rhodri was in town all along. And Brutius told me about the bastard who tried to break in. Pyxis is all right, but I want Draco in the atrium every night."

"Yes, sir." Coir clutched him a little harder.

"Brutius said that Rhodri's been caught and there's a curfew. I don't know why Gwyna, Hefin and Stricta are here, but I'm glad to see them, and glad they're safe. That's been my main worry."

I held Gwyna's eyes, and she allowed me a small smile.

"I'm sorry the house isn't larger, and we've had to make some adjustments in the sleeping arrangements. I hope everything's been satisfactory?"

I pointed the last remark at Bilicho, and he blushed a deeper shade of red, but this time looked at me.

"You're all part of this household and this family. Forget the arguments and help one another, and explain to me what the hell's been going on." I grinned lopsidedly. "The *dominus* is at home."

This time I didn't stop Gwyna from running to me and brushing a warm hand against my cheek. Bilicho smiled and nearly split his face in two. Draco stood at attention. Coir let go of his hand, bit her lip and looked stubborn.

I sat on the couch, Gwyna next to me, and Bilicho took the basket chair. Draco and Coir stood, until I asked them to sit. They looked nervous. Slaves weren't supposed to sleep together—at least without permission. I was only worried for Draco's sake. I'd talk to Coir later, alone, and make sure she wasn't just trying to make me jealous.

"Now—what happened? One at a time."

Bilicho answered. "Mollius was here earlier. They caught Rhodri at a small shack across the river, by the grove and close to his house."

"Was he hurt?"

He started to shake his head, thought better of it, and replied. "I don't think so. They're holding him for questioning."

That meant they'd send a *quaesitor* in tomorrow to torture

219

the poor bastard. I'd have to get there early. Gwyna squeezed my arm.

"Bilicho—how's your head?"

"Hard and thick. Like always."

I stared at him. "Maybe you've found a better doctor."

He turned as red as a beet and said nothing. I laughed. "C'mon, out with it, how did Stricta get here?"

He studied the floor and was quiet. No one else said anything. Then the fire lit his face and I finally saw it, and I knew. Bilicho was in love. I looked at him like I'd never seen him before. The tough, thick skin glowed like a baby's. Stricta had made him twenty years younger and three calluses softer. I wondered how long—and remembered his questions, his concern for her, and knew it had been awhile.

I bit my lip to keep from smiling too much. "I'm glad she's here. I've been worried about her."

"It was the only decision to make. After that son-of-a-bitch tried to break in here, and after Caelius threatened to send the *vigiles* after Draco—"

"Caelius threatened Draco?"

The big man spoke up. "That's why the—the Mistress"—he only stumbled a little—Coir looked sour—"is here. When I was watching her house as you ordered, *Dominus,* she sent word to me through little Hefin not to let Caelius in. So first I scared him off, and then the next day he brought Lupo with him, and we pretended to fight, and Lupo pretended to lose." He pointed to a faint shadow over his left eye. "See? Just a light blow."

Gwyna's face fell. "My father, Ardur. He agreed to let Caelius have me. He was rambling, not in his right mind. He's getting weaker by the day. And I—I left him."

"You had to. Was it after the fight with Lupo that Caelius threatened to bring the *vigiles?*"

Draco nodded vigorously. "The day after the intruder. The

Mistress and Bilicho thought it would be safer for her and the little boy to come here. And I could make sure no one climbs the wall again."

"And when did Stricta arrive?"

Gwyna looked pointedly at Bilicho, who looked at the floor again. Draco and Coir studied a cobweb on the wall.

"Bilicho?"

He cleared his throat. "After you left and someone tried to break in, I was worried. I slipped a message to Stricta when I was on my rounds, ferreting out things. Good information, too!" he added.

I nodded. "Go on."

He pinched his face a little. "I didn't tell anyone what I was doing."

Gwyna interrupted him. "I didn't even know the woman was in the house until this afternoon!"

I was beginning to see. "And?"

"There was a procession, part of Ra's birthday today. So they had a little parade yesterday. Anyway, I told Stricta to break away and come here. It seemed like the only chance."

Evidently Bilicho had been doing his Egyptian homework.

"Good idea."

He looked at me gratefully.

"But I didn't know about it until I found the woman coming out of his bedroom. If I'm staying in the same house as a whore, I'd at least like to know about it."

The air between Gwyna and Bilicho was hot and curdled and full of resentment. I rubbed my cheek until I remembered it hurt.

"Bilicho didn't tell you because you've got your own worries. And it's dangerous: keeping Stricta here is a crime. He was trying to protect you, Gwyna." I looked into her eyes. "She may've been forced to work for Caelius, but she's not a whore."

Her hand crept away. She was so damn proud. I turned to Draco.

"Draco—thank you for understanding that Gwyna is more than a guest here. She is to be treated as your mistress. What she asks you to do, you do without question."

I aimed the last words at Coir, who looked guilty but not terribly sorry. Gwyna stared at Coir's hand clutching Draco's arm but kept her mouth shut. The full stories would come out later, but maybe in the meantime I could get some sleep.

"Bilicho, has Stricta—?"

A large bang on the door made everybody jump. Draco was up before I could lift an eyebrow. Which was about all I could lift. After what I'd heard and seen, nothing would shock me, except maybe Domitian walking in dressed as a Vestal.

Brutius trotted in from the entryway, and before he could announce who it was, Saturninus followed. He wasn't anybody's idea of a virgin.

"Agricola sent word that you're here."

"I came back a day early. Meditor's arrested the man I was looking for."

He nodded. "I know. He's due to be questioned tomorrow. Agricola's already writing the story of what to tell Domitian."

I felt Gwyna's hand on my arm again. "So they're pinning it on Rhodri? That's definite?"

Saturninus shrugged into his beard. "I don't think they'll look beyond him, unless it's to one of his native friends."

God, I needed sleep. And yet here was Saturninus, and I knew it wasn't a social call.

I grumbled and groaned. "So what do you want from me?"

He grinned. "Your initiation. The temple."

"Isn't it a waste of time, if you've got the guilty man?"

He looked at me closely. "You look like shit." Then he caught himself, and apologized to Gywna. "Sorry."

She looked at him cooly. "I've heard worse. And I've said worse."

He raised his eyebrows. "Well, I can see you have ample reasons for staying at home, Arcturus, and you look none too fresh. Smell a little bad, too. But if you think this Rhodri character didn't off the Syrian, someone did, and someone in the temple, like as not. You know that. It's not like you to be so bitter."

"It's not like me to ride a hundred and twenty miles in three days straight, either."

"What's wrong, old man? Getting a little stiff?"

He chewed the end of his mustache, and shot a glance at Gwyna with the last remark.

I stared at him, and finally broke into laughter. "You win. You always do."

I leaned over to kiss her lightly on the cheek, and whispered, "I don't know when I'll be home. We can talk tomorrow." She squeezed my arm in reply, and rewarded Saturninus with a smile. Everyone liked him—you couldn't help it.

I stood up. "Tomorrow I want to hear everything—what Caelius did, said, what you found out, Bilicho, and most importantly I want to hear from Stricta."

Bilicho looked up at me, and we understood one another.

Brutius held out a cleaner mantle. Everyone was drifting off to bed. Gwyna was smiling at Bilicho. It was my home again.

On the way out the door I said: "Don't you people ever do anything at a decent hour?"

"This is a decent hour, my dour friend, if you've still got blood in your veins. And if you don't, we'll replace it with a stronger vintage."

There were two horses tied up outside, and I nearly fell over backwards when I saw them. "We're going to ride? Do you know how sore my ass is?"

"Why? You been letting somebody pound it for you? And you with that nice piece of—"

"Saturninus." That was enough. He shut up.

I gingerly mounted the large chestnut. He was a legionary horse, and a stallion, and proud. He was a good horse, but I missed Nimbus.

It didn't take us long to ride to the mithraeum. The streets were empty, except for *vigiles* and an extra ration of soldiers. I felt native eyes glaring at us, but I didn't see anyone. By the time we got there, two soldiers with torches were waiting for us, or maybe guarding the entrance. They held the reins and took the horses when we dismounted, while I sucked in some night air before climbing down that dank dirt stairway.

At the foot of the stairs were two more soldiers. I noticed, with some surprise, that Arian was one of them.

"Arcturus, this is your partner. He will explain to you how everything works, and what you must do and how you must respond in the actual initiation. That's supposed to be tomorrow night, God willing. I'm supposed to tell you something about Mithras."

Arian and the other legionnaire vanished into the inner part of the temple, where Maecenas had been laid out only six nights before. Six nights. If time was going by so slowly, why did I have so little of it?

Saturninus started lecturing to me in a sing-song voice, stuff he'd been taught, stuff he wasn't sure he believed, but stuff that was necessary for him, and now me, to know.

I absorbed what I could. Some of it was similar to what the Druids teach—particularly the stars. But they had a very hierarchical system, with grades like Lion, and Bride-Groom, and Courier of the Sun, and Persian—all pseudo-Eastern and mysterious. *Pater* was the highest post—that was Agricola. As usual, I was starting on the bottom, and frankly didn't have much ambition to move up. I liked the camaraderie in what he told me, but not the climbing. It reminded me too much of the *cursus honorum,* and if I hadn't climbed a ladder for Rome I wasn't about to do it for Mithras.

After I'd spent about an hour with Saturninus—and at the conclusion, we enjoyed a few swigs off a wine skin—I discovered that Mithras, like Bacchus, enjoyed a show. Saturninus nodded off in a corner and told me to go to the inner part of the temple where Arian was waiting. The other soldier left when I walked in. Must be a two-man performance.

The *signifer* smiled at me. "I volunteered for this. I wanted to apologize."

"Forget it."

"No, I mean it," he insisted. "I was out of line. I'm glad you're going to be part of the temple."

I looked around the black gloom, the thick soil and stone oppressing me. "Yeah. I am, too. I'm still trying to find out what happened. You know, how the body got here."

He glanced involuntarily at the slab. I couldn't see any traces of blood. They must have scrubbed for days.

"Is that why you're hurt? Your face—"

"I ran into a tree out of town. They make them big in the country."

Arian gave me a funny look, then decided to laugh.

"I'm dead tired; I've been on my feet for too long. So if I say or do something strange, it's the exhaustion, not me."

He smiled, the confident, innocent smile of a young man who has seen some, but not all, that the world has to offer. "All right. I'll remember."

From behind him, he pulled out a short sword and a scabbard. I looked at it a little doubtfully. He chuckled.

"Don't worry. Saturninus explained about the death-act, right? Mithras likes us to act out what he does for us in real life.

Tomorrow night, you'll stand in front of that carving—" he pointed with the sword to a relief on the wall of Mithras slaying the bull, a scorpion biting his ankles, and a few other figures thrown in. It was flanked by another relief of two young men holding torches, one up, one down.

"—And I'll take this sword, and it'll look as if I'm running it through you. Then I kneel, and say a prayer to Mithras, and everyone joins in, and then you get up."

"If the prayers work."

He laughed. "It's a trick sword. The blade collapses when it's pushed into something. But sometimes we like to put a little pouch of blood in the novice's tunic, so that he can pop it when the sword is supposed to hit, and it looks more real." He chuckled again. "Sometimes we don't tell the novice."

"You really like this sort of play-acting, huh? What do the other grades get to go through?"

He frowned. "Well, I'm not really supposed to tell you. But that pit over there—" he pointed again "—is part of another initiation."

"Gives me something to look forward to. All right, how does this thing work?"

I reached for the sword, but for some reason couldn't pry it from the scabbard. Arian laughed again. He was in a good mood tonight.

"I'll demonstrate. See—" Even he had a little trouble taking it out of the scabbard, but he wriggled it free. "—you stand over here, there'll be lights behind the carving. There are little holes in the stone to imitate the stars," he explained.

"Then I'll stand up next to you, and take the sword out—I'll make sure it's oiled by tomorrow—and hold it against your stomach like this"—he held it against his own—"and then just a hard push—"

I watched as his eyes widened in shock, and looked down to

see a red stain starting to spread under his tunic. I was about to congratulate him on the performance when he stumbled against the carving, and I saw the sword quiver as he moved. It wasn't an act. Arian had stabbed himself, and was dying right in front of me.

Twenty-Two

I must have yelled or screamed or made a noise, because Saturninus and the other soldier came running. I was holding on to Arian, trying to lead him to the slab. Another body in the mithraeum—but this one, goddamn it, was still alive.

"Saturninus—help me get him on this thing. Careful—don't move the knife. You—rip up a tunic or something and get me some cloth. All right—take his feet. Arian, I'm going to bend your knees close to your chest—it'll help with the bleeding and the pain. Get me a bag for his head—I need to prop it. Any more wine? Get it for me."

The other soldier came back with some torn pieces of a dirty tunic, probably his own. Saturninus hurried with the wine bag, and I laid it beside Arian and started to cut the cloth of his tunic around the knife. He was trying to look, his eyes glassy and scared, but he wasn't in shock. Not yet.

"I need a blanket, too, and hurry. Saturninus—the fort. Bring back a flat-bed cart. I need to take this knife out at the hospital and explore the wound."

I took a deep breath. I was exhausted, and my hands weren't as steady as they'd need to be. "You—more light over here."

I covered his chest with a blanket, asked for another, and used that for his knees. The bleeding was slowing down a little, and I was praying the knife hadn't cut through his liver or kidneys. It stood in the wound, slightly quivering with his every breath, which was becoming a little more jagged as he began to realize what had happened.

I bit my lip. I didn't have anything to stop the flow if I took it out, and keeping it in the wound kept the bleeding down and dirt out. But leaving it in ran the risk of it grazing an organ or worsening the damage. He had a strong muscular wall, so I was betting on the knife getting lodged in that, before it could slice off a piece of his pancreas. I'd stabilize it, not remove it.

I pulled the cloth away from the wound very slowly. A little of the tunic was inside it.

I looked up at him. "I don't think it's very deep. We've got to take you to the hospital before I can be sure. Hold on to the sides of the altar—this may hurt."

What little wine Saturninus had left flowed over his stomach and around the knife and mixed with the coagulating blood. I took some of the cloth the other soldier had torn off and placed it like packing around the blade, trying to keep it in place.

Arian moved his left leg without knowing it, and I yelled to the other soldier: "Goddamn it, hold his legs steady for him. That's it."

He whispered: "Am I going to die?"

"Eventually. Not tonight."

I moved above him and opened his mouth. I didn't see any sign of blood in his spit. I could also get a good view of his belly from here, to see if it was swelling at all. Swelling meant bleeding inside, damaged organs, and probable death. It looked mildly enlarged. Something was leaking inside, then, and I only hoped I could find what it was and sew it up and keep him alive. I still had faith in his stomach muscles.

I went back to the wound and leaned over and sniffed. I didn't smell shit. The big intestine was probably all right. He was starting to shiver, and I took off my mantle and covered him with it. Losing blood in that cold, damp place would send anyone into shock, but I needed him still and quiet, not trembling. Where the hell was Saturninus?

The other soldier was standing in front of the carving, mumbling some sort of prayer to Mithras. The god got him into this, maybe he could get him out. I wouldn't turn down any help.

I rubbed my shaggy face, and wished I had a decent bandage and a pair of forceps. Arian was closing his eyes, either trying to control his breathing or starting to fade.

I leaned over him. "Listen. You took a sword that was meant for me. You're not going to die. I promise you. I'll wrestle with that bastard Pluto, I'll pull Mithras' cap over his face and kill the bull myself—I'll do whatever I need to do to keep you alive. But you've got to help. Keep talking to me and stay awake."

His blue eyes looked enormous. "All right. But it hurts."

"Of course it hurts. So do most things in life. Wait until you get married and your wife has her first son. You think *signiferes* are tough."

I kept him awake with talk that didn't mean anything but could mean everything until Saturninus arrived. Somehow, between the three of us, we got him up the ladder. Saturninus—big, bold, burly Saturninus—had me strap him on his back like a baby, and crab-walked up the dirt, clawing at each stair with his fingernails. I held Arian's feet, and kept him as even as possible so that the knife wouldn't move. The other soldier kept praying, vowing who knew what to who knew whom if Arian lived. Maybe one of the gods was in the mood for a bribe.

I sat in the cart with him, hovering over the knife like a broody hen. I packed it firmly with more cloth once we were in the wagon, but cursed every time the rear wheel hit a rock.

The hospital was ready for us. One of the *capsarii*, Flavius, was waiting for me. He was from the Ninth Legion, like Arian.

"Got the bandages ready? Good. We have any *sanguinaria*? Is it mixed with vinegar? Mix it then, and quick."

After we lifted Arian up on the table, I told Saturninus and the other one to go. Saturninus said he'd wait for me. Agricola would need to be told. I guess my initiation was going to be postponed.

Flavius asked: "Are you going to open it up?"

"I think he's got a small cut inside somewhere. If I don't find it, he'll get a fever and die."

After that, he didn't say much. I leaned over to Arian, who had his eyes closed again.

"Wake up, *Signifer.* I'm going to pull out the knife."

His eyes lifted themselves with difficulty. "Will it hurt?"

"Not as much as the bet you lost last month."

He tried to smile, and while he was in the middle of it I grasped the sword handle with both hands and pulled it out, as straight and fast and quick as I could. It made a slight sucking sound when it came out, and blood started flowing immediately.

I threw it aside and with some forceps pried away the tunic from the punctured flesh. Arian was grasping the sides of the table again. Flavius stood by with some vinegar and *sanguinaria,* and I poured it like a man giving out wine on his wedding day.

Now I could see the wound. It was thin—the blade hadn't twisted, and had gone in cleanly. But his belly was still swollen. Not much, but enough.

Flavius pulled either side of it open, while I held a lamp over it. I sniffed again. Still no odor of shit. But a faint whiff of something other than blood. Bile, and maybe a little bit of food.

"Arian—what did you eat tonight?"

"A beef flank." He was breathing hard. "We were celebrating."

Beef. The unmistakable odor of partly digested beef. There was a nick in the little intestine.

"You've got a small cut in your gut inside. I need to find it

231

and sew it up. I'll probably have to open this stab wound up a little bit."

He whispered: "All right."

Flavius brought me more of the vinegar mixture. I told him to lay out some honey, if they had any. He gave me a funny look, but did as I asked. I guess they usually used it for bee stings and superficial cuts and scrapes. He'd learn something, then.

I picked up one of the scalpels and very quickly sliced some horizontal cuts around the opening. I kept pouring the vinegar until the entire wound smelled like Mollius' apartment. I stopped to wipe my forehead with the back of my hand. I was sweating.

The path of the blade was straight and in a limited area. But intestines twist up worse than the Gordian knot—and that meant some fold underneath could've been punctured. My hands were shaking, and I stopped again. No time, Arcturus, no time for nerves. One deep breath, and in I went.

The gods must've been smiling on Arian that night, or maybe the bribe of the other soldier had been big enough. I probed for less than a minute, and found the glancing slice on the red-pink intestine tube, a slice and a nick that would've kept leaking fluid until Arian's stomach looked pregnant, while his gut was rotting from the inside. He would've died. And if I'd been able to remove the sword from its sheath, I would almost certainly be dead already.

I doused him again with the vinegar. Then I took some flax thread, and very slowly, very patiently, sewed up the small cut on the intestine. It was slippery, and very messy work. My hands didn't shake. Flavius watched attentively, with the bandages prepared.

I doused him again. I'd probably used up their monthly supply of vinegar and *sanguinaria*, if the *praefectus castrorum* was typical of that miserly breed. After thoroughly searching the wound once more, I sewed up the puncture and the extra incisions I'd made. Finally, I turned to Flavius for the honey. I smelled it, to make sure it was a good type, and then lathered it over the stitches and layered the fresh linen bandages on top.

"Change these every day, and keep him in the hospital for at least ten days. If he has any swelling in the stomach, or any fever at all—any, you understand—get me immediately. Who's the *medicus* on duty tomorrow?"

"Cleones."

"A Greek? I don't know him. But tell him what I told you. This man is my patient, and I want him looked after with particular care."

Flavius nodded. Any doubts he'd been harboring had apparently dissolved when I found the cut. Intestine wounds are notorious.

"Arian."

His eyelids fluttered. He was very nearly unconscious.

"Arian. You're going to be all right. You need to stay in the hospital for a few days, so we can make sure you don't develop a fever. I'll be checking on you."

He blinked his eyes at me, but I didn't know if he understood.

"Give him some *opos*—a small dose—for the pain if he needs it when he wakes up. Call another *capsarius* and move him to a bed."

I breathed a deep, deep breath, and washed my hands in a jar of water. The blood under my fingernails made them itch. I picked up the sword from the floor and put on my mantle, and walked outside into the cold. Cheated the bastard yet again. I wondered how many lucky throws I had coming, and whether or not they were all used up.

Saturninus was waiting for me with the horses.

"I can't see Agricola tonight. I'm at my limit, and beyond it.

I'm going home to sleep. But when you talk to him, remind him where Rhodri is. And tell him someone tried to break into my house while I was gone, and this sword"—I held it up—"was meant for me."

"Someone switched it. Someone in this camp, and someone in the temple."

"Obviously. And Rhodri's been pissing on himself all this time in Meditor's jail, waiting for the *quaesitor*. So ask the governor, Saturninus, if he wouldn't mind holding off the torture, at least until I speak to the man. I don't want to have to save his life to get his testimony."

Saturninus' teeth gleamed in the dark. "Better than you having to save your own. Lucky that Arian took it for you."

"Yeah. But not for him. Will you tell Agricola, please?"

He grunted. "Whatever you say, Arcturus. We'll have to postpone your initiation."

I managed to pull myself aboard the stallion, groaning all the way. "Believe me, Saturninus, that's the least of my worries."

We got home somehow, and I slipped off. I couldn't remember when I'd been so weary, so empty of everything. I kept the sword and told Saturninus I'd see him a lot sooner than I wanted to. He just showed me his teeth, and took the bridle of the red horse and cantered off toward the palace.

It was earlier than it'd been last night, when Nimbus and I found the meadow. I hoped I would sleep just as well, but I didn't care, so long as I slept. The house was quiet. I tried the door—bolted this time. I knocked gently, and after a few moments, Brutius opened it, rubbing his eyes and yawning.

"Draco outside?"

"Yes, Master. I put a compress on Pyxis, too."

"Good. I'm too tired to mix a painkiller tonight—I'll give you one tomorrow."

He nodded, and held the lamp for me while we walked

through the hall to my room. I'd never seen a more glorious sight than my own green-blanketed bed, unless it was the blonde woman lying asleep under the covers.

I held my finger to my lips, and took the lamp from Brutius. He retreated on tiptoe, and I stood a minute, luxuriating in the sight of her. Her breathing was a gentle motion, like a cradle rocking, and when I climbed in next to her and held her close, it hushed me to sleep like a favorite lullaby.

Twenty-Three

I didn't wake up until I felt a soft hand brushing hair away from my cheek. I mumbled: "Not now, Coir."

I woke up when a voice answered dryly: "I'm not Coir."

I opened an eye. She was sitting on the bed, dressed in a plain white muslin *stola*. I turned pink, and sat upright. "How long have you been up?"

"Since dawn. It's about an hour after. Mollius is here waiting for you."

I scratched my chin. "I'm, uh—"

"I know." There was a amused smile on her lips. "I'd already guessed."

I was up, and getting dressed. Gwyna watched with what I hoped was interest, though I was so dirty and sore I couldn't blame her if it wasn't. "We need to talk, about that, about Caelius, about everything."

She raised an eyebrow. "Well, as far as 'that' is concerned, I think Draco's taken care of it. Everything else can wait until you've seen Rhodri."

I glanced over while I was cinching a belt over a tunic that was cleaner than I was. "Don't worry about him so much."

Her cheeks got a little red. "He risked himself for me, and he's a friend. I have every right to worry about him, Arcturus, he's sitting in a jail waiting to be subjected to God knows what kind of torture this very instant."

She used my Roman name. Not a good sign. "Yeah. I know.

But something happened last night that I think will help keep the *quaesitores* at bay for a bit. Someone tried to kill me."

She grasped my arm while I was strapping on a sword. "What happened? Are you all right?"

A small part of me—well, a rather large part, actually—was gratified. I was tired of Rhodri, and I hadn't even met the bastard yet. "I'm all right, but a man nearly died taking a sword that was meant for me. Someone at the fort was responsible, someone either in or who knows about the temple. Someone who can't be Rhodri."

She folded herself up in my arms and pulled my head to her mouth. The kiss felt like a long drink of cool water after a week in a sand pit. When she finished, she looked up at me, and asked: "Is that better than Coir?"

She already knew the answer, so I didn't give it to her. At least in words. When she finally pushed me away, I was breathing hard.

"You have work to do, Ardur."

I grunted like one of Circe's pigs, unable to talk.

She smiled, that smile that is the personal prerogative of beautiful women. "Go on. And be careful."

When I closed the door, she was vigorously shaking out my blankets. I thought about firing up the *caldarium* later.

Bilicho's door was shut, but I heard voices in the dining room. Venutius was ready with breakfast, and Mollius was standing in front of the fire, looking surprisingly alert. Coir was helping Venutius. I assumed Brutius and Draco were still asleep from staying up all night. But where was Bilicho?

"Are you ready, Arcturus? I know you had a rough night. I heard about the temple."

"Yeah. I've got the sword with me. It's not an army issue."

"Let's see it."

Mollius looked it over while I sucked down some of Venutius' oats and honey. I felt like I hadn't eaten for days. A door slammed, and a few minutes later Bilicho poked a sleepy head into the dining room.

"How did it go last night?"

"Fine. I wasn't killed."

He thought I was joking until he saw Mollius' face and the sword in his hand. "What happened?"

"Part of the initiation involves getting stabbed with a trick sword. Only someone didn't like the trick part, and switched it out for a real one, with a point. Arian, the *signifer* that gave me a hard time on the way back from the mithraeum the first night—you remember—he was showing me how to use it, and he took the blade instead. He's at the hospital; his gut had a hole in it I had to sew up."

"Will he live?"

"He should. You never know."

Bilicho gave a low whistle. "At least they can't blame Rhodri. Will they let him go?"

"Maybe. I doubt it. You know Meditor. Mollius and I are going there now. I'd like to talk to Stricta when I get back."

His forehead creased with worry. "She wants to talk. But Arcturus—she's not in good health. She won't eat, she's as thin as a papyrus leaf." He turned a little pink. "She can't sleep nights, either."

"I'll take a look at her. Probably just nerves. She's been through a lot."

"More than you know." I couldn't remember ever seeing Bilicho like this. I wondered how long he'd known her, and when it finally hit him, and how long the dazed look would stay on his face. I hoped I didn't look that witless.

When Mollius and I walked outside, a light drizzle was falling on Londinium, not enough to clean the city, but enough to bring out the smells.

"That sword—it looks like an auxiliary man's. Maybe someone from Dalmatia or Thrace."

"Yeah, it looked like that to me, too. How's the curfew going?"

"Makes 'em mad as hell. I don't blame them. Meditor is an asshole."

"One of the biggest. And he's shitting on us."

"Not just us. On every Brit who's not a citizen—and that's most—and the whole idea of why Agricola supposedly put in the *vigiles* to begin with."

"I know, Mollius. Your *pietas*, again."

He looked at me, and said: "I found some things out about Caelius Prato."

"Tell me."

"Do you think he was involved last night?"

"I don't know. I'm fairly sure he didn't try to break into my house—the others told you about that yesterday. He's a physical coward, hides behind rank and power and poor giant Lupo. He didn't actually go to Meditor and complain about Draco, did he?"

Mollius shook his head.

"I didn't think so. He's in too deep and about to get buried. There's no business between him and the fort?"

Mollius shook his head again. "Only the regular traffic between soldiers and whores. He wouldn't know a barracks from a bathhouse. Somebody inside got to that sword."

"Somebody who knew where it was kept and knew what it was for and knew who was supposed to use it. Me."

"That leaves him out of it but good. Your Caelius Prato has conspicuously avoided the military path. He's an equestrian, the third son of some ne'er-do-well who lost senatorial rank under Titus. He's spent time in the East—Judea, and generally is careful to keep his nose clean. Stays out of court, for example. He's been running Lupo's for a year."

"Where did he get the money? A dead aunt?"

Mollius frowned. "I don't know. I haven't been able to find out. It would take considerable capital—buying Lupo, and all the women."

"Try to find out for me, would you?"

"Do you think it's important?"

"Mollius, I always think money is important."

We were at the jail, a plain, grim-looking building in the back end of the forum next to the basilica. Roman jails weren't built very well, because no one ever stayed in them very long. They were just a waiting room on the way to the cemetery.

"I'm leaving now, Arcturus. I don't want Meditor to see me with you."

"Good idea. You should be out finding natives to harass, anyway."

He gave me his crooked smile, and turned back toward the west end of town. I was glad to see him like this. I walked in, and a bored *vigil* greeted me.

"*Salve.* What do you want?"

"Your superior's head on a spit, but that's not likely to happen. Where is he?"

He was easily confused. "Who?"

"Meditor. Med-i-tor. Chief *vigil* and all-around asshole."

"You shouldn't talk that way."

"Yeah, but I can't seem to stop. So where is he?"

"Upstairs. In the office. With a *beneficarius.*"

Must be Avitus. "Thanks. Has the torture started yet?"

"Of the prisoner?"

"Yes. Mine started when I walked in here."

He looked confused again. "The native hasn't been questioned yet."

"Thanks again." I left and entered the Basilica Claudia,

named after the glorious Emperor with the too-small head. Meditor was on the second floor. There were some soldiers and what looked like merchants waiting on the steps, probably for some legal wrangle. They'd scratched a gameboard into the rock and were playing a game of *terni lapilli*. I watched two red pieces get caught by three blues, and walked up to see Meditor.

I didn't knock. When I opened the door, Avitus was trying to explain something to him, and Meditor was turning red and shaking his head. "*Salvete,* gentlemen. Or gentleman. I'm here to talk to your prisoner, Meditor."

He allowed himself a full minute to gloat in my face. "The prisoner that you traveled over a hundred miles to find? The prisoner that you said isn't guilty, and yet we've found weapons in his house? The prisoner that—"

"—is an innocent man, and whom you're holding without any reason at all, except for the fact that you're a bully and an idiot. Yes, that prisoner."

We stared at each other, and Avitus smoothly intervened. "I've just been telling Meditor what happened to you last night, Favonianus. Agricola is holding off the *quaesitor* until you can talk to him."

"Just one? Make sure it's a good one, Meditor—maybe the one that tortured those German mutineers last year."

"You mind your own business."

"This is my business. Avitus just told you what happened. Your boy was locked up in that hole last night—he didn't try to kill me."

"That would hardly be a crime."

I pushed my nose into his face. "Look at me, Meditor. I've been beat up, nearly killed twice, gone without sleep for days, and had to save a good man's life by stitching up a quarter-inch slash in his gut. You give me one more word, one more reason, and I'll rip your goddamn head off and shove it up your ass and

241

no one—no one!—will give a damn."

Avitus plucked at my elbow. "C'mon, Arcturus. Talk to the prisoner."

I stared at the pinched slits that passed for eyes in Meditor's bald head.

"He's still guilty, your native pretty boy. Sure, maybe he's in league with someone—we've always known there're two involved. It's a set-up to make him look innocent."

I stared, but found no sign of anything but hatred. That must be what kept Meditor upright. It sure wasn't intelligence. I shrugged off Avitus' hand, and followed him out the door and down the steps.

"You shouldn't let him get to you like that."

I didn't say anything.

The same dumb guard looked surprised when I walked in with the *beneficarius*. "This man is here to interview the prisoner." The guard nodded. Avitus leaned over to me and whispered: "We haven't been able to get anything out of him."

I grunted, and followed the soldier to the back of the prison. The door was barred with a block of wood that weighed more than I did. He was holding a lamp and a torch, and gave the torch to me. There weren't any windows in the jail. He set the lamp on the floor, drew his sword, and banged the hilt on the door.

"Stand back—there's someone here for you."

There was no answer from within, so he shrugged and pried up the block, grunting with the effort, still holding on to his *gladius*. He opened the door wide enough for me to fit through it, and I could barely glimpse a shadowy figure in the corner of a room so black it looked like a grave. The stench of piss and shit assaulted my nostrils. They hadn't even given the poor bastard a slop bucket.

I walked in, letting my eyes and his adjust to the yellow-orange glare of the torch. The blackness swallowed it up, and I was glad for a stronger light than a lamp.

I heard a shuffle, and a man stumbled toward me. He was young, beneath the grime and the pain on his face. Young and handsome. I suppressed a momentary twinge of jealousy. He must wonder what the hell she saw in me, what with my unshaven chin and black eye and still-swollen cheek.

The guard was still in the doorway, trying to listen. I didn't speak Latin.

"I'm Arcturus."

"I know who you are. Go away."

"I've gone through a lot for you. And not just for you."

He glared at me through the light, and knew what I meant.

"Your friend nearly killed me."

"I'm sorry he failed."

"No, you're not. You're not a murderer. You're an arrogant, spoiled young bastard, but you're no killer."

"How do you know?"

"You didn't kill my freedman when you had a chance. And I know more than you think. Like it or not, I'm your only chance—and not a very good one—of saving your skin. They've got a *quaesitor* on hold, waiting to put you through it."

"Let 'em. I won't talk."

"You will when they fry your skin with a hot iron, or hold a knife up to your eye. They can keep you alive for a long time, Rhodri. This isn't a game."

"I never said it was."

We were silent for a moment. "Look, the only way I can help you is if you tell me what you know. Someone is behind this. A Roman. All the Britons are suffering right now, because the chief of the *vigiles* is a bully and a moron, and Agricola's afraid of a civil war. You're an easy target—and you're making it easier for them."

He clenched his jaw, and still said nothing. I was getting exasperated.

"Maybe you like sitting in the dark in your own shit and piss, but I don't." I groped in the pouch of my tunic with one hand. The guard leaned forward, expecting me to pull out a *ballista*. Instead, my fingers clutched the *anguinum*, the little token Lugh had given me. I held it in my palm in front of Rhodri.

"Your friend the blacksmith gave this to me. He said you'd talk to me if you saw it."

He was surprised. "Lugh gave you this?"

"Yes. After he tried to kill me."

His mouth actually turned up a little at the corner. "He's a hard man in a fight."

"Yeah. But he won't be in any more until his ribs heal."

He studied me, more respect in his eyes than before.

"I want to hate you."

"Feel free. Many do."

"Then why are you trying to help me?"

"Because it's the right thing to do."

He screwed his face up tight. "Not because of—her?"

"I'd try to help you whether she was involved or not."

He paused again, as if we were sitting on a bar stool or under a tree, not in a black cess pit. Finally, he spoke.

"I believe you. I don't have to like you to accept help in a just cause."

"No—as I said, I'm not particularly fond of you, either. So as long as we've got that clear, tell me what you know."

He took a deep breath. Some air blew in from the crack in the door.

"How much do you know already?"

"I know why you did what you did, and I know you and Madoc must've followed the killers to the mithraeum and waited until Maecenas was reburied. Then you dug him up, and left him on top the temple."

He nodded. "We were trying to find the money. I knew he had it—I saw it that night. And we left the body on the temple as an insult to the Romans."

"Didn't you think that the murderers would also be interested?"

"Madoc said so. He said it might draw them out. I didn't care, I just wanted to sully that filthy temple."

Rash, brash and overconfident. I was beginning to like him despite myself.

"What happened when you ran upstairs, after you started the quarrel?"

"That was all planned. Gwyna—" He paused, and looked at me, and swallowed his jealousy. "Gywna was supposed to drug the Syrian, and I was going to come a couple of hours later, stage a fight and run up and steal the money. Not hurt him, you understand. Madoc thought most of it up, along with her. But when I got to the landing, Maecenas was lying face down on the floor in his own doorway. Dead."

"How did you know?"

"I walked over and felt his neck. There was a blood stain on his back, and a rip in his robe. I figured he'd been stabbed, and then I panicked because I could be caught there and blamed."

"Was he holding anything in his hand? Any papers?"

Rhodri shook his head. "Nothing that I can remember."

"So then you ran?"

"I started to. But then I remembered the money. So I tried to be quiet and stepped over him and walked into his room. But there was a man already in there, hiding."

I leaned forward eagerly. "What did he look like?"

"A Roman soldier. He had a green scarf with a gold pin on. Dark, thin, and nervous."

"Not smooth-faced, pleasant-looking?"

"No. But when I saw him, I got scared and tried to run out, and that's when the other one showed up, the smooth-faced one."

"Where was he?"

"He must've come up a different way, or from another room, and was standing looking at Maecenas. He tried to block me, but I just ran like hell out the back and down the stairway into the alley. The other one, the dark one, couldn't catch me."

"Then what happened?"

"There was a wagon in the back, standing close to the rear door, with a man on horseback, holding another horse. He was muffled up, so I couldn't see his face, but I could tell he was on the small side, and his horse's gear was decked out with silver bosses. Rich man's stuff."

"Did he see you?"

"I think so. I ran again, around the corner to where Madoc was waiting for me. He'd seen the whole thing, and told me that the skinny one had gone upstairs, and then we watched while the smooth-faced one and the skinny one both hauled Maecenas down and into the wagon. The small man on the horse spoke a few words to the dark one, and the smooth one grabbed at his reins and made him angry, it looked like. Then we heard a pig squeal. Madoc said it was from the cart—he'd heard it earlier."

"How long had they been there?"

"They were there when Madoc got to the waiting place, so before we started the fight or right at the same time."

I grunted. "What did you do then?"

"We followed, at a safe distance. We knew about the temple. It's built near an old shrine of ours, a well. The dark one opened the earth floor and put the body on a blanket and dragged it down. Maecenas lost a slipper, and the small man picked it up and put it in his cloak. Then the other one took the piglet—it was trussed up in the back—and slit its throat over a jar, and let it drip for a bit. Then he went down the hole with the jar, and came back up with it empty, and took the wagon and went in the direction of the fort. The other man went back towards town."

"They forgot about the money."

"Yes, but Madoc and I didn't. We stayed out there in the dark, and saw the Romans and your freedman and you and waited until it was safe again."

"Would you be able to recognize the dark man again if you saw him?"

"Probably. I can't really forget that night. I've tried."

I rubbed my eyes. "I don't blame you. But your memory may save your life."

"I don't know if it's worth saving."

"Quit feeling sorry for yourself."

"That's easy for you to say. You've got her."

"No one really has Gwyna. She's her own woman. I didn't ask for her, but yes, I'm glad she loves me. But don't talk like a fool. There'll be other women."

"Not like her."

So I lied and said: "Yes, there will be."

He just looked at me. I turned to leave. "One more question: you said you saw the money that night. Where was it?"

"I thought it was in the room. But when I saw the man hiding, I backed out, and that's when I ran into the other one. He was standing over the body, and staring at a large pouch hanging at its side that I'd missed at first. I figured that was the money, but all I wanted to do was run."

He hung his head. "I didn't want Gwyna to know I'd been a coward."

"Rhodri, you're one of the bravest men I've ever met. And she knows it. Why do you think I hate your guts?"

He smiled at me then, his face twisting up beneath the grime.

I left him in the hole, feeling as bad as it smelled. The guard looked at me suspiciously.

"What were you holding in your hand?"

"A shovel."

He just shook his head, and led me back to the front.

Avitus was waiting, and Meditor had come in to gloat.

"He's practically an eyewitness, Avitus."

"That's because he's the murderer," Meditor leered.

I ignored him. I had better things to do. I drew Avitus aside. "Look, there are three men involved. One of them is Marcus Caelius Prato, the one I told you about. The other one is a soldier, probably a legionary officer. He's dark and thin, was wearing a green scarf and a gold pin. I found part of a *fibulae* when I searched the room, so that tallies. It seems as though he's the actual murderer. But there's a third man, smaller but richer. Someone from Londinium, possibly a merchant. I've got a lead about Maecenas and a silver mine I asked Bilicho to check into, but haven't had a chance to follow up yet. The soldier is probably the link to the temple. Does that match anyone you know?"

He shook his head doubtfully. "Not off-hand. But it's not much of a description."

"Rhodri said he could identify him if he saw him."

Avitus leaned in close. "You know Meditor. He's not going to give him up and we can't bring five hundred men in here."

I scratched my chin. "I may be able to find another witness. A woman. One Meditor doesn't know about. Would that work?"

"Sure, if you can take her to the fort."

"You don't need to look at all five hundred. The man would either be a part of the temple, or in the *contubernium* of someone who is. He'd be bunked close by Arian's room, if not actually in it. I assume you've checked that?"

"Yes. The other seven men are in the clear."

"All right, then. It's someone nearby, someone thin, dark, probably an *optio* or maybe a lower level centurion. Maybe a messenger, or a high-ranking clerk, one of the *immunes*. But it's someone in that fort, and you can find him."

"We have a better chance, at any rate."

"And another thing—he may be a Christian."

Avitus looked a little doubtful. "Whatever you say, Favonianus."

"Come get me when you've got some men who might fit. And for God's sake, don't let Meditor torture that poor bastard. I know squatting in jail isn't supposed to be the punishment, but you should see it in there. That's enough torture for any man, especially an innocent one."

I left him to deal with Meditor. Avitus didn't trust me completely, but he trusted Meditor less, and at heart he was a decent man.

I walked home in a hurry, not even feeling the light rain falling in a steady, endless drizzle. I could sense the net closing in, smell the fear in my opponent. Rhodri was in jail. Why kill me unless it was to prevent me from talking to him? Of the three men he described, the soldier was the most likely to try to break in to my house, the one who could most obviously switch swords.

It was a stupid idea. It limited the field too much. Maybe he thought it up on his own. Desperate men always move too quickly, and desperation makes them dangerous. Dangerous but stupid. I wondered what his next move would be . . . Caelius was a possibility. I'd have to get dirtier and see Caelius. But Stricta first.

I reached home sooner than anyone expected me. Gwyna was in the kitchen, watching Venutius, who was enjoying the attention. Hefin and Brutius were out with the animals. I'd have to remember to make a mixture for Pyxis tonight. Coir was at the marketplace—Gwyna was probably relieved to get her out of the house. Draco was just waking up, and Bilicho was sitting in front of the fire, a worried expression on his weathered face.

He stood up when I walked in. "What happened?"

"I talked to Rhodri." Gwyna came out to join us. She held her hand out, and I took it, and then she asked me simply: "How is he?"

"I've tried to convince them not to hold the *quaestio*. He gave me what he knows—a description of the murderer. There are three of them involved—Caelius, a thin, dark-complected legionary of some type, and another man, someone wealthy. Meditor won't free him to make an identification, but I thought if Stricta—if she'd seen anything—"

"She has. But she won't talk to me. There's something wrong. She just sits on the bed and hugs herself and rocks back and forth." Bilicho held his face in his hands, staring at the fire.

"Maybe you can get her to talk, Arcturus. I can't." His brown curls, tinged with grey, drooped as much as his wide mouth.

"Let me go, Ardur."

Gwyna surprised me. "You? But you—"

"I need to apologize to Stricta. I didn't understand why she was here or who she was. And perhaps this is something she could better tell a woman."

Bilicho and I gaped at her. She smiled that smile again, and glided out of the room toward the back. Bilicho scratched his nose. We were both quiet for awhile, but quiet together. Then he spoke. "I haven't touched her, you know. She's been sleeping in my bed—or lying in it is a better word—and I've held her a few times while she cried, but I've never touched her."

"How long have you known her?"

He turned red. "About three months. I—I visited her at Lupo's a few times."

"Why didn't you mention it? I wouldn't have teased you so often."

He mumbled something about her being a slave, and working in a whorehouse, and I let it go. Then he looked up again.

"I do love her, Arcturus. I guess it was you who made me think about it, you and Gwyna. I started to think about how nice it would be to have a woman of my own, someone to take care of me and fix my clothes, and put up with my temper, someone to keep me warm at night, somebody to fight with. Someone to laugh at my jokes." He grinned. "You've done a pretty good job of some of those things over the years, but it's not the same thing. A man wants his own, once he's free. You know how it is."

"I know how it is. But don't think she'll laugh at your jokes."

He grinned at me again. It wouldn't be the same, but it would be the same, because we were friends.

Gwyna was back before we could get embarrassed again. "She's all right, Bilicho. I think she'll eat some broth."

He stood up, fiddling with the hem of his tunic. "What was wrong with her?"

She looked serious for a moment, and then said: "She'll tell you herself. But she'll be fine, now. Just—love her." She looked up at me. "That's all the healing that's necessary."

Bilicho practically flew to his room. We were by ourselves. I rewarded myself by kissing her for a long time. Then she pulled away. "Aren't you forgetting to ask me something? Stricta saw someone."

"I knew it. What did she say?"

"The day before Maecenas was murdered, she saw a thin, dark soldier talking to Caelius. Caelius got very angry when he saw her looking, so she remembered it. The next night, Maecenas—requested her—after I left. Luckily for the poor woman, he couldn't perform. I give myself partial credit.

"She heard a pig squeal outside, and went to look out the window. When she turned around, the soldier was standing there with Caelius, who was surprised to see her. He thought she'd left. He told her to remember that she'd been with Maecenas all night, if anyone asked. She went downstairs, and that's all she saw.

"But a little later, she heard noises upstairs, and Caelius came down and—and hit her. He told her that if she repeated anything she'd seen or heard, they'd mutilate her. I don't want to say how, you can use your imagination. Then he had the idea to get Galla to pretend to be Stricta, because they were friends, and nobody would pay attention to Galla, anyway, because she was a drunk.

"Galla talked too much, as you know. Caelius found out, and—beat her to death. Stricta had been planning to kill herself, but she wanted to avenge her friend. So she used a little of the poison to drug a customer who'd paid for the whole night, and left while Caelius was still . . ." She shuddered. "The rest you know."

I held her at arm's length. "Have I told you today how beautiful you are?"

"No. But don't start, Ardur, I feel terrible hearing that poor woman's story, and knowing that man wanted to—wanted to—"

"Yes, I know. And I know you miss your father. As soon as I can catch my breath we'll see him. If he gave you to Caelius, it was only because he was ill, and his mind was clouded."

She twisted a ring on her finger. "I think Caelius has some sort of hold on him. He wouldn't listen to me, wouldn't believe me when I told him Hefin and I would be in danger. All he could think of was the money."

I took her hand. "That was the illness talking. Not your father."

She looked at me doubtfully, and I kissed her head. "I'm

right. You'll see."

A loud banging on the door drew Draco from the kitchen where he was eating.

He was at the front door in a few strides, a determined look on his face. He came in the dining room a few minutes later, his mouth still full of oat cake. "It's a message, sir."

I unrolled the scrap of papyrus, and recognized Avitus' handwriting. It said: "Have a few to check. Bring the woman." I grunted and showed it to Gwyna. "Draco, I need to go to the fort. It's still a few hours until dark, but I'd like you to stay here. I need to take Stricta." I looked at Gwyna. "I'd better get Bilicho."

A tap on his door brought him out immediately. "Yes, Arcturus?"

"I'm sorry, Bilicho. I just got a message from Avitus. They've found some men who answer Rhodri's description, and Stricta is the only one who can identify the right one. Can she come?"

A thin brown hand grasped Bilicho's shoulder, and he turned. Stricta stepped into the hallway, meeting my eyes with that peculiar grace that was all her own. She was too thin, like a stripped leaf in the winter time. But her eyes were clear, and they were strong.

"Of course I'll come, Arcturus." She spoke Latin with a pronounced Greek accent. Bilicho would have to learn Greek now. I told her so in that language, and she laughed, a low, throaty sound that seemed to fill his chest with enough pride and joy to make him float to the ceiling. I was getting even for all the times he'd given me those funny looks.

"What did you say?"

"I told Stricta you'd have to learn Greek."

"Can you teach me?"

"I think she can teach you better," and winked at him. He blushed. He was hopeless.

Stricta took her green cloak. It covered most of her face. I nudged Bilicho in the ribs. "Keep an eye out, now. Don't get so soft that you're not good for anything."

"What are you talking about? I'm as hard as a rock."

I leaned over and whispered: "Yes, but in all the wrong places."

He blushed an even deeper red, and said: "You're as bad as Antonius."

Stricta said nothing. She knew we were scoundrels.

We arrived at the fort a little over an hour later. I didn't want to hurry. Stricta was physically weak, and I was worried about her, though I didn't tell Bilicho that. When I gave my name to the guard, they told us to go straight to the *principia,* the officers' building, and the most formal one in the fort.

There seemed to be a lot of activity, and the thin woman with the stained green cloak drew attention we didn't need. Bilicho and I flanked her.

The *primus pilus* was there to greet us, along with Quintus Claudius Corvus, Agricola's head of staff. Avitus was beside him.

"That was quick. It took longer to get here than to receive your message."

"When you left I found I had one myself. Seems one of our temple members told his centurion that one of the men in his *contubernium* had been asking a lot of questions about the temple, and the rites, and so on. It made him nervous. The fellow is a *frumentarius,* and of course our man worried that if he didn't tell him what he wanted to know, he wouldn't get his daily ration."

"What's the man like? Does he know why he's here?"

Corvus replied, "He's been told there's a change in the ration order. We also picked some other men who might fit the description Avitus sent us. They've joined him in the office there." He nodded to his left.

"As for what he's like, he's been a very honest *frumentarius*. He travels to the city frequently, deals with merchants, and is always searching for better bargains for our fort. Our main foodstuffs are supplied by conscript, of course, but the men get tired of oats and barley. He's tried to liven up the diet."

"But what is he like, Corvus? How does he act? What gods does he worship?"

Corvus shook his thick head. "No one seems to know much about him. His name is Sextus Narbo. He's a very intense man, very single-minded, a good soldier. He keeps himself to himself. Not a bad idea, if you ask me."

I nodded. Avitus said: "Where's your eyewitness?"

I held Stricta gently by the elbow. "She's here, gentlemen. Let's get on with it."

We walked toward the room on the left. The doorway was open, and the soldier standing guard at it saluted Corvus and Avitus, and stood aside.

Inside, there were five men sitting in front of a desk, most looking bored. Some were thin, some were dark, one or two were both. But one—and only one—stared at us as we walked in. His eyes burned like coals, and even from a distance I could tell they were an uncommon brown-green, more like an animal's than a human's. There was something familiar about him—I wondered if I'd seen him before. He made me uncomfortable. I kept my back stiff to keep from squirming.

He wasn't wearing a green scarf and a gold pin. Just a tunic, and they'd taken his sword. But he was poised to run or strike. I could feel it. He was the man.

Corvus and Avitus both looked at Stricta. She slowly removed her hood. Bilicho and I held on to her. I could feel her body weaken, but her resolve was stronger. With a long finger that didn't tremble, she pointed at him and said in a low voice:

"That is the man."

Panic seized him. He looked around the room for a place to hide, found nothing, and bolted for the door. He made it past Corvus, but not the two guards. They held him, struggling, his face hard and bitter and full of something else—something fanatic. I'd seen faces like that in Rome during the Magna Mater celebrations, men in fits of ecstasy who would try to castrate themselves out of love for the goddess. He didn't look like a *gallus,* but the madness was there.

With a crook of his finger, Corvus sent two soldiers to search his belongings. The *primus pilus,* whom I hadn't met, was trying to question him and getting nowhere. Bilicho's arm was around Stricta, and she leaned into him.

Very soon, one of the soldiers came running in. He was holding up a shoe, a fancy thing that belonged to a dead Syrian by the name of Vibius Maecenas. Things didn't look good for Sextus Narbo.

TWENTY-FOUR

Narbo wouldn't talk. Among his clothes they found a green scarf and a gold pin of Apollo, with one of the points of his crown broken. Stricta recognized them immediately. Again, the back of my neck tingled. I put it down to not having bathed.

He was being held in a small room in the *principia*. Corvus didn't want word to spread among the others, particularly if they connected him to the temple pollution. He wouldn't last the night.

He assigned two tough-looking guards, senior men, to watch him. They confronted him with the slipper, and he just shook his head. Corvus asked him: "Why did you kill the Syrian? Why did you put him in the temple? Are you protecting someone? Answer me!"

Narbo just looked at him dully, his thin face held tight, his flesh sallow and his eyes burnt out. Whatever flame was inside him wasn't lit by threats.

When Corvus came out of the room exasperated, I asked if I could question him. The short, dark chief-of-staff raised an eyebrow. "Why do you think he'll talk to you?"

"I don't know. He tried to kill me. That gives us a kind of bond, I guess."

He frowned. But Corvus was no Meditor. "Well, go ahead and try. We'll piece this thing together bit-by-bit if we have to, but if we can get any information out of him it'll save us a lot of time and effort. I don't want to have to use the *quaesitor*. The man is an officer."

My tongue hurt when I bit it. "Thanks."

I walked into the room and sat down on a folding chair. Narbo was standing up, still, not even pacing. Any fight had been used up in trying to escape.

I watched him. He stared straight ahead, his cheek and eyelids twitching a little, trying to fight the impulse to claw the wall. He was the kind of insane that was nearly undetectable—as long as no one got too close. That's what made my skin want to crawl off in a corner and scratch itself.

"So why did you kill him? The message or the money?"

The shock of the question didn't work. He stared at me and wriggled his little finger. I rubbed my chin and began again.

"I'm the man you tried to kill. My dog's all right, too, though I should kick you in the teeth for that."

Still nothing. He was blanker than a new wax tablet. I was getting nowhere, so I took a chance.

"Are you a Christian?"

The fire flickered on. The green in his eyes started to smolder, and he stood straighter, looking ahead, but not at me, not at the wall, at something I couldn't see that wasn't there.

"Iesus Christus is the one true god. All others will fail."

"Is that why you did this? For your god?"

"Iesus Christus is the one true god. He is the Alpha and the Omega. All others will fail."

"Did he tell you to do this?"

"Iesus Christus is the one true god. All others will fail."

"Most gods don't like murder."

"Iesus Christus is the one—"

"Yeah, I know. So why did you kill the Syrian?"

"All others will fail. It is his plan, it is his will. Iesus Christus is the one—"

I got up to leave before I got sick. Someone, somewhere, had an invisible leash on the poor bastard, a leash called Iesus Christus. He wouldn't talk. He didn't know how to. Someone had put him up to this, someone had used him and squeezed him until there was nothing left but a dry husk of a man repeating some small words of comfort that served as reason and explanation and defense. Maybe he'd even helped plan some of it, once upon a time, but he was beyond planning, now. He wasn't even here.

When I came out of the room, the bad taste in my mouth was made worse by seeing Meditor. I turned to Corvus. "You heard Narbo."

He scratched an eyebrow. "I did. What was it you asked him? Something about a message and money?"

"Ask Agricola. I can't talk about it here." He looked at me thoughtfully, his coal-black eyes searching my face. Meditor felt the need to interrupt.

"Are you going to allow me to question—"

Corvus snapped around. He didn't like Meditor, either. Practically no one did. And yet he lived, or at least pretended to. "No, I am not. This is an internal affair of the *cohors praetoria*. We have our own methods of handling things."

"The Druid probably put him up to it. Both of them anti-Rome, both hating the Emperor and Agricola. If you'd only let me take him to the jail—"

"I said no, Meditor. Now kindly quit wasting my time, and go back to beating up drunks for racing tips."

Meditor glowed a very attractive shade of red, and turned so fast his heel left a mark on the floor. Avitus, Bilicho, Stricta and Corvus and I watched him retreat into the distance with varying degrees of pleasure.

"I'll stay in touch as I learn more, Corvus."

We grasped arms, and left, Avitus staying behind to make plans on what to do with Narbo. There weren't many choices.

The hospital was on the road home, so I stopped by to check on Arian. He was asleep, but his head was cool, and his cheeks were a healthy pink. He'd be all right. Cleones watched me, and then asked as I left: "You're Arcturus? Agricola's *medicus,* and the one who operated on this boy last night?"

He was about forty or fifty, with grizzled grey hair that smelled of scented oil. His Latin was a little sing-song, with a light accent. "Yes. Please keep using honey on the wound."

He nodded. "I'd like to talk to you sometime. You're quite gifted."

I smiled. "Thanks. I'm just lucky."

He shook his head and said evenly: "There is no luck, and if there is, we make our own. Be seeing you."

"*Vale.*"

Greeks were like that. Always curious, always with a philosophy to peddle. Bilicho and Stricta were waiting for me. He was holding her up. She was weak and wrung out, and we needed to get her home before dark.

They talked softly together on the way home and I decided not to throw a wet bucket of urgency at them. I was getting desperate to hear what Bilicho had found while I was gone—other than Stricta—but I figured I could spare them an hour or two of peace.

We were only a few blocks from my house when I saw a familiar bundle of rags leaning against a corner wall.

I turned to Bilicho and said: "Madoc's over there, and I want to talk to him. Go on home with Stricta. Tell Gwyna I'm going to see the governor before I come home for the evening." He nodded, peering through the thick mist at the Druid. Rain had stopped falling, but was still hanging around like an unwanted guest. He held on to Stricta's elbow as if she were a cross between a newborn kitten and a cult statue. He'd be lucky if he remembered where we lived. Stricta smiled at me, tired, her face drawn, the fine lines around her mouth deep. She'd see him home.

I crossed the street to where Madoc was waiting. He inclined his head to me, and I did the same. Then I said: "How did you know he was a Christian?"

He fished around in one of the many folds in the rags, and pulled out a bronze disk. It looked like a coin, but was perforated in the top so that it could be hung on a string. The design struck on it was Greek—the letters chi and rho, with an alpha and an omega at the sides.

"This was in the dirt by the doorway. He must have lost it when he carried the Syrian down the stairs. I found it when we followed them."

"What does it mean?"

He shook his head. "I'm not sure. But it is the symbol of their faith, and I know these letters—" He pointed to the alpha and the omega "—mean the beginning and the end of all things, which is how they think of their god."

"He babbled something about an alpha and an omega when I questioned him. He's no good, Madoc. His mind's gone."

He nodded. "I feared as much. He bore all the signs."

I wasn't surprised. I wasn't surprised that a Druid knew more about another religion than I did, either. They made it their business to know things, and acquiring knowledge and passing it on was their life's work. That's what made them so dangerous. That, and a long, native memory, and the fact that they could fight like hell.

"You know anything else about Iesus Christus?"

"Only a little. The faith sprang up in Rome and Judea. They have many wandering priests in the deserts, not unlike our own. He was one such, but his followers proclaim him as the one true God, a son of the First Creator. Some of them refuse to worship any others, though some just add him to the list of those to whom they pray. They are supposed to be gentle enough. They don't care for us because we believe the truth is revealed through death. They believe the truth is revealed after death. A small difference."

"So they hate the Old Believers because you roast criminals in baskets—"

Madoc's eyebrows raised slightly at the description.

"—and they hate the Romans because of Nero."

"And also because they must pray to the Emperor. And for the same reasons others hate the Romans. Nero killed many of them, just as Agricola and Paulinus killed our folk at Mona. But not all of them hate as much as the soldier. This I've discovered since talking to you last."

I shook my head. "And let's not forget Narbo is a Roman *and* a Christian, and maybe that's enough to make the poor son-of-a-bitch lose his mind. Meanwhile, Rhodri's still in the dark, pissing on himself. You heard I saw him this morning?"

"Yes. I hope you will be able to free him. That is why I wanted to talk to you."

"Could you recognize the third man who was with Caelius and the Christian that night?"

"No. He kept his face well-wrapped. But he was a wealthy man, and he seemed to hold a power over the others."

"I thought so. Someone's pulling the strings like a puppet show in front of the amphitheater. Narbo will never talk."

"No. His kind welcome death. It may be the most merciful thing for him."

"I just don't know why the hell this was done. Why those three men killed Maecenas. It doesn't make sense."

"Such a killing never does. But you will find the truth."

"I'm glad you trust me. Now." I grinned. "How did Bilicho do that night? I'm sure you saw him; he must've been behind you, trying to follow the tracks."

Madoc turned down the corners of his mouth and shrugged. "He wasn't a bad tracker—for a Roman."

I laughed. I wasn't sure which part would irritate Bilicho more.

"You have with you one of our tokens."

"The *anguinum*. That's what convinced Rhodri to speak to me."

"Take care of it, Ardur. You may need it again sometime."

I rubbed my sore cheek. "So long as I don't have to fight Lugh."

Madoc allowed himself a rare smile. "He is a good man." Then he turned, and with a small gesture of farewell, seemed to vanish into the street itself. I'd have to learn that trick sometime.

I decided to go straight to the palace. I'd talk to Agricola, try to convince him not to torture Rhodri. They owned Narbo or what was left of him, and not even Meditor could connect the two. Of course, there was only Stricta's identification, and politicians and whores, though familiar bedfellows, generally didn't appear together in court.

The palace was busy. It was about an hour before sunset, and tomorrow was the last day of the year. The procurator's staff would be working all night, and tomorrow, too—interest rates were due on the first. The Empire glutted on credit and loans, and grew more bloated every year. War was always good for business.

I sent word in to Agricola through a secretary. I waited, watching the accountants and the translators and the bookkeepers and the lawyers bustle in and out of the offices, the record room, leading people in, leading people out. There was an eternal feeling about it, like the flooding of the Nile. A thousand years later, the same scene would be taking place. I hoped I'd have this solved by then.

The secretary came back and ushered me through a hallway

into one of the workrooms. Inside, Agricola was hunched over a desk with tablets and styli and papyrus sheets and ink all over it, and Iavolenus Priscus, his red hair gleaming in the lamp light, was hunched over it with him, writing furiously.

Each of them looked up briefly when I entered, but kept going.

"What are you doing?"

Priscus answered. "Writing to the Emperor, Arcturus. We're concocting a story to explain why the governor here can't answer the message he's not supposed to know anything about." He stood up and pointed a stylus at me. "What do you think? They murdered him and threw the body in the river and no one has been able to find it? All that was left was one shoe and the top portion of a dispatch box . . ."

"Very creative, Priscus. Sounds like a Greek novel. I take it you're blaming this on Rhodri and the Christian."

"Well, they are in custody. It's convenient that way."

"One of them is innocent."

Agricola was cross. He put down his stylus with a thump. "Arcturus, I'm tired of hearing how innocent this native is. He may be innocent of the murder—or he may not. But he's not innocent of plotting revolts against Rome."

"Neither are many Romans. At the moment, sir, neither are you."

He stood up, his brown eyes flashing, his hands clenched into fists on the table.

"If you're suggesting—"

"I'm suggesting, Governor, that you're doing what you have to do, and I understand and support you. I don't care what you tell Domitian. You can tell him I did it, if it helps. But we don't know the extent of your danger until we find out why this man was killed. We now know we are dealing with three people: Narbo, the Christian; Marcus Caelius Prato, the owner of Lupo's; and someone else, someone with money.

"Narbo will never talk. Ask Corvus, if you don't believe me. Torture won't help. He's insane. Someone put him up to this. I don't think it was Caelius, though he's been to Judea, and maybe Narbo has, too. Caelius isn't wealthy—but a year ago he got the funds to open Lupo's. No one knows from where, and now he's suddenly flush enough to pay off Urien's debts? Where'd he get the money? And why?"

"That's your business."

"I know. And I'll find out. But you're still in danger until I do. If someone connects you—or one of your staff—with Narbo, it will look like you arranged for him to kill Maecenas, because you have the best motive. So far, we've been able to hush that up. But for how much longer? What if the papers resurface? You were going to be removed as governor. The dispatch was stolen, but a lot of money was left. And if any of this gets out to your enemies—either openly or on the sly—it will be all too easy for the Emperor to accuse you of treason."

The governor sat back down, slowly. Priscus pulled at his moustache, and looked at me like I was an unfriendly witness. He answered softly: "Has it occurred to you, Arcturus, that if we don't get a response to the Emperor soon, it won't matter what actually happened? That whoever is behind this may already have sent word to the Emperor that Maecenas was killed?"

"I know that. But the more you know, the safer you'll be. You'll know how to frame an answer. The Emperor will believe what he wants to believe. He always does. If he's out to get rid of Agricola, there's not much we can do to prevent it. But if he has an ounce of reason or sense left, he'll stall, because he knows how popular the governor is with the men. And he's busy with the Rhenus. He won't risk war unless he can really prove your guilt. And that will give us time to find the truth."

"Maybe he's right, Priscus." Agricola held his head in his hands and they were shaking. "Maybe we should wait."

The red-haired man shook his head stubbornly. "Let's work on a response. We may not need it—if Arcturus produces this mysterious third man for us—but it will help keep us focused."

The governor looked at me, his brown eyes bleary. He wasn't looking well. I'd seen him without food, without clean water, cut, shot, sore and exhausted. But not like this. "What do you want from me, Arcturus?"

"Just your trust, which I hope I have already. And your word that you won't torture Rhodri. The jail is miserable, but he's safer in there. He's one of two people, other than Caelius, who's seen this third man. When I get a lead, I'll need your help. I might have to send a message to you, and if it sounds strange, please just do what I ask."

He rubbed his forehead. "I was hoping it was all over. Maybe I wanted it to be."

I added gently: "I wish it were. Meanwhile, it would help the city's morale if you tell Meditor to end the curfew. They have one Briton and one Roman in official custody. That should be enough to prove it wasn't a British conspiracy, and yet not lose any face."

"All right."

I walked to the desk, and picked up his arm. It was heavy and lifeless. "You need rest. That's your doctor speaking. And here's the prognosis: Agricola is the greatest man of his time. He will complete the exploration and conquest of Britannia, and he will be remembered that way. He's going to live happily for many, many years, raise a handsome son, and enjoy the peace and prosperity he's fought for. That's your future, Governor. Don't argue with your doctor."

"I generally don't. I find I lose too easily."

The words helped him a little. I left them puzzling over a

document I hoped they'd never have to send. Lying to Domitian—or if he thought you were lying—was treason. If someone had done what Priscus suggested, and sent word to the Emperor about Maecenas, Domitian would automatically blame Agricola—he had the best of all reasons to kill the message and the messenger. But if Agricola then told him a different story, he'd use it as proof of a premeditated conspiracy to revolt, and have the governor arrested and killed. Wait or lie? We were foundering between Scylla and Charybdis, and the goddamn ship was leaking.

It was dark when I got home. It was always dark when I got home. I tapped on the outside door, and Brutius answered it. "*Dominus*—you're here!"

"I'm surprised myself. How's Pyxis?"

"Much better. The compresses have helped, and she's eating well. I don't think she will need the pain draught tonight." There was still straw from the kennel floor clinging to his brown curls.

I grinned. "Good." Agitated voices drifted in from the examination room.

"Is someone waiting?" Before he could answer, I pushed open the curtain.

Draco and Coir were arguing. When Draco saw me, he let go of Coir's shoulders, turned pink, saluted, and strode from the room. Coir watched him go, the corners of her mouth pinched, her tousled hair more tousled than usual.

"Wait, Coir. I want to talk to you."

She stood looking down at the floor, but her body was defiant. Brutius retreated into the *triclinium*. We were alone. I walked over to her.

"Yes, Master?"

She made it sound like a name you wouldn't want to use around your mother. I cleared my throat. "I'm glad you and

Draco are . . . together."

She met my eyes, then. "He's a good man."

"Yes, he is. I just wanted to let you know that I'm—I've—you're an excellent servant, and I want you to be happy, and if I can do something—"

"You can set me free."

"What?" I'd been expecting to buy her a new coat. I ran my fingers through my hair and took a deep breath.

"That's what Draco and I were arguing about. He doesn't think we're ready for freedom, neither one of us, but I told him I think we are. He says he couldn't support me, and he couldn't even support himself because he eats too much, to keep up his strength, and what would he do if he weren't your bodyguard, and what would you do, and I said we'd find a way. We'd go back to my village. But he's set against it."

I chewed my lip a little. "Well, he's got a point, Coir. You've learned a great deal, but the more you learn, the better your chances."

Her jawline was as stubborn as the curl sticking up in the wrong direction. "That may be, Master, but you asked. So I told you."

I held her chin in my face, and she lifted it as far away as she could.

"I'm sorry. I don't know how to say it without hurting you—I've already hurt you. I'll always care about you, Coir. But not the way you hoped." This was harder than I expected, and I tried not to shuffle. "Draco is a better man for you. I don't want you to leave, but if it will make you happy we'll talk about it. You, Draco and I."

She lowered her chin, and I removed my hand and rubbed my neck. "I was hoping you'd want to stay on, together with Draco."

"In the same house? With—her?"

"Gwyna. She's your *Domina.*" She looked into my eyes and knew better than to say anything else about "her."

"Well—" She unbent a little. "He is a good man. And he says he loves me." She smiled a small smile of power. "He says he always has."

"We can find a bigger room for you, rearrange things."

She giggled, a strange sound coming from Coir. "He says he likes it small." She suddenly flashed her eyes up at me and got businesslike again. "I'll stay. I want to keep learning."

I nodded, and wondered when she had become so cold.

"Will Bilicho live here? With Stricta?"

"I don't know. Have you seen them?"

She giggled again. "They're in his room."

I turned red. "All right. I'm glad you changed your mind."

She nodded. "Thank you, Master. I hope—she—feels the same way."

Coir walked out of the room, her head erect. I was hoping like hell for the same thing.

"She" was in the *triclinium* waiting for me, and for a second I felt like Lugh had stomach-punched me. She was wearing the aqua tunic I'd first seen her in. I couldn't keep my thoughts off her. Someone had started the furnace, and even my feet were getting hot.

Hefin was sitting beside her, innocent of the looks we exchanged over his head. I don't remember what I ate. All I could smell was lavender, and the sweetness of her skin, and I chewed and swallowed but didn't taste much other than anticipation. She complimented Venutius, which was what he'd been waiting for, and, like the man of the world that he was, he retreated to his domain and left us alone.

Hefin chattered about the dogs, the cats, playing with Brutius. All I could hear was the rustle of silk between her thighs, against her breasts. Her eyes crinkled at me. She was enjoying

269

herself. Finally, she sent Hefin to her room, and we were alone.

She led me to the *caldarium*. There were towels and some oil and a strigil waiting. And then she started to undress me.

"Wait—your *stola*—you'll get it wet—"

"I didn't know you worried about my wardrobe, Ardur." She was pressed against me, uncinching my belt. "You do smell a little like a goat."

"Keep leaning on me and I'll look like one, too."

She laughed, and kept going, and soon was standing in front of me, eyeing me critically. "Turn around."

On her tiptoes, she carefully lifted off the leather cord that held my mother's medallion. Then she turned me around again.

"You have a large bruise on your back. Get in the water."

I climbed in, while she wetted a cloth. Then she told me to stand up, and applied it to my side. I didn't know I hurt so much. She dripped the water down my back, squeezing the cloth against me gently with a squishing sound. It was about all I could take.

"Gwyna—"

"Now your hair."

She poured a pitcher over my head, while I sputtered. Twigs and grass fell out on my shoulders and chest. "You look like a wildman from the mountains."

I growled at her. "Maybe I am."

She scrubbed my neck with a rough sponge, and rubbed some salt all over me. Then she told me to rinse, and I did, and she beckoned me out. "You need oil."

"Wild men don't need oil. Come here."

She smiled and ignored me and said nothing. Her dress was getting wet, and I was getting out of control. I tried to take some deep breaths while she used her hands to spread oil on my back and chest. Then she went lower.

"Gwyna—!"

"You can control yourself, Ardur. You're a doctor, remember?"

I gritted my teeth. Finally, she finished, and started gently scraping with a strigil. The sound of it against my skin seemed loud, but my breathing was even louder. I couldn't look at her anymore.

"Get in and rinse."

I did as she directed, saying nothing. I swam to the other side and back. I needed the exercise. She was waiting with an open towel when I stepped out, and patted me dry. I was red all over, and not from the hot water.

"One more thing." She guided me to a folding chair. "Sit down. I'm going to shave you."

"What—"

"I'm quite good at it." She coated my days-old beard with oil, and deftly picked up a razor from a tray. "Lean your head back."

She was very good at it. Little by little, she scraped the dirty beard away from my chin and neck and upper lip. Then she rinsed me off with water—squeezing a towel and letting it run down my cheeks this time—and with her hands rubbed some oil into my entire face.

When she was done, she took me by the hand and led me through the back entrance directly into the bedroom. She stood before me, her silk gown clinging to her body, her hair damp and slightly curly from the moisture.

My hands were trembling. I started to undress her, but I couldn't stop them from shaking. She helped, and stepped out of her *stola*. I stood and looked at her.

I said: "Turn around." She did. But before she could complete a circle, I'd picked her up, and placed her on the bed, and her body was as I'd dreamed it would be. The moon blushed, and I didn't care where we were going, so long as I was with her, and I forgot everything but the taste of her skin

and the smell of her hair and how very, very good it was to be
alive.

TWENTY-FIVE

I woke up before dawn, and she was pressed against me, warm against my skin. I caressed the small of her back and her shoulders, and found her hips, and pulled her closer. I could feel her nipples. They were hard and I was getting there. She pushed herself on top of me, and then her hands were busy and then her mouth, and then she put her hands above her head, and mine were busy, too.

I made it last for as long as I could, which was never long enough. We clung to one another, her body hot, damp with the moist perfume of her skin still draped on mine. We went back to sleep.

I got out of bed late that morning, and thought: I could get used to this. But Agricola's face hung over us, and the face of the man who'd give anything to be in my place. And the other face, too, the strangely familiar man with the unfamiliar god, alone, staring at a wall, waiting for death and deliverance. So we got up and went in to breakfast.

Bilicho and Stricta were already there. The floor was still warm from the night before, though I doubted it would ever feel as cold as it used to. They were smiling, I was smiling, Gwyna was smiling, and we all looked ridiculous.

I said: "Brutius, tell Draco to come in here when he's through with his exercises." I could hear him outside, grunting. At least I hoped he was doing his exercises.

The food surprised me. Boiled eggs, fried wheat cakes, dates and dried plums. Maybe Venutius liked having more mouths to feed. Or maybe Gwyna hid the *garum*.

Hefin ran in like Hannibal was chasing him, and his sister hushed him, and told him to eat in the kitchen with Venutius and Brutius. He sulked a little, and threw us a couple of resentful looks on the way out. What the hell was I going to do with a ten-year-old? I bit into a wheat cake and decided to think about it later. After Maecenas. After Caelius. After we talked to Urien, and settled everything. And after I found out what happened at home while I was getting my kidneys crushed by Lugh.

"All right, Bilicho—start at the beginning, five days ago."

He looked ten years younger when Stricta smiled at him like that. Bilicho. Venus was going to get a big offering this year.

He swallowed the date in his mouth, and sipped some *mulsum*. "Not a lot to tell, Arcturus—I hope you're not disappointed. I never had the chance to follow up."

"Just tell me what happened." I wrestled my eyes away from Gwyna's hand reaching for a plum.

"Well—the first thing I did was—was check on Stricta." He turned red and looked at her. "I was worried someone might figure out she was at the temple. The priest didn't like me much, but when I told him I was your freedman—the doctor who'd been there before—he let me see her." He fumbled for her hand. "She was too thin, and I could see she wasn't sleeping. I told her you were away, and things were moving fast, and to be careful. Then I left."

"Next?"

"I went to see a silversmith I'd met once—remember that poison case a couple of years ago? Anyway, I figured he might know something about a mine and Maecenas without me trying to look up records. He didn't have anything, but he gave me the name of a lead dealer—a middleman, he buys up leaky pipes and old metal and then melts them down and probably resells

274

them as new. Anyway, he was more helpful."

He sipped again, and wiped his mouth. Stricta still didn't have much of an appetite, but she'd at least eaten a date and a cake. The raw edges of her face were beginning to smooth out. Bilicho leaned into her, and brushed her leg without knowing it, as if to make sure she was still there.

"He knew the Syrian by description, not by name. Said he used to buy lead from him. Our Maecenas was a mine contractor—probably the kind that underbids the lease from the government, then hires the cheapest labor or slaves about to croak their last in order to turn a profit.

"It was a good mine, too, somewhere in the hills near Aquae Sulis. The dealer's geography wasn't as specific as it might've been. At first the mine threw up some ore, but it ran out of silver about a year ago—lead was lead was lead. That's when Maecenas leased it. There's been a glut on the market, though, and it closed down about four months ago."

"Did your lead merchant know if Maecenas had any other business interests?"

Bilicho shrugged. "He was a little vague. Thought he'd remembered something about a perfume warehouse in Africa. He wasn't sure."

"Was the mine leased by Maecenas alone, or was he part of a *societas?*"

"I didn't ask. Does it matter?"

"It might. I'd like to know who his business partners were, if he had any."

He nodded. "I'll try to find out."

"So then what did you do?"

"Well, I was near the forum, so I thought I'd go see a banker and ask him about the money. There's one that doesn't cut your left leg off to mortgage the right one. Naturally, he does a small business, but I figured he'd know who'd use coins like that. On the way to his shop I ran into Mollius."

Draco came in from the back, breathing hard, and looking nervous. I called him over. "Sit down, Draco. I want to hear what happened when I was gone."

Coir was nowhere in sight. I snuck a glance at Gwyna. She was smiling again. I pulled my eyes away. Bilicho bit into an egg and somehow made it noisy. Then he continued.

"So Mollius said he'd ask around about Caelius, because you'd told him what Caelius had done." He looked at Stricta like she might break. "He wanted to help, and that gave me more time with the *argentarius*. Then we split up, and I got to the shop."

"What did the *argentarius* say?"

"Not a lot. He wanted to see the money, but you had it locked up, and I knew better than to show cash to a banker. Gold makes 'em go into rut, even the good ones. So Gleuco—that's his name—starts to pick his teeth, and hem and haw, and says he hadn't known Maecenas himself, you understand, but he was very surprised to find him carrying that much money, and that only a few of the large financiers would carry that much, the ones that could do business with equestrians and senators, not like him who had to be content to loan money to freedmen and slaves, and he went on like that for a while.

"So I said to him, 'Which financiers?' and he got vaguer. He said money like that almost certainly came from Rome, because it was the improved coinage. And only army paymasters and very rich merchants and big investors and government types— not small, honest *argentarii*—would carry that much around, and even then they'd use it to pay interest to another banker. Big people don't pay little people with that kind of money. That's why they go to money-changers, so they can get it in useful denominations.

"So I asked him again who the financiers were, and he waved

his hands around and said that the only ones he knew never stayed in Britannia for the winter. They went to Rome or southern Gaul, or some place more civilized than Londinium. And that was all I could get out of him."

I grunted. "It's enough. We're looking for someone who knew Caelius, and Maecenas and Narbo. An odd assortment of men. Not your typical investment dinner-party guests. So then what did you do?"

"I decided to spy on Caelius—go down to Lupo's and see if I could dig up anything. But when I got there, the place was shut tighter than a Vestal's—" He realized Stricta was next to him, and suddenly went pink. "Anyway, it was closed."

"So where was Caelius?"

"At my house, Ardur." Gwyna shivered a little. "He'd come that morning to see my father."

She looked up from the floor, and said it quietly. "I'm worried about him. He's been troubled lately, since the governor's visit. He was so happy—then more ill than ever. He won't let Meuric move him away from the fire, and he won't talk to me, or anyone.

"When Caelius showed up that morning, he gave my father receipts proving that the debts were paid. He left about half an hour later. I tried to stay out of his sight.

"Then my father called me in, and said that I was to marry Caelius. When I showed on my face what I felt, he got angry. He said he'd thought of everything. I wasn't to worry."

She looked down at her hands. "I am worried about him, Ardur."

"We'll see him, talk to him. Is that when you sent a message to Draco?"

She nodded. "Yes. I knew he was outside, and I thought if he could keep Caelius from coming in the house until you were home and could reason with my father—oh, I didn't know what to do, I was in a panic, and I couldn't stand to have that bastard in our home again. I was worried he'd try to hurt Hefin. So I sent Meuric outside to tell Draco to keep him away."

"And Caelius came back?"

"He tried." It was Bilicho who replied. "I followed him to Urien's in the afternoon. I'd given up on finding him, and was on my way home, but happened to pass by a jeweler's—an expensive shop. He was inside, looking at necklaces—jet and gold, lapis and gold, the nice stuff. I didn't want to let go once I'd caught the son-of-a-bitch, so I just tracked him straight back—to Gywna's. He'd bought the jet and gold one, I guess as a bribe for her."

Her face was hard. "I hope someone chokes him with it."

"So you stopped him, Draco?"

The large man spoke up promptly. "Yes, Master. I got in his way, and told him that no one inside wished to see him. He was very angry, but didn't do anything except threaten to have me flogged, and worse. He didn't know me from when we went that day, but he kept staring like he was trying to remember where he'd seen me."

"I watched the whole thing. It really got to Caelius, having Gwyna in his grasp and not being able to walk in and get her."

She squirmed, hearing Bilicho talking about it.

He said: "Draco and I thought it over, and we figured it would be best for him to stay the night, so I went home and sent Coir out with a couple of blankets for him. He slept in front of the door."

Draco hung his head. "That was the night somebody tried to break in."

Bilicho frowned, and squeezed Stricta's hand. "I was asleep. Still a little groggy from the headache, I guess. But I heard a crash—it was Brutius knocking over one of Venutius' pots—and I got up, and he was trembling all over and could barely talk.

Someone—he didn't see what size he was or anything—had tried to climb over the back wall, and had kicked Pyxis pretty hard.

"She was yelping, and he was starting to cry, and you weren't here and neither was Draco, and none of us slept any more that night. I checked all the outside rooms the next day to make sure he hadn't taken any poison or anything, but I guess Pyxis scared him off."

"I'm sure it was Narbo."

"I'm not shedding any tears when he's dead. Anyway, that worried me. And I was scared, and started thinking—about Stricta. And I didn't tell anybody about it, because she's still a slave, and if Caelius found out where she was, he'd tell Meditor.

"Meditor would cut off his own balls and sacrifice them to Jove if he could get something on you. Not that they'd bring much. But hiding a slave—even one that's maybe helping the governor—is a big, big something. I figured if I kept my mouth shut, no one would get in trouble except me. And I'm used to it." He looked at Stricta. Then he turned back to me, with a plea in his face.

"Someone was after us, or you, or the money, or something, and I wanted—I wanted her where I could look after her. So I got up early, and walked to the temple, and bribed the priest into smuggling in a note. I hoped she could read Latin. And she could. My Latin, anyway." They looked at each other, and I coughed.

What we were doing wasn't legal. Hiding a fugitive slave flouted the laws of the Roman Empire. I scratched my chin with my thumbnail. Not like the perfectly legal act of Caelius killing Galla.

"Stricta has to stay here, out-of-sight. When this is settled—when Caelius is settled—I think I can get her freed. As thanks for services rendered to the governor."

Stricta's soft voice answered me. Her deep-set brown eyes studied each of us in turn. "I will never be able to thank you—to thank all of you—for giving—for giving me life back."

Bilicho squeezed her hand, and they stared at each other again. I hurried it along, because they didn't look like they were going to wait for us to leave.

I asked: "How did you get away?"

"The procession. When we walked in front of the governor's palace, I pretended to fall, and slipped through the crowd. Some of the others helped me. Then I found my way here. To you. To Bil-i-cho."

She pronounced each syllable separately, and he beamed.

"What about you, Draco? When did Caelius come back?"

"The next morning. With Lupo. Lupo hates him. He would kill him if he could—and please forgive me for saying it, *Dominus*. All the other slaves would be killed if Lupo did, so he obeys.

"When he wrestled me, he didn't hold me with any strength. And he whispered to punch him in the left side of his face, where a tooth was loose. Caelius would beat him, but Lupo wouldn't help him get in the house. So we pretended to fight, and he pretended to lose."

Draco looked thoughtful for a moment. "There were a lot of people in the streets. The odds were on Lupo, five to one, so some people weren't happy with how it ended. A woman tried to throw a chamber pot on me, but I ducked and some of it hit Caelius. He was very angry."

I grinned. "I bet. Is that when he threatened you with the *vigiles?*"

"Yes. But the Mistress came out as soon as he left, with the little boy, and said she'd come home with me and wait for you."

Gywna shook her head. "I'd watched as much as I could

from the window. I tried to reason with my father, but he wouldn't talk to me. He kept saying he knew what he was doing, and when I tried to tell him what Caelius was capable of, he wouldn't talk at all. I'd already packed some clothes, so I said good-bye to him and took Hefin and left the house when I knew Caelius was gone." She looked far away for a moment. "I hope—" She paused, while we looked at her. Or at least I looked at her. She bit her lip. "Never mind, Ardur."

"So you came here, and the next day you found Stricta here, too." She turned red, and Stricta turned red, so I hurried on. "Whom Bilicho was hiding to protect everybody, and then Mollius came and told you Rhodri was arrested and then I got home."

"Yes. And now you must tell us what to do, Ardur."

I scratched my head. "I wish I knew. We still don't know why Maecenas was murdered, even if we have a good idea how. But the place to begin is Caelius. Maybe I can scare him into talking. I think he may be blackmailing someone—the man we don't know, the one with the money. That necklace wasn't a cheap little souvenir of Londinium. And then there's his payment of your father's debts." I looked at her. "We'll start there, in fact. You and I will go to Urien. He may know something about Caelius that can help us. Bilicho, can you find out about the mine? If Maecenas had any business partners?"

"I'll try."

"Good." I scratched my head again. "I keep thinking I've seen Narbo somewhere."

"He probably followed you. That's how he knew you were out of town, and why he decided to try to rob us that night."

"Yeah. Maybe."

Gwyna and I left a little later. The sun was smiling weakly, as if it were glad to be alive. It felt good after the drizzle the day before, but we kept our heads covered anyway. She was wearing an old cloak of mine which was much too big, but it kept her face and body better hidden than anything of her own.

The streets weren't busy but we didn't talk. I could feel how anxious she was to see her father. So was I. Caelius had some kind of hold on the old man, and I was going to break it. Along with Caelius himself.

The house was quiet. It looked forlorn, like a maiden aunt whose dinner guests all leave at once. I knocked on the door, and after a few moments Meuric answered. He was slightly out of breath and not too pleased to see me. But Gwyna stepped forward, and he said with surprise: "My lady! Your father will be happy you're home! He was talking about you this morning, before he sent me with the message."

She brushed past him, in a hurry.

I asked: "What message?"

His mouth turned down in a strong grimace, and he spit out the door before shutting it. "To that man. The one he betrothed my lady to."

"Caelius? What was it?"

Before he could answer, I heard a noise, not particularly loud, but one I'd heard before. Gwyna had gone ahead of me, into the main room by the fire. It was a rumbling cross between a groan and a gasp, a noise that was heavier than a gold throne and more final than a handful of dirt over a coffin. I ran.

She was standing in front of Urien. He looked like he was sleeping. But the posture was wrong. He'd tried to get up, maybe tried to call for help. His legs wouldn't work, so he'd slumped over, as if he were cold and the fire was warming him. But nothing would ever warm him again. There was a knife wound in his side, and a slow drip of blood had made a pool on the wooden floor.

She was in shock and breathing hard, her eyes wide and dry and empty. I knelt down. He was still breathing, but it wouldn't be for long. His pale, milky eyes were still open. He was watching his daughter and then he looked at me.

"Gwyna—he wants to say something."

She moved very deliberately, as if any motion would make her crack and fall apart, and knelt by him, the hem of the cloak slowly soaking her father's blood from the floor. Urien's breath was ragged. He'd been bleeding for a while. The sharp features were beginning to blur, and the hawk-blind eyes groped for something to hold on to, something to see, but were slipping backward into nothing.

"Daughter." A dry, rattling gasp. Then more breaths. Not many left. His eyes moved to me. I could feel him trying, feel him taxing his body for one last battle.

"Caelius. Wrong message."

He closed his eyes, and I thought we'd lost him. I picked up his hand, and Gwyna was holding her mouth and shaking all over. But he opened them again, and there was less worry on his face. Maybe even a little peace.

"Daughter. Proud." She broke down then, and sobbed, still shaking, and held on to him, the blood of his wound brushing a macabre pattern on her cloak.

"Why don't you do something? He's dying, goddamn it, Ardur, my father is dying!"

I shook my head and stroked her hair. Meuric stood by, frozen and numb, the dull gold of Urien's prize of valor gleaming in the firelight. He never regained consciousness. His fierce face relaxed into what he must have been before he was sick, before he was old and bitter and disappointed and lonely. Before he lost his money, before he lost his wife. He died in his daughter's arms.

Meuric said: "I was in the kitchen. Sioned is at the market, buying some food. I thought he was sleeping." His bearded face crumpled, and his mouth opened to make a wail, but no sound came out.

"Tell me the message you took."

He looked at me but didn't see me. But he was an old servant, and servants are trained to respond.

"That he was to come see him. The Master. He did at once, returned here with me. I left them alone together."

"Was that the last time you saw Urien?"

He stared down at the old man's body. Gwyna was cradling it in her arms, a low keening sound coming from her lips. He didn't need to answer me.

Sioned opened the door, and started to walk into the room and stopped. Her knees began to fold underneath her, and I strode over and held her up by the arm.

"Your master's dead. Murdered. I'm going to settle the one who did it. Take care of her. You and Meuric—lay him out. Put his best clothes on him."

She nodded, again her training keeping her upright. She walked slowly over to Gwyna, and put her arms around her. Gwyna started to sob into Sioned's chest, and they held on to one another, rocking back and forth. Meuric watched dully, his stained beard ragged in the flickering light.

"Meuric. Leave the women here. Go to my house—the big one by the river—and tell my freedman what happened. Tell him I'm going to see Caelius. Can you remember that?"

He nodded dumbly.

"Go. And hurry."

He hovered for a moment, and then turned, and walked out the door. I hoped he could find my house. But I knew he couldn't hurry, and I didn't care. I wanted to deal with Caelius by myself.

Twenty-Six

People must have passed me on the way. I didn't see any. I could only see one face, belonging to the smooth, pleasant, well-bred Marcus Caelius Prato.

The whorehouse was still closed. A sign announced that it would be reopening with new girls after the Kalends. I tried the door. It was bolted. So I started kicking it, and by the time I had one plank out, Pigeon-Chest opened it, looking terrified.

"Where is he?"

"W-Who? Lupo? He's—"

"You know goddamn well who I mean. Caelius."

He trembled a little. "Upstairs."

"Show me."

I followed him to the landing. The hallway still stank. He walked to the left, and then I saw how Caelius had appeared so suddenly, in front of Rhodri, staring at the pouch on Maecenas' side.

Right by the stairs was what I thought was a wall. I'd never looked at it closely; I'd tried not to look closely at much in that place. But there was a thin gap, door height, cut into the wall, and a little latch to hold it in place.

Pigeon-Chest watched me, trying not to wet his pants. I said: "Don't knock."

He twisted the latch, and with his fingernails, pried open the door a little. I shoved him out of the way and walked through.

It was a small room, a room from which Caelius could see

everything that happened, or at least a body being dragged downstairs and a man getting scared and hiding in a room, and another man running into him. There were peepholes facing the hallway, peepholes to watch the whores through in the adjacent room. He'd seen Narbo use the knife. He'd seen the other man, too, had spoken to him and made him angry. If the rooms in between this one and Maecenas' were empty, he could've seen everything.

Right now, he wasn't seeing much. He was lying on his side on the floor, and his throat had been slit, and not by an expert.

The rattling sound didn't bother me much. I wanted to watch him die. People usually paid for the privilege. And standing in the corner, holding a bloody knife, was Lupo, the giant, Lupo, the slave Caelius hid behind. He looked down at him, his eyes glazed, and watched his master's blood drain.

I walked toward Caelius. I thought of Urien, and Gwyna, and I stood there, staring into his eyes. They knew better than to beg, but they did anyway. Then I thought of Galla. And I was glad it was slow, and messy.

Then I thought of Bilicho.

I knelt by the bastard, and propped him up. I said: "This is for myself, Caelius. You're not worth mercy."

I wrapped his open throat with a mantle still lying on the ground. He must've worn it when he killed Urien. He'd lost too much blood; I wouldn't be able to save him, even if I could make myself. The rattling gasps were getting weaker.

"You're on the way to hell, Caelius. You'll get a senator's seat for the games, finally—the ones that last forever. Maybe you'll even be a main act."

I leaned closer to his face. All I could smell was blood.

"Don't drag along the innocent. Show some pity for once in your worthless, goddamn life. Maybe you'll get a little yourself. I can't give you any. You're not good enough, and neither am I."

The gasps were shorter now. The mantle was turning red. It wouldn't be long.

"It's your last chance. Save yourself a day's worth of pain. Who did this to you? I know it wasn't Lupo. He wouldn't have been so sloppy."

His eyes burned into mine. He still had a little fire left over for hate. But fear, fear of that dark place Romans see when they can't sleep at night, the place of childhood nightmares and grown-up pain, crept behind them. He couldn't talk, so he did what he could.

Grunting with pain and effort, he forced his fingers to crawl, groping toward a coin on the floor. It was a gold *aureus*, like the ones I'd found on Maecenas. His fingers grasped it, and he closed his eyes, spent, and then opened them again. They were getting glassy. Then he opened his palm, the coin sweaty, and looked at me as if the doors were shutting at last. There were no peepholes in hell.

I closed his eyes. Lupo was still staring down, holding the knife, when I heard heavy breathing behind me, and running footsteps, and Mollius was there. The doors were shutting on all of us.

The *vigil* was out of breath. "My God, Arcturus. What happened?"

"Not what you think. I didn't kill him. Neither did Lupo." I stood up, and gently removed the knife from the big man's hand. It was a short, thin blade of exquisite workmanship. Expensive. A collector's piece.

"How did you get here so fast?"

"I was at your house. To tell you the curfew was lifted." He was staring at Caelius still holding the coin in his palm.

"Where was Bilicho?"

"Out somewhere. Then the old man came by—he was going from house to house, I thought he was a beggar. Draco recognized him, and he told us Urien had been killed and you'd gone to see Caelius Prato."

"Caelius killed Urien."

"How do you know?"

"Ask the old man. Urien sent Caelius a message to come see him, he did, and that's the last Meuric saw Urien alive. Then Caelius came back here, met someone who can afford beautiful daggers, demanded more money, got it for a few seconds, and then collected a little interest."

Pigeon-Chest was standing behind the door, his jaw open.

"You there. Come in here."

He obeyed.

"Your master is dead."

He was silent for a few minutes, his puffy chest heaving. Then he looked up. "I'm glad he's dead." He and Lupo met each other's eyes for a moment.

"Did you see anything?"

He shook his head. "He left this morning when the old man came, and was nervous-like when he got back. Paced up and down, up and down, in this room. Told me to go downstairs and stay there."

"Any other slaves? Girls downstairs?"

"Only three left. He's been selling them off for labor. Wanted a whole new group next year—he's been boasting about making the place into a real palace."

"Anyone else?"

"Just me and Grotius. The one who runs the bar. We keep to ourselves and do what he says. He's got ways to make you hurt." The little man shivered.

"Did anyone else come in?"

He thought a minute. "No one by the front way. Except you. But before that, I heard him go down the backstairs. I think he came up with someone else, because I heard him raise his voice a little."

"Did you hear what he said?"

"No. He sounded scared." He said it with amazement. The slave killer had been scared of something.

"Then it was quiet again. Then Lupo said he was going upstairs to ask him." He turned toward the big man, who looked small huddled in the corner, staring at his reflection in the puddle of blood.

"Why did you come upstairs, Lupo? What did you want to ask him?"

He spoke heavily. "To sell me. But I saw man leaving—down backstairs. Very quiet. So I knock. No answer. Then I open door." His eyes kept getting pulled back to Caelius' half-sawn throat.

"Could you see the face of the man who left?"

He shook his massive head, and blinked his one eye. "It was covered. Dark cloak, very fine."

"Why did you pick up the knife?"

"Don't know."

Mollius spoke quietly. "I'm going to have to report this, Arcturus."

"They'll arrest Lupo."

"I know."

The giant was still staring dumbly at the body. It was strange to see something you'd dreamed of doing happen, done by someone else.

"Do what you have to do, Mollius. We'll all do what we have to do."

He reddened for a moment, studied me, and turned on his heel and left. A shrill whistle was starting to escape from somewhere inside Pigeon-Chest.

"But if he's arrested, they'll kill all of us! All of us!"

"Did you ever see him speak to a thin, dark soldier? A legionary?"

He was wringing his hands together and starting to yelp. "They'll kill us, they'll torture us!"

I slapped him across the face, and he quieted down. "Did you see such a soldier?"

"I—I think so."

"He liked to wear a bright gold pin and a green scarf."

"Y-yes. I know the one. He's been here, off and on, for a few months. And—and the night before the Syrian came, he—the Master—told me to take a message to the soldier. To come here."

"That was when?"

"Last day of the Saturnalia. We had a big party."

"Did you go to the fort?"

He nodded.

"Did the soldier come?"

"He got here late, but we still had lots of people because of the festival. He talked to the Master for a long time. Then he came back the next day, and was here when the Syrian arrived. He went straight upstairs to see him. I don't know how long he stayed."

"Did you give that end room to the Syrian on purpose?"

"The M-Master told me to. And all the rooms in between this one and it, he told me to keep empty."

The peepholes. Every room would have them. "Did you see him again? The soldier."

"No. I didn't see him that—that night. I—I cleaned up the room, though, afterward. He told us to tell anyone who asked that the Syrian had left. And—and he hit Stricta. I think he was angry, because she saw something that night, but she never told us."

"How much blood was there?"

"A little in the room, and some in the hallway to the stairway and down." He started to whine again. "What will happen to us?"

I said: "I'll do what I can."

I left them there, the big man and Pigeon-Chest. The *vigiles* would come, and they'd take them and hold them, and torture them, and then not believe them, and then kill them and the women and the bar man. Any crime that smacked of even a possibility of slaves killing a master—no matter how vile the master might be—the Romans were always eager to see through to the end. There were no innocent slaves in Rome.

I walked back to Urien's house. Gwyna wasn't crying. The shock was protecting her. They'd laid Urien on his bed, dressed in his best clothes, a moth-eaten robe with a mink fur edge wrapped around him. They stood and stared at him, the old man and his wife and the daughter. There was no comfort I could give her. There was no comfort in death.

We walked home in silence. When we opened the door, Brutius handed me a message. It was from Corvus. I read it, quickly. Then I took Gwyna to see Stricta, who was waiting for her in Bilicho's room. The dark Egyptian held the blonde woman, while they both cried together in a bond of shared pain that is a wholly feminine thing. I shut myself in my bedroom, and opened the chest.

I kneeled, and let the gold coins I'd found on Maecenas trickle through my hands. I looked at the scrap of message I pried from his stiff fingers. I rolled around the broken point of Apollo's crown on my palm. The *latrunculi* game was almost over, and all the moves were blocked except one.

Four people dead. Only two of them deserved it.

A man driven mad. A bravely foolish one in jail.

A cracked skull, a black eye, some broken ribs. A soldier's punctured gut.

An injured dog. A woman in mourning.

And now, six more people—slaves—to be killed. More death. It had to end now.

There was a scratch on the door and it was Bilicho. He'd been told.

"Caelius and Maecenas were partners in the mine."

I nodded, absentmindedly. I was writing out two messages. Bilicho waited, as I rolled and sealed them with wax and my ring, and he watched me, puzzled.

"Deliver these for me."

He raised an eyebrow when he read the names.

"Are you sure? Arcturus, have you—have you figured all this out? Who's behind it? Who the third man is?"

My smile was painful, and a little twisted. "Rome, Bilicho. Rome is the third man."

He looked at me with worry on his face.

"I'll explain later. Just go."

He left, and I lay in my bed for a while, staring at the ceiling.

Twenty-Seven

It was dark when I got up, and I wondered where Gwyna was. She was sitting in the *triclinium*, her hands still and simple in her lap, staring at the fire.

"I have to go."

She turned to look at me, and asked the question as if she didn't care about the answer.

"Where?"

"It doesn't matter. This business." I sat next to her and held her hands. "I want you to know something. Your father was trying to protect you. That's why he was killed."

A spark of life came into her face.

"You think so?"

"I know so. He had some sort of plan against Caelius—him letting you marry him was part of it. He was trying to take care of you. He always did."

She looked at me, and her eyes filled with tears. "Thank you, Ardur."

I held her hand to my lips and left. I wasn't sure whether it had happened that way, but it didn't matter. Urien changed his mind—that's why Caelius killed him. It didn't matter to anyone when he'd changed it—anyone except his daughter. So the record would stand like I said it did.

The streets were empty, and the air was cold. The last day of the year. *Vale*, a.u.c. 836. *Ave*, 837: *morituri te salutamus*. The guard at the procurator's palace let me in immediately. The entrance hall was as still as the city. Except for Domitian. There he was, gloating quietly, the man behind it all.

I turned left toward the large record room. It was the heart of Roman bureaucracy, a center of the palace. Four doors, one on every wall, opened to other pathways, even to the apartments, in case someone felt the need to file something in the middle of the night.

Standing in front of the room, waiting for me, was the procurator, Numerius Sallustius Lucullus.

"Arcturus—I got your message. I can't believe it. I won't believe it. Even if you have proof, do you know what you're doing? The Emperor won't believe you. Agricola is one of his best generals—it doesn't make any sense."

"I don't expect him to believe me. That's why I need you. You deal with him directly. If I have to take down the governor—my patron, my friend, the man who's been like a father to me—I need someone powerful to back me up. I don't like this any more than you do."

He nodded, the lines around his mouth grim. "Let's go in. What are we looking for?"

"A piece of the document. It was brought in today—one of the temple soldiers found it with Narbo's things. He must've been holding on to it like an insurance policy."

"What do you mean?"

"It's from the message Maecenas was carrying—and proof that the governor had Narbo kill him. Agricola would do anything to stay in power—and the Emperor was going to remove him, send him packing. This paper proves it. And Narbo will talk, if we confront him with it."

Lucullus shut the door carefully behind him, and walked to the center of the room, his brow wrinkled, shaking his head.

"How do you know it's in here, in my records room? If it's so dangerous to him, why wouldn't the governor destroy it immediately?"

"Can you tell me a better place to hide a record than a record room? Not even you could find it, if you didn't know where to look. I had my man plant it earlier today. I haven't seen it yet. The governor doesn't know—no one knows except us and the soldier who found it, and neither he nor my slave can read. But we need to get it before the soldier talks. I've only got so much money." I licked my lips and tasted sweat. "I made sure of everything before I got you involved."

The little man's face crumpled, while his eyes searched the rolls of documents. "I don't like it, Arcturus. Not at all. And before I agree to anything, I want to see this paper. Where is it? Where do we start?"

I waited a minute, while his eyes flicked back and forth, and made my voice soft. "A long time ago. With a little boy playing soldier, a little boy who always dreamed of leading an army."

He stopped then, and turned to me, a funny look on his face. "What are you talking about?"

"Or maybe six years ago. When Agricola was made governor, and year after year after year went by, and he stayed on. While you watched."

Lucullus' eyes got harder and he forgot about the document.

"Or maybe the day when Domitian appointed you procurator. You, born a senator, to a lowly equestrian job. No armies for you, Lucullus. You got to push around numbers. And you hated it."

His hand went toward his sword. I pretended not to notice.

"Of course, that was before you realized how much money you could make as a procurator. Money was almost as good as an army command. Because money let you buy things. It let you control things. People, for instance. You collected them . . . along with your weapons."

He tried to bluff. He wasn't sure how much of it was a guess.

"What is this, Arcturus? A game?"

I wiped my hand across my forehead. It was hot in the room. He gripped the sword hilt tighter.

"Yeah, a game. A game of ambition and greed called your life. You figured you'd studied battles for long enough. It was time to lead one for a change. But the gutless Emperor didn't listen, did he, Lucullus? He wouldn't give you what you deserved. So you decided to take it for yourself."

His forehead wrinkled like the sum didn't total. I wondered how long he was going to keep up the act. "If you're accusing me of something—"

"Conspiracy. Murder. Treason. If I think of any more, I'll let you know."

He inhaled sharply, making a shrill sound while his cheeks sucked air. His eyes kept getting pulled to my sword. By now, my hand was on it. Sweat was starting to crawl out of his forehead. His voice was the dry whisper of snakeskin.

"You can't prove anything. And there's nothing to prove."

I eyed him thoughtfully. "Maybe I'm not looking for proof."

His eyes strayed back down to my sword again, before he dragged them to my face, a little defiantly. "What is it exactly that you think you know? And know enough to be crucified for?"

The sweat was starting to drip down my back, but I couldn't afford to squirm. Not now.

"You collect people, Lucullus. Ones you can twist into tools until they're broken. A year ago, you gave a mine contract to a freedman and sometime messenger whose loyalty to Domitian came cheap. Or so you thought. And you set him up in partnership with a cruel bastard who craved power however he could get it—a little like you, except he liked to get his hands dirty. He wanted his family's money and position back. Your sense of humor made you stick him in a whorehouse."

He let go of his sword pommel and leaned against a record shelf. Some tax records fell and skidded to the floor. He didn't pick them up. His voice was even.

"Awarding contracts is my job."

I nodded. "Sure. But you want a bigger job. So you kept collecting. That poor son-of-a-bitch Narbo. He was easy, because he didn't want money. So you whispered in his ear, about his god, his fellow believers. And you spread some rumors about Domitian killing Christians, and that made it easy. You owned Narbo, almost as much as his god did.

"You got him to the fort, so he'd be close by. You used him to do what you can't do: kill like an expert. Narbo was your best weapon. I even saw him the day I came to question you."

I raised my hand to my chin in a fluid motion and the procurator's right jerked back down to his pommel. I scratched where the beard was growing and stared hard at him.

"Then you tried to buy someone else. An old native chieftain named Urien. You used Caelius to bring him in . . . and Caelius had his own reasons for getting close. Urien thought the world had forgotten him, and he wanted a little attention. And Caelius flattered him, made him feel important and special."

He was busy trying to swallow the spittle on his lips.

"Maecenas, Caelius, Narbo and Urien. Those are the ones I know about. They were your tools, your *latrunculi* pieces. And a few months ago, after Domitian's triumph, you figured out how to work it. So you put them into play. You heard rumors, Lucullus—the garbage you dislike so much."

His breath was coming out harder, and I felt his arms tense. But he still didn't say anything.

"While Domitian's captives shuffled through Rome, you thought up a plan. Maecenas could get the commission for delivery. You could promise him money, women . . . even a particular woman. And you know, it might have worked. Except for Urien. You never really owned him. He was able to get out a few words after Caelius stabbed him. Caelius was in a hurry, and never thought the old man could last that long.

"Urien said 'Wrong message.' And, after a while, I understood."

He made a move, but I was on him with my sword against his throat. He small teeth shrank against his lips and he stared at me, stared at the *gladius*. I lowered the blade to his stomach, and kept going.

"Nothing made sense. Why Maecenas was killed, why the message wasn't found. Until I realized what Urien meant. Maecenas wasn't carrying orders to remove the governor. He was carrying an order from the Emperor to keep Agricola here—indefinitely."

I lowered the sword to the ground. "End of the game, Lucullus. You lose."

He glared for a moment, his shoulders thrust forward in front of his narrow chest. Then he relaxed suddenly, leaning against the wall. His voice was the wheezy sound of dry bones crunching. And it chilled me.

"I've always enjoyed *latrunculi*. But you're out of your element, and this isn't a game. It's politics." He looked at me with contempt. "And you're not a killer."

I reached over and pulled his sword out. It was ornate and gold-plated, with rubies in the hilt.

"Don't be too sure of me. I'm full of surprises."

He smiled sourly. His eyelids drooped, but his grey eyes never left my face.

"I don't like making mistakes. They're messy, and I don't like mess. So tell me the rest—what you *think* you know. Maybe I'll have your woman sold to a better class of whorehouse."

My hand went for his throat before I could stop it. His face was starting to turn purple, and when I pried my fingers off, he staggered and knocked a few more tablets over, his chest gulping like a beached fish.

"You're no killer," he croaked. "You're weak, like all your kind. You're going to die, Arcturus. You can kill me now and hope you won't get caught, or I'll have you hung upside down with nails in your wrists. There won't be anything left to bury, and no one left to bury it."

I took a step closer. "You forget about the money."

He choked, and spat out something on the floor. His eyes got bigger. "What do you mean?"

"The money you hoarded at Domitian's triumph. The money Narbo forgot when he killed Maecenas. The money he tried to steal when he broke into my house. That money. It left a trail, and you're at the end of it."

His breath was slowing down, and he leaned backwards, bracing himself, his palms making sweaty marks on the wall.

"All right. That's—that's useful to me. Not that you can do anything about it. What else?"

There was still a little fear in his face. But not enough. I unclenched my left fist, and started to walk back and forth in front of him, while his little grey eyes tried to follow.

"You're arrogant. You overlook people. You started a phony rumor about Agricola's recall when you found out Domitian's plans at the triumph. Maecenas was a good informer, and he'd get more, if he could convince the Emperor to let him deliver the message in person. His bait was plenty of *aurei* and Urien's daughter." I rubbed my jaw. "Urien didn't like that."

"That old bast—"

I took another step toward him and his mouth shut tight. "Urien was sick and bitter, and got some pleasure from being involved and important again. Caelius used him to help spread the gossip—and to get close to Gwyna. But that didn't mean the old man would sell out his daughter. Maybe he wanted to play it both ways. So he encouraged her not to see me in a way that all but guaranteed she would. And that still worked for you. Because she unknowingly fed me the wrong information. The false rumor."

I paused. His smile was strained, and he licked his lips but this time said nothing.

"But then Agricola went to see the old man. And he started to change his mind, about the governor, about Caelius. His daughter told him what Caelius had done to a whore he owned. And Urien figured he could trap Caelius, because he had been a real general, once upon a time. But he forgot he couldn't fight anymore. So Caelius did what he always did—he struck him down, and sent word to you."

Lucullus stared at me for a minute, hesitating. Then his face relaxed, and got chatty, as if it were dinner conversation. "Caelius was rash. He wouldn't listen. And he irritated me, killing that whore. Needless, and too much attention." He gave me a patronizing look. "I won't pretend you weren't a nuisance, with all that fretting over slaves and natives. Caelius' mistake made it worse."

I spoke carefully. "What happened with Maecenas? Did he want more money?"

Lucullus sighed, as if he'd just discovered an error in a long column of computation.

"Always more money. Like Caelius. When Narbo saw him the night he arrived, he told him he'd sell off the message to the highest bidder—Agricola or his friends would be glad to know his job was so secure."

"So Maecenas tried to cross you, and you decided to kill him and the message. But why the mithraeum?"

He was in a talkative, indulgent mood now. "The temple was Narbo's idea. He was to get Maecenas to show him the papers—so we knew Domitian hadn't changed his mind. Then

300

he'd stab Maecenas. I wanted the body left at the whorehouse, so it would look like a simple robbery, but Caelius wanted more money for that. So Narbo thought of the mithraeum."

Lucullus shrugged, and ran his tongue over his teeth.

"He hated how popular Mithras is with the soldiers. The more I thought about it, the more I liked it. Agricola's temple would be defiled, and his men might even come to suspect him of something. Or at least each other. The native New Year was a lucky coincidence—and those knots Narbo used were a helpful touch."

He frowned. "But then that native interfered, and Narbo panicked. He was dragging the body down the hallway, and the fight broke out, and he got scared and hid, and the boy saw him. And worst of all, he forgot to take the money."

"Smart of you to figure out I had it. But not so smart to send Narbo."

He shrugged. "You weren't there. It was worth a chance. Not like the sword switch. That was his idea. Although from what I understand, it very nearly worked." He looked at me as if looking would make me go away. "He and Caelius were getting worried. But if they'd just waited—"

"They'd already turned on you. Maybe you're not the general you think you are. They wanted more money, and kept biting your ankles until they got it. Or you killed them. It would've been cheaper to pay."

I looked at him thoughtfully. "I wondered why Agricola's enemies weren't running to tell the Emperor. If Maecenas' murder meant big trouble for the governor, why keep quiet? An enemy wouldn't kill a messenger bringing bad news. Much safer to sit and wait for the message. Of course, it made sense when I realized what the message actually was."

The smile was brittle. "No one likes mistakes, but the great ones always learn. I'm not too proud to learn, even from you.

And nothing you've said will ever matter to anyone else."

I said it gently, and took my sword out once more. "I'm not done, Lucullus." His eyes focused on the edge of it. He was sweating again.

"You want to be governor. You've waited for six years, and you weren't going to wait for six years more. Even if it meant causing a civil war. It was time for your rightful place in the world, and nothing—not Maecenas' greed, not Caelius' blackmail, not Narbo's madness—nothing was going to stop you."

I took another step closer, and he retreated, his eyes thin and tight. My fist hurt from where it was holding the sword. He wasn't sure what I was capable of anymore. I wasn't sure, either.

"You planted that slipper on Narbo during one of your meetings. If anyone found it, they'd know they caught the killer—and stop looking for anyone else. And then there was Rhodri. He wasn't part of your plan, but he worked for you, anyway. He was native, he was there, he had motive, and he ran. Narbo and Rhodri. Two sacrificial calves, ready for your war god. Two deaths for Maecenas' murder would be enough. Everyone would forget the third man. Why should they believe a madman, a Roman hater and an Egyptian whore? Yeah, Lucullus—I don't know what Caelius told you, but Stricta got away."

He leaned against the wall, and raised a hand to wipe his forehead. The fingers were trembling. "Are you through?"

"Not yet. Because now we come to tonight. You couldn't be sure Narbo wouldn't talk, babble something about the plan. And it worried you. So you got a message to him earlier today, something that probably told him Domitian was killing Christians again, and suggesting he not wait to join them. Yeah—the message worked, since you're keeping track.

"But then I sent you another message, and you were puzzled. What if Narbo *hadn't* killed himself? What if the orders he'd snatched from Maecenas' fingers weren't destroyed? You couldn't risk the real will of the Emperor coming to light, not after all your planning."

I stood over him, and thought about how easy it would be. His eyes searched the room again, this time looking for an escape.

"You couldn't get word from the fort, to see if your plan had worked. Everyone's celebrating the end of the year, and besides—Corvus was smart enough to keep the hanging a secret. To everyone but a few, including me. We'd have eventually traced the message you sent him. Another mistake. Like killing Caelius. Amateur job, particularly leaving the knife behind."

His shoulder blades touched the wall. His mouth pulled open into a grimace, while a drop of sweat rolled down his cheek and fell in.

"No, Lucullus, you're desperate. You've murdered two men in one day because you got scared and you wanted to save an *aureus* or two when you could've afforded a few more months of blackmail."

I got in his face, and his eyes were big and his breath was shallow and this time I could smell the fear on him.

"You're no soldier. You're a money-pusher. You're good at using people. Too bad you ran out."

He raised his face to mine, trying hard to breathe, trying not to watch the sword. "What exactly do you think you can do about it?"

"Let Agricola know."

He was silent for a minute, then he almost fell, and wrapped his arms around his chest and laughed. When he was done, he wiped his eyes. Relief smoothed his face again.

"It's over. You don't have anything left. I told you, Arcturus, this isn't *latrunculi.* It's politics. Why did you bring me here? I admit, it's a clumsy trap, and one I fell into. But you don't have many choices. Only one, really. You can kill me, and die yourself, and that's all you can do. And you won't kill me. You can't." He let himself bask in it, gloating a little.

"You think the governor will believe you? And if he did, do you think he can do something about it? So some people got killed. So what? A whore? A pimp? A freedman even Domitian won't overly miss? No one cares. They'll think the slaves murdered Caelius. Narbo killed himself, and saved me the trouble, and even if they trace the messenger, he won't know who I was. Nor will they care to find out. It's over and done with. Agricola will face Domitian with a lie—responding to the wrong message in the wrong way—Domitian will get suspicious, and recall him. Or they'll start a war. Either way, I've still won. He'll make me governor. I'll get command."

I took a step backwards. His face was flushed, his eyes bright, his smile secure. I felt sick.

"I wonder how many more of you are out there. Every crooked law suit, every burned down building. Every trumped-up war." I looked at him. "It's your face I'll see, Lucullus. You and all the small grey men just like you."

He laughed again. "You won't be seeing much of anything, Arcturus. You're so—British. I told you—this is politics. Agricola would've done the same thing."

A door on the right wall opened, and the governor stepped inside. "*Salve,* Lucullus."

The procurator turned pale, and pressed himself backward, his hands and feet flat against the wall. Avitus stepped quietly out of the other door behind him, and stood blocking it. The governor didn't look at me; he stared at Lucullus.

"I think you should go back to Rome. You're not feeling well—unable to perform your duties. Have the Emperor appoint an interim procurator for however long he wishes me to stay. We still don't know how long that will be, do we?"

I counted five beats. Avitus' eyes were fixed on Lucullus. The procurator looked from one to the other and sucked his cheek. "Why should I?"

"Because I don't think you'd be comfortable in Britannia. At least while I'm still governor. You might meet with an accident."

He whispered: "You wouldn't dare."

Agricola replied with a shrug: "Others would."

Avitus took a step closer. The governor looked up at me. "You can go now, Arcturus."

"Remember what I asked."

He nodded. "I'll see that it's done."

Lucullus' eyes darted back and forth. He seemed smaller than he did a minute ago, small and grey and brown and full of venom. He muttered to Agricola: "You'd have done the same thing."

I walked out. I couldn't hear what the governor answered. I didn't want to.

I left them discussing politics. Lucullus would obey, because he had no choice. He was out of people to use, and he didn't want to fall in the street and break his neck. Domitian would appoint an interim procurator, and look at all of them with fresh suspicion in his eyes. And Rome would go on, the same scenes reenacted in different cities, greed and power and lust and money and desperate people, all tools in the hands of the right men.

They'd get their page in the annals, the mention in the history books, holding death by the throat through eternity by the grace of a papyrus leaf. It's funny how many men will kill for the sake of immortality.

The light was warm, and they were waiting for me when I walked in the door.

Epilogue

The rain was falling lightly on the third day after the Kalends of Ianuarius, the new year 837. In Britannia, the water dampened the ground, but in Rome it formed puddles that lashed and eventually broke against the Emperor's palace, leaving a small, wet stain.

We were celebrating the *cena novendialis,* the last day of mourning for Galla. Venutius prepared a feast: roasted pigeon, stuffed hare, oysters and boiled venison, honey-cakes, chestnuts and dates. The wine was the best my cellars had.

Urien had gone to his god the day before. The pyre was tall, stocked with seasoned oak and yew. Gwyna, Hefin and I, together with Meuric and Sioned, watched until our eyes burned and we could see the gold of his *phalerae* start to melt. A lot of natives came.

Rhodri was there, too, and we grasped arms, and he didn't look at her until she put her hand on his shoulder, and then he had to, but he'd have to go away somewhere. It was too hard to look at her and not have her. Madoc spoke a few words for Urien, and laid mistletoe on the ashes.

The rite was Trinovantian, but the gravesite would be Roman. I commissioned a replica of his house to be built in the cemetery. We'd load it with jars of mead and salt pork, and the pokers and prongs that always kept his fire burning. His tombstone would talk about the battles he'd fought for Claudius. Agricola was coming for the *cena.*

The governor wasn't there today. The business of Empire building had been put aside: it was time to take it up again. Roads, temples, plans for the summer. But Galla had a full crowd. Bilicho and Stricta, of course, and Draco and Coir and Brutius and Venutius. And Lupo, and Caelius' last three whores, and Pigeon-Chest and the barkeep. I never did know their names.

They were free. I'd asked Agricola to free them and give the whorehouse to Lupo. It would be his in more than name, now, and a much cleaner business. The women would keep a percentage of their earnings, and who knows—maybe find a better life.

Gwyna and I planned to hold a ceremony after Urien's mourning. We didn't need one: she was a citizen, thanks to her father. But it was something we wanted to do, and it would be easier on Hefin that way. Stricta was officially a freedwoman, and she and Bilicho could follow us into the terrifying world of matrimony.

We'd talked about what to do with Urien's house. Then Gwyna thought of giving it to them as a wedding present. Bilicho liked living with me—in fact, I wasn't sure if anyone else could stand living with him—but a man needs his own place. It was still close enough for me to see him more often than I'd like.

I heard a shout, and it was Mollius. He was late, holding half a bottle of Falernian. He'd started celebrating too early, but we were glad to see him, and he turned red when one of the whores welcomed him with a kiss.

The procurator had left for Rome. Agricola sent a carefully worded official dispatch describing how Vibius Maecenas had been robbed and killed, the murderer caught, and part of the original message found. He said he was hoping the Emperor was pleased with his progress, and would allow him to finish the task of conquering all of Britannia.

He knew Lucullus would back up the story. Avitus was sailing with him. He also knew he'd be lucky to stay on another year. Domitian was notorious for disliking the unexpected. The death of Maecenas was a bad omen, if not outright treason.

Maybe he'd claim the freedman disappeared—he sailed and turned around, he ran into the wrong port—anything, no matter how implausible, so long as it didn't look like the Emperor wasn't god.

He wouldn't trust Agricola like that again. And he probably wouldn't offer him Syria, the most prestigious post for a *legatus*. I hoped it wouldn't matter to the governor too much.

What mattered to me was what I had around me. The light was starting to fade: Venutius and Coir were arranging the rest of the food on Galla's grave. I thought I saw a ragged figure move into the elongating shadows from a nearby tree.

A Catullus poem kept running through my mind. "The sun may fall, and rise again: once the brief light dims for us, there's but one long night for sleeping." I squeezed Gwyna's hand, and kissed her. She looked surprised, her cheeks flushing, and smiled.

The sun was up.

AUTHOR'S NOTE

I'm going to try to keep this what it claims to be: a note, rather than a thesis. There is a lot of history in *Nox Dormienda* and the Arcturus Mystery series, and I know some of you would like to know how much.

The short answer, of course, is that it is fiction. Made up. Invented. And of course, that's the truth. But what I've tried to do is insinuate a genuine feel for Roman culture in the first century C.E., a flavor and a taste that's based on many long years of studying works in the original languages, analyzing archaeology reports, and poring over history books. In short, while the events and most of the characters in *Nox Dormienda* are fictional, much of the background is not.

My mantra as a writer is if isn't impossible, I can use it. This is the opposite of my mantra as a scholar. Classicists question everything: dates, remains, names, even Greek particles. As a writer, however, I've chosen bits and pieces of history that will fit my story: there was a Temple of Isis in Londinium, for example, but we're not entirely sure how early it was established. Since it was plausibly around in 83 C.E., it appears in *Nox Dormienda*. Some scholars think the remains of a big building by the river are not the governor's palace; many do. I like thinking it is, and—as a writer—I can make it so. I usually try to go with the majority opinion, and I prefer the plausible to the possible. Sometimes, though, I have to settle for the merely "not impossible."

As for the real characters, other than Agricola and Domitian, Sallustius Lucullus, Saturninus, and Iavolenus Priscus are all documented, historical figures. I gave Sallustius his *praenomen* of Numerius, though. And if you are the type who wants to see how the story ends (and maybe the tenth or eleventh book of the Arcturus Mystery series), you can look him up in Dio Cassius.

Arcturus' fathers are also both real people. You can see their gravestones (Classicianus' in the British Museum, Facilis' in the Colchester Castle Museum), and more on Classicianus at the Museum of London. Narcissus and Verecundus were historical, too: they really did set up Facilis' gravestone.

We know a little about most of these people. How they serve the story—and in some cases, how they serve Agricola—is completely made-up. There aren't many sources for this era, unlike, say, late Republican Rome. The main sources are Tacitus' *Agricola* (of course), Dio Cassius and Suetonius, as well as inscriptions and slightly later evidence like the wonderful Vindolanda tablets.

If you develop a taste for Roman Britain, and delve into the many excellent secondary history sources available, you'll find questions about the dating. The exact dates of Agricola's service—at least the date of his removal—are open to dispute. *Nox Dormienda* is one version. Part of the plot was inspired by a particular passage in Tacitus' *Agricola*.

For telling time, Arcturus uses a.u.c. (*ab urbe condita*), which, along with many other phrases, you can find in the glossary after these pages. I use "C.E." in place of "A.D." because that is how I was trained; it stands for "Common Era."

As a doctor, Arcturus embraces an herbalist tradition based on folk medicine, modern medicine, and Roman and Greek techniques. He studied under Dioscorides (whom he mentions) and who really was a famous herbalist and healer. Arcturus is the only ancient physician I'd trust with my health, however, and even he makes mistakes.

The language in *Nox Dormienda* is not rated G. This, too, is historical. There are always layers of language, and in Latin, rough street vernacular can be found everywhere from graffiti to poetry. Rome was a vulgar culture, not unlike our own. Some characters, of course, will be a bit more vulgar than others.

Various bits of Latin are peppered throughout the story, in the hope that readers will savor their sounds and maybe decide to learn the language. The native words and names in the book are all derived from Welsh, which is the closest linguistic descendant to what the natives spoke.

For those of you who'd like more history, Arcturus-style, you can find a chronology of his life (up to this point), and other assorted bonus material (Venutius' recipes—don't try them at home!) on my website, www.kellistanley.com.

One final note on the style. *Nox Dormienda* is an attempt to inject Roman Britain with a shot of noir. By noir, I mean the classic private eye language of Chandler, Hammett, and the snappy-tough dialogue of films from the period. The noir style is born from urban life, and Rome defined *urbanitas* for centuries. Ancient Roman culture, was, in essence, a noir culture. All they lacked were cigarettes and scotch.

Only readers can tell an author if she's successful, especially when she's trying something new. "Roman Noir" is as new as this book, and I'm guessing you've read to this point either because you loved it or hated it. Obviously, Arcturus and I hope it's the former. If you did like *Nox Dormienda,* or have any questions, please write and let me know. Undoubtedly, some mistakes crept in, but I hope they don't get in the way.

It's a crowded market out there, and it's always helpful if you let the publisher or your favorite bookstore or library know you liked it, too. Arcturus wants to keep working, and is planning to return in *Maledictus.*

On behalf of him, Bilicho, Gwyna and everyone else—thanks for reading *Nox Dormienda.*

GLOSSARY

Simple translations and definitions are offered below. For more detailed information, you can try one of the sources listed at the end of the glossary.

AD ASTRA IN AETERNUM: "To the stars for all eternity."

AMICUS: "Friend," and politically a member of an inner circle of supporters.

AMINNIAN: A particularly good (and expensive) Italian wine.

AMPHORA: A large jar, and a unit of measurement.

ANGUINUM: Literally, "snaky": an *anguinum ovum*, which is what Lugh gives Arcturus, was a "snake-stone," supposedly created by serpent spit. Druids carried or wore one as an emblem of honor.

AS/SESTERTIUS/DENARIUS/AUREUS: Roman money in order of value.

AUC/a.u.c.: *ab urbe condita*, "From the founding of the city." One method of annual timekeeping in Rome.

BALLISTA: A Roman catapult.

BENEFICARIUS: A legionary on special service, and usually an older, more experienced soldier. Avitus is essentially a spy and very trusted adjutant for Agricola.

CALDARIUM: The hot, heated pool in a Roman bath.

CAMULODUNUM: Modern Colchester.

CAPSARIUS: A medical orderly who dressed wounds.

CENA/CENA NOVENDIALIS: A *cena* was a dinner, and a

cena novendialis was a feast for the recently departed, held nine days after the funeral, and marking the end of official mourning.

CLOACA MAXIMA: The largest sewer in Rome.

COHORS PRAETORIA: A select group of about one thousand soldiers from various Legions and Auxiliaries who acted as the governor's bodyguard, and were stationed at the fort outside of Londinium.

CONTUBERNIUM: A group of eight soldiers that shared a tent (while on campaign) or barracks.

CURSUS HONORUM: High-ranking young men with ability were expected to run the "course of honor," which involved holding a series of ever-advancing political offices.

DEFRUCTUM: A thick, sweet drink boiled down from grape juice into a syrup.

DIUS FIDIUS: A Roman deity who oversaw the sanctity of oaths and certain contracts.

DIVUS: Divine, holy. What most Emperors became after they died.

DOMINUS: Master.

DRUVID: Native British for Druid.

DUBRIS: Dover

DUROVERNUM: Canterbury.

EQUES: A knight in the social order or a cavalryman like Quatio.

FALERNIAN: One of the best and most famous wines in ancient Rome.

FAMES: The name of Verecundus' puppy means "hunger."

FELIX: *Felix* means "successful" or "happy," and no one wants to meet a happy executioner.

FIBULA: A Roman safety pin, used to close cloaks and other types of clothing.

FLAMEN: An ancient variety of priest, dedicated to a

particular Roman deity. They were famous for their bizarre, old-fashioned costume and sanctity of office.

FRIGIDARIUM: The cold pool in a Roman bath.

FRUMENTARIUS: A soldier excused from fighting in order to perform the administrative duty of acquiring and distributing food.

FUGITIVARIUS: A bounty-hunter out to capture runaway slaves.

GALLUS: A begging priest of the Magna Mater, who may or may not have been a self-made eunuch.

GARUM: A very popular condiment and spice used in many Roman dishes, made from liquefied fish guts. Similar to anchovy sauce.

GLADIUS: A two-edged Roman sword.

HARUSPEX: A man who practiced divination by examining the livers of sacrificed animals.

HEMINA: A unit of measure, about half a pint.

HOMO SINE PECUNIA MORTIS IMAGO: "A man without money is the image of death."

HORREA: A Roman warehouse.

IATROS: Greek for *medicus.*

IMMUNES: Soldier-specialists (like doctors, armorers, etc.) excused from actual fighting.

INSULA: An island, a city block, or (in this case) a tenement complex.

ISEUM: A temple to Isis.

KALENDS: The first of the month in the Roman calendar.

KRATER: A large-bodied jar, traditionally used by the Greeks to hold and mix wine and water.

KYLIX: A shallow Greek drinking cup with two handles.

LARES/LARARIUM: The *Lares* were Roman deities that protected the household and family; a *Lararium* was their altar.

LATRUNCULI: A Roman board game, very similar to chess, in which a king is blocked and captured.

LEGATUS: A deputy or representative; an ambassador, general, or the governor of an imperial province.

LEGATUS IURIDICUS: A legal advisor to the governor.

MAGNA MATER: A major Roman goddess imported from the East, sometimes known as Cybele.

MEDDYGON: "Doctor" in the native language.

MEDICUS: A doctor. Some people might mean it as an insult.

MITHRAEUM: A temple to Mithras, sometimes above ground, sometimes not.

MITHRAS REGNET: "Let Mithras reign!"

MONA: The modern island of Anglesey in northern Wales, and the headquarters of the British Druids.

MORITURI TE SALUTAMUS: "We who are about to die salute you." Famously addressed to the Emperor Claudius by a group of prisoners sentenced to fight a staged sea battle.

MORS IANUA VITAE: "Death is the doorway to life."

MULSUM: A salutary cocktail of honeyed wine and spices, served before or early in the dinner.

NUMA: The legendary second king of Rome, famous for his religiosity and dour abstemiousness.

NUMEN: A divine power, will or god, in particular the divine spirit of the (living) Emperor.

OCEANUS BRITANNICUS: The Channel.

OPTIO: An officer in the legion directly below a centurion.

OPOS: Greek for opium; the juice of the wild poppy was also known as *lacrimae papaver*, "tears of the poppy." Poppy derivatives were often used as sleep-aids and painkillers.

PALLA: A mantle worn by respectable Roman women, rectangular in shape, and reaching at least to the calf.

PATER: Father.

PATERFAMILIAS: The head of the family.

PATHICE: The vocative (direct address) form of the word *pathicus,* which was a pejorative term for the passive partner in a sex act between two men.

PHALERAE: A kind of chest-harness decorated with metal disks, worn by soldiers and given as an award for valor. Urien's is made of gold.

PIETAS: Nearly impossible to define: it means a lot more than piety. More like a sacred obligation and duty based on who and what you were.

PILUM: A spear or javelin.

POSCA: Diluted vinegar and herbs: the cheapest sort of alcohol.

PRAEFECTUS CASTRORUM: A career soldier who was responsible for the operational running of the fort.

PRAEFECTUS VIGILIUM: Head of the *vigiles.*

PRAENOMEN: The first of the typically three names of a Roman citizen; the given name.

PRIMUS PILUS: The head or chief centurion of the fort.

PRINCEPS PRAETORII: The head of the governor's staff, usually a senior centurion.

PRINCIPIA: Headquarters building.

PUGIO: A legionary dagger.

QUAESITOR: An investigator or inquisitor; a slight euphemism for a torturer.

QUAESTIO: A questioning, investigation, or criminal court case; here, it means interrogation by a professional torturer.

QUAESTOR: Traditionally the first rung of the Roman political ladder; basically, an elected Senatorial official who assisted the governor by holding some financial or military responsibilities for the province.

RETIARIUS: A type of gladiator who fought with a net.

RHENUS: The Rhine river.

ROSTRA: Literally, the plural form of the word for the prow or beak of a ship; in practice, it was the "Speaker's Corner" of the Forum, where candidates, orators, and officials made announcements and speeches.

SAGUM: A cloak generally worn by soldiers.

SALUTATIO: The formal morning visit of the people who wanted something from you (if you were important enough).

SALVE/SALVETE: Singular and plural forms of the common Roman greeting. Literally means, "Be well!"

SANGUINARIA: A liquid herbal concoction that helped stop bleeding.

SATURNALIA: A celebration and festival of the god Saturn, held in December, complete with reciprocal gift-giving and extreme conviviality.

SIGNIFER: The soldier who held and protected the Legion's standard.

SILENUS: A mythical figure. He was a drunk, fat, bearded old man who followed Dionysus (Bacchus) around, and highly popular in ancient Greek art.

SILPHIUM: A type of fennel that grew in modern-day Libya, and was highly, highly prized for its culinary and medicinal attributes. By Nero's era, the quasi-legendary *silphium* was apparently extinct.

SILVANUS: A god of the wild places—especially forests.

SINGULAR: Men singled out and chosen to serve an official—in this case, Agricola.

SISTRA: Plural for *sistrum*, a kind of rattle.

SOCIETAS: A company or business partnership.

SPECULATOR: A spy, examiner or special agent for the military; also an executioner.

SPONSUS: The man a woman was engaged to; the fiancé.

STOLA: A somewhat dated fashion choice, only Roman matrons could wear this feminine version of the toga. It featured a plunging neckline, was belted below the breast, and was worn over a tunic.

TERNI LAPILI: A Roman board game played with markers.

THERMAE: The Baths.

TOGA PRAETEXTA: A toga with a small purple stripe on the edges, worn by the sons of Roman citizens before they reached adulthood.

TRICLINIUM: The dining room.

VALE/VALETE: Singular and plural forms of address for "good-bye." Literally means, "Be strong!"

VAPPA: A very cheap, watered down, Roman wine.

VIGILES: The fire/watch/police force of Rome. Singular term is *vigil*.

ZEUXIS: A nearly legendary ancient Greek painter, who lived about six hundred years before the events of *Nox Dormienda*.

REFERENCES

The Internet can be a fertile place for exploration, but nothing beats a good book. If you're intrigued by Latin or the world of *Nox Dormienda,* you can explore a few of the following resources. You can find more at www.kellistanley.com. If you're stuck and don't know where else to turn, you can also write Bilicho at this address: AskBilicho@kellistanley.com. If he's not too busy investigating things for Arcturus or learning Greek from Stricta, he will try to help you with your question.

Adkins, Lesley, and Roy A. Adkins. 1998. *Handbook to Life in Ancient Rome.* New York: Oxford University Press.

Croom, A. T. 2002. *Roman Clothing and Fashion.* Charleston, S.C.: Tempus Publishing.

Dalby, Andrew. 2003. *Food in the Ancient World from A to Z.* New York: Routledge.

Hornblower, Simon, ed. 1996. *The Oxford Classical Dictionary.* 3rd ed. Oxford: Oxford University Press.

Scullard, H. H. 1995. *Roman Britain: Outpost of the Empire.* New York: Thames and Hudson.

Webster, Graham. 1998. *The Roman Imperial Army.* 3rd ed. Norman: University of Oklahoma Press.

Any edition of the Lewis and Short Latin Dictionary.

ABOUT THE AUTHOR

Kelli Stanley likes fog, which is a good thing because she lives in San Francisco. In addition to writing Roman Noir, she holds a Master's Degree in Classics. As a scholar, she writes and lectures internationally on a variety of subjects from Sallust to Superman, and her published work can be found in academic books and journals.

Kelli also likes to travel on trains, play with her dog, listen to New Orleans jazz, talk to the cat, and swig strong bourbon on cold nights. Occasionally, she will sing "See What the Boys in the Backroom Will Have" in the shower.

Her favorite film is *Casablanca*—she always gets choked up over the "Marseillaise" scene. Favorite writers include Raymond Chandler, Thomas Hardy, Catullus and Shakespeare.

She loves to write, teach, talk, and travel. She also loves nature, and all kinds of animals, something she shares with Arcturus. She is currently working on her third Arcturus novel, and is researching a second series set in San Francisco in 1939.

To read an interview with her, find out more about her next book, *Maledictus,* and discover the history and research behind the world of Roman Noir, visit Kelli's website at www.kelli stanley.com.